JONATHAN SWIFT COLLECTION

JONATHAN SWIFT

CONTENTS

GULLIVER'S TRAVELS

THE PUBLISHER TO THE READER

[AS GIVEN IN THE ORIGINAL EDITION.]

The author of these Travels, Mr. Lemuel Gulliver, is my ancient and intimate friend; there is likewise some relation between us on the mother's side. About three years ago, Mr. Gulliver growing weary of the concourse of curious people coming to him at his house in Redriff, made a small purchase of land, with a convenient house, near Newark, in Nottinghamshire, his native country; where he now lives retired, yet in good esteem among his neighbours.

Although Mr. Gulliver was born in Nottinghamshire, where his father dwelt, yet I have heard him say his family came from Oxfordshire; to confirm which, I have observed in the churchyard at Banbury in that county, several tombs and monuments of the Gullivers.

Before he quitted Redriff, he left the custody of the following papers in my hands, with the liberty to dispose of them as I should think fit. I have carefully perused them three times. The style is very plain and simple; and the only fault I find is, that the author, after the manner of travellers, is a little too circumstantial. There is an air of truth apparent through the whole; and indeed the author was so distinguished for his veracity, that it became a sort of proverb among his neighbours at Redriff, when any one affirmed a thing, to say, it was as true as if Mr. Gulliver had spoken it.

By the advice of several worthy persons, to whom, with the author's permission, I communicated these papers, I now venture to send them into the world, hoping they may be, at least for some time, a better entertainment to our young noblemen, than the common scribbles of politics and party.

This volume would have been at least twice as large, if I had not made bold to strike out innumerable passages relating to the winds and tides, as well as to the variations and bearings in the several voyages, together with the minute descriptions of the management of the ship in storms, in the style of sailors; likewise the account of longitudes and latitudes; wherein I have reason to apprehend, that Mr. Gulliver may be a little dissatisfied. But I was resolved to fit the work as much as possible to the general capacity of readers. However, if my own ignorance in sea affairs shall have led me to commit some mistakes, I alone am answerable for them. And if any traveller hath a curiosity to see the whole work at large, as it came from the hands of the author, I will be ready to gratify him.

As for any further particulars relating to the author, the reader will receive satisfaction from the first pages of the book.

RICHARD SYMPSON.

A LETTER FROM CAPTAIN GULLIVER TO HIS COUSIN SYMPSON

WRITTEN IN THE YEAR 1727

I hope you will be ready to own publicly, whenever you shall be called to it, that by your great and frequent urgency you prevailed on me to publish a very loose and uncorrect account of my travels, with directions to hire some young gentleman of either university to put them in order, and correct the style, as my cousin Dampier did, by my advice, in his book called "A Voyage round the world." But I do not remember I gave you power to consent that any thing should be omitted, and much less that any thing should be inserted; therefore, as to the latter, I do here renounce every thing of that kind; particularly a paragraph about her majesty Queen Anne, of most pious and glorious memory; although I did reverence and esteem her more than any of human species. But you, or your interpolator, ought to have considered, that it was not my inclination, so was it not decent to praise any animal of our composition before my master *Houyhnhnm*: And besides, the fact was altogether false; for to my knowledge, being in England during some part of her majesty's reign, she did govern by a chief minister; nay even by two successively, the first whereof was the lord of Godolphin, and the second the lord of Oxford; so that you have made me say the thing that was not. Likewise in the account of the academy of projectors, and several passages of my discourse to my master *Houyhnhnm*, you have either omitted some material circumstances, or minced or changed them in such a manner, that I do hardly know my own work. When I formerly hinted to you something of this in a letter, you were pleased to answer that you were afraid of giving offence; that people in power were very watchful over the press, and apt not only to interpret, but to punish every thing which looked like an *innuendo* (as I think you call it). But, pray how could that which I spoke so many years ago, and at about five thousand leagues distance, in another reign, be applied to any of the *Yahoos*, who now are said to govern the herd; especially at a time when I little thought, or feared, the unhappiness of living under them? Have not I the most reason to complain, when I see these very *Yahoos* carried by *Houyhnhnms* in a vehicle, as if they were brutes, and those the rational creatures? And indeed to avoid so monstrous and detestable a sight was one principal motive of my retirement hither.

Thus much I thought proper to tell you in relation to yourself, and to the trust I reposed in you.

I do, in the next place, complain of my own great want of judgment, in being prevailed upon by the entreaties and false reasoning of you and some others, very much against my own opinion, to suffer my travels to be published. Pray bring to your mind how often I desired you to consider, when you insisted on the motive of public good, that the *Yahoos* were a species of animals utterly incapable of amendment by precept or example: and so it has proved; for, instead of seeing a full stop put to all abuses and corruptions, at least in this little island, as I had reason to expect; behold, after above six months warning, I cannot learn that my book has produced one single effect according to my intentions. I desired you would let me know, by a letter, when party and faction were extinguished; judges learned and upright; pleaders honest and modest, with some tincture of common sense, and Smithfield blazing with pyramids of law books; the young nobility's education entirely changed; the physicians banished; the female *Yahoos* abounding in virtue, honour, truth, and good sense; courts and levees of great ministers thoroughly weeded and swept; wit, merit, and learning rewarded; all disgracers of the press in prose and verse condemned to eat nothing but their own cotton, and quench their thirst with their own ink. These, and a thousand other reformations, I firmly counted upon by your encouragement; as indeed they were plainly deducible from the precepts delivered in my book. And it must be owned, that seven months were a sufficient time to correct every vice and folly to which *Yahoos* are subject, if their natures had been capable of the least disposition to virtue or wisdom. Yet, so far have you been from answering my expectation in any of your letters; that on the contrary you are loading our carrier every week with libels, and keys, and reflections, and memoirs, and second parts; wherein I see myself accused of reflecting upon great state folk; of degrading human nature (for so they have still the confidence to style it), and of abusing the female sex. I find likewise that the writers of those bundles are not agreed among themselves; for some of them will not allow me to be the author of my own travels; and others make me author of books to which I am wholly a stranger.

I find likewise that your printer has been so careless as to confound the times, and mistake the dates, of my several voyages and returns; neither assigning the true year, nor the true month, nor day of the month: and I hear the original manuscript is all destroyed since the publication of my book; neither have I any copy left: however, I have sent you some corrections, which you may insert, if ever there should be a second edition: and yet I cannot stand to them; but shall leave that matter to my judicious and candid readers to adjust it as they please.

I hear some of our sea *Yahoos* find fault with my sea-language, as not proper in many parts, nor now in use. I cannot help it. In my first voyages, while I was young, I was instructed by the oldest mariners, and learned to speak as they did. But I have since found that the sea *Yahoos* are apt, like the land ones, to become new-fangled in their words, which the latter change every year; insomuch, as I remember upon each return to my own country their old dialect was so altered, that I could hardly understand the new. And I observe, when any *Yahoo* comes from London out of curiosity to visit me at my house, we neither of us are able to deliver our conceptions in a manner intelligible to the other.

If the censure of the *Yahoos* could any way affect me, I should have great reason to complain, that some of them are so bold as to think my book of travels a mere fiction out of mine own brain, and have gone so far as to drop hints, that the *Houyhnhnms* and *Yahoos* have no more existence than the inhabitants of Utopia.

Indeed I must confess, that as to the people of *Lilliput*, *Brobdingrag* (for so the word should have been spelt, and not erroneously *Brobdingnag*), and *Laputa*, I have never yet heard of any *Yahoo* so presumptuous as to dispute their being, or the facts I have related concerning them; because the truth immediately strikes every reader with conviction. And is there less probability in my account of the *Houyhnhnms* or *Yahoos*, when it is manifest as to the latter, there are so many thousands even in this country, who only differ from their brother brutes in *Houyhnhnmland*, because they use a sort of jabber, and do not go naked? I wrote for their amendment, and not their approbation. The united praise of the whole race would be of less consequence to me, than the neighing of those two degenerate *Houyhnhnms* I keep in my stable; because from these, degenerate as they are, I still improve in some virtues without any mixture of vice.

Do these miserable animals presume to think, that I am so degenerated as to defend my veracity? *Yahoo* as I am, it is well known through all *Houyhnhnmland*, that, by the instructions and example of my illustrious master, I was able in the compass of two years (although I confess with the utmost difficulty) to remove that infernal habit of lying, shuffling, deceiving, and equivocating, so deeply rooted in the very souls of all my species; especially the Europeans.

I have other complaints to make upon this vexatious occasion; but I forbear troubling myself or you any further. I must freely confess, that since my last return, some corruptions of my *Yahoo* nature have revived in me by conversing with a few of your species, and particularly those of my own family, by an unavoidable necessity; else I should never have attempted so absurd a project as that of reforming the *Yahoo* race in this kingdom: But I have now done with all such visionary schemes for ever.

April 2, 1727

𝕴 I 𝕴

A VOYAGE TO LILLIPUT

CHAPTER 1: THE AUTHOR GIVES SOME ACCOUNT OF
HIMSELF AND FAMILY. HIS FIRST INDUCEMENTS TO
TRAVEL. HE IS SHIPWRECKED, AND SWIMS FOR HIS LIFE.
GETS SAFE ON SHORE IN THE COUNTRY OF LILLIPUT; IS
MADE A PRISONER, AND CARRIED UP THE COUNTRY.

My father had a small estate in Nottinghamshire: I was the third of five sons. He sent me to Emanuel College in Cambridge at fourteen years old, where I resided three years, and applied myself close to my studies; but the charge of maintaining me, although I had a very scanty allowance, being too great for a narrow fortune, I was bound apprentice to Mr. James Bates, an eminent surgeon in London, with whom I continued four years. My father now and then sending me small sums of money, I laid them out in learning navigation, and other parts of the mathematics, useful to those who intend to travel, as I always believed it would be, some time or other, my fortune to do. When I left Mr. Bates, I went down to my father: where, by the assistance of him and my uncle John, and some other relations, I got forty pounds, and a promise of thirty pounds a year to maintain me at Leyden: there I studied physic two years and seven months, knowing it would be useful in long voyages.

Soon after my return from Leyden, I was recommended by my good master, Mr. Bates, to be surgeon to the Swallow, Captain Abraham Pannel, commander; with whom I continued three years and a half, making a voyage or two into the Levant, and some other parts. When I came back I resolved to settle in London;

to which Mr. Bates, my master, encouraged me, and by him I was recommended to several patients. I took part of a small house in the Old Jewry; and being advised to alter my condition, I married Mrs. Mary Burton, second daughter to Mr. Edmund Burton, hosier, in Newgate-street, with whom I received four hundred pounds for a portion.

But my good master Bates dying in two years after, and I having few friends, my business began to fail; for my conscience would not suffer me to imitate the bad practice of too many among my brethren. Having therefore consulted with my wife, and some of my acquaintance, I determined to go again to sea. I was surgeon successively in two ships, and made several voyages, for six years, to the East and West Indies, by which I got some addition to my fortune. My hours of leisure I spent in reading the best authors, ancient and modern, being always provided with a good number of books; and when I was ashore, in observing the manners and dispositions of the people, as well as learning their language; wherein I had a great facility, by the strength of my memory.

The last of these voyages not proving very fortunate, I grew weary of the sea, and intended to stay at home with my wife and family. I removed from the Old Jewry to Fetter Lane, and from thence to Wapping, hoping to get business among the sailors; but it would not turn to account. After three years expectation that things would mend, I accepted an advantageous offer from Captain William Prichard, master of the Antelope, who was making a voyage to the South Sea. We set sail from Bristol, May 4, 1699, and our voyage was at first very prosperous.

It would not be proper, for some reasons, to trouble the reader with the particulars of our adventures in those seas; let it suffice to inform him, that in our passage from thence to the East Indies, we were driven by a violent storm to the north-west of Van Diemen's Land. By an observation, we found ourselves in the latitude of 30 degrees 2 minutes south. Twelve of our crew were dead by immoderate labour and ill food; the rest were in a very weak condition. On the 5th of November, which was the beginning of summer in those parts, the weather being very hazy, the seamen spied a rock within half a cable's length of the ship; but the wind was so strong, that we were driven directly upon it, and immediately split. Six of the crew, of whom I was one, having let down the boat into the sea, made a shift to get clear of the ship and the rock. We rowed, by my computation, about three leagues, till we were able to work no longer, being already spent with labour while we were in the ship. We therefore trusted ourselves to the mercy of the waves, and in about half an hour the boat was overset by a sudden flurry from the north. What became of my companions in the boat, as well as of those who escaped on the rock, or were left in the vessel, I cannot tell; but conclude they were all lost. For my own part, I swam as fortune directed me, and was pushed forward by wind and tide. I often let my legs drop, and could feel no bottom; but when I was almost gone, and able to struggle no longer, I found myself within my depth; and by this time the storm was much abated. The declivity was so small, that I walked near a mile before I got to the shore, which I conjectured was about eight o'clock in the evening. I then advanced forward near half a mile, but could not discover any sign of houses or inhabitants; at least I was in so weak a condition, that I did not observe them. I was extremely tired, and with that, and the heat of the weather, and about half a pint of brandy that I drank as I left the ship, I found myself much inclined to sleep. I lay down on the grass, which was very short and soft, where I slept sounder than ever I remembered to have done in my life, and, as I reckoned, about nine hours; for when I awaked, it was just day-light. I attempted to rise, but was not able to stir: for, as I happened to lie on my back, I found my arms and legs were strongly fastened on each side to the ground; and my hair, which was long and thick, tied down in the same manner. I likewise felt several slender ligatures across my body, from my arm-pits to my thighs. I could only look upwards; the sun began to grow hot, and the light offended my eyes. I heard a confused noise about me; but in the posture I lay, could see nothing except the sky. In a little time I felt something alive moving on my left leg, which advancing gently forward over my breast, came almost up to my chin; when, bending my eyes downwards as much as I could, I perceived it to be a human creature not six inches high, with a bow and arrow in his hands, and a quiver at his back. In the mean time, I felt at least forty more of the same kind (as I conjectured) following the first. I was in the utmost astonishment, and roared so loud, that they all ran back in a fright; and some of them, as I was afterwards told, were hurt with the falls they got by leaping from my sides upon the ground. However, they soon returned, and one of them, who ventured so far as to get a full sight of my face, lifting up his hands and eyes by way of admiration, cried out in a shrill but distinct voice, *Hekinah degul*: the others repeated the same words several times, but then I knew not what they meant. I lay all this while, as the reader may believe, in great uneasiness. At length, struggling to get loose, I had the fortune to break the strings, and wrench out the pegs that fastened my left arm to the ground; for, by lifting it up to my face, I discovered the methods they had taken to bind me, and at the same time with a violent pull, which gave me excessive pain, I a little loosened the strings that tied down my hair on the left side, so that I was just able to turn my head about two inches. But the creatures ran off a second time, before I could seize them; whereupon there was a great shout in a very shrill accent, and after it ceased I heard one of them cry aloud *Tolgo phonac*; when in an instant I felt above a hundred arrows discharged on my left hand, which, pricked me like so many needles; and besides, they shot another flight into the air, as we do bombs in Europe, whereof many, I suppose, fell on my body, (though I felt them not), and some on my face, which I immediately covered with my left hand.

When this shower of arrows was over, I fell a groaning with grief and pain; and then striving again to get loose, they discharged another volley larger than the first, and some of them attempted with spears to stick me in the sides; but by good luck I had on a buff jerkin, which they could not pierce. I thought it the most prudent method to lie still, and my design was to continue so till night, when, my left hand being already loose, I could easily free myself: and as for the inhabitants, I had reason to believe I might be a match for the greatest army they could bring against me, if they were all of the same size with him that I saw. But fortune disposed otherwise of me. When the people observed I was quiet, they discharged no more arrows; but, by the noise I heard, I knew their numbers increased; and about four yards from me, over against my right ear, I heard a knocking for above an hour, like that of people at work; when turning my head that way, as well as the pegs and strings would permit me, I saw a stage erected about a foot and a half from the ground, capable of holding four of the inhabitants, with two or three ladders to mount it: from whence one of them, who seemed to be a person of quality, made me a long speech, whereof I understood not one syllable. But I should have mentioned, that before the principal person began his oration, he cried out three times, *Langro dehul san* (these words and the former were afterwards repeated and explained to me); whereupon, immediately, about fifty of the inhabitants came and cut the strings that fastened the left side of my head, which gave me the liberty of turning it to the right, and of observing the person and gesture of him that was to speak. He appeared to be of a middle age, and taller than any of the other three who attended him, whereof one was a page that held up his train, and seemed to be somewhat longer than my middle finger; the other two stood one on each side to support him. He acted every part of an orator, and I could observe many periods of threatenings, and others of promises, pity, and kindness. I answered in a few words, but in the most submissive manner, lifting up my left hand, and both my eyes to the sun, as calling him for a witness; and being almost famished with hunger, having not eaten a morsel for some hours before I left the ship, I found the demands of nature so strong upon me, that I could not forbear showing my impatience (perhaps against the strict rules of decency) by putting my finger frequently to my mouth, to signify that I wanted food. The *hurgo* (for so they call a great lord, as I afterwards learnt) understood me very well. He descended from the stage, and commanded that several ladders should be applied to my sides, on which above a hundred of the inhabitants mounted and walked towards my mouth, laden with baskets full of meat, which had been provided and sent thither by the king's orders, upon the first intelligence he received of me. I observed there was the flesh of several animals, but could not distinguish them by the taste. There were shoulders, legs, and loins, shaped like those of mutton, and very well dressed, but smaller than the wings of a lark. I ate them by two or three at a mouthful, and took three loaves at a time, about the bigness of musket bullets. They supplied me as fast as they could, showing a thousand marks of wonder and astonishment at my bulk and appetite. I then made another sign, that I wanted drink. They found by my eating that a small quantity would not suffice me; and being a most ingenious people, they slung up, with great dexterity, one of their largest hogsheads, then rolled it towards my hand, and beat out the top; I drank it off at a draught, which I might well do, for it did not hold half a pint, and tasted like a small wine of Burgundy, but much more delicious. They brought me a second hogshead, which I drank in the same manner, and made signs for more; but they had none to give me. When I had performed these wonders, they shouted for joy, and danced upon my breast, repeating several times as they did at first, *Hekinah degul*. They made me a sign that I should throw down the two hogsheads, but first warning the people below to stand out of the way, crying aloud, *Borach mevolah*; and when they saw the vessels in the air, there was a universal shout of *Hekinah degul*. I confess I was often tempted, while they were passing backwards and forwards on my body, to seize forty or fifty of the first that came in my reach, and dash them against the ground. But the remembrance of what I had felt, which probably might not be the worst they could do, and the promise of honour I made them—for so I interpreted my submissive behaviour— soon drove out these imaginations. Besides, I now considered myself as bound by the laws of hospitality, to a people who had treated me with so much expense and magnificence. However, in my thoughts I could not sufficiently wonder at the intrepidity of these diminutive mortals, who durst venture to mount and walk upon my body, while one of my hands was at liberty, without trembling at the very sight of so prodigious a creature as I must appear to them. After some time, when they observed that I made no more demands for meat, there appeared before me a person of high rank from his imperial majesty. His excellency, having mounted on the small of my right leg, advanced forwards up to my face, with about a dozen of his retinue; and producing his credentials under the signet royal, which he applied close to my eyes, spoke about ten minutes without any signs of anger, but with a kind of determinate resolution, often pointing forwards, which, as I afterwards found, was towards the capital city, about half a mile distant; whither it was agreed by his majesty in council that I must be conveyed. I answered in few words, but to no purpose, and made a sign with my hand that was loose, putting it to the other (but over his excellency's head for fear of hurting him or his train) and then to my own head and body, to signify that I desired my liberty. It appeared that he understood me well enough, for he shook his head by way of disapprobation, and held his hand in a posture to show that I must be carried as a prisoner. However, he made other signs to let me understand that I should have meat and drink enough, and very good treatment. Whereupon I once more thought of attempting to break my bonds; but again, when I felt the smart of their arrows upon my face and hands, which were all in blisters, and many of the darts still sticking in them, and observing likewise that the number of my enemies increased, I gave tokens to let them know that they might do with me what they pleased. Upon this, the *hurgo* and his train withdrew, with much civility and cheerful countenances. Soon after I heard a general shout, with frequent repetitions of the words *Peplom selan*; and I felt great numbers of people on my left side relaxing the cords to such a degree, that I was able to turn upon my right, and to ease myself with making water; which I very plentifully did, to the great astonishment of the people; who, conjecturing by my motion what I was going to do, immediately opened to the right and left on that side, to avoid the torrent, which fell with such noise and violence from me. But before this, they had daubed my face and both my hands with a sort of ointment, very pleasant to the smell, which, in a few minutes, removed all the smart of their arrows. These circumstances, added to the refreshment I had received by their victuals and drink, which were very nourishing, disposed me to sleep. I slept about eight hours, as I was afterwards assured; and it was no wonder, for the physicians, by the emperor's order, had mingled a sleepy potion in the hogsheads of wine.

It seems, that upon the first moment I was discovered sleeping on the ground, after my landing, the emperor had early notice of it by an express; and determined in council, that I should be tied in the manner I have related, (which was done in the night while I slept;) that plenty of meat and drink should be sent to me, and a machine prepared to carry me to the capital city.

This resolution perhaps may appear very bold and dangerous, and I am confident would not be imitated by any prince in Europe on the like occasion. However, in my opinion, it was extremely prudent, as well as generous: for, supposing these people had endeavoured to kill me with their spears and arrows, while I was asleep, I should certainly have awaked with the first sense of smart, which might so far have roused my rage and strength, as to have enabled me to break the strings wherewith I was tied; after which, as they were not able to make resistance, so they could expect no mercy.

These people are most excellent mathematicians, and arrived to a great perfection in mechanics, by the countenance and encouragement of the emperor, who is a renowned patron of learning. This prince has several machines fixed on wheels, for the carriage of trees and other great weights. He often builds his largest men of war, whereof some are nine feet long, in the woods where the timber grows, and has them carried on these engines three or four hundred yards to the sea. Five hundred carpenters and engineers were immediately set at work to prepare the greatest engine they had. It was a frame of wood raised three inches from the ground, about seven feet long, and four wide, moving upon twenty-two wheels. The shout I heard was upon the arrival of this engine, which, it seems, set out in four hours after my landing. It was brought parallel to me, as I lay. But the principal difficulty was to raise and place me in this vehicle. Eighty poles, each of one foot high, were erected for this purpose, and very strong cords, of the bigness of packthread, were fastened by hooks to many bandages, which the workmen had girt round my neck, my hands, my body, and my legs. Nine hundred of the strongest men were employed to draw up these cords, by many pulleys fastened on the poles; and thus, in less than three hours, I was raised and slung into the engine, and there tied fast. All this I was told; for, while the operation was performing, I lay in a profound sleep, by the force of that soporiferous medicine infused into my liquor. Fifteen hundred of the emperor's largest horses, each about four inches and a half high, were employed to draw me towards the metropolis, which, as I said, was half a mile distant.

About four hours after we began our journey, I awaked by a very ridiculous accident; for the carriage being stopped a while, to adjust something that was out of order, two or three of the young natives had the curiosity to see how I looked when I was asleep; they climbed up into the engine, and advancing very softly to my face, one of them, an officer in the guards, put the sharp end of his half-pike a good way up into my left nostril, which tickled my nose like a straw, and made me sneeze violently; whereupon they stole off unperceived, and it was three weeks before I knew the cause of my waking so suddenly. We made a long march the remaining part of the day, and, rested at night with five hundred guards on each side of me, half with torches, and half with bows and arrows, ready to shoot me if I should offer to stir. The next morning at sun-rise we continued our march, and arrived within two hundred yards of the city gates about noon. The emperor, and all his court, came out to meet us; but his great officers would by no means suffer his majesty to endanger his person by mounting on my body.

At the place where the carriage stopped there stood an ancient temple, esteemed to be the largest in the whole kingdom; which, having been polluted some years before by an unnatural murder, was, according to the zeal of those people, looked upon as profane, and therefore had been applied to common use, and all the ornaments and furniture carried away. In this edifice it was determined I should lodge. The great gate fronting to the north was about four feet high, and almost two feet wide, through which I could easily creep. On each side of the gate was a small window, not above six inches from the ground: into that on the left side, the king's smith conveyed fourscore and eleven chains, like those that hang to a lady's watch in Europe, and almost as large, which were locked to my left leg with six-and-thirty padlocks. Over against this temple, on the other side of the great highway, at twenty feet distance, there was a turret at least five feet high. Here the emperor ascended, with many principal lords of his court, to have an opportunity of viewing me, as I was told, for I could not see them. It was reckoned that above a hundred thousand inhabitants came out of the town upon the same errand; and, in spite of my guards, I believe there could not be fewer than ten thousand at several times, who mounted my body by the help of ladders. But a proclamation was soon issued, to forbid it upon pain of death. When the workmen found it was impossible for me to break loose, they cut all the strings that bound me; whereupon I rose up, with as melancholy a disposition as ever I had in my life. But the noise and astonishment of the people, at seeing me rise and walk, are not to be expressed. The chains that held my left leg were about two yards long, and gave me not only the liberty of walking backwards and forwards in a semicircle, but, being fixed within four inches of the gate, allowed me to creep in, and lie at my full length in the temple.

CHAPTER 2: THE EMPEROR OF LILLIPUT, ATTENDED BY SEVERAL OF THE NOBILITY, COMES TO SEE THE AUTHOR IN HIS CONFINEMENT. THE EMPEROR'S PERSON AND HABIT DESCRIBED. LEARNED MEN APPOINTED TO TEACH THE AUTHOR THEIR LANGUAGE. HE GAINS FAVOUR BY HIS MILD DISPOSITION. HIS POCKETS ARE SEARCHED, AND HIS SWORD AND PISTOLS TAKEN FROM HIM.

When I found myself on my feet, I looked about me, and must confess I never beheld a more entertaining prospect. The country around appeared like a continued garden, and the enclosed fields, which were generally forty feet square, resembled so many beds of flowers. These fields were intermingled with woods of half a stang,[1] and the tallest trees, as I could judge, appeared to be seven feet high. I viewed the town on my left hand, which looked like the painted scene of a city in a theatre.

I had been for some hours extremely pressed by the necessities of nature; which was no wonder, it being almost two days since I had last disburdened myself. I was under great difficulties between urgency and shame. The best expedient I could think of, was to creep into my house, which I accordingly did; and shutting the gate after me, I went as far as the length of my chain would suffer, and discharged my body of that uneasy load. But this was the only time I was ever guilty of so uncleanly an action; for which I cannot but hope the candid reader will give some allowance, after he has maturely and impartially considered my case, and the distress I was in. From this time my constant practice was, as soon as I rose, to perform that business in open air, at the full extent of my chain; and due care was taken every morning before company came, that the offensive matter should be carried off in wheel-barrows, by two servants appointed for that purpose. I would not have dwelt so long upon a circumstance that, perhaps, at first sight, may appear not very momentous, if I had not thought it necessary to justify my character, in point of cleanliness, to the world; which, I am told, some of my maligners have been pleased, upon this and other occasions, to call in question.

When this adventure was at an end, I came back out of my house, having occasion for fresh air. The emperor was already descended from the tower, and advancing on horseback towards me, which had like to have cost him dear; for the beast, though very well trained, yet wholly unused to such a sight, which appeared as if a mountain moved before him, reared up on its hinder feet: but that prince, who is an excellent horseman, kept his seat, till his attendants ran in, and held the bridle, while his majesty had time to dismount. When he alighted, he surveyed me round with great admiration; but kept beyond the length of my chain. He ordered his cooks and butlers, who were already prepared, to give me victuals and drink, which they pushed forward in a sort of vehicles upon wheels, till I could reach them. I took these vehicles and soon emptied them all; twenty of them were filled with meat, and ten with liquor; each of the former afforded me two or three good mouthfuls; and I emptied the liquor of ten vessels, which was contained in earthen vials, into one vehicle, drinking it off at a draught; and so I did with the rest. The empress, and young princes of the blood of both sexes, attended by many ladies, sat at some distance in their chairs; but upon the accident that happened to the emperor's horse, they alighted, and came near his person, which I am now going to describe. He is taller by almost the breadth of my nail, than any of his court; which alone is enough to strike an awe into the beholders. His features are strong and masculine, with an Austrian lip and arched nose, his complexion olive, his countenance erect, his body and limbs well proportioned, all his motions graceful, and his deportment majestic. He was then past his prime, being twenty-eight years and three quarters old, of which he had reigned about seven in great felicity, and generally victorious. For the better convenience of beholding him, I lay on my side, so that my face was parallel to his, and he stood but three yards off: however, I have had him since many times in my hand, and therefore cannot be deceived in the description. His dress was very plain and simple, and the fashion of it between the Asiatic and the European; but he had on his head a light helmet of gold, adorned with jewels, and a plume on the crest. He held his sword drawn in his hand to defend himself, if I should happen to break loose; it was almost three inches long; the hilt and scabbard were gold enriched with diamonds. His voice was shrill, but very clear and articulate; and I could distinctly hear it when I stood up. The ladies and courtiers were all most magnificently clad; so that the spot they stood upon seemed to resemble a petticoat spread upon the ground, embroidered with figures of gold and silver.

His imperial majesty spoke often to me, and I returned answers: but neither of us could understand a syllable. There were several of his priests and lawyers present (as I conjectured by their habits), who were commanded to address themselves to me; and I spoke to them in as many languages as I had the least smattering of, which were High and Low Dutch, Latin, French, Spanish, Italian, and Lingua Franca, but all to no purpose. After about two hours the court retired, and I was left with a strong guard, to prevent the impertinence, and probably the malice of the rabble, who were very impatient to crowd about me as near as they durst; and some of them had the impudence to shoot their arrows at me, as I sat on the ground by the door of my house, whereof one very narrowly missed my left eye. But the colonel ordered six of the ringleaders to be seized, and thought no punishment so proper as to deliver them bound into my hands; which some of his soldiers accordingly did, pushing them forward with the butt-ends of their pikes into my reach. I took them all in my right hand, put five of them into my coat-pocket; and as to the sixth, I made a countenance as if I would eat him alive. The poor man squalled terribly, and the colonel and his officers were in much pain, especially when they saw me take out my penknife: but I soon put them out of fear; for, looking mildly, and immediately cutting the strings he was bound with, I set him gently on the ground, and away he ran. I treated the rest in the same manner, taking them one by one out of my pocket; and I observed both the soldiers and people were highly delighted at this mark of my clemency, which was represented very much to my advantage at court.

Towards night I got with some difficulty into my house, where I lay on the ground, and continued to do so about a fortnight; during which time, the emperor gave orders to have a bed prepared for me. Six hundred beds of the common measure were brought in carriages, and worked up in my house; a hundred and fifty of their beds, sewn together, made up the breadth and length; and these were four double: which, however, kept me but very indifferently from the hardness of the floor, that was of smooth stone. By the same computation, they provided me with sheets, blankets, and coverlets, tolerable enough for one who had been so long inured to hardships.

As the news of my arrival spread through the kingdom, it brought prodigious numbers of rich, idle, and curious people to see me; so that the villages were almost emptied; and great neglect of tillage and household affairs must have ensued, if his imperial majesty had not provided, by several proclamations and orders of state, against this inconveniency. He directed that those who had already beheld me should return home, and not presume to come within fifty yards of my house, without license from the court; whereby the secretaries of state got considerable fees.

In the mean time the emperor held frequent councils, to debate what course should be taken with me; and I was afterwards assured by a particular friend, a person of great quality, who was as much in the secret as any, that the court was under many difficulties concerning me. They apprehended my breaking loose; that my diet would be very expensive, and might cause a famine. Sometimes they determined to starve me; or at least to shoot me in the face and hands with poisoned arrows, which would soon despatch me; but again they considered, that the stench of so large a carcass might produce a plague in the metropolis, and probably spread through the whole kingdom. In the midst of these consultations, several officers of the army went to the door of the great council-chamber, and two of them being admitted, gave an account of my behaviour to the six criminals above-mentioned; which made so favourable an impression in the breast of his majesty and the whole board, in my behalf, that an imperial commission was issued out, obliging all the villages, nine hundred yards round the city, to deliver in every morning six beeves, forty sheep, and other victuals for my sustenance; together with a proportionable quantity of bread, and wine, and other liquors; for the due payment of which, his majesty gave assignments upon his treasury:—for this prince lives chiefly upon his own demesnes; seldom, except upon great occasions, raising any subsidies upon his subjects, who are bound to attend him in his wars at their own expense. An establishment was also made of six hundred persons to be my domestics, who had board-wages allowed for their maintenance, and tents built for them very conveniently on each side of my door. It was likewise ordered, that three hundred tailors should make me a suit of clothes, after the fashion of the country; that six of his majesty's greatest scholars should be employed to instruct me in their language; and lastly, that the emperor's horses, and those of the nobility and troops of guards, should be frequently exercised in my sight, to accustom themselves to me. All these orders were duly put in execution; and in about three weeks I made a great progress in learning their language; during which time the emperor frequently honoured me with his visits, and was pleased to assist my masters in teaching me. We began already to converse together in some sort; and the first words I learnt, were to express my desire "that he would please give me my liberty;" which I every day repeated on my knees. His answer, as I could comprehend it, was, "that this must be a work of time, not to be thought on without the advice of his council, and that first I must *lumos kelmin pesso desmar lon emposo;*" that is, swear a peace with him and his kingdom. However, that I should be used with all kindness. And he advised me to "acquire, by my patience and discreet behaviour, the good opinion of himself and his subjects." He desired "I would not take it ill, if he gave orders to certain proper officers to search me; for probably I might carry about me several weapons, which must needs be dangerous things, if they answered the bulk of so prodigious a person." I said, "His majesty should be satisfied; for I was ready to strip myself, and turn up my pockets before him." This I delivered part in words, and part in signs. He replied, "that, by the laws of the kingdom, I must be searched by two of his officers; that he knew this could not be done without my consent and assistance; and he had so good an opinion of my generosity and justice, as to trust their persons in my hands; that whatever they took from me, should be returned when I left the country, or paid for at the rate which I would set upon them." I took up the two officers in my hands, put them first into my coat-pockets, and then into every other pocket about me, except my two fobs, and another secret pocket, which I had no mind should be searched, wherein I had some little necessaries that were of no consequence to any but myself. In one of my fobs there was a silver watch, and in the other a small quantity of gold in a purse. These gentlemen, having pen, ink, and paper, about them, made an exact inventory of every thing they saw; and when they had done, desired I would set them down, that they might deliver it to the emperor. This inventory I afterwards translated into English, and is, word for word, as follows:

"*Imprimis*: In the right coat-pocket of the great man-mountain" (for so I interpret the words *quinbus flestrin*,) "after the strictest search, we found only one great piece of coarse-cloth, large enough to be a foot-cloth for your majesty's chief room of state. In the left pocket we saw a huge silver chest, with a cover of the same metal, which we, the searchers, were not able to lift. We desired it should be opened, and one of us stepping into it, found himself up to the mid leg in a sort of dust, some part whereof flying up to our faces set us both a sneezing for several times together. In his right waistcoat-pocket we found a prodigious bundle of white thin substances, folded one over another, about the bigness of three men, tied with a strong cable, and marked with black figures; which we humbly conceive to be writings, every letter almost half as large as the palm of our hands. In the left there was a sort of engine, from the back of which were extended twenty long poles, resembling the pallisados before your majesty's court: wherewith we conjecture the man-mountain combs his head; for we did not always trouble him with questions, because we found it a great difficulty to make him understand us. In the large pocket, on the right side of his middle cover" (so I translate the word *ranfulo*, by which they meant my breeches,) "we saw a hollow pillar of iron, about the length of a man, fastened to a strong piece of timber larger than the pillar; and upon one side of the pillar, were huge pieces of iron sticking out, cut into strange figures, which we know not what to make of. In the left pocket, another engine of the same kind. In the smaller pocket on the right side, were several round flat pieces of white and red metal, of different bulk; some of the white, which seemed to be silver, were so large and heavy, that my comrade and I could hardly lift them. In the left pocket were two black pillars irregularly shaped: we could not, without difficulty, reach the top of them, as we stood at the bottom of his pocket. One of them was covered, and seemed all of a piece: but at the upper end of the other there appeared a white round substance, about twice the bigness of our heads. Within each of these was enclosed a prodigious plate of steel; which, by our orders, we obliged him to show us, because we apprehended they might be dangerous engines. He took them out of their cases, and told us, that in his own country his practice was to shave his beard with one of these, and cut his meat with the other. There were two pockets which we could not enter: these he called his fobs; they were two large slits cut into the top of his middle cover, but squeezed close by the pressure of his belly. Out of the right fob hung a great silver chain, with a wonderful kind of engine at the bottom. We directed him to draw out whatever was at the end of that chain; which appeared to be a globe, half silver, and half of some transparent metal; for, on the transparent side, we saw certain strange figures circularly drawn, and thought we could touch them, till we found our fingers stopped by the lucid substance. He put this engine into our ears, which made an incessant noise, like that of a water-mill: and we conjecture it is either some unknown animal, or the god that he worships; but we are more inclined to the latter opinion, because he assured us, (if we understood him right, for he expressed himself very imperfectly) that he seldom did any thing without consulting it. He called it his oracle, and said, it pointed out the time for every action of his life. From the left fob he took out a net almost large enough for a fisherman, but contrived to open and shut like a purse, and served him for the same use: we found therein several massy pieces of yellow metal, which, if they be real gold, must be of immense value.

"Having thus, in obedience to your majesty's commands, diligently searched all his pockets, we observed a girdle about his waist made of the hide of some prodigious animal, from which, on the left side, hung a sword of the length of five men; and on the right, a bag or pouch divided into two cells, each cell capable of holding three of your majesty's subjects. In one of these cells were several globes, or balls, of a most ponderous metal, about the bigness of our heads, and requiring a strong hand to lift them: the other cell contained a heap of certain black grains, but of no great bulk or weight, for we could hold above fifty of them in the palms of our hands.

"This is an exact inventory of what we found about the body of the man-mountain, who used us with great civility, and due respect to your majesty's commission. Signed and sealed on the fourth day of the eighty-ninth moon of your majesty's auspicious reign.

CLEFRIN FRELOCK, MARSI FRELOCK."

When this inventory was read over to the emperor, he directed me, although in very gentle terms, to deliver up the several particulars. He first called for my scimitar, which I took out, scabbard and all. In the mean time he ordered three thousand of his choicest troops (who then attended him) to surround me at a distance, with their bows and arrows just ready to discharge; but I did not observe it, for mine eyes were wholly fixed upon his majesty. He then desired me to draw my scimitar, which, although it had got some rust by the sea water, was, in most parts, exceeding bright. I did so, and immediately all the troops gave a shout between terror and surprise; for the sun shone clear, and the reflection dazzled their eyes, as I waved the scimitar to and fro in my hand. His majesty, who is a most magnanimous prince, was less daunted than I could expect: he ordered me to return it into the scabbard, and cast it on the ground as gently as I could, about six feet from the end of my chain. The next thing he demanded was one of the hollow iron pillars; by which he meant my pocket pistols. I drew it out, and at his desire, as well as I could, expressed to him the use of it; and charging it only with powder, which, by the closeness of my pouch, happened to escape wetting in the sea (an inconvenience against which all prudent mariners take special care to provide,) I first cautioned the emperor not to be afraid, and then I let it off in the air. The astonishment here was much greater than at the sight of my scimitar. Hundreds fell down as if they had been struck dead; and even the emperor, although he stood his ground, could not recover himself for some time. I delivered up both my pistols in the same manner as I had done my scimitar, and then my pouch of powder and bullets; begging him that the former might be kept from fire, for it would kindle with the smallest spark, and blow up his imperial palace into the air. I likewise delivered up my watch, which the emperor was very curious to see, and commanded two of his tallest yeomen of the guards to bear it on a pole upon their shoulders, as draymen in England do a barrel of ale. He was amazed at the continual noise it made, and the motion of the minute-hand, which he could easily discern; for their sight is much more acute than ours: he asked the opinions of his learned men about it, which were various and remote, as the reader may well imagine without my repeating; although indeed I could not very perfectly understand them. I then gave up my silver and copper money, my purse, with nine large pieces of gold, and some smaller ones; my knife and razor, my comb and silver snuff-box, my handkerchief and journal-book. My scimitar, pistols, and pouch, were conveyed in carriages to his majesty's stores; but the rest of my goods were returned me.

I had as I before observed, one private pocket, which escaped their search, wherein there was a pair of spectacles (which I sometimes use for the weakness of mine eyes,) a pocket perspective, and some other little conveniences; which, being of no consequence to the emperor, I did not think myself bound in honour to discover, and I apprehended they might be lost or spoiled if I ventured them out of my possession.

CHAPTER 3: THE AUTHOR DIVERTS THE EMPEROR, AND HIS NOBILITY OF BOTH SEXES, IN A VERY UNCOMMON MANNER. THE DIVERSIONS OF THE COURT OF LILLIPUT DESCRIBED. THE AUTHOR HAS HIS LIBERTY GRANTED HIM UPON CERTAIN CONDITIONS.

My gentleness and good behaviour had gained so far on the emperor and his court, and indeed upon the army and people in general, that I began to conceive hopes of getting my liberty in a short time. I took all possible methods to cultivate this favourable disposition. The natives came, by degrees, to be less apprehensive of any danger from me. I would sometimes lie down, and let five or six of them dance on my hand; and at last the boys and girls would venture to come and play at hide-and-seek in my hair. I had now made a good progress in understanding and speaking the language. The emperor had a mind one day to entertain me with several of the country shows, wherein they exceed all nations I have known, both for dexterity and magnificence. I was diverted with none so much as that of the rope-dancers, performed upon a slender white thread, extended about two feet, and twelve inches from the ground. Upon which I shall desire liberty, with the reader's patience, to enlarge a little.

This diversion is only practised by those persons who are candidates for great employments, and high favour at court. They are trained in this art from their youth, and are not always of noble birth, or liberal education. When a great office is vacant, either by death or disgrace (which often happens,) five or six of those candidates petition the emperor to entertain his majesty and the court with a dance on the rope; and whoever jumps the highest, without falling, succeeds in the office. Very often the chief ministers themselves are commanded to show their skill, and to convince the emperor that they have not lost their faculty. Flimnap, the treasurer, is allowed to cut a caper on the straight rope, at least an inch higher than any other lord in the whole empire. I have seen him do the summerset several times together, upon a trencher fixed on a rope which is no thicker than a common packthread in England. My friend Reldresal, principal secretary for private affairs, is, in my opinion, if I am not partial, the second after the treasurer; the rest of the great officers are much upon a par.

These diversions are often attended with fatal accidents, whereof great numbers are on record. I myself have seen two or three candidates break a limb. But the danger is much greater, when the ministers themselves are commanded to show their dexterity; for, by contending to excel themselves and their fellows, they strain so far that there is hardly one of them who has not received a fall, and some of them two or three. I was assured that, a year or two before my arrival, Flimnap would infallibly have broke his neck, if one of the king's cushions, that accidentally lay on the ground, had not weakened the force of his fall.

There is likewise another diversion, which is only shown before the emperor and empress, and first minister, upon particular occasions. The emperor lays on the table three fine silken threads of six inches long; one is blue, the other red, and the third green. These threads are proposed as prizes for those persons whom the emperor has a mind to distinguish by a peculiar mark of his favour. The ceremony is performed in his majesty's great chamber of state, where the candidates are to undergo a trial of dexterity very different from the former, and such as I have not observed the least resemblance of in any other country of the new or old world. The emperor holds a stick in his hands, both ends parallel to the horizon, while the candidates advancing, one by one, sometimes leap over the stick, sometimes creep under it, backward and forward, several times, according as the stick is advanced or depressed. Sometimes the emperor holds one end of the stick, and his first minister the other; sometimes the minister has it entirely to himself. Whoever performs his part with most agility, and holds out the longest in leaping and creeping, is rewarded with the blue-coloured silk; the red is given to the next, and the green to the third, which they all wear girt twice round about the middle; and you see few great persons about this court who are not adorned with one of these girdles.

The horses of the army, and those of the royal stables, having been daily led before me, were no longer shy, but would come up to my very feet without starting. The riders would leap them over my hand, as I held it on the ground; and one of the emperor's huntsmen, upon a large courser, took my foot, shoe and all; which was indeed a prodigious leap. I had the good fortune to divert the emperor one day after a very extraordinary manner. I desired he would order several sticks of two feet high, and the thickness of an ordinary cane, to be brought me; whereupon his majesty commanded the master of his woods to give directions accordingly; and the next morning six woodmen arrived with as many carriages, drawn by eight horses to each. I took nine of these sticks, and fixing them firmly in the ground in a quadrangular figure, two feet and a half square, I took four other sticks, and tied them parallel at each corner, about two feet from the ground; then I fastened my handkerchief to the nine sticks that stood erect; and extended it on all sides, till it was tight as the top of a drum; and the four parallel sticks, rising about five inches higher than the handkerchief, served as ledges on each side. When I had finished my work, I desired the emperor to let a troop of his best horses twenty-four in number, come and exercise upon this plain. His majesty approved of the proposal, and I took them up, one by one, in my hands, ready mounted and armed, with the proper officers to exercise them. As soon as they got into order they divided into two parties, performed mock skirmishes, discharged blunt arrows, drew their swords, fled and pursued, attacked and retired, and in short discovered the best military discipline I ever beheld. The parallel sticks secured them and their horses from falling over the stage; and the emperor was so much delighted, that he ordered this entertainment to be repeated several days, and once was pleased to be lifted up and give the word of command; and with great difficulty persuaded even the empress herself to let me hold her in her close chair within two yards of the stage, when she was able to take a full view of the whole performance. It was my good fortune, that no ill accident happened in these entertainments; only once a fiery horse, that belonged to one of the captains, pawing with his hoof, struck a hole in my handkerchief, and his foot slipping, he overthrew his rider and himself; but I immediately relieved them both, and covering the hole with one hand, I set down the troop with the other, in the same manner as I took them up. The horse that fell was strained in the left shoulder, but the rider got no hurt; and I repaired my handkerchief as well as I could: however, I would not trust to the strength of it any more, in such dangerous enterprises.

About two or three days before I was set at liberty, as I was entertaining the court with this kind of feat, there arrived an express to inform his majesty, that some of his subjects, riding near the place where I was first taken up, had seen a great black substance lying on the around, very oddly shaped, extending its edges round, as wide as his majesty's bedchamber, and rising up in the middle as high as a man; that it was no living creature, as they at first apprehended, for it lay on the grass without motion; and some of them had walked round it several times; that, by mounting upon each other's shoulders, they had got to the top, which was flat and even, and, stamping upon it, they found that it was hollow within; that they humbly conceived it might be something belonging to the man-mountain; and if his majesty pleased, they would undertake to bring it with only five horses. I presently knew what they meant, and was glad at heart to receive this intelligence. It seems, upon my first reaching the shore after our shipwreck, I was in such confusion, that before I came to the place where I went to sleep, my hat, which I had fastened with a string to my head while I was rowing, and had stuck on all the time I was swimming, fell off after I came to land; the string, as I conjecture, breaking by some accident, which I never observed, but thought my hat had been lost at sea. I entreated his imperial majesty to give orders it might be brought to me as soon as possible, describing to him the use and the nature of it: and the next day the waggoners arrived with it, but not in a very good condition; they had bored two holes in the brim, within an inch and half of the edge, and fastened two hooks in the holes; these hooks were tied by a long cord to the harness, and thus my hat was dragged along for above half an English mile; but, the ground in that country being extremely smooth and level, it received less damage than I expected.

Two days after this adventure, the emperor, having ordered that part of his army which quarters in and about his metropolis, to be in readiness, took a fancy of diverting himself in a very singular manner. He desired I would stand like a Colossus, with my legs as far asunder as I conveniently could. He then commanded his general (who was an old experienced leader, and a great patron of mine) to draw up the troops in close order, and march them under me; the foot by twenty-four abreast, and the horse by sixteen, with drums beating, colours flying, and pikes advanced. This body consisted of three thousand foot, and a thousand horse. His majesty gave orders, upon pain of death, that every soldier in his march should observe the strictest decency with regard to my person; which however could not prevent some of the younger officers from turning up their eyes as they passed under me: and, to confess the truth, my breeches were at that time in so ill a condition, that they afforded some opportunities for laughter and admiration.

I had sent so many memorials and petitions for my liberty, that his majesty at length mentioned the matter, first in the cabinet, and then in a full council; where it was opposed by none, except Skyresh Bolgolam, who was pleased, without any provocation, to be my mortal enemy. But it was carried against him by the whole board, and confirmed by the emperor. That minister was *galbet*, or admiral of the realm, very much in his master's confidence, and a person well versed in affairs, but of a morose and sour complexion. However, he was at length persuaded to comply; but prevailed that the articles and conditions upon which I should be set free, and to which I must swear, should be drawn up by himself. These articles were brought to me by Skyresh Bolgolam in person attended by two under-secretaries, and several persons of distinction. After they were read, I was demanded to swear to the performance of them; first in the manner of my own country, and afterwards in the method prescribed by their laws; which was, to hold my right foot in my left hand, and to place the middle finger of my right hand on the crown of my head, and my thumb on the tip of my right ear. But because the reader may be curious to have some idea of the style and manner of expression peculiar to that people, as well as to know the article upon which I recovered my liberty, I have made a translation of the whole instrument, word for word, as near as I was able, which I here offer to the public.

"Golbasto Momarem Evlame Gurdilo Shefin Mully Ully Gue, most mighty Emperor of Lilliput, delight and terror of the universe, whose dominions extend five thousand *blustrugs* (about twelve miles in circumference) to the extremities of the globe; monarch of all monarchs, taller than the sons of men; whose feet press down to the centre, and whose head strikes against the sun; at whose nod the princes of the earth shake their knees; pleasant as the spring, comfortable as the summer, fruitful as autumn, dreadful as winter: his most sublime majesty proposes to the man-mountain, lately arrived at our celestial dominions, the following articles, which, by a solemn oath, he shall be obliged to perform:—

"1st, The man-mountain shall not depart from our dominions, without our license under our great seal.

"2d, He shall not presume to come into our metropolis, without our express order; at which time, the inhabitants shall have two hours warning to keep within doors.

"3d, The said man-mountain shall confine his walks to our principal high roads, and not offer to walk, or lie down, in a meadow or field of corn.

"4th, As he walks the said roads, he shall take the utmost care not to trample upon the bodies of any of our loving subjects, their horses, or carriages, nor take any of our subjects into his hands without their own consent.

"5th, If an express requires extraordinary despatch, the man-mountain shall be obliged to carry, in his pocket, the messenger and horse a six days journey, once in every moon, and return the said messenger back (if so required) safe to our imperial presence.

"6th, He shall be our ally against our enemies in the island of Blefuscu, and do his utmost to destroy their fleet, which is now preparing to invade us.

"7th, That the said man-mountain shall, at his times of leisure, be aiding and assisting to our workmen, in helping to raise certain great stones, towards covering the wall of the principal park, and other our royal buildings.

"8th, That the said man-mountain shall, in two moons' time, deliver in an exact survey of the circumference of our dominions, by a computation of his own paces round the coast.

"Lastly, That, upon his solemn oath to observe all the above articles, the said man-mountain shall have a daily allowance of meat and drink sufficient for the support of 1724 of our subjects, with free access to our royal person, and other marks of our favour. Given at our palace at Belfaborac, the twelfth day of the ninety-first moon of our reign."

I swore and subscribed to these articles with great cheerfulness and content, although some of them were not so honourable as I could have wished; which proceeded wholly from the malice of Skyresh Bolgolam, the high-admiral: whereupon my chains were immediately unlocked, and I was at full liberty. The emperor himself, in person, did me the honour to be by at the whole ceremony. I made my acknowledgements by prostrating myself at his majesty's feet: but he commanded me to rise; and after many gracious expressions, which, to avoid the censure of vanity, I shall not repeat, he added, "that he hoped I should prove a useful servant, and well deserve all the favours he had already conferred upon me, or might do for the future."

The reader may please to observe, that, in the last article of the recovery of my liberty, the emperor stipulates to allow me a quantity of meat and drink sufficient for the support of 1724 Lilliputians. Some time after, asking a friend at court how they came to fix on that determinate number, he told me that his majesty's mathematicians, having taken the height of my body by the help of a quadrant, and finding it to exceed theirs in the proportion of twelve to one, they concluded from the similarity of their bodies, that mine must contain at least 1724 of theirs, and consequently would require as much food as was necessary to support that number of Lilliputians. By which the reader may conceive an idea of the ingenuity of that people, as well as the prudent and exact economy of so great a prince.

CHAPTER 4: MILDENDO, THE METROPOLIS OF LILLIPUT, DESCRIBED, TOGETHER WITH THE EMPEROR'S PALACE. A CONVERSATION BETWEEN THE AUTHOR AND A PRINCIPAL SECRETARY, CONCERNING THE AFFAIRS OF THAT EMPIRE. THE AUTHOR'S OFFERS TO SERVE THE EMPEROR IN HIS WARS.

The first request I made, after I had obtained my liberty, was, that I might have license to see Mildendo, the metropolis; which the emperor easily granted me, but with a special charge to do no hurt either to the inhabitants or their houses. The people had notice, by proclamation, of my design to visit the town. The wall which encompassed it is two feet and a half high, and at least eleven inches broad, so that a coach and horses may be driven very safely round it; and it is flanked with strong towers at ten feet distance. I stepped over the great western gate, and passed very gently, and sidling, through the two principal streets, only in my short waistcoat, for fear of damaging the roofs and eaves of the houses with the skirts of my coat. I walked with the utmost circumspection, to avoid treading on any stragglers who might remain in the streets, although the orders were very strict, that all people should keep in their houses, at their own peril. The garret windows and tops of houses were so crowded with spectators, that I thought in all my travels I had not seen a more populous place. The city is an exact square, each side of the wall being five hundred feet long. The two great streets, which run across and divide it into four quarters, are five feet wide. The lanes and alleys, which I could not enter, but only view them as I passed, are from twelve to eighteen inches. The town is capable of holding five hundred thousand souls: the houses are from three to five stories: the shops and markets well provided.

The emperor's palace is in the centre of the city where the two great streets meet. It is enclosed by a wall of two feet high, and twenty feet distance from the buildings. I had his majesty's permission to step over this wall; and, the space being so wide between that and the palace, I could easily view it on every side. The outward court is a square of forty feet, and includes two other courts: in the inmost are the royal apartments, which I was very desirous to see, but found it extremely difficult; for the great gates, from one square into another, were but eighteen inches high, and seven inches wide. Now the buildings of the outer court were at least five feet high, and it was impossible for me to stride over them without infinite damage to the pile, though the walls were strongly built of hewn stone, and four inches thick. At the same time the emperor had a great desire that I should see the magnificence of his palace; but this I was not able to do till three days after, which I spent in cutting down with my knife some of the largest trees in the royal park, about a hundred yards distant from the city. Of these trees I made two stools, each about three feet high, and strong enough to bear my weight. The people having received notice a second time, I went again through the city to the palace with my two stools in my hands. When I came to the side of the outer court, I stood upon one stool, and took the other in my hand; this I lifted over the roof, and gently set it down on the space between the first and second court, which was eight feet wide. I then stept over the building very conveniently from one stool to the other, and drew up the first after me with a hooked stick. By this contrivance I got into the inmost court; and, lying down upon my side, I applied my face to the windows of the middle stories, which were left open on purpose, and discovered the most splendid apartments that can be imagined. There I saw the empress and the young princes, in their several lodgings, with their chief attendants about them. Her imperial majesty was pleased to smile very graciously upon me, and gave me out of the window her hand to kiss.

But I shall not anticipate the reader with further descriptions of this kind, because I reserve them for a greater work, which is now almost ready for the press; containing a general description of this empire, from its first erection, through along series of princes; with a particular account of their wars and politics, laws, learning, and religion; their plants and animals; their peculiar manners and customs, with other matters very curious and useful; my chief design at present being only to relate such events and transactions as happened to the public or to myself during a residence of about nine months in that empire.

One morning, about a fortnight after I had obtained my liberty, Reldresal, principal secretary (as they style him) for private affairs, came to my house attended only by one servant. He ordered his coach to wait at a distance, and desired I would give him an hours audience; which I readily consented to, on account of his quality and personal merits, as well as of the many good offices he had done me during my solicitations at court. I offered to lie down that he might the more conveniently reach my ear, but he chose rather to let me hold him in my hand during our conversation. He began with compliments on my liberty; said "he might pretend to some merit in it;" but, however, added, "that if it had not been for the present situation of things at court, perhaps I might not have obtained it so soon. For," said he, "as flourishing a condition as we may appear to be in to foreigners, we labour under two mighty evils: a violent faction at home, and the danger of an invasion, by a most potent enemy, from abroad. As to the first, you are to understand, that for about seventy moons past there have been two struggling parties in this empire, under the names of *Tramecksan* and *Slamecksan*, from the high and low heels of their shoes, by which they distinguish themselves. It is alleged, indeed, that the high heels are most agreeable to our ancient constitution; but, however this be, his majesty has determined to make use only of low heels in the administration of the government, and all offices in the gift of the crown, as you cannot but observe; and particularly that his majesty's imperial heels are lower at least by a *drurr* than any of his court (*drurr* is a measure about the fourteenth part of an inch). The animosities between these two parties run so high, that they will neither eat, nor drink, nor talk with each other. We compute the *Tramecksan*, or high heels, to exceed us in number; but the power is wholly on our side. We apprehend his imperial highness, the heir to the crown, to have some tendency towards the high heels; at least we can plainly discover that one of his heels is higher than the other, which gives him a hobble in his gait. Now, in the midst of these intestine disquiets, we are threatened with an invasion from the island of Blefuscu, which is the other great empire of the universe, almost as large and powerful as this of his majesty. For as to what we have heard you affirm, that there are other kingdoms and states in the world inhabited by human creatures as large as yourself, our philosophers are in much doubt, and would rather conjecture that you dropped from the moon, or one of the stars; because it is certain, that a hundred mortals of your bulk would in a short time destroy all the fruits and cattle of his majesty's dominions: besides, our histories of six thousand moons make no mention of any other regions than the two great empires of Lilliput and Blefuscu. Which two mighty powers have, as I was going to tell you, been engaged in a most obstinate war for six-and-thirty moons past. It began upon the following occasion. It is allowed on all hands, that the primitive way of breaking eggs, before we eat them, was upon the larger end; but his present majesty's grandfather, while he was a boy, going to eat an egg, and breaking it according to the ancient practice, happened to cut one of his fingers. Whereupon the emperor his father published an edict, commanding all his subjects, upon great penalties, to break the smaller end of their eggs. The people so highly resented this law, that our histories tell us, there have been six rebellions raised on that account; wherein one emperor lost his life, and another his crown. These civil commotions were constantly fomented by the monarchs of Blefuscu; and when they were quelled, the exiles always fled for refuge to that empire. It is computed that eleven thousand persons have at several times suffered death, rather than submit to break their eggs at the smaller end. Many hundred large volumes have been published upon this controversy: but the books of the Big-endians have been long forbidden, and the whole party rendered incapable by law of holding employments. During the course of these troubles, the emperors of Blefuscu did frequently expostulate by their ambassadors, accusing us of making a schism in religion, by offending against a fundamental doctrine of our great prophet Lustrog, in the fifty-fourth chapter of the Blundecral (which is their Alcoran). This, however, is thought to be a mere strain upon the text; for the words are these: 'that all true believers break their eggs at the convenient end.' And which is the convenient end, seems, in my humble opinion to be left to every man's conscience, or at least in the power of the chief magistrate to determine. Now, the Big-endian exiles have found so much credit in the emperor of Blefuscu's court, and so much private assistance and encouragement from their party here at home, that a bloody war has been carried on between the two empires for six-and-thirty moons, with various success; during which time we have lost forty capital ships, and a much a greater number of smaller vessels, together with thirty thousand of our best seamen and soldiers; and the damage received by the enemy is reckoned to be somewhat greater than ours. However, they have now equipped a numerous fleet, and are just preparing to make a descent upon us; and his imperial majesty, placing great confidence in your valour and strength, has commanded me to lay this account of his affairs before you."

I desired the secretary to present my humble duty to the emperor; and to let him know, "that I thought it would not become me, who was a foreigner, to interfere with parties; but I was ready, with the hazard of my life, to defend his person and state against all invaders."

CHAPTER 5: THE AUTHOR, BY AN EXTRAORDINARY STRATAGEM, PREVENTS AN INVASION. A HIGH TITLE OF HONOUR IS CONFERRED UPON HIM. AMBASSADORS ARRIVE FROM THE EMPEROR OF BLEFUSCU, AND SUE FOR PEACE. THE EMPRESS'S APARTMENT ON FIRE BY AN ACCIDENT; THE AUTHOR INSTRUMENTAL IN SAVING THE REST OF THE PALACE.

The empire of Blefuscu is an island situated to the north-east of Lilliput, from which it is parted only by a channel of eight hundred yards wide. I had not yet seen it, and upon this notice of an intended invasion, I avoided appearing on that side of the coast, for fear of being discovered, by some of the enemy's ships, who had received no intelligence of me; all intercourse between the two empires having been strictly forbidden during the war, upon pain of death, and an embargo laid by our emperor upon all vessels whatsoever. I communicated to his majesty a project I had formed of seizing the enemy's whole fleet; which, as our scouts assured us, lay at anchor in the harbour, ready to sail with the first fair wind. I consulted the most experienced seamen upon the depth of the channel, which they had often plumbed; who told me, that in the middle, at high-water, it was seventy *glumgluffs* deep, which is about six feet of European measure; and the rest of it fifty *glumgluffs* at most. I walked towards the north-east coast, over against Blefuscu, where, lying down behind a hillock, I took out my small perspective glass, and viewed the enemy's fleet at anchor, consisting of about fifty men of war, and a great number of transports: I then came back to my house, and gave orders (for which I had a warrant) for a great quantity of the strongest cable and bars of iron. The cable was about as thick as packthread and the bars of the length and size of a knitting-needle. I trebled the cable to make it stronger, and for the same reason I twisted three of the iron bars together, bending the extremities into a hook. Having thus fixed fifty hooks to as many cables, I went back to the north-east coast, and putting off my coat, shoes, and stockings, walked into the sea, in my leathern jerkin, about half an hour before high water. I waded with what haste I could, and swam in the middle about thirty yards, till I felt ground. I arrived at the fleet in less than half an hour. The enemy was so frightened when they saw me, that they leaped out of their ships, and swam to shore, where there could not be fewer than thirty thousand souls. I then took my tackling, and, fastening a hook to the hole at the prow of each, I tied all the cords together at the end. While I was thus employed, the enemy discharged several thousand arrows, many of which stuck in my hands and face, and, beside the excessive smart, gave me much disturbance in my work. My greatest apprehension was for mine eyes, which I should have infallibly lost, if I had not suddenly thought of an expedient. I kept, among other little necessaries, a pair of spectacles in a private pocket, which, as I observed before, had escaped the emperor's searchers. These I took out and fastened as strongly as I could upon my nose, and thus armed, went on boldly with my work, in spite of the enemy's arrows, many of which struck against the glasses of my spectacles, but without any other effect, further than a little to discompose them. I had now fastened all the hooks, and, taking the knot in my hand, began to pull; but not a ship would stir, for they were all too fast held by their anchors, so that the boldest part of my enterprise remained. I therefore let go the cord, and leaving the hooks fixed to the ships, I resolutely cut with my knife the cables that fastened the anchors, receiving about two hundred shots in my face and hands; then I took up the knotted end of the cables, to which my hooks were tied, and with great ease drew fifty of the enemy's largest men of war after me.

The Blefuscudians, who had not the least imagination of what I intended, were at first confounded with astonishment. They had seen me cut the cables, and thought my design was only to let the ships run adrift or fall foul on each other: but when they perceived the whole fleet moving in order, and saw me pulling at the end, they set up such a scream of grief and despair as it is almost impossible to describe or conceive. When I had got out of danger, I stopped awhile to pick out the arrows that stuck in my hands and face; and rubbed on some of the same ointment that was given me at my first arrival, as I have formerly mentioned. I then took off my spectacles, and waiting about an hour, till the tide was a little fallen, I waded through the middle with my cargo, and arrived safe at the royal port of Lilliput.

The emperor and his whole court stood on the shore, expecting the issue of this great adventure. They saw the ships move forward in a large half-moon, but could not discern me, who was up to my breast in water. When I advanced to the middle of the channel, they were yet more in pain, because I was under water to my neck. The emperor concluded me to be drowned, and that the enemy's fleet was approaching in a hostile manner: but he was soon eased of his fears; for the channel growing shallower every step I made, I came in a short time within hearing, and holding up the end of the cable, by which the fleet was fastened, I cried in a loud voice, "Long live the most puissant king of Lilliput!" This great prince received me at my landing with all possible encomiums, and created me a *nardac* upon the spot, which is the highest title of honour among them.

His majesty desired I would take some other opportunity of bringing all the rest of his enemy's ships into his ports. And so unmeasureable is the ambition of princes, that he seemed to think of nothing less than reducing the whole empire of Blefuscu into a province, and governing it, by a viceroy; of destroying the Big-endian exiles, and compelling that people to break the smaller end of their eggs, by which he would remain the sole monarch of the whole world. But I endeavoured to divert him from this design, by many arguments drawn from the topics of policy as well as justice; and I plainly protested, "that I would never be an instrument of bringing a free and brave people into slavery." And, when the matter was debated in council, the wisest part of the ministry were of my opinion.

This open bold declaration of mine was so opposite to the schemes and politics of his imperial majesty, that he could never forgive me. He mentioned it in a very artful manner at council, where I was told that some of the wisest appeared, at least by their silence, to be of my opinion; but others, who were my secret enemies, could not forbear some expressions which, by a side-wind, reflected on me. And from this time began an intrigue between his majesty and a junto of ministers, maliciously bent against me, which broke out in less than two months, and had like to have ended in my utter destruction. Of so little weight are the greatest services to princes, when put into the balance with a refusal to gratify their passions.

About three weeks after this exploit, there arrived a solemn embassy from Blefuscu, with humble offers of a peace, which was soon concluded, upon conditions very advantageous to our emperor, wherewith I shall not trouble the reader. There were six ambassadors, with a train of about five hundred persons, and their entry was very magnificent, suitable to the grandeur of their master, and the importance of their business. When their treaty was finished, wherein I did them several good offices by the credit I now had, or at least appeared to have, at court, their excellencies, who were privately told how much I had been their friend, made me a visit in form. They began with many compliments upon my valour and generosity, invited me to that kingdom in the emperor their master's name, and desired me to show them some proofs of my prodigious strength, of which they had heard so many wonders; wherein I readily obliged them, but shall not trouble the reader with the particulars.

When I had for some time entertained their excellencies, to their infinite satisfaction and surprise, I desired they would do me the honour to present my most humble respects to the emperor their master, the renown of whose virtues had so justly filled the whole world with admiration, and whose royal person I resolved to attend, before I returned to my own country. Accordingly, the next time I had the honour to see our emperor, I desired his general license to wait on the Blefuscudian monarch, which he was pleased to grant me, as I could perceive, in a very cold manner; but could not guess the reason, till I had a whisper from a certain person, "that Flimnap and Bolgolam had represented my intercourse with those ambassadors as a mark of disaffection;" from which I am sure my heart was wholly free. And this was the first time I began to conceive some imperfect idea of courts and ministers.

It is to be observed, that these ambassadors spoke to me, by an interpreter, the languages of both empires differing as much from each other as any two in Europe, and each nation priding itself upon the antiquity, beauty, and energy of their own tongue, with an avowed contempt for that of their neighbour; yet our emperor, standing upon the advantage he had got by the seizure of their fleet, obliged them to deliver their credentials, and make their speech, in the Lilliputian tongue. And it must be confessed, that from the great intercourse of trade and commerce between both realms, from the continual reception of exiles which is mutual among them, and from the custom, in each empire, to send their young nobility and richer gentry to the other, in order to polish themselves by seeing the world, and understanding men and manners; there are few persons of distinction, or merchants, or seamen, who dwell in the maritime parts, but what can hold conversation in both tongues; as I found some weeks after, when I went to pay my respects to the emperor of Blefuscu, which, in the midst of great misfortunes, through the malice of my enemies, proved a very happy adventure to me, as I shall relate in its proper place.

The reader may remember, that when I signed those articles upon which I recovered my liberty, there were some which I disliked, upon account of their being too servile; neither could anything but an extreme necessity have forced me to submit. But being now a *nardac* of the highest rank in that empire, such offices were looked upon as below my dignity, and the emperor (to do him justice), never once mentioned them to me. However, it was not long before I had an opportunity of doing his majesty, at least as I then thought, a most signal service. I was alarmed at midnight with the cries of many hundred people at my door; by which, being suddenly awaked, I was in some kind of terror. I heard the word *Burglum* repeated incessantly: several of the emperor's court, making their way through the crowd, entreated me to come immediately to the palace, where her imperial majesty's apartment was on fire, by the carelessness of a maid of honour, who fell asleep while she was reading a romance. I got up in an instant; and orders being given to clear the way before me, and it being likewise a moonshine night, I made a shift to get to the palace without trampling on any of the people. I found they had already applied ladders to the walls of the apartment, and were well provided with buckets, but the water was at some distance. These buckets were about the size of large thimbles, and the poor people supplied me with them as fast as they could: but the flame was so violent that they did little good. I might easily have stifled it with my coat, which I unfortunately left behind me for haste, and came away only in my leathern jerkin. The case seemed wholly desperate and deplorable; and this magnificent palace would have infallibly been burnt down to the ground, if, by a presence of mind unusual to me, I had not suddenly thought of an expedient. I had, the evening before, drunk plentifully of a most delicious wine called *glimigrim*, (the Blefuscudians call it *flunec*, but ours is esteemed the better sort,) which is very diuretic. By the luckiest chance in the world, I had not discharged myself of any part of it. The heat I had contracted by coming very near the flames, and by labouring to quench them, made the wine begin to operate by urine; which I voided in such a quantity, and applied so well to the proper places, that in three minutes the fire was wholly extinguished, and the rest of that noble pile, which had cost so many ages in erecting, preserved from destruction.

It was now day-light, and I returned to my house without waiting to congratulate with the emperor: because, although I had done a very eminent piece of service, yet I could not tell how his majesty might resent the manner by which I had performed it: for, by the fundamental laws of the realm, it is capital in any person, of what quality soever, to make water within the precincts of the palace. But I was a little comforted by a message from his majesty, "that he would give orders to the grand justiciary for passing my pardon in form:" which, however, I could not obtain; and I was privately assured, "that the empress, conceiving the greatest abhorrence of what I had done, removed to the most distant side of the court, firmly resolved that those buildings should never be repaired for her use: and, in the presence of her chief confidents could not forbear vowing revenge."

CHAPTER 6: OF THE INHABITANTS OF LILLIPUT; THEIR LEARNING, LAWS, AND CUSTOMS; THE MANNER OF EDUCATING THEIR CHILDREN. THE AUTHOR'S WAY OF LIVING IN THAT COUNTRY. HIS VINDICATION OF A GREAT LADY.

Although I intend to leave the description of this empire to a particular treatise, yet, in the mean time, I am content to gratify the curious reader with some general ideas. As the common size of the natives is somewhat under six inches high, so there is an exact proportion in all other animals, as well as plants and trees: for instance, the tallest horses and oxen are between four and five inches in height, the sheep an inch and half, more or less: their geese about the bigness of a sparrow, and so the several gradations downwards till you come to the smallest, which to my sight, were almost invisible; but nature has adapted the eyes of the Lilliputians to all objects proper for their view: they see with great exactness, but at no great distance. And, to show the sharpness of their sight towards objects that are near, I have been much pleased with observing a cook pulling a lark, which was not so large as a common fly; and a young girl threading an invisible needle with invisible silk. Their tallest trees are about seven feet high: I mean some of those in the great royal park, the tops whereof I could but just reach with my fist clenched. The other vegetables are in the same proportion; but this I leave to the reader's imagination.

I shall say but little at present of their learning, which, for many ages, has flourished in all its branches among them: but their manner of writing is very peculiar, being neither from the left to the right, like the Europeans, nor from the right to the left, like the Arabians, nor from up to down, like the Chinese, but aslant, from one corner of the paper to the other, like ladies in England.

They bury their dead with their heads directly downward, because they hold an opinion, that in eleven thousand moons they are all to rise again; in which period the earth (which they conceive to be flat) will turn upside down, and by this means they shall, at their resurrection, be found ready standing on their feet.

The learned among them confess the absurdity of this doctrine; but the practice still continues, in compliance to the vulgar.

There are some laws and customs in this empire very peculiar; and if they were not so directly contrary to those of my own dear country, I should be tempted to say a little in their justification. It is only to be wished they were as well executed. The first I shall mention, relates to informers. All crimes against the state, are punished here with the utmost severity; but, if the person accused makes his innocence plainly to appear upon his trial, the accuser is immediately put to an ignominious death; and out of his goods or lands the innocent person is quadruply recompensed for the loss of his time, for the danger he underwent, for the hardship of his imprisonment, and for all the charges he has been at in making his defence; or, if that fund be deficient, it is largely supplied by the crown. The emperor also confers on him some public mark of his favour, and proclamation is made of his innocence through the whole city.

They look upon fraud as a greater crime than theft, and therefore seldom fail to punish it with death; for they allege, that care and vigilance, with a very common understanding, may preserve a man's goods from thieves, but honesty has no defence against superior cunning; and, since it is necessary that there should be a perpetual intercourse of buying and selling, and dealing upon credit, where fraud is permitted and connived at, or has no law to punish it, the honest dealer is always undone, and the knave gets the advantage. I remember, when I was once interceding with the emperor for a criminal who had wronged his master of a great sum of money, which he had received by order and ran away with; and happening to tell his majesty, by way of extenuation, that it was only a breach of trust, the emperor thought it monstrous in me to offer as a defence the greatest aggravation of the crime; and truly I had little to say in return, farther than the common answer, that different nations had different customs; for, I confess, I was heartily ashamed.[2]

Although we usually call reward and punishment the two hinges upon which all government turns, yet I could never observe this maxim to be put in practice by any nation except that of Lilliput. Whoever can there bring sufficient proof, that he has strictly observed the laws of his country for seventy-three moons, has a claim to certain privileges, according to his quality or condition of life, with a proportionable sum of money out of a fund appropriated for that use: he likewise acquires the title of *snilpall*, or legal, which is added to his name, but does not descend to his posterity. And these people thought it a prodigious defect of policy among us, when I told them that our laws were enforced only by penalties, without any mention of reward. It is upon this account that the image of Justice, in their courts of judicature, is formed with six eyes, two before, as many behind, and on each side one, to signify circumspection; with a bag of gold open in her right hand, and a sword sheathed in her left, to show she is more disposed to reward than to punish.

In choosing persons for all employments, they have more regard to good morals than to great abilities; for, since government is necessary to mankind, they believe, that the common size of human understanding is fitted to some station or other; and that Providence never intended to make the management of public affairs a mystery to be comprehended only by a few persons of sublime genius, of which there seldom are three born in an age: but they suppose truth, justice, temperance, and the like, to be in every man's power; the practice of which virtues, assisted by experience and a good intention, would qualify any man for the service of his country, except where a course of study is required. But they thought the want of moral virtues was so far from being supplied by superior endowments of the mind, that employments could never be put into such dangerous hands as those of persons so qualified; and, at least, that the mistakes committed by ignorance, in a virtuous disposition, would never be of such fatal consequence to the public weal, as the practices of a man, whose inclinations led him to be corrupt, and who had great abilities to manage, to multiply, and defend his corruptions.

In like manner, the disbelief of a Divine Providence renders a man incapable of holding any public station; for, since kings avow themselves to be the deputies of Providence, the Lilliputians think nothing can be more absurd than for a prince to employ such men as disown the authority under which he acts.

In relating these and the following laws, I would only be understood to mean the original institutions, and not the most scandalous corruptions, into which these people are fallen by the degenerate nature of man. For, as to that infamous practice of acquiring great employments by dancing on the ropes, or badges of favour and distinction by leaping over sticks and creeping under them, the reader is to observe, that they were first introduced by the grandfather of the emperor now reigning, and grew to the present height by the gradual increase of party and faction.

Ingratitude is among them a capital crime, as we read it to have been in some other countries: for they reason thus; that whoever makes ill returns to his benefactor, must needs be a common enemy to the rest of mankind, from whom he has received no obligation, and therefore such a man is not fit to live.

Their notions relating to the duties of parents and children differ extremely from ours. For, since the conjunction of male and female is founded upon the great law of nature, in order to propagate and continue the species, the Lilliputians will needs have it, that men and women are joined together, like other animals, by the motives of concupiscence; and that their tenderness towards their young proceeds from the like natural principle: for which reason they will never allow that a child is under any obligation to his father for begetting him, or to his mother for bringing him into the world; which, considering the miseries of human life, was neither a benefit in itself, nor intended so by his parents, whose thoughts, in their love encounters, were otherwise employed. Upon these, and the like reasonings, their opinion is, that parents are the last of all others to be trusted with the education of their own children; and therefore they have in every town public nurseries, where all parents, except cottagers and labourers, are obliged to send their infants of both sexes to be reared and educated, when they come to the age of twenty moons, at which time they are supposed to have some rudiments of docility. These schools are of several kinds, suited to different qualities, and both sexes. They have certain professors well skilled in preparing children for such a condition of life as befits the rank of their parents, and their own capacities, as well as inclinations. I shall first say something of the male nurseries, and then of the female.

The nurseries for males of noble or eminent birth, are provided with grave and learned professors, and their several deputies. The clothes and food of the children are plain and simple. They are bred up in the principles of honour, justice, courage, modesty, clemency, religion, and love of their country; they are always employed in some business, except in the times of eating and sleeping, which are very short, and two hours for diversions consisting of bodily exercises. They are dressed by men till four years of age, and then are obliged to dress themselves, although their quality be ever so great; and the women attendant, who are aged proportionably to ours at fifty, perform only the most menial offices. They are never suffered to converse with servants, but go together in smaller or greater numbers to take their diversions, and always in the presence of a professor, or one of his deputies; whereby they avoid those early bad impressions of folly and vice, to which our children are subject. Their parents are suffered to see them only twice a year; the visit is to last but an hour; they are allowed to kiss the child at meeting and parting; but a professor, who always stands by on those occasions, will not suffer them to whisper, or use any fondling expressions, or bring any presents of toys, sweetmeats, and the like.

The pension from each family for the education and entertainment of a child, upon failure of due payment, is levied by the emperor's officers.

The nurseries for children of ordinary gentlemen, merchants, traders, and handicrafts, are managed proportionably after the same manner; only those designed for trades are put out apprentices at eleven years old, whereas those of persons of quality continue in their exercises till fifteen, which answers to twenty-one with us: but the confinement is gradually lessened for the last three years.

In the female nurseries, the young girls of quality are educated much like the males, only they are dressed by orderly servants of their own sex; but always in the presence of a professor or deputy, till they come to dress themselves, which is at five years old. And if it be found that these nurses ever presume to entertain the girls with frightful or foolish stories, or the common follies practised by chambermaids among us, they are publicly whipped thrice about the city, imprisoned for a year, and banished for life to the most desolate part of the country. Thus the young ladies are as much ashamed of being cowards and fools as the men, and despise all personal ornaments, beyond decency and cleanliness: neither did I perceive any difference in their education made by their difference of sex, only that the exercises of the females were not altogether so robust; and that some rules were given them relating to domestic life, and a smaller compass of learning was enjoined them: for their maxim is, that among peoples of quality, a wife should be always a reasonable and agreeable companion, because she cannot always be young. When the girls are twelve years old, which among them is the marriageable age, their parents or guardians take them home, with great expressions of gratitude to the professors, and seldom without tears of the young lady and her companions.

In the nurseries of females of the meaner sort, the children are instructed in all kinds of works proper for their sex, and their several degrees: those intended for apprentices are dismissed at seven years old, the rest are kept to eleven.

The meaner families who have children at these nurseries, are obliged, besides their annual pension, which is as low as possible, to return to the steward of the nursery a small monthly share of their gettings, to be a portion for the child; and therefore all parents are limited in their expenses by the law. For the Lilliputians think nothing can be more unjust, than for people, in subservience to their own appetites, to bring children into the world, and leave the burthen of supporting them on the public. As to persons of quality, they give security to appropriate a certain sum for each child, suitable to their condition; and these funds are always managed with good husbandry and the most exact justice.

The cottagers and labourers keep their children at home, their business being only to till and cultivate the earth, and therefore their education is of little consequence to the public: but the old and diseased among them, are supported by hospitals; for begging is a trade unknown in this empire.

And here it may, perhaps, divert the curious reader, to give some account of my domestics, and my manner of living in this country, during a residence of nine months, and thirteen days. Having a head mechanically turned, and being likewise forced by necessity, I had made for myself a table and chair convenient enough, out of the largest trees in the royal park. Two hundred sempstresses were employed to make me shirts, and linen for my bed and table, all of the strongest and coarsest kind they could get; which, however, they were forced to quilt together in several folds, for the thickest was some degrees finer than lawn. Their linen is usually three inches wide, and three feet make a piece. The sempstresses took my measure as I lay on the ground, one standing at my neck, and another at my mid-leg, with a strong cord extended, that each held by the end, while a third measured the length of the cord with a rule of an inch long. Then they measured my right thumb, and desired no more; for by a mathematical computation, that twice round the thumb is once round the wrist, and so on to the neck and the waist, and by the help of my old shirt, which I displayed on the ground before them for a pattern, they fitted me exactly. Three hundred tailors were employed in the same manner to make me clothes; but they had another contrivance for taking my measure. I kneeled down, and they raised a ladder from the ground to my neck; upon this ladder one of them mounted, and let fall a plumb-line from my collar to the floor, which just answered the length of my coat: but my waist and arms I measured myself. When my clothes were finished, which was done in my house (for the largest of theirs would not have been able to hold them), they looked like the patch-work made by the ladies in England, only that mine were all of a colour.

I had three hundred cooks to dress my victuals, in little convenient huts built about my house, where they and their families lived, and prepared me two dishes a-piece. I took up twenty waiters in my hand, and placed them on the table: a hundred more attended below on the ground, some with dishes of meat, and some with barrels of wine and other liquors slung on their shoulders; all which the waiters above drew up, as I wanted, in a very ingenious manner, by certain cords, as we draw the bucket up a well in Europe. A dish of their meat was a good mouthful, and a barrel of their liquor a reasonable draught. Their mutton yields to ours, but their beef is excellent. I have had a sirloin so large, that I have been forced to make three bites of it; but this is rare. My servants were astonished to see me eat it, bones and all, as in our country we do the leg of a lark. Their geese and turkeys I usually ate at a mouthful, and I confess they far exceed ours. Of their smaller fowl I could take up twenty or thirty at the end of my knife.

One day his imperial majesty, being informed of my way of living, desired "that himself and his royal consort, with the young princes of the blood of both sexes, might have the happiness," as he was pleased to call it, "of dining with me." They came accordingly, and I placed them in chairs of state, upon my table, just over against me, with their guards about them. Flimnap, the lord high treasurer, attended there likewise with his white staff; and I observed he often looked on me with a sour countenance, which I would not seem to regard, but ate more than usual, in honour to my dear country, as well as to fill the court with admiration. I have some private reasons to believe, that this visit from his majesty gave Flimnap an opportunity of doing me ill offices to his master. That minister had always been my secret enemy, though he outwardly caressed me more than was usual to the moroseness of his nature. He represented to the emperor "the low condition of his treasury; that he was forced to take up money at a great discount; that exchequer bills would not circulate under nine per cent. below par; that I had cost his majesty above a million and a half of *sprugs*" (their greatest gold coin, about the bigness of a spangle) "and, upon the whole, that it would be advisable in the emperor to take the first fair occasion of dismissing me."

I am here obliged to vindicate the reputation of an excellent lady, who was an innocent sufferer upon my account. The treasurer took a fancy to be jealous of his wife, from the malice of some evil tongues, who informed him that her grace had taken a violent affection for my person; and the court scandal ran for some time, that she once came privately to my lodging. This I solemnly declare to be a most infamous falsehood, without any grounds, further than that her grace was pleased to treat me with all innocent marks of freedom and friendship. I own she came often to my house, but always publicly, nor ever without three more in the coach, who were usually her sister and young daughter, and some particular acquaintance; but this was common to many other ladies of the court. And I still appeal to my servants round, whether they at any time saw a coach at my door, without knowing what persons were in it. On those occasions, when a servant had given me notice, my custom was to go immediately to the door, and, after paying my respects, to take up the coach and two horses very carefully in my hands (for, if there were six horses, the postillion always unharnessed four,) and place them on a table, where I had fixed a movable rim quite round, of five inches high, to prevent accidents. And I have often had four coaches and horses at once on my table, full of company, while I sat in my chair, leaning my face towards them; and when I was engaged with one set, the coachmen would gently drive the others round my table. I have passed many an afternoon very agreeably in these conversations. But I defy the treasurer, or his two informers (I will name them, and let them make the best of it) Clustril and Drunlo, to prove that any person ever came to me *incognito*, except the secretary Reldresal, who was sent by express command of his imperial majesty, as I have before related. I should not have dwelt so long upon this particular, if it had not been a point wherein the reputation of a great lady is so nearly concerned, to say nothing of my own; though I then had the honour to be a *nardac*, which the treasurer himself is not; for all the world knows, that he is only a *glumglum*, a title inferior by one degree, as that of a marquis is to a duke in England; yet I allow he preceded me in right of his post. These false informations, which I afterwards came to the knowledge of by an accident not proper to mention, made the treasurer show his lady for some time an ill countenance, and me a worse; and although he was at last undeceived and reconciled to her, yet I lost all credit with him, and found my interest decline very fast with the emperor himself, who was, indeed, too much governed by that favourite.

CHAPTER 7: THE AUTHOR, BEING INFORMED OF A DESIGN TO ACCUSE HIM OF HIGH-TREASON, MAKES HIS ESCAPE TO BLEFUSCU. HIS RECEPTION THERE.

Before I proceed to give an account of my leaving this kingdom, it may be proper to inform the reader of a private intrigue which had been for two months forming against me.

I had been hitherto, all my life, a stranger to courts, for which I was unqualified by the meanness of my condition. I had indeed heard and read enough of the dispositions of great princes and ministers, but never expected to have found such terrible effects of them, in so remote a country, governed, as I thought, by very different maxims from those in Europe.

When I was just preparing to pay my attendance on the emperor of Blefuscu, a considerable person at court (to whom I had been very serviceable, at a time when he lay under the highest displeasure of his imperial majesty) came to my house very privately at night, in a close chair, and, without sending his name, desired admittance. The chairmen were dismissed; I put the chair, with his lordship in it, into my coat-pocket: and, giving orders to a trusty servant, to say I was indisposed and gone to sleep, I fastened the door of my house, placed the chair on the table, according to my usual custom, and sat down by it. After the common salutations were over, observing his lordship's countenance full of concern, and inquiring into the reason, he desired "I would hear him with patience, in a matter that highly concerned my honour and my life." His speech was to the following effect, for I took notes of it as soon as he left me:—

"You are to know," said he, "that several committees of council have been lately called, in the most private manner, on your account; and it is but two days since his majesty came to a full resolution.

"You are very sensible that Skyresh Bolgolam" (*galbet*, or high-admiral) "has been your mortal enemy, almost ever since your arrival. His original reasons I know not; but his hatred is increased since your great success against Blefuscu, by which his glory as admiral is much obscured. This lord, in conjunction with Flimnap the high-treasurer, whose enmity against you is notorious on account of his lady, Limtoc the general, Lalcon the chamberlain, and Balmuff the grand justiciary, have prepared articles of impeachment against you, for treason and other capital crimes."

This preface made me so impatient, being conscious of my own merits and innocence, that I was going to interrupt him; when he entreated me to be silent, and thus proceeded:—

"Out of gratitude for the favours you have done me, I procured information of the whole proceedings, and a copy of the articles; wherein I venture my head for your service.

"Articles of Impeachment against QUINBUS FLESTRIN, (the Man-Mountain.)
ARTICLE I.

"'Whereas, by a statute made in the reign of his imperial majesty Calin Deffar Plune, it is enacted, that, whoever shall make water within the precincts of the royal palace, shall be liable to the pains and penalties of high-treason; notwithstanding, the said Quinbus Flestrin, in open breach of the said law, under colour of extinguishing the fire kindled in the apartment of his majesty's most dear imperial consort, did maliciously, traitorously, and devilishly, by discharge of his urine, put out the said fire kindled in the said apartment, lying and being within the precincts of the said royal palace, against the statute in that case provided, etc. against the duty, etc.

ARTICLE II.

"'That the said Quinbus Flestrin, having brought the imperial fleet of Blefuscu into the royal port, and being afterwards commanded by his imperial majesty to seize all the other ships of the said empire of Blefuscu, and reduce that empire to a province, to be governed by a viceroy from hence, and to destroy and put to death, not only all the Big-endian exiles, but likewise all the people of that empire who would not immediately forsake the Big-endian heresy, he, the said Flestrin, like a false traitor against his most auspicious, serene, imperial majesty, did petition to be excused from the said service, upon pretence of unwillingness to force the consciences, or destroy the liberties and lives of an innocent people.

ARTICLE III.

"'That, whereas certain ambassadors arrived from the Court of Blefuscu, to sue for peace in his majesty's court, he, the said Flestrin, did, like a false traitor, aid, abet, comfort, and divert, the said ambassadors, although he knew them to be servants to a prince who was lately an open enemy to his imperial majesty, and in an open war against his said majesty.

ARTICLE IV.

"'That the said Quinbus Flestrin, contrary to the duty of a faithful subject, is now preparing to make a voyage to the court and empire of Blefuscu, for which he has received only verbal license from his imperial majesty; and, under colour of the said license, does falsely and traitorously intend to take the said voyage, and thereby to aid, comfort, and abet the emperor of Blefuscu, so lately an enemy, and in open war with his imperial majesty aforesaid.'

"There are some other articles; but these are the most important, of which I have read you an abstract.

"In the several debates upon this impeachment, it must be confessed that his majesty gave many marks of his great lenity; often urging the services you had done him, and endeavouring to extenuate your crimes. The treasurer and admiral insisted that you should be put to the most painful and ignominious death, by setting fire to your house at night, and the general was to attend with twenty thousand men, armed with poisoned arrows, to shoot you on the face and hands. Some of your servants were to have private orders to strew a poisonous juice on your shirts and sheets, which would soon make you tear your own flesh, and die in the utmost torture. The general came into the same opinion; so that for a long time there was a majority against you; but his majesty resolving, if possible, to spare your life, at last brought off the chamberlain.

"Upon this incident, Reldresal, principal secretary for private affairs, who always approved himself your true friend, was commanded by the emperor to deliver his opinion, which he accordingly did; and therein justified the good thoughts you have of him. He allowed your crimes to be great, but that still there was room for mercy, the most commendable virtue in a prince, and for which his majesty was so justly celebrated. He said, the friendship between you and him was so well known to the world, that perhaps the most honourable board might think him partial; however, in obedience to the command he had received, he would freely offer his sentiments. That if his majesty, in consideration of your services, and pursuant to his own merciful disposition, would please to spare your life, and only give orders to put out both your eyes, he humbly conceived, that by this expedient justice might in some measure be satisfied, and all the world would applaud the lenity of the emperor, as well as the fair and generous proceedings of those who have the honour to be his counsellors. That the loss of your eyes would be no impediment to your bodily strength, by which you might still be useful to his majesty; that blindness is an addition to courage, by concealing dangers from us; that the fear you had for your eyes, was the greatest difficulty in bringing over the enemy's fleet, and it would be sufficient for you to see by the eyes of the ministers, since the greatest princes do no more.

"This proposal was received with the utmost disapprobation by the whole board. Bolgolam, the admiral, could not preserve his temper, but, rising up in fury, said, he wondered how the secretary durst presume to give his opinion for preserving the life of a traitor; that the services you had performed were, by all true reasons of state, the great aggravation of your crimes; that you, who were able to extinguish the fire by discharge of urine in her majesty's apartment (which he mentioned with horror), might, at another time, raise an inundation by the same means, to drown the whole palace; and the same strength which enabled you to bring over the enemy's fleet, might serve, upon the first discontent, to carry it back; that he had good reasons to think you were a Big-endian in your heart; and, as treason begins in the heart, before it appears in overt-acts, so he accused you as a traitor on that account, and therefore insisted you should be put to death.

"The treasurer was of the same opinion: he showed to what straits his majesty's revenue was reduced, by the charge of maintaining you, which would soon grow insupportable; that the secretary's expedient of putting out your eyes, was so far from being a remedy against this evil, that it would probably increase it, as is manifest from the common practice of blinding some kind of fowls, after which they fed the faster, and grew sooner fat; that his sacred majesty and the council, who are your judges, were, in their own consciences, fully convinced of your guilt, which was a sufficient argument to condemn you to death, without the formal proofs required by the strict letter of the law.

"But his imperial majesty, fully determined against capital punishment, was graciously pleased to say, that since the council thought the loss of your eyes too easy a censure, some other way may be inflicted hereafter. And your friend the secretary, humbly desiring to be heard again, in answer to what the treasurer had objected, concerning the great charge his majesty was at in maintaining you, said, that his excellency, who had the sole disposal of the emperor's revenue, might easily provide against that evil, by gradually lessening your establishment; by which, for want of sufficient for you would grow weak and faint, and lose your appetite, and consequently, decay, and consume in a few months; neither would the stench of your carcass be then so dangerous, when it should become more than half diminished; and immediately upon your death five or six thousand of his majesty's subjects might, in two or three days, cut your flesh from your bones, take it away by cart-loads, and bury it in distant parts, to prevent infection, leaving the skeleton as a monument of admiration to posterity.

"Thus, by the great friendship of the secretary, the whole affair was compromised. It was strictly enjoined, that the project of starving you by degrees should be kept a secret; but the sentence of putting out your eyes was entered on the books; none dissenting, except Bolgolam the admiral, who, being a creature of the empress, was perpetually instigated by her majesty to insist upon your death, she having borne perpetual malice against you, on account of that infamous and illegal method you took to extinguish the fire in her apartment.

"In three days your friend the secretary will be directed to come to your house, and read before you the articles of impeachment; and then to signify the great lenity and favour of his majesty and council, whereby you are only condemned to the loss of your eyes, which his majesty does not question you will gratefully and humbly submit to; and twenty of his majesty's surgeons will attend, in order to see the operation well performed, by discharging very sharp-pointed arrows into the balls of your eyes, as you lie on the ground.

"I leave to your prudence what measures you will take; and to avoid suspicion, I must immediately return in as private a manner as I came."

His lordship did so; and I remained alone, under many doubts and perplexities of mind.

It was a custom introduced by this prince and his ministry (very different, as I have been assured, from the practice of former times,) that after the court had decreed any cruel execution, either to gratify the monarch's resentment, or the malice of a favourite, the emperor always made a speech to his whole council, expressing his great lenity and tenderness, as qualities known and confessed by all the world. This speech was immediately published throughout the kingdom; nor did any thing terrify the people so much as those encomiums on his majesty's mercy; because it was observed, that the more these praises were enlarged and insisted on, the more inhuman was the punishment, and the sufferer more innocent. Yet, as to myself, I must confess, having never been designed for a courtier, either by my birth or education, I was so ill a judge of things, that I could not discover the lenity and favour of this sentence, but conceived it (perhaps erroneously) rather to be rigorous than gentle. I sometimes thought of standing my trial, for, although I could not deny the facts alleged in the several articles, yet I hoped they would admit of some extenuation. But having in my life perused many state-trials, which I ever observed to terminate as the judges thought fit to direct, I durst not rely on so dangerous a decision, in so critical a juncture, and against such powerful enemies. Once I was strongly bent upon resistance, for, while I had liberty the whole strength of that empire could hardly subdue me, and I might easily with stones pelt the metropolis to pieces; but I soon rejected that project with horror, by remembering the oath I had made to the emperor, the favours I received from him, and the high title of *nardac* he conferred upon me. Neither had I so soon learned the gratitude of courtiers, to persuade myself, that his majesty's present seventies acquitted me of all past obligations.

At last, I fixed upon a resolution, for which it is probable I may incur some censure, and not unjustly; for I confess I owe the preserving of mine eyes, and consequently my liberty, to my own great rashness and want of experience; because, if I had then known the nature of princes and ministers, which I have since observed in many other courts, and their methods of treating criminals less obnoxious than myself, I should, with great alacrity and readiness, have submitted to so easy a punishment. But hurried on by the precipitancy of youth, and having his imperial majesty's license to pay my attendance upon the emperor of Blefuscu, I took this opportunity, before the three days were elapsed, to send a letter to my friend the secretary, signifying my resolution of setting out that morning for

Blefuscu, pursuant to the leave I had got; and, without waiting for an answer, I went to that side of the island where our fleet lay. I seized a large man of war, tied a cable to the prow, and, lifting up the anchors, I stripped myself, put my clothes (together with my coverlet, which I carried under my arm) into the vessel, and, drawing it after me, between wading and swimming arrived at the royal port of Blefuscu, where the people had long expected me: they lent me two guides to direct me to the capital city, which is of the same name. I held them in my hands, till I came within two hundred yards of the gate, and desired them "to signify my arrival to one of the secretaries, and let him know, I there waited his majesty's command." I had an answer in about an hour, "that his majesty, attended by the royal family, and great officers of the court, was coming out to receive me." I advanced a hundred yards. The emperor and his train alighted from their horses, the empress and ladies from their coaches, and I did not perceive they were in any fright or concern. I lay on the ground to kiss his majesty's and the empress's hands. I told his majesty, "that I was come according to my promise, and with the license of the emperor my master, to have the honour of seeing so mighty a monarch, and to offer him any service in my power, consistent with my duty to my own prince;" not mentioning a word of my disgrace, because I had hitherto no regular information of it, and might suppose myself wholly ignorant of any such design; neither could I reasonably conceive that the emperor would discover the secret, while I was out of his power; wherein, however, it soon appeared I was deceived.

I shall not trouble the reader with the particular account of my reception at this court, which was suitable to the generosity of so great a prince; nor of the difficulties I was in for want of a house and bed, being forced to lie on the ground, wrapped up in my coverlet.

CHAPTER 8: THE AUTHOR, BY A LUCKY ACCIDENT, FINDS MEANS TO LEAVE BLEFUSCU; AND, AFTER SOME DIFFICULTIES, RETURNS SAFE TO HIS NATIVE COUNTRY.

Three days after my arrival, walking out of curiosity to the north-east coast of the island, I observed, about half a league off in the sea, somewhat that looked like a boat overturned. I pulled off my shoes and stockings, and, wailing two or three hundred yards, I found the object to approach nearer by force of the tide; and then plainly saw it to be a real boat, which I supposed might by some tempest have been driven from a ship. Whereupon, I returned immediately towards the city, and desired his imperial majesty to lend me twenty of the tallest vessels he had left, after the loss of his fleet, and three thousand seamen, under the command of his vice-admiral. This fleet sailed round, while I went back the shortest way to the coast, where I first discovered the boat. I found the tide had driven it still nearer. The seamen were all provided with cordage, which I had beforehand twisted to a sufficient strength. When the ships came up, I stripped myself, and waded till I came within a hundred yards off the boat, after which I was forced to swim till I got up to it. The seamen threw me the end of the cord, which I fastened to a hole in the fore-part of the boat, and the other end to a man of war; but I found all my labour to little purpose; for, being out of my depth, I was not able to work. In this necessity I was forced to swim behind, and push the boat forward, as often as I could, with one of my hands; and the tide favouring me, I advanced so far that I could just hold up my chin and feel the ground. I rested two or three minutes, and then gave the boat another shove, and so on, till the sea was no higher than my arm-pits; and now, the most laborious part being over, I took out my other cables, which were stowed in one of the ships, and fastened them first to the boat, and then to nine of the vessels which attended me; the wind being favourable, the seamen towed, and I shoved, until we arrived within forty yards of the shore; and, waiting till the tide was out, I got dry to the boat, and by the assistance of two thousand men, with ropes and engines, I made a shift to turn it on its bottom, and found it was but little damaged.

I shall not trouble the reader with the difficulties I was under, by the help of certain paddles, which cost me ten days making, to get my boat to the royal port of Blefuscu, where a mighty concourse of people appeared upon my arrival, full of wonder at the sight of so prodigious a vessel. I told the emperor "that my good fortune had thrown this boat in my way, to carry me to some place whence I might return into my native country; and begged his majesty's orders for getting materials to fit it up, together with his license to depart;" which, after some kind expostulations, he was pleased to grant.

I did very much wonder, in all this time, not to have heard of any express relating to me from our emperor to the court of Blefuscu. But I was afterward given privately to understand, that his imperial majesty, never imagining I had the least notice of his designs, believed I was only gone to Blefuscu in performance of my promise, according to the license he had given me, which was well known at our court, and would return in a few days, when the ceremony was ended. But he was at last in pain at my long absence; and after consulting with the treasurer and the rest of that cabal, a person of quality was dispatched with the copy of the articles against me. This envoy had instructions to represent to the monarch of Blefuscu, "the great lenity of his master, who was content to punish me no farther than with the loss of mine eyes; that I had fled from justice; and if I did not return in two hours, I should be deprived of my title of *nardac*, and declared a traitor." The envoy further added, "that in order to maintain the peace and amity between both empires, his master expected that his brother of Blefuscu would give orders to have me sent back to Lilliput, bound hand and foot, to be punished as a traitor."

The emperor of Blefuscu, having taken three days to consult, returned an answer consisting of many civilities and excuses. He said, "that as for sending me bound, his brother knew it was impossible; that, although I had deprived him of his fleet, yet he owed great obligations to me for many good offices I had done him in making the peace. That, however, both their majesties would soon be made easy; for I had found a prodigious vessel on the shore, able to carry me on the sea, which he had given orders to fit up, with my own assistance and direction; and he hoped, in a few weeks, both empires would be freed from so insupportable an encumbrance."

With this answer the envoy returned to Lilliput; and the monarch of Blefuscu related to me all that had passed; offering me at the same time (but under the strictest confidence) his gracious protection, if I would continue in his service; wherein, although I believed him sincere, yet I resolved never more to put any confidence in princes or ministers, where I could possibly avoid it; and therefore, with all due acknowledgments for his favourable intentions, I humbly begged to be excused. I told him, "that since fortune, whether good or evil, had thrown a vessel in my way, I was resolved to venture myself on the ocean, rather than be an occasion of difference between two such mighty monarchs." Neither did I find the emperor at all displeased; and I discovered, by a certain accident, that he was very glad of my resolution, and so were most of his ministers.

These considerations moved me to hasten my departure somewhat sooner than I intended; to which the court, impatient to have me gone, very readily contributed. Five hundred workmen were employed to make two sails to my boat, according to my directions, by quilting thirteen folds of their strongest linen together. I was at the pains of making ropes and cables, by twisting ten, twenty, or thirty of the thickest and strongest of theirs. A great stone that I happened to find, after a long search, by the sea-shore, served me for an anchor. I had the tallow of three hundred cows, for greasing my boat, and other uses. I was at incredible pains in cutting down some of the largest timber-trees, for oars and masts, wherein I was, however, much assisted by his majesty's ship-carpenters, who helped me in smoothing them, after I had done the rough work.

In about a month, when all was prepared, I sent to receive his majesty's commands, and to take my leave. The emperor and royal family came out of the palace; I lay down on my face to kiss his hand, which he very graciously gave me: so did the empress and young princes of the blood. His majesty presented me with fifty purses of two hundred *sprugs* a-piece, together with his picture at full length, which I put immediately into one of my gloves, to keep it from being hurt. The ceremonies at my departure were too many to trouble the reader with at this time.

I stored the boat with the carcases of a hundred oxen, and three hundred sheep, with bread and drink proportionable, and as much meat ready dressed as four hundred cooks could provide. I took with me six cows and two bulls alive, with as many ewes and rams, intending to carry them into my own country, and propagate the breed. And to feed them on board, I had a good bundle of hay, and a bag of corn. I would gladly have taken a dozen of the natives, but this was a thing the emperor would by no means permit; and, besides a diligent search into my pockets, his majesty engaged my honour "not to carry away any of his subjects, although with their own consent and desire."

Having thus prepared all things as well as I was able, I set sail on the twenty-fourth day of September 1701, at six in the morning; and when I had gone about four-leagues to the northward, the wind being at south-east, at six in the evening I descried a small island, about half a league to the north-west. I advanced forward, and cast anchor on the lee-side of the island, which seemed to be uninhabited. I then took some refreshment, and went to my rest. I slept well, and as I conjectured at least six hours, for I found the day broke in two hours after I awaked. It was a clear night. I ate my breakfast before the sun was up; and heaving anchor, the wind being favourable, I steered the same course that I had done the day before, wherein I was directed by my pocket compass. My intention was to reach, if possible, one of those islands which I had reason to believe lay to the north-east of Van Diemen's Land. I discovered nothing all that day; but upon the next, about three in the afternoon, when I had by my computation made twenty-four leagues from Blefuscu, I descried a sail steering to the south-east; my course was due east. I hailed her, but could get no answer; yet I found I gained upon her, for the wind slackened. I made all the sail I could, and in half an hour she spied me, then hung out her ancient, and discharged a gun. It is not easy to express the joy I was in, upon the unexpected hope of once more seeing my beloved country, and the dear pledges I left in it. The ship slackened her sails, and I came up with her between five and six in the evening, September 26th; but my heart leaped within me to see her English colours. I put my cows and sheep into my coat-pockets, and got on board with all my little cargo of provisions. The vessel was an English merchantman, returning from Japan by the North and South seas; the captain, Mr. John Biddel, of Deptford, a very civil man, and an excellent sailor.

We were now in the latitude of 30 degrees south; there were about fifty men in the ship; and here I met an old comrade of mine, one Peter Williams, who gave me a good character to the captain. This gentleman treated me with kindness, and desired I would let him know what place I came from last, and whither I was bound; which I did in a few words, but he thought I was raving, and that the dangers I underwent had disturbed my head; whereupon I took my black cattle and sheep out of my pocket, which, after great astonishment, clearly convinced him of my veracity. I then showed him the gold given me by the emperor of Blefuscu, together with his majesty's picture at full length, and some other rarities of that country. I gave him two purses of two hundreds *sprugs* each, and promised, when we arrived in England, to make him a present of a cow and a sheep big with young.

I shall not trouble the reader with a particular account of this voyage, which was very prosperous for the most part. We arrived in the Downs on the 13th of April, 1702. I had only one misfortune, that the rats on board carried away one of my sheep; I found her bones in a hole, picked clean from the flesh. The rest of my cattle I got safe ashore, and set them a-grazing in a bowling-green at Greenwich, where the fineness of the grass made them feed very heartily, though I had always feared the contrary: neither could I possibly have preserved them in so long a voyage, if the captain had not allowed me some of his best biscuit, which, rubbed to powder, and mingled with water, was their constant food. The short time I continued in England, I made a considerable profit by showing my cattle to many persons of quality and others: and before I began my second voyage, I sold them for six hundred pounds. Since my last return I find the breed is considerably increased, especially the sheep, which I hope will prove much to the advantage of the woollen manufacture, by the fineness of the fleeces.

I stayed but two months with my wife and family, for my insatiable desire of seeing foreign countries, would suffer me to continue no longer. I left fifteen hundred pounds with my wife, and fixed her in a good house at Redriff. My remaining stock I carried with me, part in money and part in goods, in hopes to improve my fortunes. My eldest uncle John had left me an estate in land, near Epping, of about thirty pounds a-year; and I had a long lease of the Black Bull in Fetter-Lane, which yielded me as much more; so that I was not in any danger of leaving my family upon the parish. My son Johnny, named so after his uncle, was at the grammar-school, and a towardly child. My daughter Betty (who is now well married, and has children) was then at her needle-work. I took leave of my wife, and boy and girl, with tears on both sides, and went on board the Adventure, a merchant ship of three hundred tons, bound for Surat, captain John Nicholas, of Liverpool, commander. But my account of this voyage must be referred to the Second Part of my Travels.

---

1. A stang is a pole or perch; sixteen feet and a half.
2. An act of parliament has been since passed by which some breaches of trust have been made capital.

2

A VOYAGE TO BROBDINGNAG

CHAPTER 1: A GREAT STORM DESCRIBED; THE LONG BOAT SENT TO FETCH WATER; THE AUTHOR GOES WITH IT TO DISCOVER THE COUNTRY. HE IS LEFT ON SHORE, IS SEIZED BY ONE OF THE NATIVES, AND CARRIED TO A FARMER'S HOUSE. HIS RECEPTION, WITH SEVERAL ACCIDENTS THAT HAPPENED THERE. A DESCRIPTION OF THE INHABITANTS.

Having been condemned, by nature and fortune, to active and restless life, in two months after my return, I again left my native country, and took shipping in the Downs, on the 20th day of June, 1702, in the Adventure, Captain John Nicholas, a Cornish man, commander, bound for Surat. We had a very prosperous gale, till we arrived at the Cape of Good Hope, where we landed for fresh water; but discovering a leak, we unshipped our goods and wintered there; for the captain falling sick of an ague, we could not leave the Cape till the end of March. We then set sail, and had a good voyage till we passed the Straits of Madagascar; but having got northward of that island, and to about five degrees south latitude, the winds, which in those seas are observed to blow a constant equal gale between the north and west, from the beginning of December to the beginning of May, on the 19th of April began to blow with much greater violence, and more westerly than usual, continuing so for twenty days together: during which time, we were driven a little to the east of the Molucca Islands, and about three degrees northward of the line, as our captain found by an observation he took the 2nd of May, at which time the wind ceased, and it was a perfect calm, whereat I was not a little rejoiced. But he, being a man well experienced in the navigation of those seas, bid us all prepare against a storm, which accordingly happened the day following: for the southern wind, called the southern monsoon, began to set in.

Finding it was likely to overblow, we took in our sprit-sail, and stood by to hand the fore-sail; but making foul weather, we looked the guns were all fast, and handed the mizen. The ship lay very broad off, so we thought it better spooning before the sea, than trying or hulling. We reefed the fore-sail and set him, and hauled aft the fore-sheet; the helm was hard a-weather. The ship wore bravely. We belayed the fore down-haul; but the sail was split, and we hauled down the yard, and got the sail into the ship, and unbound all the things clear of it. It was a very fierce storm; the sea broke strange and dangerous. We hauled off upon the laniard of the whip-staff, and helped the man at the helm. We would not get down our top-mast, but let all stand, because she scudded before the sea very well, and we knew that the top-mast being aloft, the ship was the wholesomer, and made better way through the sea, seeing we had sea-room. When the storm was over, we set fore-sail and main-sail, and brought the ship to. Then we set the mizen, main-top-sail, and the fore-top-sail. Our course was east-north-east, the wind was at south-west. We got the starboard tacks aboard, we cast off our weather-braces and lifts; we set in the lee-braces, and hauled forward by the weather-bowlings, and hauled them tight, and belayed them, and hauled over the mizen tack to windward, and kept her full and by as near as she would lie.

During this storm, which was followed by a strong wind west-south-west, we were carried, by my computation, about five hundred leagues to the east, so that the oldest sailor on board could not tell in what part of the world we were. Our provisions held out well, our ship was staunch, and our crew all in good health; but we lay in the utmost distress for water. We thought it best to hold on the same course, rather than turn more northerly, which might have brought us to the north-west part of Great Tartary, and into the Frozen Sea.

On the 16th day of June, 1703, a boy on the top-mast discovered land. On the 17th, we came in full view of a great island, or continent (for we knew not whether;) on the south side whereof was a small neck of land jutting out into the sea, and a creek too shallow to hold a ship of above one hundred tons. We cast anchor within a league of this creek, and our captain sent a dozen of his men well armed in the long-boat, with vessels for water, if any could be found. I desired his leave to go with them, that I might see the country, and make what discoveries I could. When we came to land we saw no river or spring, nor any sign of inhabitants. Our men therefore wandered on the shore to find out some fresh water near the sea, and I walked alone about a mile on the other side, where I observed the country all barren and rocky. I now began to be weary, and seeing nothing to entertain my curiosity, I returned gently down towards the creek; and the sea being full in my view, I saw our men already got into the boat, and rowing for life to the ship. I was going to holla after them, although it had been to little purpose, when I observed a huge creature walking after them in the sea, as fast as he could: he waded not much deeper than his knees, and took prodigious strides: but our men had the start of him half a league, and, the sea thereabouts being full of sharp-pointed rocks, the monster was not able to overtake the boat. This I was afterwards told, for I durst not stay to see the issue of the adventure; but ran as fast as I could the way I first went, and then climbed up a steep hill, which gave me some prospect of the country. I found it fully cultivated; but that which first surprised me was the length of the grass, which, in those grounds that seemed to be kept for hay, was about twenty feet high.

I fell into a high road, for so I took it to be, though it served to the inhabitants only as a foot-path through a field of barley. Here I walked on for some time, but could see little on either side, it being now near harvest, and the corn rising at least forty feet. I was an hour walking to the end of this field, which was fenced in with a hedge of at least one hundred and twenty feet high, and the trees so lofty that I could make no computation of their altitude. There was a stile to pass from this field into the next. It had four steps, and a stone to cross over when you came to the uppermost. It was impossible for me to climb this stile, because every step was six-feet high, and the upper stone about twenty. I was endeavouring to find some gap in the hedge, when I discovered one of the inhabitants in the next field, advancing towards the stile, of the same size with him whom I saw in the sea pursuing our boat. He appeared as tall as an ordinary spire steeple, and took about ten yards at every stride, as near as I could guess. I was struck with the utmost fear and astonishment, and ran to hide myself in the corn, whence I saw him at the top of the stile looking back into the next field on the right hand, and heard him call in a voice many degrees louder than a speaking-trumpet: but the noise was so high in the air, that at first I certainly thought it was thunder. Whereupon seven monsters, like himself, came towards him with reaping-hooks in their hands, each hook about the largeness of six scythes. These people were not so well clad as the first, whose servants or labourers they seemed to be; for, upon some words he spoke, they went to reap the corn in the field where I lay. I kept from them at as great a distance as I could, but was forced to move with extreme difficulty, for the stalks of the corn were sometimes not above a foot distant, so that I could hardly squeeze my body betwixt them. However, I made a shift to go forward, till I came to a part of the field where the corn had been laid by the rain and wind. Here it was impossible for me to advance a step; for the stalks were so interwoven, that I could not creep through, and the beards of the fallen ears so strong and pointed, that they pierced through my clothes into my flesh. At the same time I heard the reapers not a hundred yards behind me. Being quite dispirited with toil, and wholly overcome by grief and despair, I lay down between two ridges, and heartily wished I might there end my days. I bemoaned my desolate widow and fatherless children. I lamented my own folly and willfulness, in attempting a second voyage, against the advice of all my friends and relations. In this terrible agitation of mind, I could not forbear thinking of Lilliput, whose inhabitants looked upon me as the greatest prodigy that ever appeared in the world; where I was able to draw an imperial fleet in my hand, and perform those other actions, which will be recorded for ever in the chronicles of that empire, while posterity shall hardly believe them, although attested by millions. I reflected what a mortification it must prove to me, to appear as inconsiderable in this nation, as one single Lilliputian would be among us. But this I conceived was to be the least of my misfortunes; for, as human creatures are observed to be more savage and cruel in proportion to their bulk, what could I expect but to be a morsel in the mouth of the first among these enormous barbarians that should happen to seize me? Undoubtedly philosophers are in the right, when they tell us that nothing is great or little otherwise than by comparison. It might have pleased fortune, to have let the Lilliputians find some nation, where the people were as diminutive with respect to them, as they were to me. And who knows but that even this prodigious race of mortals might be equally overmatched in some distant part of the world, whereof we have yet no discovery.

Scared and confounded as I was, I could not forbear going on with these reflections, when one of the reapers, approaching within ten yards of the ridge where I lay, made me apprehend that with the next step I should be squashed to death under his foot, or cut in two with his reaping-hook. And therefore, when he was again about to move, I screamed as loud as fear could make me: whereupon the huge creature trod short, and, looking round about under him for some time, at last espied me as I lay on the ground. He considered awhile, with the caution of one who endeavours to lay hold on a small dangerous animal in such a manner that it shall not be able either to scratch or bite him, as I myself have sometimes done with a weasel in England. At length he ventured to take me behind, by the middle, between his fore-finger and thumb, and brought me within three yards of his eyes, that he might behold my shape more perfectly. I guessed his meaning, and my good fortune gave me so much presence of mind, that I resolved not to struggle in the least as he held me in the air above sixty feet from the ground, although he grievously pinched my sides, for fear I should slip through his fingers. All I ventured was to raise mine eyes towards the sun, and place my hands together in a supplicating posture, and to speak some words in a humble melancholy tone, suitable to the condition I then was in: for I apprehended every moment that he would dash me against the ground, as we usually do any little hateful animal, which we have a mind to destroy. But my good star would have it, that he appeared pleased with my voice and gestures, and began to look upon me as a curiosity, much wondering to hear me pronounce articulate words, although he could not understand them. In the mean time I was not able to forbear groaning and shedding tears, and turning my head towards my sides; letting him know, as well as I could, how cruelly I was hurt by the pressure of his thumb and finger. He seemed to apprehend my meaning; for, lifting up the lappet of his coat, he put me gently into it, and immediately ran along with me to his master, who was a substantial farmer, and the same person I had first seen in the field.

The farmer having (as I suppose by their talk) received such an account of me as his servant could give him, took a piece of a small straw, about the size of a walking-staff, and therewith lifted up the lappets of my coat; which it seems he thought to be some kind of covering that nature had given me. He blew my hairs aside to take a better view of my face. He called his hinds about him, and asked them, as I afterwards learned, whether they had ever seen in the fields any little creature that resembled me. He then placed me softly on the ground upon all fours, but I got immediately up, and walked slowly backward and forward, to let those people see I had no intent to run away. They all sat down in a circle about me, the better to observe my motions. I pulled off my hat, and made a low bow towards the farmer. I fell on my knees, and lifted up my hands and eyes, and spoke several words as loud as I could: I took a purse of gold out of my pocket, and humbly presented it to him. He received it on the palm of his hand, then applied it close to his eye to see what it was, and afterwards turned it several times with the point of a pin (which he took out of his sleeve,) but could make nothing of it. Whereupon I made a sign that he should place his hand on the ground. I then took the purse, and, opening it, poured all the gold into his palm. There were six Spanish pieces of four pistoles each, beside twenty or thirty smaller coins. I saw him wet the tip of his little finger upon his tongue, and take up one of my largest pieces, and then another; but he seemed to be wholly ignorant what they were. He made me a sign to put them again into my purse, and the purse again into my pocket, which, after offering it to him several times, I thought it best to do.

The farmer, by this time, was convinced I must be a rational creature. He spoke often to me; but the sound of his voice pierced my ears like that of a water-mill, yet his words were articulate enough. I answered as loud as I could in several languages, and he often laid his ear within two yards of me: but all in vain, for we were wholly unintelligible to each other. He then sent his servants to their work, and taking his handkerchief out of his pocket, he doubled and spread it on his left hand, which he placed flat on the ground with the palm upward, making me a sign to step into it, as I could easily do, for it was not above a foot in thickness. I thought it my part to obey, and, for fear of falling, laid myself at full length upon the handkerchief, with the remainder of which he lapped me up to the head for further security, and in this manner carried me home to his house. There he called his wife, and showed me to her; but she screamed and ran back, as women in England do at the sight of a toad or a spider. However, when she had a while seen my behaviour, and how well I observed the signs her husband made, she was soon reconciled, and by degrees grew extremely tender of me.

It was about twelve at noon, and a servant brought in dinner. It was only one substantial dish of meat (fit for the plain condition of a husbandman,) in a dish of about four-and-twenty feet diameter. The company were, the farmer and his wife, three children, and an old grandmother. When they were sat down, the farmer placed me at some distance from him on the table, which was thirty feet high from the floor. I was in a terrible fright, and kept as far as I could from the edge, for fear of falling. The wife minced a bit of meat, then crumbled some bread on a trencher, and placed it before me. I made her a low bow, took out my knife and fork, and fell to eat, which gave them exceeding delight. The mistress sent her maid for a small dram cup, which held about two gallons, and filled it with drink; I took up the vessel with much difficulty in both hands, and in a most respectful manner drank to her ladyship's health, expressing the words as loud as I could in English, which made the company laugh so heartily, that I was almost deafened with the noise. This liquor tasted like a small cider, and was not unpleasant. Then the master made me a sign to come to his trencher side; but as I walked on the table, being in great surprise all the time, as the indulgent reader will easily conceive and excuse, I happened to stumble against a crust, and fell flat on my face, but received no hurt. I got up immediately, and observing the good people to be in much concern, I took my hat (which I held under my arm out of good manners,) and waving it over my head, made three huzzas, to show I had got no mischief by my fall. But advancing forward towards my master (as I shall henceforth call him,) his youngest son, who sat next to him, an arch boy of about ten years old, took me up by the legs, and held me so high in the air, that I trembled every limb: but his father snatched me from him, and at the same time gave him such a box on the left ear, as would have felled an European troop of horse to the earth, ordering him to be taken from the table. But being afraid the boy might owe me a spite, and well remembering how mischievous all children among us naturally are to sparrows, rabbits, young kittens, and puppy dogs, I fell on my knees, and pointing to the boy, made my master to understand, as well as I could, that I desired his son might be pardoned. The father complied, and the lad took his seat again, whereupon I went to him, and kissed his hand, which my master took, and made him stroke me gently with it.

In the midst of dinner, my mistress's favourite cat leaped into her lap. I heard a noise behind me like that of a dozen stocking-weavers at work; and turning my head, I found it proceeded from the purring of that animal, who seemed to be three times larger than an ox, as I computed by the view of her head, and one of her paws, while her mistress was feeding and stroking her. The fierceness of this creature's countenance altogether discomposed me; though I stood at the farther end of the table, above fifty feet off; and although my mistress held her fast, for fear she might give a spring, and seize me in her talons. But it happened there was no danger, for the cat took not the least notice of me when my master placed me within three yards of her. And as I have been always told, and found true by experience in my travels, that flying or discovering fear before a fierce animal, is a certain way to make it pursue or attack you, so I resolved, in this dangerous juncture, to show no manner of concern. I walked with intrepidity five or six times before the very head of the cat, and came within half a yard of her; whereupon she drew herself back, as if she were more afraid of me: I had less apprehension concerning the dogs, whereof three or four came into the room, as it is usual in farmers' houses; one of which was a mastiff, equal in bulk to four elephants, and another a greyhound, somewhat taller than the mastiff, but not so large.

When dinner was almost done, the nurse came in with a child of a year old in her arms, who immediately spied me, and began a squall that you might have heard from London-Bridge to Chelsea, after the usual oratory of infants, to get me for a plaything. The mother, out of pure indulgence, took me up, and put me towards the child, who presently seized me by the middle, and got my head into his mouth, where I roared so loud that the urchin was frighted, and let me drop, and I should infallibly have broke my neck, if the mother had not held her apron under me. The nurse, to quiet her babe, made use of a rattle which was a kind of hollow vessel filled with great stones, and fastened by a cable to the child's waist: but all in vain; so that she was forced to apply the last remedy by giving it suck. I must confess no object ever disgusted me so much as the sight of her monstrous breast, which I cannot tell what to compare with, so as to give the curious reader an idea of its bulk, shape, and colour. It stood prominent six feet, and could not be less than sixteen in circumference. The nipple was about half the bigness of my head, and the hue both of that and the dug, so varied with spots, pimples, and freckles, that nothing could appear more nauseous: for I had a near sight of her, she sitting down, the more conveniently to give suck, and I standing on the table. This made me reflect upon the fair skins of our English ladies, who appear so beautiful to us, only because they are of our own size, and their defects not to be seen but through a magnifying glass; where we find by experiment that the smoothest and whitest skins look rough, and coarse, and ill-coloured.

I remember when I was at Lilliput, the complexion of those diminutive people appeared to me the fairest in the world; and talking upon this subject with a person of learning there, who was an intimate friend of mine, he said that my face appeared much fairer and smoother when he looked on me from the ground, than it did upon a nearer view, when I took him up in my hand, and brought him close, which he confessed was at first a very shocking sight. He said, "he could discover great holes in my skin; that the stumps of my beard were ten times stronger than the bristles of a boar, and my complexion made up of several colours altogether disagreeable:" although I must beg leave to say for myself, that I am as fair as most of my sex and country, and very little sunburnt by all my travels. On the other side, discoursing of the ladies in that emperor's court, he used to tell me, "one had freckles; another too wide a mouth; a third too large a nose;" nothing of which I was able to distinguish. I confess this reflection was obvious enough; which, however, I could not forbear, lest the reader might think those vast creatures were actually deformed: for I must do them the justice to say, they are a comely race of people, and particularly the features of my master's countenance, although he was but a farmer, when I beheld him from the height of sixty feet, appeared very well proportioned.

When dinner was done, my master went out to his labourers, and, as I could discover by his voice and gesture, gave his wife strict charge to take care of me. I was very much tired, and disposed to sleep, which my mistress perceiving, she put me on her own bed, and covered me with a clean white handkerchief, but larger and coarser than the main-sail of a man-of-war.

I slept about two hours, and dreamt I was at home with my wife and children, which aggravated my sorrows when I awaked, and found myself alone in a vast room, between two and three hundred feet wide, and above two hundred high, lying in a bed twenty yards wide. My mistress was gone about her household affairs, and had locked me in. The bed was eight yards from the floor. Some natural necessities required me to get down; I durst not presume to call; and if I had, it would have been in vain, with such a voice as mine, at so great a distance from the room where I lay to the kitchen where the family kept. While I was under these circumstances, two rats crept up the curtains, and ran smelling backwards and forwards on the bed. One of them came up almost to my face, whereupon I rose in a fright, and drew out my hanger to defend myself. These horrible animals had the boldness to attack me on both sides, and one of them held his fore-feet at my collar; but I had the good fortune to rip up his belly before he could do me any mischief. He fell down at my feet; and the other, seeing the fate of his comrade, made his escape, but not without one good wound on the back, which I gave him as he fled, and made the blood run trickling from him. After this exploit, I walked gently to and fro on the bed, to recover my breath and loss of spirits. These creatures were of the size of a large mastiff, but infinitely more nimble and fierce; so that if I had taken off my belt before I went to sleep, I must have infallibly been torn to pieces and devoured. I measured the tail of the dead rat, and found it to be two yards long, wanting an inch; but it went against my stomach to drag the carcass off the bed, where it lay still bleeding; I observed it had yet some life, but with a strong slash across the neck, I thoroughly despatched it.

Soon after my mistress came into the room, who seeing me all bloody, ran and took me up in her hand. I pointed to the dead rat, smiling, and making other signs to show I was not hurt; whereat she was extremely rejoiced, calling the maid to take up the dead rat with a pair of tongs, and throw it out of the window. Then she set me on a table, where I showed her my hanger all bloody, and wiping it on the lappet of my coat, returned it to the scabbard. I was pressed to do more than one thing which another could not do for me, and therefore endeavoured to make my mistress understand, that I desired to be set down on the floor; which after she had done, my bashfulness would not suffer me to express myself farther, than by pointing to the door, and bowing several times. The good woman, with much difficulty, at last perceived what I would be at, and taking me up again in her hand, walked into the garden, where she set me down. I went on one side about two hundred yards, and beckoning to her not to look or to follow me, I hid myself between two leaves of sorrel, and there discharged the necessities of nature.

I hope the gentle reader will excuse me for dwelling on these and the like particulars, which, however insignificant they may appear to groveling vulgar minds, yet will certainly help a philosopher to enlarge his thoughts and imagination, and apply them to the benefit of public as well as private life, which was my sole design in presenting this and other accounts of my travels to the world; wherein I have been chiefly studious of truth, without affecting any ornaments of learning or of style. But the whole scene of this voyage made so strong an impression on my mind, and is so deeply fixed in my memory, that, in committing it to paper I did not omit one material circumstance: however, upon a strict review, I blotted out several passages of less moment which were in my first copy, for fear of being censured as tedious and trifling, whereof travellers are often, perhaps not without justice, accused.

CHAPTER 2: A DESCRIPTION OF THE FARMER'S DAUGHTER. THE AUTHOR CARRIED TO A MARKET-TOWN, AND THEN TO THE METROPOLIS. THE PARTICULARS OF HIS JOURNEY.

My mistress had a daughter of nine years old, a child of towardly parts for her age, very dexterous at her needle, and skilful in dressing her baby. Her mother and she contrived to fit up the baby's cradle for me against night: the cradle was put into a small drawer of a cabinet, and the drawer placed upon a hanging shelf for fear of the rats. This was my bed all the time I staid with those people, though made more convenient by degrees, as I began to learn their language and make my wants known. This young girl was so handy, that after I had once or twice pulled off my clothes before her, she was able to dress and undress me, though I never gave her that trouble when she would let me do either myself. She made me seven shirts, and some other linen, of as fine cloth as could be got, which indeed was coarser than sackcloth; and these she constantly washed for me with her own hands. She was likewise my school-mistress, to teach me the language: when I pointed to any thing, she told me the name of it in her own tongue, so that in a few days I was able to call for whatever I had a mind to. She was very good-natured, and not above forty feet high, being little for her age. She gave me the name of *Grildrig*, which the family took up, and afterwards the whole kingdom. The word imports what the Latins call *nanunculus*, the Italians *homunceletino*, and the English *mannikin*. To her I chiefly owe my preservation in that country: we never parted while I was there; I called her my *Glumdalclitch*, or little nurse; and should be guilty of great ingratitude, if I omitted this honourable mention of her care and affection towards me, which I heartily wish it lay in my power to requite as she deserves, instead of being the innocent, but unhappy instrument of her disgrace, as I have too much reason to fear.

It now began to be known and talked of in the neighbourhood, that my master had found a strange animal in the field, about the bigness of a *splacnuck*, but exactly shaped in every part like a human creature; which it likewise imitated in all its actions; seemed to speak in a little language of its own, had already learned several words of theirs, went erect upon two legs, was tame and gentle, would come when it was called, do whatever it was bid, had the finest limbs in the world, and a complexion fairer than a nobleman's daughter of three years old. Another farmer, who lived hard by, and was a particular friend of my master, came on a visit on purpose to inquire into the truth of this story. I was immediately produced, and placed upon a table, where I walked as I was commanded, drew my hanger, put it up again, made my reverence to my master's guest, asked him in his own language how he did, and told him *he was welcome*, just as my little nurse had instructed me. This man, who was old and dim-sighted, put on his spectacles to behold me better; at which I could not forbear laughing very heartily, for his eyes appeared like the full moon shining into a chamber at two windows. Our people, who discovered the cause of my mirth, bore me company in laughing, at which the old fellow was fool enough to be angry and out of countenance. He had the character of a great miser; and, to my misfortune, he well deserved it, by the cursed advice he gave my master, to show me as a sight upon a market-day in the next town, which was half an hour's riding, about two-and-twenty miles from our house. I guessed there was some mischief when I observed my master and his friend whispering together, sometimes pointing at me; and my fears made me fancy that I overheard and understood some of their words. But the next morning Glumdalclitch, my little nurse, told me the whole matter, which she had cunningly picked out from her mother. The poor girl laid me on her bosom, and fell a weeping with shame and grief. She apprehended some mischief would happen to me from rude vulgar folks, who might squeeze me to death, or break one of my limbs by taking me in their hands. She had also observed how modest I was in my nature, how nicely I regarded my honour, and what an indignity I should conceive it, to be exposed for money as a public spectacle, to the meanest of the people. She said, her papa and mamma had promised that Grildrig should be hers; but now she found they meant to serve her as they did last year, when they pretended to give her a lamb, and yet, as soon as it was fat, sold it to a butcher. For my own part, I may truly affirm, that I was less concerned than my nurse. I had a strong hope, which never left me, that I should one day recover my liberty: and as to the ignominy of being carried about for a monster, I considered myself to be a perfect stranger in the country, and that such a misfortune could never be charged upon me as a reproach, if ever I should return to England, since the king of Great Britain himself, in my condition, must have undergone the same distress.

My master, pursuant to the advice of his friend, carried me in a box the next market-day to the neighbouring town, and took along with him his little daughter, my nurse, upon a pillion behind him. The box was close on every side, with a little door for me to go in and out, and a few gimlet holes to let in air. The girl had been so careful as to put the quilt of her baby's bed into it, for me to lie down on. However, I was terribly shaken and discomposed in this journey, though it was but of half an hour: for the horse went about forty feet at every step and trotted so high, that the agitation was equal to the rising and falling of a ship in a great storm, but much more frequent. Our journey was somewhat farther than from London to St. Alban's. My master alighted at an inn which he used to frequent; and after consulting awhile with the inn-keeper, and making some necessary preparations, he hired the *grultrud*, or crier, to give notice through the town of a strange creature to be seen at the sign of the Green Eagle, not so big as a *splacnuck* (an animal in that country very finely shaped, about six feet long,) and in every part of the body resembling a human creature, could speak several words, and perform a hundred diverting tricks.

I was placed upon a table in the largest room of the inn, which might be near three hundred feet square. My little nurse stood on a low stool close to the table, to take care of me, and direct what I should do. My master, to avoid a crowd, would suffer only thirty people at a time to see me. I walked about on the table as the girl commanded; she asked me questions, as far as she knew my understanding of the language reached, and I answered them as loud as I could. I turned about several times to the company, paid my humble respects, said *they were welcome*, and used some other speeches I had been taught. I took up a thimble filled with liquor, which Glumdalclitch had given me for a cup, and drank their health, I drew out my hanger, and flourished with it after the manner of fencers in England. My nurse gave me a part of a straw, which I exercised as a pike, having learnt the art in my youth. I was that day shown to twelve sets of company, and as often forced to act over again the same fopperies, till I was half dead with weariness and vexation; for those who had seen me made such wonderful reports, that the people were ready to break down the doors to come in. My master, for his own interest, would not suffer any one to touch me except my nurse; and to prevent danger, benches were set round the table at such a distance as to put me out of every body's reach. However, an unlucky school-boy aimed a hazel nut directly at my head, which very narrowly missed me; otherwise it came with so much violence, that it would have infallibly knocked out my brains, for it was almost as large as a small pumpkin, but I had the satisfaction to see the young rogue well beaten, and turned out of the room.

My master gave public notice that he would show me again the next market-day; and in the meantime he prepared a convenient vehicle for me, which he had reason enough to do; for I was so tired with my first journey, and with entertaining company for eight hours together, that I could hardly stand upon my legs, or speak a word. It was at least three days before I recovered my strength; and that I might have no rest at home, all the neighbouring gentlemen from a hundred miles round, hearing of my fame, came to see me at my master's own house. There could not be fewer than thirty persons with their wives and children (for the country is very populous;) and my master demanded the rate of a full room whenever he showed me at home, although it were only to a single family; so that for some time I had but little ease every day of the week (except Wednesday, which is their Sabbath,) although I were not carried to the town.

My master, finding how profitable I was likely to be, resolved to carry me to the most considerable cities of the kingdom. Having therefore provided himself with all things necessary for a long journey, and settled his affairs at home, he took leave of his wife, and upon the 17th of August, 1703, about two months after my arrival, we set out for the metropolis, situate near the middle of that empire, and about three thousand miles distance from our house. My master made his daughter Glumdalclitch ride behind him. She carried me on her lap, in a box tied about her waist. The girl had lined it on all sides with the softest cloth she could get, well quilted underneath, furnished it with her baby's bed, provided me with linen and other necessaries, and made everything as convenient as she could. We had no other company but a boy of the house, who rode after us with the luggage.

My master's design was to show me in all the towns by the way, and to step out of the road for fifty or a hundred miles, to any village, or person of quality's house, where he might expect custom. We made easy journeys, of not above seven or eight score miles a-day; for Glumdalclitch, on purpose to spare me, complained she was tired with the trotting of the horse. She often took me out of my box, at my own desire, to give me air, and show me the country, but always held me fast by a leading-string. We passed over five or six rivers, many degrees broader and deeper than the Nile or the Ganges: and there was hardly a rivulet so small as the Thames at London-bridge. We were ten weeks in our journey, and I was shown in eighteen large towns, besides many villages, and private families.

On the 26th day of October we arrived at the metropolis, called in their language *Lorbrulgrud*, or Pride of the Universe. My master took a lodging in the principal street of the city, not far from the royal palace, and put out bills in the usual form, containing an exact description of my person and parts. He hired a large room between three and four hundred feet wide. He provided a table sixty feet in diameter, upon which I was to act my part, and pallisadoed it round three feet from the edge, and as many high, to prevent my falling over. I was shown ten times a-day, to the wonder and satisfaction of all people. I could now speak the language tolerably well, and perfectly understood every word, that was spoken to me. Besides, I had learnt their alphabet, and could make a shift to explain a sentence here and there; for Glumdalclitch had been my instructor while we were at home, and at leisure hours during our journey. She carried a little book in her pocket, not much larger than a Sanson's Atlas; it was a common treatise for the use of young girls, giving a short account of their religion: out of this she taught me my letters, and interpreted the words.

CHAPTER 3: THE AUTHOR SENT FOR TO COURT. THE QUEEN BUYS HIM OF HIS MASTER THE FARMER, AND PRESENTS HIM TO THE KING. HE DISPUTES WITH HIS MAJESTY'S GREAT SCHOLARS. AN APARTMENT AT COURT PROVIDED FOR THE AUTHOR. HE IS IN HIGH FAVOUR WITH THE QUEEN. HE STANDS UP FOR THE HONOUR OF HIS OWN COUNTRY. HIS QUARRELS WITH THE QUEEN'S DWARF.

The frequent labours I underwent every day, made, in a few weeks, a very considerable change in my health: the more my master got by me, the more insatiable he grew. I had quite lost my stomach, and was almost reduced to a skeleton. The farmer observed it, and concluding I must soon die, resolved to make as good a hand of me as he could. While he was thus reasoning and resolving with himself, a *sardral*, or gentleman-usher, came from court, commanding my master to carry me immediately thither for the diversion of the queen and her ladies. Some of the latter had already been to see me, and reported strange things of my beauty, behaviour, and good sense. Her majesty, and those who attended her, were beyond measure delighted with my demeanour. I fell on my knees, and begged the honour of kissing her imperial foot; but this gracious princess held out her little finger towards me, after I was set on the table, which I embraced in both my arms, and put the tip of it with the utmost respect to my lip. She made me some general questions about my country and my travels, which I answered as distinctly, and in as few words as I could. She asked, "whether I could be content to live at court?" I bowed down to the board of the table, and humbly answered "that I was my master's slave: but, if I were at my own disposal, I should be proud to devote my life to her majesty's service." She then asked my master, "whether he was willing to sell me at a good price?" He, who apprehended I could not live a month, was ready enough to part with me, and demanded a thousand pieces of gold, which were ordered him on the spot, each piece being about the bigness of eight hundred moidores; but allowing for the proportion of all things between that country and Europe, and the high price of gold among them, was hardly so great a sum as a thousand guineas would be in England. I then said to the queen, "since I was now her majesty's most humble creature and vassal, I must beg the favour, that Glumdalclitch, who had always tended me with so much care and kindness, and understood to do it so well, might be admitted into her service, and continue to be my nurse and instructor."

Her majesty agreed to my petition, and easily got the farmer's consent, who was glad enough to have his daughter preferred at court, and the poor girl herself was not able to hide her joy. My late master withdrew, bidding me farewell, and saying he had left me in a good service; to which I replied not a word, only making him a slight bow.

The queen observed my coldness; and, when the farmer was gone out of the apartment, asked me the reason. I made bold to tell her majesty, "that I owed no other obligation to my late master, than his not dashing out the brains of a poor harmless creature, found by chance in his fields: which obligation was amply recompensed, by the gain he had made in showing me through half the kingdom, and the price he had now sold me for. That the life I had since led was laborious enough to kill an animal of ten times my strength. That my health was much impaired, by the continual drudgery of entertaining the rabble every hour of the day; and that, if my master had not thought my life in danger, her majesty would not have got so cheap a bargain. But as I was out of all fear of being ill-treated under the protection of so great and good an empress, the ornament of nature, the darling of the world, the delight of her subjects, the phoenix of the creation, so I hoped my late master's apprehensions would appear to be groundless; for I already found my spirits revive, by the influence of her most august presence."

This was the sum of my speech, delivered with great improprieties and hesitation. The latter part was altogether framed in the style peculiar to that people, whereof I learned some phrases from Glumdalclitch, while she was carrying me to court.

The queen, giving great allowance for my defectiveness in speaking, was, however, surprised at so much wit and good sense in so diminutive an animal. She took me in her own hand, and carried me to the king, who was then retired to his cabinet. His majesty, a prince of much gravity and austere countenance, not well observing my shape at first view, asked the queen after a cold manner "how long it was since she grew fond of a *splacnuck*?" for such it seems he took me to be, as I lay upon my breast in her majesty's right hand. But this princess, who has an infinite deal of wit and humour, set me gently on my feet upon the scrutoire, and commanded me to give his majesty an account of myself, which I did in a very few words: and Glumdalclitch who attended at the cabinet door, and could not endure I should be out of her sight, being admitted, confirmed all that had passed from my arrival at her father's house.

The king, although he be as learned a person as any in his dominions, had been educated in the study of philosophy, and particularly mathematics; yet when he observed my shape exactly, and saw me walk erect, before I began to speak, conceived I might be a piece of clock-work (which is in that country arrived to a very great perfection) contrived by some ingenious artist. But when he heard my voice, and found what I delivered to be regular and rational, he could not conceal his astonishment. He was by no means satisfied with the relation I gave him of the manner I came into his kingdom, but thought it a story concerted between Glumdalclitch and her father, who had taught me a set of words to make me sell at a better price. Upon this imagination, he put several other questions to me, and still received rational answers: no otherwise defective than by a foreign accent, and an imperfect knowledge in the language, with some rustic phrases which I had learned at the farmer's house, and did not suit the polite style of a court.

His majesty sent for three great scholars, who were then in their weekly waiting, according to the custom in that country. These gentlemen, after they had a while examined my shape with much nicety, were of different opinions concerning me. They all agreed that I could not be produced according to the regular laws of nature, because I was not framed with a capacity of preserving my life, either by swiftness, or climbing of trees, or digging holes in the earth. They observed by my teeth, which they viewed with great exactness, that I was a carnivorous animal; yet most quadrupeds being an overmatch for me, and field mice, with some others, too nimble, they could not imagine how I should be able to support myself, unless I fed upon snails and other insects, which they offered, by many learned arguments, to evince that I could not possibly do. One of these virtuosi seemed to think that I might be an embryo, or abortive birth. But this opinion was rejected by the other two, who observed my limbs to be perfect and finished; and that I had lived several years, as it was manifest from my beard, the stumps whereof they plainly discovered through a magnifying glass. They would not allow me to be a dwarf, because my littleness was beyond all degrees of comparison; for the queen's favourite dwarf, the smallest ever known in that kingdom, was near thirty feet high. After much debate, they concluded unanimously, that I was only *relplum scalcath*, which is interpreted literally *lusus naturæ*; a determination exactly agreeable to the modern philosophy of Europe, whose professors, disdaining the old evasion of occult causes, whereby the followers of Aristotle endeavoured in vain to disguise their ignorance, have invented this wonderful solution of all difficulties, to the unspeakable advancement of human knowledge.

After this decisive conclusion, I entreated to be heard a word or two. I applied myself to the king, and assured his majesty, "that I came from a country which abounded with several millions of both sexes, and of my own stature; where the animals, trees, and houses, were all in proportion, and where, by consequence, I might be as able to defend myself, and to find sustenance, as any of his majesty's subjects could do here; which I took for a full answer to those gentlemen's arguments." To this they only replied with a smile of contempt, saying, "that the farmer had instructed me very well in my lesson." The king, who had a much better understanding, dismissing his learned men, sent for the farmer, who by good fortune was not yet gone out of town. Having therefore first examined him privately, and then confronted him with me and the young girl, his majesty began to think that what we told him might possibly be true. He desired the queen to order that a particular care should be taken of me; and was of opinion that Glumdalclitch should still continue in her office of tending me, because he observed we had a great affection for each other. A convenient apartment was provided for her at court: she had a sort of governess appointed to take care of her education, a maid to dress her, and two other servants for menial offices; but the care of me was wholly appropriated to herself. The queen commanded her own cabinet-maker to contrive a box, that might serve me for a bedchamber, after the model that Glumdalclitch and I should agree upon. This man was a most ingenious artist, and according to my direction, in three weeks finished for me a wooden chamber of sixteen feet square, and twelve high, with sash-windows, a door, and two closets, like a London bed-chamber. The board, that made the ceiling, was to be lifted up and down by two hinges, to put in a bed ready furnished by her majesty's upholsterer, which Glumdalclitch took out every day to air, made it with her own hands, and letting it down at night, locked up the roof over me. A nice workman, who was famous for little curiosities, undertook to make me two chairs, with backs and frames, of a substance not unlike ivory, and two tables, with a cabinet to put my things in. The room was quilted on all sides, as well as the floor and the ceiling, to prevent any accident from the carelessness of those who carried me, and to break the force of a jolt, when I went in a coach. I desired a lock for my door, to prevent rats and mice from coming in. The smith, after several attempts, made the smallest that ever was seen among them, for I have known a larger at the gate of a gentleman's house in England. I made a shift to keep the key in a pocket of my own, fearing Glumdalclitch might lose it. The queen likewise ordered the thinnest silks that could be gotten, to make me clothes, not much thicker than an English blanket, very cumbersome till I was accustomed to them. They were after the fashion of the kingdom, partly resembling the Persian, and partly the Chinese, and are a very grave and decent habit.

The queen became so fond of my company, that she could not dine without me. I had a table placed upon the same at which her majesty ate, just at her left elbow, and a chair to sit on. Glumdalclitch stood on a stool on the floor near my table, to assist and take care of me. I had an entire set of silver dishes and plates, and other necessaries, which, in proportion to those of the queen, were not much bigger than what I have seen in a London toy-shop for the furniture of a baby-house: these my little nurse kept in her pocket in a silver box, and gave me at meals as I wanted them, always cleaning them herself. No person dined with the queen but the two princesses royal, the eldest sixteen years old, and the younger at that time thirteen and a month. Her majesty used to put a bit of meat upon one of my dishes, out of which I carved for myself, and her diversion was to see me eat in miniature: for the queen (who had indeed but a weak stomach) took up, at one mouthful, as much as a dozen English farmers could eat at a meal, which to me was for some time a very nauseous sight. She would craunch the wing of a lark, bones and all, between her teeth, although it were nine times as large as that of a full-grown turkey; and put a bit of bread into her mouth as big as two twelve-penny loaves. She drank out of a golden cup, above a hogshead at a draught. Her knives were twice as long as a scythe, set straight upon the handle. The spoons, forks, and other instruments, were all in the same proportion. I remember when Glumdalclitch carried me, out of curiosity, to see some of the tables at court, where ten or a dozen of those enormous knives and forks were lifted up together, I thought I had never till then beheld so terrible a sight.

It is the custom, that every Wednesday (which, as I have observed, is their Sabbath) the king and queen, with the royal issue of both sexes, dine together in the apartment of his majesty, to whom I was now become a great favourite; and at these times, my little chair and table were placed at his left hand, before one of the salt-cellars. This prince took a pleasure in conversing with me, inquiring into the manners, religion, laws, government, and learning of Europe; wherein I gave him the best account I was able. His apprehension was so clear, and his judgment so exact, that he made very wise reflections and observations upon all I said. But I confess, that, after I had been a little too copious in talking of my own beloved country, of our trade and wars by sea and land, of our schisms in religion, and parties in the state; the prejudices of his education prevailed so far, that he could not forbear taking me up in his right hand, and stroking me gently with the other, after a hearty fit of laughing, asked me, "whether I was a whig or tory?" Then turning to his first minister, who waited behind him with a white staff, near as tall as the mainmast of the Royal Sovereign, he observed "how contemptible a thing was human grandeur, which could be mimicked by such diminutive insects as I: and yet," says he, "I dare engage these creatures have their titles and distinctions of honour; they contrive little nests and burrows, that they call houses and cities; they make a figure in dress and equipage; they love, they fight, they dispute, they cheat, they betray!" And thus he continued on, while my colour came and went several times, with indignation, to hear our noble country, the mistress of arts and arms, the scourge of France, the arbitress of Europe, the seat of virtue, piety, honour, and truth, the pride and envy of the world, so contemptuously treated.

But as I was not in a condition to resent injuries, so upon mature thoughts I began to doubt whether I was injured or no. For, after having been accustomed several months to the sight and converse of this people, and observed every object upon which I cast mine eyes to be of proportionable magnitude, the horror I had at first conceived from their bulk and aspect was so far worn off, that if I had then beheld a company of English lords and ladies in their finery and birth-day clothes, acting their several parts in the most courtly manner of strutting, and bowing, and prating, to say the truth, I should have been strongly tempted to laugh as much at them as the king and his grandees did at me. Neither, indeed, could I forbear smiling at myself, when the queen used to place me upon her hand towards a looking-glass, by which both our persons appeared before me in full view together; and there could be nothing more ridiculous than the comparison; so that I really began to imagine myself dwindled many degrees below my usual size.

Nothing angered and mortified me so much as the queen's dwarf; who being of the lowest stature that was ever in that country (for I verily think he was not full thirty feet high), became so insolent at seeing a creature so much beneath him, that he would always affect to swagger and look big as he passed by me in the queen's antechamber, while I was standing on some table talking with the lords or ladies of the court, and he seldom failed of a smart word or two upon my littleness; against which I could only revenge myself by calling him brother, challenging him to wrestle, and such repartees as are usually in the mouths of court pages. One day, at dinner, this malicious little cub was so nettled with something I had said to him, that, raising himself upon the frame of her majesty's chair, he took me up by the middle, as I was sitting down, not thinking any harm, and let me drop into a large silver bowl of cream, and then ran away as fast as he could. I fell over head and ears, and, if I had not been a good swimmer, it might have gone very hard with me; for Glumdalclitch in that instant happened to be at the other end of the room, and the queen was in such a fright, that she wanted presence of mind to assist me. But my little nurse ran to my relief, and took me out, after I had swallowed above a quart of cream. I was put to bed: however, I received no other damage than the loss of a suit of clothes, which was utterly spoiled. The dwarf was soundly whipt, and as a farther punishment, forced to drink up the bowl of cream into which he had thrown me: neither was he ever restored to favour; for soon after the queen bestowed him on a lady of high quality, so that I saw him no more, to my very great satisfaction; for I could not tell to what extremities such a malicious urchin might have carried his resentment.

He had before served me a scurvy trick, which set the queen a-laughing, although at the same time she was heartily vexed, and would have immediately cashiered him, if I had not been so generous as to intercede. Her majesty had taken a marrow-bone upon her plate, and, after knocking out the marrow, placed the bone again in the dish erect, as it stood before; the dwarf, watching his opportunity, while Glumdalclitch was gone to the side-board, mounted the stool that she stood on to take care of me at meals, took me up in both hands, and squeezing my legs together, wedged them into the marrow bone above my waist, where I stuck for some time, and made a very ridiculous figure. I believe it was near a minute before any one knew what was become of me; for I thought it below me to cry out. But, as princes seldom get their meat hot, my legs were not scalded, only my stockings and breeches in a sad condition. The dwarf, at my entreaty, had no other punishment than a sound whipping.

I was frequently rallied by the queen upon account of my fearfulness; and she used to ask me whether the people of my country were as great cowards as myself? The occasion was this: the kingdom is much pestered with flies in summer; and these odious insects, each of them as big as a Dunstable lark, hardly gave me any rest while I sat at dinner, with their continual humming and buzzing about mine ears. They would sometimes alight upon my victuals, and leave their loathsome excrement, or spawn behind, which to me was very visible, though not to the natives of that country, whose large optics were not so acute as mine, in viewing smaller objects. Sometimes they would fix upon my nose, or forehead, where they stung me to the quick, smelling very offensively; and I could easily trace that viscous matter, which, our naturalists tell us, enables those creatures to walk with their feet upwards upon a ceiling. I had much ado to defend myself against these detestable animals, and could not forbear starting when they came on my face. It was the common practice of the dwarf, to catch a number of these insects in his hand, as schoolboys do among us, and let them out suddenly under my nose, on purpose to frighten me, and divert the queen. My remedy was to cut them in pieces with my knife, as they flew in the air, wherein my dexterity was much admired.

I remember, one morning, when Glumdalclitch had set me in a box upon a window, as she usually did in fair days to give me air (for I durst not venture to let the box be hung on a nail out of the window, as we do with cages in England), after I had lifted up one of my sashes, and sat down at my table to eat a piece of sweet cake for my breakfast, above twenty wasps, allured by the smell, came flying into the room, humming louder than the drones of as many bagpipes. Some of them seized my cake, and carried it piecemeal away; others flew about my head and face, confounding me with the noise, and putting me in the utmost terror of their stings. However, I had the courage to rise and draw my hanger, and attack them in the air. I dispatched four of them, but the rest got away, and I presently shut my window. These insects were as large as partridges: I took out their stings, found them an inch and a half long, and as sharp as needles. I carefully preserved them all; and having since shown them, with some other curiosities, in several parts of Europe, upon my return to England I gave three of them to Gresham College, and kept the fourth for myself.

CHAPTER 4: THE COUNTRY DESCRIBED. A PROPOSAL FOR CORRECTING MODERN MAPS. THE KING'S PALACE; AND SOME ACCOUNT OF THE METROPOLIS. THE AUTHOR'S WAY OF TRAVELLING. THE CHIEF TEMPLE DESCRIBED.

I now intend to give the reader a short description of this country, as far as I travelled in it, which was not above two thousand miles round Lorbrulgrud, the metropolis. For the queen, whom I always attended, never went farther when she accompanied the king in his progresses, and there staid till his majesty returned from viewing his frontiers. The whole extent of this prince's dominions reaches about six thousand miles in length, and from three to five in breadth: whence I cannot but conclude, that our geographers of Europe are in a great error, by supposing nothing but sea between Japan and California; for it was ever my opinion, that there must be a balance of earth to counterpoise the great continent of Tartary; and therefore they ought to correct their maps and charts, by joining this vast tract of land to the north-west parts of America, wherein I shall be ready to lend them my assistance.

The kingdom is a peninsula, terminated to the north-east by a ridge of mountains thirty miles high, which are altogether impassable, by reason of the volcanoes upon the tops: neither do the most learned know what sort of mortals inhabit beyond those mountains, or whether they be inhabited at all. On the three other sides, it is bounded by the ocean. There is not one seaport in the whole kingdom: and those parts of the coasts into which the rivers issue, are so full of pointed rocks, and the sea generally so rough, that there is no venturing with the smallest of their boats; so that these people are wholly excluded from any commerce with the rest of the world. But the large rivers are full of vessels, and abound with excellent fish; for they seldom get any from the sea, because the sea fish are of the same size with those in Europe, and consequently not worth catching; whereby it is manifest, that nature, in the production of plants and animals of so extraordinary a bulk, is wholly confined to this continent, of which I leave the reasons to be determined by philosophers. However, now and then they take a whale that happens to be dashed against the rocks, which the common people feed on heartily. These whales I have known so large, that a man could hardly carry one upon his shoulders; and sometimes, for curiosity, they are brought in hampers to Lorbrulgrud; I saw one of them in a dish at the king's table, which passed for a rarity, but I did not observe he was fond of it; for I think, indeed, the bigness disgusted him, although I have seen one somewhat larger in Greenland.

The country is well inhabited, for it contains fifty-one cities, near a hundred walled towns, and a great number of villages. To satisfy my curious reader, it may be sufficient to describe Lorbrulgrud. This city stands upon almost two equal parts, on each side the river that passes through. It contains above eighty thousand houses, and about six hundred thousand inhabitants. It is in length three *glomglungs* (which make about fifty-four English miles,) and two and a half in breadth; as I measured it myself in the royal map made by the king's order, which was laid on the ground on purpose for me, and extended a hundred feet: I paced the diameter and circumference several times barefoot, and, computing by the scale, measured it pretty exactly.

The king's palace is no regular edifice, but a heap of buildings, about seven miles round: the chief rooms are generally two hundred and forty feet high, and broad and long in proportion. A coach was allowed to Glumdalclitch and me, wherein her governess frequently took her out to see the town, or go among the shops; and I was always of the party, carried in my box; although the girl, at my own desire, would often take me out, and hold me in her hand, that I might more conveniently view the houses and the people, as we passed along the streets. I reckoned our coach to be about a square of Westminster-hall, but not altogether so high: however, I cannot be very exact. One day the governess ordered our coachman to stop at several shops, where the beggars, watching their opportunity, crowded to the sides of the coach, and gave me the most horrible spectacle that ever a European eye beheld. There was a woman with a cancer in her breast, swelled to a monstrous size, full of holes, in two or three of which I could have easily crept, and covered my whole body. There was a fellow with a wen in his neck, larger than five wool-packs; and another, with a couple of wooden legs, each about twenty feet high. But the most hateful sight of all, was the lice crawling on their clothes. I could see distinctly the limbs of these vermin with my naked eye, much better than those of a European louse through a microscope, and their snouts with which they rooted like swine. They were the first I had ever beheld, and I should have been curious enough to dissect one of them, if I had had proper instruments, which I unluckily left behind me in the ship, although, indeed, the sight was so nauseous, that it perfectly turned my stomach.

Besides the large box in which I was usually carried, the queen ordered a smaller one to be made for me, of about twelve feet square, and ten high, for the convenience of travelling; because the other was somewhat too large for Glumdalclitch's lap, and cumbersome in the coach; it was made by the same artist, whom I directed in the whole contrivance. This travelling-closet was an exact square, with a window in the middle of three of the squares, and each window was latticed with iron wire on the outside, to prevent accidents in long journeys. On the fourth side, which had no window, two strong staples were fixed, through which the person that carried me, when I had a mind to be on horseback, put a leathern belt, and buckled it about his waist. This was always the office of some grave trusty servant, in whom I could confide, whether I attended the king and queen in their progresses, or were disposed to see the gardens, or pay a visit to some great lady or minister of state in the court, when Glumdalclitch happened to be out of order; for I soon began to be known and esteemed among the greatest officers, I suppose more upon account of their majesties' favour, than any merit of my own. In journeys, when I was weary of the coach, a servant on horseback would buckle on my box, and place it upon a cushion before him; and there I had a full prospect of the country on three sides, from my three windows. I had, in this closet, a field-bed and a hammock, hung from the ceiling, two chairs and a table, neatly screwed to the floor, to prevent being tossed about by the agitation of the horse or the coach. And having been long used to sea-voyages, those motions, although sometimes very violent, did not much discompose me.

Whenever I had a mind to see the town, it was always in my travelling-closet; which Glumdalclitch held in her lap in a kind of open sedan, after the fashion of the country, borne by four men, and attended by two others in the queen's livery. The people, who had often heard of me, were very curious to crowd about the sedan, and the girl was complaisant enough to make the bearers stop, and to take me in her hand, that I might be more conveniently seen.

I was very desirous to see the chief temple, and particularly the tower belonging to it, which is reckoned the highest in the kingdom. Accordingly one day my nurse carried me thither, but I may truly say I came back disappointed; for the height is not above three thousand feet, reckoning from the ground to the highest pinnacle top; which, allowing for the difference between the size of those people and us in Europe, is no great matter for admiration, nor at all equal in proportion (if I rightly remember) to Salisbury steeple. But, not to detract from a nation, to which, during my life, I shall acknowledge myself extremely obliged, it must be allowed, that whatever this famous tower wants in height, is amply made up in beauty and strength: for the walls are near a hundred feet thick, built of hewn stone, whereof each is about forty feet square, and adorned on all sides with statues of gods and emperors, cut in marble, larger than the life, placed in their several niches. I measured a little finger which had fallen down from one of these statues, and lay unperceived among some rubbish, and found it exactly four feet and an inch in length. Glumdalclitch wrapped it up in her handkerchief, and carried it home in her pocket, to keep among other trinkets, of which the girl was very fond, as children at her age usually are.

The king's kitchen is indeed a noble building, vaulted at top, and about six hundred feet high. The great oven is not so wide, by ten paces, as the cupola at St. Paul's: for I measured the latter on purpose, after my return. But if I should describe the kitchen grate, the prodigious pots and kettles, the joints of meat turning on the spits, with many other particulars, perhaps I should be hardly believed; at least a severe critic would be apt to think I enlarged a little, as travellers are often suspected to do. To avoid which censure I fear I have run too much into the other extreme; and that if this treatise should happen to be translated into the language of Brobdingnag (which is the general name of that kingdom,) and transmitted thither, the king and his people would have reason to complain that I had done them an injury, by a false and diminutive representation.

His majesty seldom keeps above six hundred horses in his stables: they are generally from fifty-four to sixty feet high. But, when he goes abroad on solemn days, he is attended, for state, by a military guard of five hundred horse, which, indeed, I thought was the most splendid sight that could be ever beheld, till I saw part of his army in battalia, whereof I shall find another occasion to speak.

CHAPTER 5: SEVERAL ADVENTURERS THAT HAPPENED TO THE AUTHOR. THE EXECUTION OF A CRIMINAL. THE AUTHOR SHOWS HIS SKILL IN NAVIGATION.

I should have lived happy enough in that country, if my littleness had not exposed me to several ridiculous and troublesome accidents; some of which I shall venture to relate. Glumdalclitch often carried me into the gardens of the court in my smaller box, and would sometimes take me out of it, and hold me in her hand, or set me down to walk. I remember, before the dwarf left the queen, he followed us one day into those gardens, and my nurse having set me down, he and I being close together, near some dwarf apple trees, I must needs show my wit, by a silly allusion between him and the trees, which happens to hold in their language as it does in ours. Whereupon, the malicious rogue, watching his opportunity, when I was walking under one of them, shook it directly over my head, by which a dozen apples, each of them near as large as a Bristol barrel, came tumbling about my ears; one of them hit me on the back as I chanced to stoop, and knocked me down flat on my face; but I received no other hurt, and the dwarf was pardoned at my desire, because I had given the provocation.

Another day, Glumdalclitch left me on a smooth grass-plot to divert myself, while she walked at some distance with her governess. In the meantime, there suddenly fell such a violent shower of hail, that I was immediately by the force of it, struck to the ground: and when I was down, the hailstones gave me such cruel bangs all over the body, as if I had been pelted with tennis-balls; however, I made a shift to creep on all fours, and shelter myself, by lying flat on my face, on the lee-side of a border of lemon-thyme, but so bruised from head to foot, that I could not go abroad in ten days. Neither is this at all to be wondered at, because nature, in that country, observing the same proportion through all her operations, a hailstone is near eighteen hundred times as large as one in Europe; which I can assert upon experience, having been so curious as to weigh and measure them.

But a more dangerous accident happened to me in the same garden, when my little nurse, believing she had put me in a secure place (which I often entreated her to do, that I might enjoy my own thoughts,) and having left my box at home, to avoid the trouble of carrying it, went to another part of the garden with her governess and some ladies of her acquaintance. While she was absent, and out of hearing, a small white spaniel that belonged to one of the chief gardeners, having got by accident into the garden, happened to range near the place where I lay: the dog, following the scent, came directly up, and taking me in his mouth, ran straight to his master wagging his tail, and set me gently on the ground. By good fortune he had been so well taught, that I was carried between his teeth without the least hurt, or even tearing my clothes. But the poor gardener, who knew me well, and had a great kindness for me, was in a terrible fright: he gently took me up in both his hands, and asked me how I did? but I was so amazed and out of breath, that I could not speak a word. In a few minutes I came to myself, and he carried me safe to my little nurse, who, by this time, had returned to the place where she left me, and was in cruel agonies when I did not appear, nor answer when she called. She severely reprimanded the gardener on account of his dog. But the thing was hushed up, and never known at court, for the girl was afraid of the queen's anger; and truly, as to myself, I thought it would not be for my reputation, that such a story should go about.

This accident absolutely determined Glumdalclitch never to trust me abroad for the future out of her sight. I had been long afraid of this resolution, and therefore concealed from her some little unlucky adventures, that happened in those times when I was left by myself. Once a kite, hovering over the garden, made a stoop at me, and if I had not resolutely drawn my hanger, and run under a thick espalier, he would have certainly carried me away in his talons. Another time, walking to the top of a fresh mole-hill, I fell to my neck in the hole, through which that animal had cast up the earth, and coined some lie, not worth remembering, to excuse myself for spoiling my clothes. I likewise broke my right shin against the shell of a snail, which I happened to stumble over, as I was walking alone and thinking on poor England.

I cannot tell whether I were more pleased or mortified to observe, in those solitary walks, that the smaller birds did not appear to be at all afraid of me, but would hop about within a yard's distance, looking for worms and other food, with as much indifference and security as if no creature at all were near them. I remember, a thrush had the confidence to snatch out of my hand, with his bill, a of cake that Glumdalclitch had just given me for my breakfast. When I attempted to catch any of these birds, they would boldly turn against me, endeavouring to peck my fingers, which I durst not venture within their reach; and then they would hop back unconcerned, to hunt for worms or snails, as they did before. But one day, I took a thick cudgel, and threw it with all my strength so luckily, at a linnet, that I knocked him down, and seizing him by the neck with both my hands, ran with him in triumph to my nurse. However, the bird, who had only been stunned, recovering himself gave me so many boxes with his wings, on both sides of my head and body, though I held him at arm's-length, and was out of the reach of his claws, that I was twenty times thinking to let him go. But I was soon relieved by one of our servants, who wrung off the bird's neck, and I had him next day for dinner, by the queen's command. This linnet, as near as I can remember, seemed to be somewhat larger than an English swan.

The maids of honour often invited Glumdalclitch to their apartments, and desired she would bring me along with her, on purpose to have the pleasure of seeing and touching me. They would often strip me naked from top to toe, and lay me at full length in their bosoms; wherewith I was much disgusted because, to say the truth, a very offensive smell came from their skins; which I do not mention, or intend, to the disadvantage of those excellent ladies, for whom I have all manner of respect; but I conceive that my sense was more acute in proportion to my littleness, and that those illustrious persons were no more disagreeable to their lovers, or to each other, than people of the same quality are with us in England. And, after all, I found their natural smell was much more supportable, than when they used perfumes, under which I immediately swooned away. I cannot forget, that an intimate friend of mine in Lilliput, took the freedom in a warm day, when I had used a good deal of exercise, to complain of a strong smell about me, although I am as little faulty that way, as most of my sex: but I suppose his faculty of smelling was as nice with regard to me, as mine was to that of this people. Upon this point, I cannot forbear doing justice to the queen my mistress, and Glumdalclitch my nurse, whose persons were as sweet as those of any lady in England.

That which gave me most uneasiness among these maids of honour (when my nurse carried me to visit then) was, to see them use me without any manner of ceremony, like a creature who had no sort of consequence: for they would strip themselves to the skin, and put on their smocks in my presence, while I was placed on their toilet, directly before their naked bodies, which I am sure to me was very far from being a tempting sight, or from giving me any other emotions than those of horror and disgust: their skins appeared so coarse and uneven, so variously coloured, when I saw them near, with a mole here and there as broad as a trencher, and hairs hanging from it thicker than packthreads, to say nothing farther concerning the rest of their persons. Neither did they at all scruple, while I was by, to discharge what they had drank, to the quantity of at least two hogsheads, in a vessel that held above three tuns. The handsomest among these maids of honour, a pleasant, frolicsome girl of sixteen, would sometimes set me astride upon one of her nipples, with many other tricks, wherein the reader will excuse me for not being over particular. But I was so much displeased, that I entreated Glumdalclitch to contrive some excuse for not seeing that young lady any more.

One day, a young gentleman, who was nephew to my nurse's governess, came and pressed them both to see an execution. It was of a man, who had murdered one of that gentleman's intimate acquaintance. Glumdalclitch was prevailed on to be of the company, very much against her inclination, for she was naturally tender-hearted: and, as for myself, although I abhorred such kind of spectacles, yet my curiosity tempted me to see something that I thought must be extraordinary. The malefactor was fixed in a chair upon a scaffold erected for that purpose, and his head cut off at one blow, with a sword of about forty feet long. The veins and arteries spouted up such a prodigious quantity of blood, and so high in the air, that the great *jet d'eau* at Versailles was not equal to it for the time it lasted: and the head, when it fell on the scaffold floor, gave such a bounce as made me start, although I was at least half an English mile distant.

The queen, who often used to hear me talk of my sea-voyages, and took all occasions to divert me when I was melancholy, asked me whether I understood how to handle a sail or an oar, and whether a little exercise of rowing might not be convenient for my health? I answered, that I understood both very well: for although my proper employment had been to be surgeon or doctor to the ship, yet often, upon a pinch, I was forced to work like a common mariner. But I could not see how this could be done in their country, where the smallest wherry was equal to a first-rate man of war among us; and such a boat as I could manage would never live in any of their rivers. Her majesty said, if I would contrive a boat, her own joiner should make it, and she would provide a place for me to sail in. The fellow was an ingenious workman, and by my instructions, in ten days, finished a pleasure-boat with all its tackling, able conveniently to hold eight Europeans. When it was finished, the queen was so delighted, that she ran with it in her lap to the king, who ordered it to be put into a cistern full of water, with me in it, by way of trial, where I could not manage my two sculls, or little oars, for want of room. But the queen had before contrived another project. She ordered the joiner to make a wooden trough of three hundred feet long, fifty broad, and eight deep; which, being well pitched, to prevent leaking, was placed on the floor, along the wall, in an outer room of the palace. It had a cock near the bottom to let out the water, when it began to grow stale; and two servants could easily fill it in half an hour. Here I often used to row for my own diversion, as well as that of the queen and her ladies, who thought themselves well entertained with my skill and agility. Sometimes I would put up my sail, and then my business was only to steer, while the ladies gave me a gale with their fans; and, when they were weary, some of their pages would blow my sail forward with their breath, while I showed my art by steering starboard or larboard as I pleased. When I had done, Glumdalclitch always carried back my boat into her closet, and hung it on a nail to dry.

In this exercise I once met an accident, which had like to have cost me my life; for, one of the pages having put my boat into the trough, the governess who attended Glumdalclitch very officiously lifted me up, to place me in the boat: but I happened to slip through her fingers, and should infallibly have fallen down forty feet upon the floor, if, by the luckiest chance in the world, I had not been stopped by a corking-pin that stuck in the good gentlewoman's stomacher; the head of the pin passing between my shirt and the waistband of my breeches, and thus I was held by the middle in the air, till Glumdalclitch ran to my relief.

Another time, one of the servants, whose office it was to fill my trough every third day with fresh water, was so careless as to let a huge frog (not perceiving it) slip out of his pail. The frog lay concealed till I was put into my boat, but then, seeing a resting-place, climbed up, and made it lean so much on one side, that I was forced to balance it with all my weight on the other, to prevent overturning. When the frog was got in, it hopped at once half the length of the boat, and then over my head, backward and forward, daubing my face and clothes with its odious slime. The largeness of its features made it appear the most deformed animal that can be conceived. However, I desired Glumdalclitch to let me deal with it alone. I banged it a good while with one of my sculls, and at last forced it to leap out of the boat.

But the greatest danger I ever underwent in that kingdom, was from a monkey, who belonged to one of the clerks of the kitchen. Glumdalclitch had locked me up in her closet, while she went somewhere upon business, or a visit. The weather being very warm, the closet-window was left open, as well as the windows and the door of my bigger box, in which I usually lived, because of its largeness and conveniency. As I sat quietly meditating at my table, I heard something bounce in at the closet-window, and skip about from one side to the other: whereat, although I was much alarmed, yet I ventured to look out, but not stirring from my seat; and then I saw this frolicsome animal frisking and leaping up and down, till at last he came to my box, which he seemed to view with great pleasure and curiosity, peeping in at the door and every window. I retreated to the farther corner of my room; or box; but the monkey looking in at every side, put me in such a fright, that I wanted presence of mind to conceal myself under the bed, as I might easily have done. After some time spent in peeping, grinning, and chattering, he at last espied me; and reaching one of his paws in at the door, as a cat does when she plays with a mouse, although I often shifted place to avoid him, he at length seized the lappet of my coat (which being made of that country silk, was very thick and strong), and dragged me out. He took me up in his right fore-foot and held me as a nurse does a child she is going to suckle, just as I have seen the same sort of creature do with a kitten in Europe; and when I offered to struggle he squeezed me so hard, that I thought it more prudent to submit. I have good reason to believe, that he took me for a young one of his own species, by his often stroking my face very gently with his other paw. In these diversions he was interrupted by a noise at the closet door, as if somebody were opening it: whereupon he suddenly leaped up to the window at which he had come in, and thence upon the leads and gutters, walking upon three legs, and holding me in the fourth, till he clambered up to a roof that was next to ours. I heard Glumdalclitch give a shriek at the moment he was carrying me out. The poor girl was almost distracted: that quarter of the palace was all in an uproar; the servants ran for ladders; the monkey was seen by hundreds in the court, sitting upon the ridge of a building, holding me like a baby in one of his forepaws, and feeding me with the other, by cramming into my mouth some victuals he had squeezed out of the bag on one side of his chaps, and patting me when I would not eat; whereat many of the rabble below could not forbear laughing; neither do I think they justly ought to be blamed, for, without question, the sight was ridiculous enough to every body but myself. Some of the people threw up stones, hoping to drive the monkey down; but this was strictly forbidden, or else, very probably, my brains had been dashed out.

The ladders were now applied, and mounted by several men; which the monkey observing, and finding himself almost encompassed, not being able to make speed enough with his three legs, let me drop on a ridge tile, and made his escape. Here I sat for some time, five hundred yards from the ground, expecting every moment to be blown down by the wind, or to fall by my own giddiness, and come tumbling over and over from the ridge to the eaves; but an honest lad, one of my nurse's footmen, climbed up, and putting me into his breeches pocket, brought me down safe.

I was almost choked with the filthy stuff the monkey had crammed down my throat: but my dear little nurse picked it out of my mouth with a small needle, and then I fell a-vomiting, which gave me great relief. Yet I was so weak and bruised in the sides with the squeezes given me by this odious animal, that I was forced to keep my bed a fortnight. The king, queen, and all the court, sent every day to inquire after my health; and her majesty made me several visits during my sickness. The monkey was killed, and an order made, that no such animal should be kept about the palace.

When I attended the king after my recovery, to return him thanks for his favours, he was pleased to rally me a good deal upon this adventure. He asked me, "what my thoughts and speculations were, while I lay in the monkey's paw; how I liked the victuals he gave me; his manner of feeding; and whether the fresh air on the roof had sharpened my stomach." He desired to know, "what I would have done upon such an occasion in my own country." I told his majesty, "that in Europe we had no monkeys, except such as were brought for curiosity from other places, and so small, that I could deal with a dozen of them together, if they presumed to attack me. And as for that monstrous animal with whom I was so lately engaged (it was indeed as large as an elephant), if my fears had suffered me to think so far as to make use of my hanger," (looking fiercely, and clapping my hand on the hilt, as I spoke) "when he poked his paw into my chamber, perhaps I should have given him such a wound, as would have made him glad to withdraw it with more haste than he put it in." This I delivered in a firm tone, like a person who was jealous lest his courage should be called in question. However, my speech produced nothing else beside a loud laughter, which all the respect due to his majesty from those about him could not make them contain. This made me reflect, how vain an attempt it is for a man to endeavour to do himself honour among those who are out of all degree of equality or comparison with him. And yet I have seen the moral of my own behaviour very frequent in England since my return; where a little contemptible varlet, without the least title to birth, person, wit, or common sense, shall presume to look with importance, and put himself upon a foot with the greatest persons of the kingdom.

I was every day furnishing the court with some ridiculous story: and Glumdalclitch, although she loved me to excess, yet was arch enough to inform the queen, whenever I committed any folly that she thought would be diverting to her majesty. The girl, who had been out of order, was carried by her governess to take the air about an hour's distance, or thirty miles from town. They alighted out of the coach near a small foot-path in a field, and Glumdalclitch setting down my travelling box, I went out of it to walk. There was a cow-dung in the path, and I must need try my activity by attempting to leap over it. I took a run, but unfortunately jumped short, and found myself just in the middle up to my knees. I waded through with some difficulty, and one of the footmen wiped me as clean as he could with his handkerchief, for I was filthily bemired; and my nurse confined me to my box, till we returned home; where the queen was soon informed of what had passed, and the footmen spread it about the court: so that all the mirth for some days was at my expense.

CHAPTER 6: SEVERAL CONTRIVANCES OF THE AUTHOR TO PLEASE THE KING AND QUEEN. HE SHOWS HIS SKILL IN MUSIC. THE KING INQUIRES INTO THE STATE OF ENGLAND, WHICH THE AUTHOR RELATES TO HIM. THE KING'S OBSERVATIONS THEREON.

I used to attend the king's levee once or twice a week, and had often seen him under the barber's hand, which indeed was at first very terrible to behold; for the razor was almost twice as long as an ordinary scythe. His majesty, according to the custom of the country, was only shaved twice a-week. I once prevailed on the barber to give me some of the suds or lather, out of which I picked forty or fifty of the strongest stumps of hair. I then took a piece of fine wood, and cut it like the back of a comb, making several holes in it at equal distances with as small a needle as I could get from Glumdalclitch. I fixed in the stumps so artificially, scraping and sloping them with my knife toward the points, that I made a very tolerable comb; which was a seasonable supply, my own being so much broken in the teeth, that it was almost useless: neither did I know any artist in that country so nice and exact, as would undertake to make me another.

And this puts me in mind of an amusement, wherein I spent many of my leisure hours. I desired the queen's woman to save for me the combings of her majesty's hair, whereof in time I got a good quantity; and consulting with my friend the cabinet-maker, who had received general orders to do little jobs for me, I directed him to make two chair-frames, no larger than those I had in my box, and to bore little holes with a fine awl, round those parts where I designed the backs and seats; through these holes I wove the strongest hairs I could pick out, just after the manner of cane chairs in England. When they were finished, I made a present of them to her majesty; who kept them in her cabinet, and used to show them for curiosities, as indeed they were the wonder of every one that beheld them. The queen would have me sit upon one of these chairs, but I absolutely refused to obey her, protesting I would rather die than place a dishonourable part of my body on those precious hairs, that once adorned her majesty's head. Of these hairs (as I had always a mechanical genius) I likewise made a neat little purse, about five feet long, with her majesty's name deciphered in gold letters, which I gave to Glumdalclitch, by the queen's consent. To say the truth, it was more for show than use, being not of strength to bear the weight of the larger coins, and therefore she kept nothing in it but some little toys that girls are fond of.

The king, who delighted in music, had frequent concerts at court, to which I was sometimes carried, and set in my box on a table to hear them: but the noise was so great that I could hardly distinguish the tunes. I am confident that all the drums and trumpets of a royal army, beating and sounding together just at your ears, could not equal it. My practice was to have my box removed from the place where the performers sat, as far as I could, then to shut the doors and windows of it, and draw the window curtains; after which I found their music not disagreeable.

I had learned in my youth to play a little upon the spinet. Glumdalclitch kept one in her chamber, and a master attended twice a-week to teach her: I called it a spinet, because it somewhat resembled that instrument, and was played upon in the same manner. A fancy came into my head, that I would entertain the king and queen with an English tune upon this instrument. But this appeared extremely difficult: for the spinet was near sixty feet long, each key being almost a foot wide, so that with my arms extended I could not reach to above five keys, and to press them down required a good smart stroke with my fist, which would be too great a labour, and to no purpose. The method I contrived was this: I prepared two round sticks, about the bigness of common cudgels; they were thicker at one end than the other, and I covered the thicker ends with pieces of a mouse's skin, that by rapping on them I might neither damage the tops of the keys nor interrupt the sound. Before the spinet a bench was placed, about four feet below the keys, and I was put upon the bench. I ran sideling upon it, that way and this, as fast as I could, banging the proper keys with my two sticks, and made a shift to play a jig, to the great satisfaction of both their majesties; but it was the most violent exercise I ever underwent; and yet I could not strike above sixteen keys, nor consequently play the bass and treble together, as other artists do; which was a great disadvantage to my performance.

The king, who, as I before observed, was a prince of excellent understanding, would frequently order that I should be brought in my box, and set upon the table in his closet: he would then command me to bring one of my chairs out of the box, and sit down within three yards distance upon the top of the cabinet, which brought me almost to a level with his face. In this manner I had several conversations with him. I one day took the freedom to tell his majesty, "that the contempt he discovered towards Europe, and the rest of the world, did not seem answerable to those excellent qualities of mind that he was master of; that reason did not extend itself with the bulk of the body; on the contrary, we observed in our country, that the tallest persons were usually the least provided with it; that among other animals, bees and ants had the reputation of more industry, art, and sagacity, than many of the larger kinds; and that, as inconsiderable as he took me to be, I hoped I might live to do his majesty some signal service." The king heard me with attention, and began to conceive a much better opinion of me than he had ever before. He desired "I would give him as exact an account of the government of England as I possibly could; because, as fond as princes commonly are of their own customs (for so he conjectured of other monarchs, by my former discourses), he should be glad to hear of any thing that might deserve imitation."

Imagine with thyself, courteous reader, how often I then wished for the tongue of Demosthenes or Cicero, that might have enabled me to celebrate the praise of my own dear native country in a style equal to its merits and felicity.

I began my discourse by informing his majesty, that our dominions consisted of two islands, which composed three mighty kingdoms, under one sovereign, beside our plantations in America. I dwelt long upon the fertility of our soil, and the temperature of our climate. I then spoke at large upon the constitution of an English parliament; partly made up of an illustrious body called the House of Peers; persons of the noblest blood, and of the most ancient and ample patrimonies. I described that extraordinary care always taken of their education in arts and arms, to qualify them for being counsellors both to the king and kingdom; to have a share in the legislature; to be members of the highest court of judicature, whence there can be no appeal; and to be champions always ready for the defence of their prince and country, by their valour, conduct, and fidelity. That these were the ornament and bulwark of the kingdom, worthy followers of their most renowned ancestors, whose honour had been the reward of their virtue, from which their posterity were never once known to degenerate. To these were joined several holy persons, as part of that assembly, under the title of bishops, whose peculiar business is to take care of religion, and of those who instruct the people therein. These were searched and sought out through the whole nation, by the prince and his wisest counsellors, among such of the priesthood as were most deservedly distinguished by the sanctity of their lives, and the depth of their erudition; who were indeed the spiritual fathers of the clergy and the people.

That the other part of the parliament consisted of an assembly called the House of Commons, who were all principal gentlemen, freely picked and culled out by the people themselves, for their great abilities and love of their country, to represent the wisdom of the whole nation. And that these two bodies made up the most august assembly in Europe; to whom, in conjunction with the prince, the whole legislature is committed.

I then descended to the courts of justice; over which the judges, those venerable sages and interpreters of the law, presided, for determining the disputed rights and properties of men, as well as for the punishment of vice and protection of innocence. I mentioned the prudent management of our treasury; the valour and achievements of our forces, by sea and land. I computed the number of our people, by reckoning how many millions there might be of each religious sect, or political party among us. I did not omit even our sports and pastimes, or any other particular which I thought might redound to the honour of my country. And I finished all with a brief historical account of affairs and events in England for about a hundred years past.

This conversation was not ended under five audiences, each of several hours; and the king heard the whole with great attention, frequently taking notes of what I spoke, as well as memorandums of what questions he intended to ask me.

When I had put an end to these long discources, his majesty, in a sixth audience, consulting his notes, proposed many doubts, queries, and objections, upon every article. He asked, "What methods were used to cultivate the minds and bodies of our young nobility, and in what kind of business they commonly spent the first and teachable parts of their lives? What course was taken to supply that assembly, when any noble family became extinct? What qualifications were necessary in those who are to be created new lords: whether the humour of the prince, a sum of money to a court lady, or a design of strengthening a party opposite to the public interest, ever happened to be the motive in those advancements? What share of knowledge these lords had in the laws of their country, and how they came by it, so as to enable them to decide the properties of their fellow-subjects in the last resort? Whether they were always so free from avarice, partialities, or want, that a bribe, or some other sinister view, could have no place among them? Whether those holy lords I spoke of were always promoted to that rank upon account of their knowledge in religious matters, and the sanctity of their lives; had never been compliers with the times, while they were common priests; or slavish prostitute chaplains to some nobleman, whose opinions they continued servilely to follow, after they were admitted into that assembly?"

He then desired to know, "What arts were practised in electing those whom I called commoners: whether a stranger, with a strong purse, might not influence the vulgar voters to choose him before their own landlord, or the most considerable gentleman in the neighbourhood? How it came to pass, that people were so violently bent upon getting into this assembly, which I allowed to be a great trouble and expense, often to the ruin of their families, without any salary or pension? because this appeared such an exalted strain of virtue and public spirit, that his majesty seemed to doubt it might possibly not be always sincere." And he desired to know, "Whether such zealous gentlemen could have any views of refunding themselves for the charges and trouble they were at by sacrificing the public good to the designs of a weak and vicious prince, in conjunction with a corrupted ministry?" He multiplied his questions, and sifted me thoroughly upon every part of this head, proposing numberless inquiries and objections, which I think it not prudent or convenient to repeat.

Upon what I said in relation to our courts of justice, his majesty desired to be satisfied in several points: and this I was the better able to do, having been formerly almost ruined by a long suit in chancery, which was decreed for me with costs. He asked, "What time was usually spent in determining between right and wrong, and what degree of expense? Whether advocates and orators had liberty to plead in causes manifestly known to be unjust, vexatious, or oppressive? Whether party, in religion or politics, were observed to be of any weight in the scale of justice? Whether those pleading orators were persons educated in the general knowledge of equity, or only in provincial, national, and other local customs? Whether they or their judges had any part in penning those laws, which they assumed the liberty of interpreting, and glossing upon at their pleasure? Whether they had ever, at different times, pleaded for and against the same cause, and cited precedents to prove contrary opinions? Whether they were a rich or a poor corporation? Whether they received any pecuniary reward for pleading, or delivering their opinions? And particularly, whether they were ever admitted as members in the lower senate?"

He fell next upon the management of our treasury; and said, "he thought my memory had failed me, because I computed our taxes at about five or six millions a-year, and when I came to mention the issues, he found they sometimes amounted to more than double; for the notes he had taken were very particular in this point, because he hoped, as he told me, that the knowledge of our conduct might be useful to him, and he could not be deceived in his calculations. But, if what I told him were true, he was still at a loss how a kingdom could run out of its estate, like a private person." He asked me, "who were our creditors; and where we found money to pay them?" He wondered to hear me talk of such chargeable and expensive wars; "that certainly we must be a quarrelsome people, or live among very bad neighbours, and that our generals must needs be richer than our kings." He asked, "what business we had out of our own islands, unless upon the score of trade, or treaty, or to defend the coasts with our fleet?" Above all, he was amazed to hear me talk of a mercenary standing army, in the midst of peace, and among a free people. He said, "if we were governed by our own consent, in the persons of our representatives, he could not imagine of whom we were afraid, or against whom we were to fight; and would hear my opinion, whether a private man's house might not be better defended by himself, his children, and family, than by half-a-dozen rascals, picked up at a venture in the streets for small wages, who might get a hundred times more by cutting their throats?"

He laughed at my "odd kind of arithmetic," as he was pleased to call it, "in reckoning the numbers of our people, by a computation drawn from the several sects among us, in religion and politics." He said, "he knew no reason why those, who entertain opinions prejudicial to the public, should be obliged to change, or should not be obliged to conceal them. And as it was tyranny in any government to require the first, so it was weakness not to enforce the second: for a man may be allowed to keep poisons in his closet, but not to vend them about for cordials."

He observed, "that among the diversions of our nobility and gentry, I had mentioned gaming: he desired to know at what age this entertainment was usually taken up, and when it was laid down; how much of their time it employed; whether it ever went so high as to affect their fortunes; whether mean, vicious people, by their dexterity in that art, might not arrive at great riches, and sometimes keep our very nobles in dependence, as well as habituate them to vile companions, wholly take them from the improvement of their minds, and force them, by the losses they received, to learn and practise that infamous dexterity upon others?"

He was perfectly astonished with the historical account gave him of our affairs during the last century; protesting "it was only a heap of conspiracies, rebellions, murders, massacres, revolutions, banishments, the very worst effects that avarice, faction, hypocrisy, perfidiousness, cruelty, rage, madness, hatred, envy, lust, malice, and ambition, could produce."

His majesty, in another audience, was at the pains to recapitulate the sum of all I had spoken; compared the questions he made with the answers I had given; then taking me into his hands, and stroking me gently, delivered himself in these words, which I shall never forget, nor the manner he spoke them in: "My little friend Grildrig, you have made a most admirable panegyric upon your country; you have clearly proved, that ignorance, idleness, and vice, are the proper ingredients for qualifying a legislator; that laws are best explained, interpreted, and applied, by those whose interest and abilities lie in perverting, confounding, and eluding them. I observe among you some lines of an institution, which, in its original, might have been tolerable, but these half erased, and the rest wholly blurred and blotted by corruptions. It does not appear, from all you have said, how any one perfection is required toward the procurement of any one station among you; much less, that men are ennobled on account of their virtue; that priests are advanced for their piety or learning; soldiers, for their conduct or valour; judges, for their integrity; senators, for the love of their country; or counsellors for their wisdom. As for yourself," continued the king, "who have spent the greatest part of your life in travelling, I am well disposed to hope you may hitherto have escaped many vices of your country. But by what I have gathered from your own relation, and the answers I have with much pains wrung and extorted from you, I cannot but conclude the bulk of your natives to be the most pernicious race of little odious vermin that nature ever suffered to crawl upon the surface of the earth."

CHAPTER 7: THE AUTHOR'S LOVE OF HIS COUNTRY. HE MAKES A PROPOSAL OF MUCH ADVANTAGE TO THE KING, WHICH IS REJECTED. THE KING'S GREAT IGNORANCE IN POLITICS. THE LEARNING OF THAT COUNTRY VERY IMPERFECT AND CONFINED. THE LAWS, AND MILITARY AFFAIRS, AND PARTIES IN THE STATE.

Nothing but an extreme love of truth could have hindered me from concealing this part of my story. It was in vain to discover my resentments, which were always turned into ridicule; and I was forced to rest with patience, while my noble and beloved country was so injuriously treated. I am as heartily sorry as any of my readers can possibly be, that such an occasion was given: but this prince happened to be so curious and inquisitive upon every particular, that it could not consist either with gratitude or good manners, to refuse giving him what satisfaction I was able. Yet thus much I may be allowed to say in my own vindication, that I artfully eluded many of his questions, and gave to every point a more favourable turn, by many degrees, than the strictness of truth would allow. For I have always borne that laudable partiality to my own country, which Dionysius Halicarnassensis, with so much justice, recommends to an historian: I would hide the frailties and deformities of my political mother, and place her virtues and beauties in the most advantageous light. This was my sincere endeavour in those many discourses I had with that monarch, although it unfortunately failed of success.

But great allowances should be given to a king, who lives wholly secluded from the rest of the world, and must therefore be altogether unacquainted with the manners and customs that most prevail in other nations: the want of which knowledge will ever produce many prejudices, and a certain narrowness of thinking, from which we, and the politer countries of Europe, are wholly exempted. And it would be hard indeed, if so remote a prince's notions of virtue and vice were to be offered as a standard for all mankind.

To confirm what I have now said, and further to show the miserable effects of a confined education, I shall here insert a passage, which will hardly obtain belief. In hopes to ingratiate myself further into his majesty's favour, I told him of "an invention, discovered between three and four hundred years ago, to make a certain powder, into a heap of which, the smallest spark of fire falling, would kindle the whole in a moment, although it were as big as a mountain, and make it all fly up in the air together, with a noise and agitation greater than thunder. That a proper quantity of this powder rammed into a hollow tube of brass or iron, according to its bigness, would drive a ball of iron or lead, with such violence and speed, as nothing was able to sustain its force. That the largest balls thus discharged, would not only destroy whole ranks of an army at once, but batter the strongest walls to the ground, sink down ships, with a thousand men in each, to the bottom of the sea, and when linked together by a chain, would cut through masts and rigging, divide hundreds of bodies in the middle, and lay all waste before them. That we often put this powder into large hollow balls of iron, and discharged them by an engine into some city we were besieging, which would rip up the pavements, tear the houses to pieces, burst and throw splinters on every side, dashing out the brains of all who came near. That I knew the ingredients very well, which were cheap and common; I understood the manner of compounding them, and could direct his workmen how to make those tubes, of a size proportionable to all other things in his majesty's kingdom, and the largest need not be above a hundred feet long; twenty or thirty of which tubes, charged with the proper quantity of powder and balls, would batter down the walls of the strongest town in his dominions in a few hours, or destroy the whole metropolis, if ever it should pretend to dispute his absolute commands." This I humbly offered to his majesty, as a small tribute of acknowledgment, in turn for so many marks that I had received, of his royal favour and protection.

The king was struck with horror at the description I had given of those terrible engines, and the proposal I had made. "He was amazed, how so impotent and grovelling an insect as I" (these were his expressions) "could entertain such inhuman ideas, and in so familiar a manner, as to appear wholly unmoved at all the scenes of blood and desolation which I had painted as the common effects of those destructive machines; whereof," he said, "some evil genius, enemy to mankind, must have been the first contriver. As for himself, he protested, that although few things delighted him so much as new discoveries in art or in nature, yet he would rather lose half his kingdom, than be privy to such a secret; which he commanded me, as I valued any life, never to mention any more."

A strange effect of narrow principles and views! that a prince possessed of every quality which procures veneration, love, and esteem; of strong parts, great wisdom, and profound learning, endowed with admirable talents, and almost adored by his subjects, should, from a nice, unnecessary scruple, whereof in Europe we can have no conception, let slip an opportunity put into his hands that would have made him absolute master of the lives, the liberties, and the fortunes of his people! Neither do I say this, with the least intention to detract from the many virtues of that excellent king, whose character, I am sensible, will, on this account, be very much lessened in the opinion of an English reader: but I take this defect among them to have risen from their ignorance, by not having hitherto reduced politics into a science, as the more acute wits of Europe have done. For, I remember very well, in a discourse one day with the king, when I happened to say, "there were several thousand books among us written upon the art of government," it gave him (directly contrary to my intention) a very mean opinion of our understandings. He professed both to abominate and despise all mystery, refinement, and intrigue, either in a prince or a minister. He could not tell what I meant by secrets of state, where an enemy, or some rival nation, were not in the case. He confined the knowledge of governing within very narrow bounds, to common sense and reason, to justice and lenity, to the speedy determination of civil and criminal causes; with some other obvious topics, which are not worth considering. And he gave it for his opinion, "that whoever could make two ears of corn, or two blades of grass, to grow upon a spot of ground where only one grew before, would deserve better of mankind, and do more essential service to his country, than the whole race of politicians put together."

The learning of this people is very defective, consisting only in morality, history, poetry, and mathematics, wherein they must be allowed to excel. But the last of these is wholly applied to what may be useful in life, to the improvement of agriculture, and all mechanical arts; so that among us, it would be little esteemed. And as to ideas, entities, abstractions, and transcendentals, I could never drive the least conception into their heads.

No law in that country must exceed in words the number of letters in their alphabet, which consists only of two and twenty. But indeed few of them extend even to that length. They are expressed in the most plain and simple terms, wherein those people are not mercurial enough to discover above one interpretation: and to write a comment upon any law, is a capital crime. As to the decision of civil causes, or proceedings against criminals, their precedents are so few, that they have little reason to boast of any extraordinary skill in either.

They have had the art of printing, as well as the Chinese, time out of mind: but their libraries are not very large; for that of the king, which is reckoned the largest, does not amount to above a thousand volumes, placed in a gallery of twelve hundred feet long, whence I had liberty to borrow what books I pleased.

The queen's joiner had contrived in one of Glumdalclitch's rooms, a kind of wooden machine five-and-twenty feet high, formed like a standing ladder; the steps were each fifty feet long. It was indeed a moveable pair of stairs, the lowest end placed at ten feet distance from the wall of the chamber. The book I had a mind to read, was put up leaning against the wall: I first mounted to the upper step of the ladder, and turning my face towards the book, began at the top of the page, and so walking to the right and left about eight or ten paces, according to the length of the lines, till I had gotten a little below the level of mine eyes, and then descending gradually till I came to the bottom: after which I mounted again, and began the other page in the same manner, and so turned over the leaf, which I could easily do with both my hands, for it was as thick and stiff as a pasteboard, and in the largest folios not above eighteen or twenty feet long.

Their style is clear, masculine, and smooth, but not florid; for they avoid nothing more than multiplying unnecessary words, or using various expressions. I have perused many of their books, especially those in history and morality. Among the rest, I was much diverted with a little old treatise, which always lay in Glumdalclitch's bed chamber, and belonged to her governess, a grave elderly gentlewoman, who dealt in writings of morality and devotion. The book treats of the weakness of human kind, and is in little esteem, except among the women and the vulgar. However, I was curious to see what an author of that country could say upon such a subject. This writer went through all the usual topics of European moralists, showing "how diminutive, contemptible, and helpless an animal was man in his own nature; how unable to defend himself from inclemencies of the air, or the fury of wild beasts: how much he was excelled by one creature in strength, by another in speed, by a third in foresight, by a fourth in industry." He added, "that nature was degenerated in these latter declining ages of the world, and could now produce only small abortive births, in comparison of those in ancient times." He said "it was very reasonable to think, not only that the species of men were originally much larger, but also that there must have been giants in former ages; which, as it is asserted by history and tradition, so it has been confirmed by huge bones and skulls, casually dug up in several parts of the kingdom, far exceeding the common dwindled race of men in our days." He argued, "that the very laws of nature absolutely required we should have been made, in the beginning of a size more large and robust; not so liable to destruction from every little accident, of a tile falling from a house, or a stone cast from the hand of a boy, or being drowned in a little brook." From this way of reasoning, the author drew several moral applications, useful in the conduct of life, but needless here to repeat. For my own part, I could not avoid reflecting how universally this talent was spread, of drawing lectures in morality, or indeed rather matter of discontent and repining, from the quarrels we raise with nature. And I believe, upon a strict inquiry, those quarrels might be shown as ill-grounded among us as they are among that people.

As to their military affairs, they boast that the king's army consists of a hundred and seventy-six thousand foot, and thirty-two thousand horse: if that may be called an army, which is made up of tradesmen in the several cities, and farmers in the country, whose commanders are only the nobility and gentry, without pay or reward. They are indeed perfect enough in their exercises, and under very good discipline, wherein I saw no great merit; for how should it be otherwise, where every farmer is under the command of his own landlord, and every citizen under that of the principal men in his own city, chosen after the manner of Venice, by ballot?

I have often seen the militia of Lorbrulgrud drawn out to exercise, in a great field near the city of twenty miles square. They were in all not above twenty-five thousand foot, and six thousand horse; but it was impossible for me to compute their number, considering the space of ground they took up. A cavalier, mounted on a large steed, might be about ninety feet high. I have seen this whole body of horse, upon a word of command, draw their swords at once, and brandish them in the air. Imagination can figure nothing so grand, so surprising, and so astonishing! it looked as if ten thousand flashes of lightning were darting at the same time from every quarter of the sky.

I was curious to know how this prince, to whose dominions there is no access from any other country, came to think of armies, or to teach his people the practice of military discipline. But I was soon informed, both by conversation and reading their histories; for, in the course of many ages, they have been troubled with the same disease to which the whole race of mankind is subject; the nobility often contending for power, the people for liberty, and the king for absolute dominion. All which, however happily tempered by the laws of that kingdom, have been sometimes violated by each of the three parties, and have more than once occasioned civil wars; the last whereof was happily put an end to by this prince's grand-father, in a general composition; and the militia, then settled with common consent, has been ever since kept in the strictest duty.

CHAPTER 8: THE KING AND QUEEN MAKE A PROGRESS TO THE FRONTIERS. THE AUTHOR ATTENDS THEM. THE MANNER IN WHICH HE LEAVES THE COUNTRY VERY PARTICULARLY RELATED. HE RETURNS TO ENGLAND.

I had always a strong impulse that I should some time recover my liberty, though it was impossible to conjecture by what means, or to form any project with the least hope of succeeding. The ship in which I sailed, was the first ever known to be driven within sight of that coast, and the king had given strict orders, that if at any time another appeared, it should be taken ashore, and with all its crew and passengers brought in a tumbril to Lorbrulgrud. He was strongly bent to get me a woman of my own size, by whom I might propagate the breed: but I think I should rather have died than undergone the disgrace of leaving a posterity to be kept in cages, like tame canary-birds, and perhaps, in time, sold about the kingdom, to persons of quality, for curiosities. I was indeed treated with much kindness: I was the favourite of a great king and queen, and the delight of the whole court; but it was upon such a foot as ill became the dignity of humankind. I could never forget those domestic pledges I had left behind me. I wanted to be among people, with whom I could converse upon even terms, and walk about the streets and fields without being afraid of being trod to death like a frog or a young puppy. But my deliverance came sooner than I expected, and in a manner not very common; the whole story and circumstances of which I shall faithfully relate.

I had now been two years in this country; and about the beginning of the third, Glumdalclitch and I attended the king and queen, in a progress to the south coast of the kingdom. I was carried, as usual, in my travelling-box, which as I have already described, was a very convenient closet, of twelve feet wide. And I had ordered a hammock to be fixed, by silken ropes from the four corners at the top, to break the jolts, when a servant carried me before him on horseback, as I sometimes desired; and would often sleep in my hammock, while we were upon the road. On the roof of my closet, not directly over the middle of the hammock, I ordered the joiner to cut out a hole of a foot square, to give me air in hot weather, as I slept; which hole I shut at pleasure with a board that drew backward and forward through a groove.

When we came to our journey's end, the king thought proper to pass a few days at a palace he has near Flanflasnic, a city within eighteen English miles of the seaside. Glumdalclitch and I were much fatigued: I had gotten a small cold, but the poor girl was so ill as to be confined to her chamber. I longed to see the ocean, which must be the only scene of my escape, if ever it should happen. I pretended to be worse than I really was, and desired leave to take the fresh air of the sea, with a page, whom I was very fond of, and who had sometimes been trusted with me. I shall never forget with what unwillingness Glumdalclitch consented, nor the strict charge she gave the page to be careful of me, bursting at the same time into a flood of tears, as if she had some forboding of what was to happen. The boy took me out in my box, about half an hours walk from the palace, towards the rocks on the sea-shore. I ordered him to set me down, and lifting up one of my sashes, cast many a wistful melancholy look towards the sea. I found myself not very well, and told the page that I had a mind to take a nap in my hammock, which I hoped would do me good. I got in, and the boy shut the window close down, to keep out the cold. I soon fell asleep, and all I can conjecture is, while I slept, the page, thinking no danger could happen, went among the rocks to look for birds' eggs, having before observed him from my window searching about, and picking up one or two in the clefts. Be that as it will, I found myself suddenly awaked with a violent pull upon the ring, which was fastened at the top of my box for the conveniency of carriage. I felt my box raised very high in the air, and then borne forward with prodigious speed. The first jolt had like to have shaken me out of my hammock, but afterward the motion was easy enough. I called out several times, as loud as I could raise my voice, but all to no purpose. I looked towards my windows, and could see nothing but the clouds and sky. I heard a noise just over my head, like the clapping of wings, and then began to perceive the woful condition I was in; that some eagle had got the ring of my box in his beak, with an intent to let it fall on a rock, like a tortoise in a shell, and then pick out my body, and devour it: for the sagacity and smell of this bird enables him to discover his quarry at a great distance, though better concealed than I could be within a two-inch board.

In a little time, I observed the noise and flutter of wings to increase very fast, and my box was tossed up and down, like a sign in a windy day. I heard several bangs or buffets, as I thought given to the eagle (for such I am certain it must have been that held the ring of my box in his beak), and then, all on a sudden, felt myself falling perpendicularly down, for above a minute, but with such incredible swiftness, that I almost lost my breath. My fall was stopped by a terrible squash, that sounded louder to my ears than the cataract of Niagara; after which, I was quite in the dark for another minute, and then my box began to rise so high, that I could see light from the tops of the windows. I now perceived I was fallen into the sea. My box, by the weight of my body, the goods that were in, and the broad plates of iron fixed for strength at the four corners of the top and bottom, floated about five feet deep in water. I did then, and do now suppose, that the eagle which flew away with my box was pursued by two or three others, and forced to let me drop, while he defended himself against the rest, who hoped to share in the prey. The plates of iron fastened at the bottom of the box (for those were the strongest) preserved the balance while it fell, and hindered it from being broken on the surface of the water. Every joint of it was well grooved; and the door did not move on hinges, but up and down like a sash, which kept my closet so tight that very little water came in. I got with much difficulty out of my hammock, having first ventured to draw back the slip-board on the roof already mentioned, contrived on purpose to let in air, for want of which I found myself almost stifled.

How often did I then wish myself with my dear Glumdalclitch, from whom one single hour had so far divided me! And I may say with truth, that in the midst of my own misfortunes I could not forbear lamenting my poor nurse, the grief she would suffer for my loss, the displeasure of the queen, and the ruin of her fortune. Perhaps many travellers have not been under greater difficulties and distress than I was at this juncture, expecting every moment to see my box dashed to pieces, or at least overset by the first violent blast, or rising wave. A breach in one single pane of glass would have been immediate death: nor could any thing have preserved the windows, but the strong lattice wires placed on the outside, against accidents in travelling. I saw the water ooze in at several crannies, although the leaks were not considerable, and I endeavoured to stop them as well as I could. I was not able to lift up the roof of my closet, which otherwise I certainly should have done, and sat on the top of it; where I might at least preserve myself some hours longer, than by being shut up (as I may call it) in the hold. Or if I escaped these dangers for a day or two, what could I expect but a miserable death of cold and hunger? I was four hours under these circumstances, expecting, and indeed wishing, every moment to be my last.

I have already told the reader that there were two strong staples fixed upon that side of my box which had no window, and into which the servant, who used to carry me on horseback, would put a leathern belt, and buckle it about his waist. Being in this disconsolate state, I heard, or at least thought I heard, some kind of grating noise on that side of my box where the staples were fixed; and soon after I began to fancy that the box was pulled or towed along the sea; for I now and then felt a sort of tugging, which made the waves rise near the tops of my windows, leaving me almost in the dark. This gave me some faint hopes of relief, although I was not able to imagine how it could be brought about. I ventured to unscrew one of my chairs, which were always fastened to the floor; and having made a hard shift to screw it down again, directly under the slipping-board that I had lately opened, I mounted on the chair, and putting my mouth as near as I could to the hole, I called for help in a loud voice, and in all the languages I understood. I then fastened my handkerchief to a stick I usually carried, and thrusting it up the hole, waved it several times in the air, that if any boat or ship were near, the seamen might conjecture some unhappy mortal to be shut up in the box.

I found no effect from all I could do, but plainly perceived my closet to be moved along; and in the space of an hour, or better, that side of the box where the staples were, and had no windows, struck against something that was hard. I apprehended it to be a rock, and found myself tossed more than ever. I plainly heard a noise upon the cover of my closet, like that of a cable, and the grating of it as it passed through the ring. I then found myself hoisted up, by degrees, at least three feet higher than I was before. Whereupon I again thrust up my stick and handkerchief, calling for help till I was almost hoarse. In return to which, I heard a great shout repeated three times, giving me such transports of joy as are not to be conceived but by those who feel them. I now heard a trampling over my head, and somebody calling through the hole with a loud voice, in the English tongue, "If there be any body below, let them speak." I answered, "I was an Englishman, drawn by ill fortune into the greatest calamity that ever any creature underwent, and begged, by all that was moving, to be delivered out of the dungeon I was in." The voice replied, "I was safe, for my box was fastened to their ship; and the carpenter should immediately come and saw a hole in the cover, large enough to pull me out." I answered, "that was needless, and would take up too much time; for there was no more to be done, but let one of the crew put his finger into the ring, and take the box out of the sea into the ship, and so into the captain's cabin." Some of them, upon hearing me talk so wildly, thought I was mad: others laughed; for indeed it never came into my head, that I was now got among people of my own stature and strength. The carpenter came, and in a few minutes sawed a passage about four feet square, then let down a small ladder, upon which I mounted, and thence was taken into the ship in a very weak condition.

The sailors were all in amazement, and asked me a thousand questions, which I had no inclination to answer. I was equally confounded at the sight of so many pigmies, for such I took them to be, after having so long accustomed mine eyes to the monstrous objects I had left. But the captain, Mr. Thomas Wilcocks, an honest worthy Shropshire man, observing I was ready to faint, took me into his cabin, gave me a cordial to comfort me, and made me turn in upon his own bed, advising me to take a little rest, of which I had great need. Before I went to sleep, I gave him to understand that I had some valuable furniture in my box, too good to be lost: a fine hammock, a handsome field-bed, two chairs, a table, and a cabinet; that my closet was hung on all sides, or rather quilted, with silk and cotton; that if he would let one of the crew bring my closet into his cabin, I would open it there before him, and show him my goods. The captain, hearing me utter these absurdities, concluded I was raving; however (I suppose to pacify me) he promised to give order as I desired, and going upon deck, sent some of his men down into my closet, whence (as I afterwards found) they drew up all my goods, and stripped off the quilting; but the chairs, cabinet, and bedstead, being screwed to the floor, were much damaged by the ignorance of the seamen, who tore them up by force. Then they knocked off some of the boards for the use of the ship, and when they had got all they had a mind for, let the hull drop into the sea, which by reason of many breaches made in the bottom and sides, sunk to rights. And, indeed, I was glad not to have been a spectator of the havoc they made, because I am confident it would have sensibly touched me, by bringing former passages into my mind, which I would rather have forgot.

I slept some hours, but perpetually disturbed with dreams of the place I had left, and the dangers I had escaped. However, upon waking, I found myself much recovered. It was now about eight o'clock at night, and the captain ordered supper immediately, thinking I had already fasted too long. He entertained me with great kindness, observing me not to look wildly, or talk inconsistently: and, when we were left alone, desired I would give him a relation of my travels, and by what accident I came to be set adrift, in that monstrous wooden chest. He said "that about twelve o'clock at noon, as he was looking through his glass, he spied it at a distance, and thought it was a sail, which he had a mind to make, being not much out of his course, in hopes of buying some biscuit, his own beginning to fall short. That upon coming nearer, and finding his error, he sent out his long-boat to discover what it was; that his men came back in a fright, swearing they had seen a swimming house. That he laughed at their folly, and went himself in the boat, ordering his men to take a strong cable along with them. That the weather being calm, he rowed round me several times, observed my windows and wire lattices that defended them. That he discovered two staples upon one side, which was all of boards, without any passage for light. He then commanded his men to row up to that side, and fastening a cable to one of the staples, ordered them to tow my chest, as they called it, toward the ship. When it was there, he gave directions to fasten another cable to the ring fixed in the cover, and to raise up my chest with pulleys, which all the sailors were not able to do above two or three feet." He said, "they saw my stick and handkerchief thrust out of the hole, and concluded that some unhappy man must be shut up in the cavity." I asked, "whether he or the crew had seen any prodigious birds in the air, about the time he first discovered me." To which he answered, "that discoursing this matter with the sailors while I was asleep, one of them said, he had observed three eagles flying towards the north, but remarked nothing of their being larger than the usual size:" which I suppose must be imputed to the great height they were at; and he could not guess the reason of my question. I then asked the captain, "how far he reckoned we might be from land?" He said, "by the best computation he could make, we were at least a hundred leagues." I assured him, "that he must be mistaken by almost half, for I had not left the country whence I came above two hours before I dropped into the sea." Whereupon he began again to think that my brain was disturbed, of which he gave me a hint, and advised me to go to bed in a cabin he had provided. I assured him, "I was well refreshed with his good entertainment and company, and as much in my senses as ever I was in my life." He then grew serious, and desired to ask me freely, "whether I were not troubled in my mind by the consciousness of some enormous crime, for which I was punished, at the command of some prince, by exposing me in that chest; as great criminals, in other countries, have been forced to sea in a leaky vessel, without provisions: for although he should be sorry to have taken so ill a man into his ship, yet he would engage his word to set me safe ashore, in the first port where we arrived." He added, "that his suspicions were much increased by some very absurd speeches I had delivered at first to his sailors, and afterwards to himself, in relation to my closet or chest, as well as by my odd looks and behaviour while I was at supper."

I begged his patience to hear me tell my story, which I faithfully did, from the last time I left England, to the moment he first discovered me. And, as truth always forces its way into rational minds, so this honest worthy gentleman, who had some tincture of learning, and very good sense, was immediately convinced of my candour and veracity. But further to confirm all I had said, I entreated him to give order that my cabinet should be brought, of which I had the key in my pocket; for he had already informed me how the seamen disposed of my closet. I opened it in his own presence, and showed him the small collection of rarities I made in the country from which I had been so strangely delivered. There was the comb I had contrived out of the stumps of the king's beard, and another of the same materials, but fixed into a paring of her majesty's thumb-nail, which served for the back. There was a collection of needles and pins, from a foot to half a yard long; four wasp stings, like joiner's tacks; some combings of the queen's hair; a gold ring, which one day she made me a present of, in a most obliging manner, taking it from her little finger, and throwing it over my head like a collar. I desired the captain would please to accept this ring in return for his civilities; which he absolutely refused. I showed him a corn that I had cut off with my own hand, from a maid of honour's toe; it was about the bigness of Kentish pippin, and grown so hard, that when I returned England, I got it hollowed into a cup, and set in silver. Lastly, I desired him to see the breeches I had then on, which were made of a mouse's skin.

I could force nothing on him but a footman's tooth, which I observed him to examine with great curiosity, and found he had a fancy for it. He received it with abundance of thanks, more than such a trifle could deserve. It was drawn by an unskilful surgeon, in a mistake, from one of Glumdalclitch's men, who was afflicted with the tooth-ache, but it was as sound as any in his head. I got it cleaned, and put it into my cabinet. It was about a foot long, and four inches in diameter.

The captain was very well satisfied with this plain relation I had given him, and said, "he hoped, when we returned to England, I would oblige the world by putting it on paper, and making it public." My answer was, "that we were overstocked with books of travels: that nothing could now pass which was not extraordinary; wherein I doubted some authors less consulted truth, than their own vanity, or interest, or the diversion of ignorant readers; that my story could contain little beside common events, without those ornamental descriptions of strange plants, trees, birds, and other animals; or of the barbarous customs and idolatry of savage people, with which most writers abound. However, I thanked him for his good opinion, and promised to take the matter into my thoughts."

He said "he wondered at one thing very much, which was, to hear me speak so loud;" asking me "whether the king or queen of that country were thick of hearing?" I told him, "it was what I had been used to for above two years past, and that I admired as much at the voices of him and his men, who seemed to me only to whisper, and yet I could hear them well enough. But, when I spoke in that country, it was like a man talking in the streets, to another looking out from the top of a steeple, unless when I was placed on a table, or held in any person's hand." I told him, "I had likewise observed another thing, that, when I first got into the ship, and the sailors stood all about me, I thought they were the most little contemptible creatures I had ever beheld." For indeed, while I was in that prince's country, I could never endure to look in a glass, after mine eyes had been accustomed to such prodigious objects, because the comparison gave me so despicable a conceit of myself. The captain said, "that while we were at supper, he observed me to look at every thing with a sort of wonder, and that I often seemed hardly able to contain my laughter, which he knew not well how to take, but imputed it to some disorder in my brain." I answered, "it was very true; and I wondered how I could forbear, when I saw his dishes of the size of a silver three-pence, a leg of pork hardly a mouthful, a cup not so big as a nut-shell;" and so I went on, describing the rest of his household-stuff and provisions, after the same manner. For, although he queen had ordered a little equipage of all things necessary for me, while I was in her service, yet my ideas were wholly taken up with what I saw on every side of me, and I winked at my own littleness, as people do at their own faults. The captain understood my raillery very well, and merrily replied with the old English proverb, "that he doubted mine eyes were bigger than my belly, for he did not observe my stomach so good, although I had fasted all day;" and, continuing in his mirth, protested "he would have gladly given a hundred pounds, to have seen my closet in the eagle's bill, and afterwards in its fall from so great a height into the sea; which would certainly have been a most astonishing object, worthy to have the description of it transmitted to future ages:" and the comparison of Phaëton was so obvious, that he could not forbear applying it, although I did not much admire the conceit.

The captain having been at Tonquin, was, in his return to England, driven north-eastward to the latitude of 44 degrees, and longitude of 143. But meeting a trade-wind two days after I came on board him, we sailed southward a long time, and coasting New Holland, kept our course west-south-west, and then south-south-west, till we doubled the Cape of Good Hope. Our voyage was very prosperous, but I shall not trouble the reader with a journal of it. The captain called in at one or two ports, and sent in his long-boat for provisions and fresh water; but I never went out of the ship till we came into the Downs, which was on the third day of June, 1706, about nine months after my escape. I offered to leave my goods in security for payment of my freight: but the captain protested he would not receive one farthing. We took a kind leave of each other, and I made him promise he would come to see me at my house in Redriff. I hired a horse and guide for five shillings, which I borrowed of the captain.

As I was on the road, observing the littleness of the houses, the trees, the cattle, and the people, I began to think myself in Lilliput. I was afraid of trampling on every traveller I met, and often called aloud to have them stand out of the way, so that I had like to have gotten one or two broken heads for my impertinence.

When I came to my own house, for which I was forced to inquire, one of the servants opening the door, I bent down to go in, (like a goose under a gate,) for fear of striking my head. My wife run out to embrace me, but I stooped lower than her knees, thinking she could otherwise never be able to reach my mouth. My daughter kneeled to ask my blessing, but I could not see her till she arose, having been so long used to stand with my head and eyes erect to above sixty feet; and then I went to take her up with one hand by the waist. I looked down upon the servants, and one or two friends who were in the house, as if they had been pigmies and I a giant. I told my wife, "she had been too thrifty, for I found she had starved herself and her daughter to nothing." In short, I behaved myself so unaccountably, that they were all of the captain's opinion when he first saw me, and concluded I had lost my wits. This I mention as an instance of the great power of habit and prejudice.

In a little time, I and my family and friends came to a right understanding: but my wife protested "I should never go to sea any more;" although my evil destiny so ordered, that she had not power to hinder me, as the reader may know hereafter. In the mean time, I here conclude the second part of my unfortunate voyages.

✦ 3 ✦

A VOYAGE TO LAPUTA,
BALNIBARBI, LUGGNAGG,
GLUBBDUBDRIB, AND JAPAN

CHAPTER 1: THE AUTHOR SETS OUT ON HIS THIRD VOYAGE. IS TAKEN BY PIRATES. THE MALICE OF A DUTCHMAN. HIS ARRIVAL AT AN ISLAND. HE IS RECEIVED INTO LAPUTA.

I had not been at home above ten days, when Captain William Robinson, a Cornish man, commander of the Hopewell, a stout ship of three hundred tons, came to my house. I had formerly been surgeon of another ship where he was master, and a fourth part owner, in a voyage to the Levant. He had always treated me more like a brother, than an inferior officer; and, hearing of my arrival, made me a visit, as I apprehended only out of friendship, for nothing passed more than what is usual after long absences. But repeating his visits often, expressing his joy to find I me in good health, asking, "whether I were now settled for life?" adding, "that he intended a voyage to the East Indies in two months," at last he plainly invited me, though with some apologies, to be surgeon of the ship; "that I should have another surgeon under me, beside our two mates; that my salary should be double to the usual pay; and that having experienced my knowledge in sea-affairs to be at least equal to his, he would enter into any engagement to follow my advice, as much as if I had shared in the command."

He said so many other obliging things, and I knew him to be so honest a man, that I could not reject this proposal; the thirst I had of seeing the world, notwithstanding my past misfortunes, continuing as violent as ever. The only difficulty that remained, was to persuade my wife, whose consent however I at last obtained, by the prospect of advantage she proposed to her children.

We set out the 5th day of August, 1706, and arrived at Fort St. George the 11th of April, 1707. We staid there three weeks to refresh our crew, many of whom were sick. From thence we went to Tonquin, where the captain resolved to continue some time, because many of the goods he intended to buy were not ready, nor could he expect to be dispatched in several months. Therefore, in hopes to defray some of the charges he must be at, he bought a sloop, loaded it with several sorts of goods, wherewith the Tonquinese usually trade to the neighbouring islands, and putting fourteen men on board, whereof three were of the country, he appointed me master of the sloop, and gave me power to traffic, while he transacted his affairs at Tonquin.

We had not sailed above three days, when a great storm arising, we were driven five days to the north-north-east, and then to the east: after which we had fair weather, but still with a pretty strong gale from the west. Upon the tenth day we were chased by two pirates, who soon overtook us; for my sloop was so deep laden, that she sailed very slow, neither were we in a condition to defend ourselves.

We were boarded about the same time by both the pirates, who entered furiously at the head of their men; but finding us all prostrate upon our faces (for so I gave order), they pinioned us with strong ropes, and setting guard upon us, went to search the sloop.

I observed among them a Dutchman, who seemed to be of some authority, though he was not commander of either ship. He knew us by our countenances to be Englishmen, and jabbering to us in his own language, swore we should be tied back to back and thrown into the sea. I spoke Dutch tolerably well; I told him who we were, and begged him, in consideration of our being Christians and Protestants, of neighbouring countries in strict alliance, that he would move the captains to take some pity on us. This inflamed his rage; he repeated his threatenings, and turning to his companions, spoke with great vehemence in the Japanese language, as I suppose, often using the word *Christianos*.

The largest of the two pirate ships was commanded by a Japanese captain, who spoke a little Dutch, but very imperfectly. He came up to me, and after several questions, which I answered in great humility, he said, "we should not die." I made the captain a very low bow, and then, turning to the Dutchman, said, "I was sorry to find more mercy in a heathen, than in a brother christian." But I had soon reason to repent those foolish words: for that malicious reprobate, having often endeavoured in vain to persuade both the captains that I might be thrown into the sea (which they would not yield to, after the promise made me that I should not die), however, prevailed so far, as to have a punishment inflicted on me, worse, in all human appearance, than death itself. My men were sent by an equal division into both the pirate ships, and my sloop new manned. As to myself, it was determined that I should be set adrift in a small canoe, with paddles and a sail, and four days' provisions; which last, the Japanese captain was so kind to double out of his own stores, and would permit no man to search me. I got down into the canoe, while the Dutchman, standing upon the deck, loaded me with all the curses and injurious terms his language could afford.

About an hour before we saw the pirates I had taken an observation, and found we were in the latitude of 46 N. and longitude of 183. When I was at some distance from the pirates, I discovered, by my pocket-glass, several islands to the south-east. I set up my sail, the wind being fair, with a design to reach the nearest of those islands, which I made a shift to do, in about three hours. It was all rocky: however I got many birds' eggs; and, striking fire, I kindled some heath and dry sea-weed, by which I roasted my eggs. I ate no other supper, being resolved to spare my provisions as much as I could. I passed the night under the shelter of a rock, strewing some heath under me, and slept pretty well.

The next day I sailed to another island, and thence to a third and fourth, sometimes using my sail, and sometimes my paddles. But, not to trouble the reader with a particular account of my distresses, let it suffice, that on the fifth day I arrived at the last island in my sight, which lay south-south-east to the former.

This island was at a greater distance than I expected, and I did not reach it in less than five hours. I encompassed it almost round, before I could find a convenient place to land in; which was a small creek, about three times the wideness of my canoe. I found the island to be all rocky, only a little intermingled with tufts of grass, and sweet-smelling herbs. I took out my small provisions and after having refreshed myself, I secured the remainder in a cave, whereof there were great numbers; I gathered plenty of eggs upon the rocks, and got a quantity of dry sea-weed, and parched grass, which I designed to kindle the next day, and roast my eggs as well as I could, for I had about me my flint, steel, match, and burning-glass. I lay all night in the cave where I had lodged my provisions. My bed was the same dry grass and sea-weed which I intended for fuel. I slept very little, for the disquiets of my mind prevailed over my weariness, and kept me awake. I considered how impossible it was to preserve my life in so desolate a place, and how miserable my end must be: yet found myself so listless and desponding, that I had not the heart to rise; and before I could get spirits enough to creep out of my cave, the day was far advanced. I walked awhile among the rocks: the sky was perfectly clear, and the sun so hot, that I was forced to turn my face from it: when all on a sudden it became obscure, as I thought, in a manner very different from what happens by the interposition of a cloud. I turned back, and perceived a vast opaque body between me and the sun moving forwards towards the island: it seemed to be about two miles high, and hid the sun six or seven minutes; but I did not observe the air to be much colder, or the sky more darkened, than if I had stood under the shade of a mountain. As it approached nearer over the place where I was, it appeared to be a firm substance, the bottom flat, smooth, and shining very bright, from the reflection of the sea below. I stood upon a height about two hundred yards from the shore, and saw this vast body descending almost to a parallel with me, at less than an English mile distance. I took out my pocket perspective, and could plainly discover numbers of people moving up and down the sides of it, which appeared to be sloping; but what those people where doing I was not able to distinguish.

The natural love of life gave me some inward motion of joy, and I was ready to entertain a hope that this adventure might, some way or other, help to deliver me from the desolate place and condition I was in. But at the same time the reader can hardly conceive my astonishment, to behold an island in the air, inhabited by men, who were able (as it should seem) to raise or sink, or put it into progressive motion, as they pleased. But not being at that time in a disposition to philosophise upon this phenomenon, I rather chose to observe what course the island would take, because it seemed for awhile to stand still. Yet soon after, it advanced nearer, and I could see the sides of it encompassed with several gradations of galleries, and stairs, at certain intervals, to descend from one to the other. In the lowest gallery, I beheld some people fishing with long angling rods, and others looking on. I waved my cap (for my hat was long since worn out) and my handkerchief toward the island; and upon its nearer approach, I called and shouted with the utmost strength of my voice; and then looking circumspectly, I beheld a crowd gather to that side which was most in my view. I found by their pointing towards me and to each other, that they plainly discovered me, although they made no return to my shouting. But I could see four or five men running in great haste, up the stairs, to the top of the island, who then disappeared. I happened rightly to conjecture, that these were sent for orders to some person in authority upon this occasion.

The number of people increased, and, in less than half an hour, the island was moved and raised in such a manner, that the lowest gallery appeared in a parallel of less then a hundred yards distance from the height where I stood. I then put myself in the most supplicating posture, and spoke in the humblest accent, but received no answer. Those who stood nearest over against me, seemed to be persons of distinction, as I supposed by their habit. They conferred earnestly with each other, looking often upon me. At length one of them called out in a clear, polite, smooth dialect, not unlike in sound to the Italian: and therefore I returned an answer in that language, hoping at least that the cadence might be more agreeable to his ears. Although neither of us understood the other, yet my meaning was easily known, for the people saw the distress I was in.

They made signs for me to come down from the rock, and go towards the shore, which I accordingly did; and the flying island being raised to a convenient height, the verge directly over me, a chain was let down from the lowest gallery, with a seat fastened to the bottom, to which I fixed myself, and was drawn up by pulleys.

CHAPTER 2: THE HUMOURS AND DISPOSITIONS OF THE LAPUTIANS DESCRIBED. AN ACCOUNT OF THEIR LEARNING. OF THE KING AND HIS COURT. THE AUTHOR'S RECEPTION THERE. THE INHABITANTS SUBJECT TO FEAR AND DISQUIETUDES. AN ACCOUNT OF THE WOMEN.

At my alighting, I was surrounded with a crowd of people, but those who stood nearest seemed to be of better quality. They beheld me with all the marks and circumstances of wonder; neither indeed was I much in their debt, having never till then seen a race of mortals so singular in their shapes, habits, and countenances. Their heads were all reclined, either to the right, or the left; one of their eyes turned inward, and the other directly up to the zenith. Their outward garments were adorned with the figures of suns, moons, and stars; interwoven with those of fiddles, flutes, harps, trumpets, guitars, harpsichords, and many other instruments of music, unknown to us in Europe. I observed, here and there, many in the habit of servants, with a blown bladder, fastened like a flail to the end of a stick, which they carried in their hands. In each bladder was a small quantity of dried peas, or little pebbles, as I was afterwards informed. With these bladders, they now and then flapped the mouths and ears of those who stood near them, of which practice I could not then conceive the meaning. It seems the minds of these people are so taken up with intense speculations, that they neither can speak, nor attend to the discourses of others, without being roused by some external action upon the organs of speech and hearing; for which reason, those persons who are able to afford it always keep a flapper (the original is *climenole*) in their family, as one of their domestics; nor ever walk abroad, or make visits, without him. And the business of this officer is, when two, three, or more persons are in company, gently to strike with his bladder the mouth of him who is to speak, and the right ear of him or them to whom the speaker addresses himself. This flapper is likewise employed diligently to attend his master in his walks, and upon occasion to give him a soft flap on his eyes; because he is always so wrapped up in cogitation, that he is in manifest danger of falling down every precipice, and bouncing his head against every post; and in the streets, of justling others, or being justled himself into the kennel.

It was necessary to give the reader this information, without which he would be at the same loss with me to understand the proceedings of these people, as they conducted me up the stairs to the top of the island, and from thence to the royal palace. While we were ascending, they forgot several times what they were about, and left me to myself, till their memories were again roused by their flappers; for they appeared altogether unmoved by the sight of my foreign habit and countenance, and by the shouts of the vulgar, whose thoughts and minds were more disengaged.

At last we entered the palace, and proceeded into the chamber of presence, where I saw the king seated on his throne, attended on each side by persons of prime quality. Before the throne, was a large table filled with globes and spheres, and mathematical instruments of all kinds. His majesty took not the least notice of us, although our entrance was not without sufficient noise, by the concourse of all persons belonging to the court. But he was then deep in a problem; and we attended at least an hour, before he could solve it. There stood by him, on each side, a young page with flaps in their hands, and when they saw he was at leisure, one of them gently struck his mouth, and the other his right ear; at which he startled like one awaked on the sudden, and looking towards me and the company I was in, recollected the occasion of our coming, whereof he had been informed before. He spoke some words, whereupon immediately a young man with a flap came up to my side, and flapped me gently on the right ear; but I made signs, as well as I could, that I had no occasion for such an instrument; which, as I afterwards found, gave his majesty, and the whole court, a very mean opinion of my understanding. The king, as far as I could conjecture, asked me several questions, and I addressed myself to him in all the languages I had. When it was found I could neither understand nor be understood, I was conducted by his order to an apartment in his palace (this prince being distinguished above all his predecessors for his hospitality to strangers), where two servants were appointed to attend me. My dinner was brought, and four persons of quality, whom I remembered to have seen very near the king's person, did me the honour to dine with me. We had two courses, of three dishes each. In the first course, there was a shoulder of mutton cut into an equilateral triangle, a piece of beef into a rhomboides, and a pudding into a cycloid. The second course was two ducks trussed up in the form of fiddles; sausages and puddings resembling flutes and hautboys, and a breast of veal in the shape of a harp. The servants cut our bread into cones, cylinders, parallelograms, and several other mathematical figures.

While we were at dinner, I made bold to ask the names of several things in their language, and those noble persons, by the assistance of their flappers, delighted to give me answers, hoping to raise my admiration of their great abilities if I could be brought to converse with them. I was soon able to call for bread and drink, or whatever else I wanted.

After dinner my company withdrew, and a person was sent to me by the king's order, attended by a flapper. He brought with him pen, ink, and paper, and three or four books, giving me to understand by signs, that he was sent to teach me the language. We sat together four hours, in which time I wrote down a great number of words in columns, with the translations over against them; I likewise made a shift to learn several short sentences; for my tutor would order one of my servants to fetch something, to turn about, to make a bow, to sit, or to stand, or walk, and the like. Then I took down the sentence in writing. He showed me also, in one of his books, the figures of the sun, moon, and stars, the zodiac, the tropics, and polar circles, together with the denominations of many plains and solids. He gave me the names and descriptions of all the musical instruments, and the general terms of art in playing on each of them. After he had left me, I placed all my words, with their interpretations, in alphabetical order. And thus, in a few days, by the help of a very faithful memory, I got some insight into their language. The word, which I interpret the flying or floating island, is in the original *Laputa*, whereof I could never learn the true etymology. *Lap*, in the old obsolete language, signifies high; and *untuh*, a governor; from which they say, by corruption, was derived *Laputa*, from *Lapuntuh*. But I do not approve of this derivation, which seems to be a little strained. I ventured to offer to the learned among them a conjecture of my own, that Laputa was *quasi lap outed*; *lap*, signifying properly, the dancing of the sunbeams in the sea, and *outed*, a wing; which, however, I shall not obtrude, but submit to the judicious reader.

Those to whom the king had entrusted me, observing how ill I was clad, ordered a tailor to come next morning, and take measure for a suit of clothes. This operator did his office after a different manner from those of his trade in Europe. He first took my altitude by a quadrant, and then, with a rule and compasses, described the dimensions and outlines of my whole body, all which he entered upon paper; and in six days brought my clothes very ill made, and quite out of shape, by happening to mistake a figure in the calculation. But my comfort was, that I observed such accidents very frequent, and little regarded.

During my confinement for want of clothes, and by an indisposition that held me some days longer, I much enlarged my dictionary; and when I went next to court, was able to understand many things the king spoke, and to return him some kind of answers. His majesty had given orders, that the island should move northeast and by east, to the vertical point over Lagado, the metropolis of the whole kingdom below, upon the firm earth. It was about ninety leagues distant, and our voyage lasted four days and a half. I was not in the least sensible of the progressive motion made in the air by the island. On the second morning, about eleven o'clock, the king himself in person, attended by his nobility, courtiers, and officers, having prepared all their musical instruments, played on them for three hours without intermission, so that I was quite stunned with the noise; neither could I possibly guess the meaning, till my tutor informed me. He said that, the people of their island had their ears adapted to hear "the music of the spheres, which always played at certain periods, and the court was now prepared to bear their part, in whatever instrument they most excelled."

In our journey towards Lagado, the capital city, his majesty ordered that the island should stop over certain towns and villages, from whence he might receive the petitions of his subjects. And to this purpose, several packthreads were let down, with small weights at the bottom. On these packthreads the people strung their petitions, which mounted up directly, like the scraps of paper fastened by school boys at the end of the string that holds their kite. Sometimes we received wine and victuals from below, which were drawn up by pulleys.

The knowledge I had in mathematics, gave me great assistance in acquiring their phraseology, which depended much upon that science, and music; and in the latter I was not unskilled. Their ideas are perpetually conversant in lines and figures. If they would, for example, praise the beauty of a woman, or any other animal, they describe it by rhombs, circles, parallelograms, ellipses, and other geometrical terms, or by words of art drawn from music, needless here to repeat. I observed in the king's kitchen all sorts of mathematical and musical instruments, after the figures of which they cut up the joints that were served to his majesty's table.

Their houses are very ill built, the walls bevil, without one right angle in any apartment; and this defect arises from the contempt they bear to practical geometry, which they despise as vulgar and mechanic; those instructions they give being too refined for the intellects of their workmen, which occasions perpetual mistakes. And although they are dexterous enough upon a piece of paper, in the management of the rule, the pencil, and the divider, yet in the common actions and behaviour of life, I have not seen a more clumsy, awkward, and unhandy people, nor so slow and perplexed in their conceptions upon all other subjects, except those of mathematics and music. They are very bad reasoners, and vehemently given to opposition, unless when they happen to be of the right opinion, which is seldom their case. Imagination, fancy, and invention, they are wholly strangers to, nor have any words in their language, by which those ideas can be expressed; the whole compass of their thoughts and mind being shut up within the two forementioned sciences.

Most of them, and especially those who deal in the astronomical part, have great faith in judicial astrology, although they are ashamed to own it publicly. But what I chiefly admired, and thought altogether unaccountable, was the strong disposition I observed in them towards news and politics, perpetually inquiring into public affairs, giving their judgments in matters of state, and passionately disputing every inch of a party opinion. I have indeed observed the same disposition among most of the mathematicians I have known in Europe, although I could never discover the least analogy between the two sciences; unless those people suppose, that because the smallest circle has as many degrees as the largest, therefore the regulation and management of the world require no more abilities than the handling and turning of a globe; but I rather take this quality to spring from a very common infirmity of human nature, inclining us to be most curious and conceited in matters where we have least concern, and for which we are least adapted by study or nature.

These people are under continual disquietudes, never enjoying a minute's peace of mind; and their disturbances proceed from causes which very little affect the rest of mortals. Their apprehensions arise from several changes they dread in the celestial bodies: for instance, that the earth, by the continual approaches of the sun towards it, must, in course of time, be absorbed, or swallowed up; that the face of the sun, will, by degrees, be encrusted with its own effluvia, and give no more light to the world; that the earth very narrowly escaped a brush from the tail of the last comet, which would have infallibly reduced it to ashes; and that the next, which they have calculated for one-and-thirty years hence, will probably destroy us. For if, in its perihelion, it should approach within a certain degree of the sun (as by their calculations they have reason to dread) it will receive a degree of heat ten thousand times more intense than that of red hot glowing iron, and in its absence from the sun, carry a blazing tail ten hundred thousand and fourteen miles long, through which, if the earth should pass at the distance of one hundred thousand miles from the nucleus, or main body of the comet, it must in its passage be set on fire, and reduced to ashes: that the sun, daily spending its rays without any nutriment to supply them, will at last be wholly consumed and annihilated; which must be attended with the destruction of this earth, and of all the planets that receive their light from it.

They are so perpetually alarmed with the apprehensions of these, and the like impending dangers, that they can neither sleep quietly in their beds, nor have any relish for the common pleasures and amusements of life. When they meet an acquaintance in the morning, the first question is about the sun's health, how he looked at his setting and rising, and what hopes they have to avoid the stroke of the approaching comet. This conversation they are apt to run into with the same temper that boys discover in delighting to hear terrible stories of spirits and hobgoblins, which they greedily listen to, and dare not go to bed for fear.

The women of the island have abundance of vivacity: they contemn their husbands, and are exceedingly fond of strangers, whereof there is always a considerable number from the continent below, attending at court, either upon affairs of the several towns and corporations, or their own particular occasions, but are much despised, because they want the same endowments. Among these the ladies choose their gallants: but the vexation is, that they act with too much ease and security; for the husband is always so rapt in speculation, that the mistress and lover may proceed to the greatest familiarities before his face, if he be but provided with paper and implements, and without his flapper at his side.

The wives and daughters lament their confinement to the island, although I think it the most delicious spot of ground in the world; and although they live here in the greatest plenty and magnificence, and are allowed to do whatever they please, they long to see the world, and take the diversions of the metropolis, which they are not allowed to do without a particular license from the king; and this is not easy to be obtained, because the people of quality have found, by frequent experience, how hard it is to persuade their women to return from below. I was told that a great court lady, who had several children,—is married to the prime minister, the richest subject in the kingdom, a very graceful person, extremely fond of her, and lives in the finest palace of the island,—went down to Lagado on the pretence of health, there hid herself for several months, till the king sent a warrant to search for her; and she was found in an obscure eating-house all in rags, having pawned her clothes to maintain an old deformed footman, who beat her every day, and in whose company she was taken, much against her will. And although her husband received her with all possible kindness, and without the least reproach, she soon after contrived to steal down again, with all her jewels, to the same gallant, and has not been heard of since.

This may perhaps pass with the reader rather for an European or English story, than for one of a country so remote. But he may please to consider, that the caprices of womankind are not limited by any climate or nation, and that they are much more uniform, than can be easily imagined.

In about a month's time, I had made a tolerable proficiency in their language, and was able to answer most of the king's questions, when I had the honour to attend him. His majesty discovered not the least curiosity to inquire into the laws, government, history, religion, or manners of the countries where I had been; but confined his questions to the state of mathematics, and received the account I gave him with great contempt and indifference, though often roused by his flapper on each side.

CHAPTER 3: A PHENOMENON SOLVED BY MODERN PHILOSOPHY AND ASTRONOMY. THE LAPUTIANS' GREAT IMPROVEMENTS IN THE LATTER. THE KING'S METHOD OF SUPPRESSING INSURRECTIONS.

I desired leave of this prince to see the curiosities of the island, which he was graciously pleased to grant, and ordered my tutor to attend me. I chiefly wanted to know, to what cause, in art or in nature, it owed its several motions, whereof I will now give a philosophical account to the reader.

The flying or floating island is exactly circular, its diameter 7837 yards, or about four miles and a half, and consequently contains ten thousand acres. It is three hundred yards thick. The bottom, or under surface, which appears to those who view it below, is one even regular plate of adamant, shooting up to the height of about two hundred yards. Above it lie the several minerals in their usual order, and over all is a coat of rich mould, ten or twelve feet deep. The declivity of the upper surface, from the circumference to the centre, is the natural cause why all the dews and rains, which fall upon the island, are conveyed in small rivulets toward the middle, where they are emptied into four large basins, each of about half a mile in circuit, and two hundred yards distant from the centre. From these basins the water is continually exhaled by the sun in the daytime, which effectually prevents their overflowing. Besides, as it is in the power of the monarch to raise the island above the region of clouds and vapours, he can prevent the falling of dews and rain whenever he pleases. For the highest clouds cannot rise above two miles, as naturalists agree, at least they were never known to do so in that country.

At the centre of the island there is a chasm about fifty yards in diameter, whence the astronomers descend into a large dome, which is therefore called *flandona gagnole*, or the astronomer's cave, situated at the depth of a hundred yards beneath the upper surface of the adamant. In this cave are twenty lamps continually burning, which, from the reflection of the adamant, cast a strong light into every part. The place is stored with great variety of sextants, quadrants, telescopes, astrolabes, and other astronomical instruments. But the greatest curiosity, upon which the fate of the island depends, is a loadstone of a prodigious size, in shape resembling a weaver's shuttle. It is in length six yards, and in the thickest part at least three yards over. This magnet is sustained by a very strong axle of adamant passing through its middle, upon which it plays, and is poised so exactly that the weakest hand can turn it. It is hooped round with a hollow cylinder of adamant, four feet yards in diameter, placed horizontally, and supported by eight adamantine feet, each six yards high. In the middle of the concave side, there is a groove twelve inches deep, in which the extremities of the axle are lodged, and turned round as there is occasion.

The stone cannot be removed from its place by any force, because the hoop and its feet are one continued piece with that body of adamant which constitutes the bottom of the island.

By means of this loadstone, the island is made to rise and fall, and move from one place to another. For, with respect to that part of the earth over which the monarch presides, the stone is endued at one of its sides with an attractive power, and at the other with a repulsive. Upon placing the magnet erect, with its attracting end towards the earth, the island descends; but when the repelling extremity points downwards, the island mounts directly upwards. When the position of the stone is oblique, the motion of the island is so too: for in this magnet, the forces always act in lines parallel to its direction.

By this oblique motion, the island is conveyed to different parts of the monarch's dominions. To explain the manner of its progress, let $A B$ represent a line drawn across the dominions of Balnibarbi, let the line $c d$ represent the loadstone, of which let d be the repelling end, and c the attracting end, the island being over C: let the stone be placed in position $c d$, with its repelling end downwards; then the island will be driven upwards obliquely towards D. When it is arrived at D, let the stone be turned upon its axle, till its attracting end points towards E, and then the island will be carried obliquely towards E; where, if the stone be again turned upon its axle till it stands in the position E F, with its repelling point downwards, the island will rise obliquely towards F, where, by directing the attracting end towards G, the island may be carried to G, and from G to H, by turning the stone, so as to make its repelling extremity to point directly downward. And thus, by changing the situation of the stone, as often as there is occasion, the island is made to rise and fall by turns in an oblique direction, and by those alternate risings and fallings (the obliquity being not considerable) is conveyed from one part of the dominions to the other.

But it must be observed, that this island cannot move beyond the extent of the dominions below, nor can it rise above the height of four miles. For which the astronomers (who have written large systems concerning the stone) assign the following reason: that the magnetic virtue does not extend beyond the distance of four miles, and that the mineral, which acts upon the stone in the bowels of the earth, and in the sea about six leagues distant from the shore, is not diffused through the whole globe, but terminated with the limits of the king's dominions; and it was easy, from the great advantage of such a superior situation, for a prince to bring under his obedience whatever country lay within the attraction of that magnet.

When the stone is put parallel to the plane of the horizon, the island stands still; for in that case the extremities of it, being at equal distance from the earth, act with equal force, the one in drawing downwards, the other in pushing upwards, and consequently no motion can ensue.

This loadstone is under the care of certain astronomers, who, from time to time, give it such positions as the monarch directs. They spend the greatest part of their lives in observing the celestial bodies, which they do by the assistance of glasses, far excelling ours in goodness. For, although their largest telescopes do not exceed three feet, they magnify much more than those of a hundred with us, and show the stars with greater clearness. This advantage has enabled them to extend their discoveries much further than our astronomers in Europe; for they have made a catalogue of ten thousand fixed stars, whereas the largest of ours do not contain above one third part of that number. They have likewise discovered two lesser stars, or satellites, which revolve about Mars; whereof the innermost is distant from the centre of the primary planet exactly three of his diameters, and the outermost, five; the former revolves in the space of ten hours, and the latter in twenty-one and a half; so that the squares of their periodical times are very near in the same proportion with the cubes of their distance from the centre of Mars; which evidently shows them to be governed by the same law of gravitation that influences the other heavenly bodies.

They have observed ninety-three different comets, and settled their periods with great exactness. If this be true (and they affirm it with great confidence) it is much to be wished, that their observations were made public, whereby the theory of comets, which at present is very lame and defective, might be brought to the same perfection with other arts of astronomy.

The king would be the most absolute prince in the universe, if he could but prevail on a ministry to join with him; but these having their estates below on the continent, and considering that the office of a favourite has a very uncertain tenure, would never consent to the enslaving of their country.

If any town should engage in rebellion or mutiny, fall into violent factions, or refuse to pay the usual tribute, the king has two methods of reducing them to obedience. The first and the mildest course is, by keeping the island hovering over such a town, and the lands about it, whereby he can deprive them of the benefit of the sun and the rain, and consequently afflict the inhabitants with dearth and diseases: and if the crime deserve it, they are at the same time pelted from above with great stones, against which they have no defence but by creeping into cellars or caves, while the roofs of their houses are beaten to pieces. But if they still continue obstinate, or offer to raise insurrections, he proceeds to the last remedy, by letting the island drop directly upon their heads, which makes a universal destruction both of houses and men. However, this is an extremity to which the prince is seldom driven, neither indeed is he willing to put it in execution; nor dare his ministers advise him to an action, which, as it would render them odious to the people, so it would be a great damage to their own estates, which all lie below; for the island is the king's demesne.

But there is still indeed a more weighty reason, why the kings of this country have been always averse from executing so terrible an action, unless upon the utmost necessity. For, if the town intended to be destroyed should have in it any tall rocks, as it generally falls out in the larger cities, a situation probably chosen at first with a view to prevent such a catastrophe; or if it abound in high spires, or pillars of stone, a sudden fall might endanger the bottom or under surface of the island, which, although it consist, as I have said, of one entire adamant, two hundred yards thick, might happen to crack by too great a shock, or burst by approaching too near the fires from the houses below, as the backs, both of iron and stone, will often do in our chimneys. Of all this the people are well apprised, and understand how far to carry their obstinacy, where their liberty or property is concerned. And the king, when he is highest provoked, and most determined to press a city to rubbish, orders the island to descend with great gentleness, out of a pretence of tenderness to his people, but, indeed, for fear of breaking the adamantine bottom; in which case, it is the opinion of all their philosophers, that the loadstone could no longer hold it up, and the whole mass would fall to the ground.

By a fundamental law of this realm, neither the king, nor either of his two eldest sons, are permitted to leave the island; nor the queen, till she is past child-bearing.

CHAPTER 4: THE AUTHOR LEAVES LAPUTA; IS CONVEYED TO BALNIBARBI; ARRIVES AT THE METROPOLIS. A DESCRIPTION OF THE METROPOLIS, AND THE COUNTRY ADJOINING. THE AUTHOR HOSPITABLY RECEIVED BY A GREAT LORD. HIS CONVERSATION WITH THAT LORD.

Although I cannot say that I was ill treated in this island, yet I must confess I thought myself too much neglected, not without some degree of contempt; for neither prince nor people appeared to be curious in any part of knowledge, except mathematics and music, wherein I was far their inferior, and upon that account very little regarded.

On the other side, after having seen all the curiosities of the island, I was very desirous to leave it, being heartily weary of those people. They were indeed excellent in two sciences for which I have great esteem, and wherein I am not unversed; but, at the same time, so abstracted and involved in speculation, that I never met with such disagreeable companions. I conversed only with women, tradesmen, flappers, and court-pages, during two months of my abode there; by which, at last, I rendered myself extremely contemptible; yet these were the only people from whom I could ever receive a reasonable answer.

I had obtained, by hard study, a good degree of knowledge in their language: I was weary of being confined to an island where I received so little countenance, and resolved to leave it with the first opportunity.

There was a great lord at court, nearly related to the king, and for that reason alone used with respect. He was universally reckoned the most ignorant and stupid person among them. He had performed many eminent services for the crown, had great natural and acquired parts, adorned with integrity and honour; but so ill an ear for music, that his detractors reported, "he had been often known to beat time in the wrong place;" neither could his tutors, without extreme difficulty, teach him to demonstrate the most easy proposition in the mathematics. He was pleased to show me many marks of favour, often did me the honour of a visit, desired to be informed in the affairs of Europe, the laws and customs, the manners and learning of the several countries where I had travelled. He listened to me with great attention, and made very wise observations on all I spoke. He had two flappers attending him for state, but never made use of them, except at court and in visits of ceremony, and would always command them to withdraw, when we were alone together.

I entreated this illustrious person, to intercede in my behalf with his majesty, for leave to depart; which he accordingly did, as he was pleased to tell me, with regret: for indeed he had made me several offers very advantageous, which, however, I refused, with expressions of the highest acknowledgment.

On the 16th of February I took leave of his majesty and the court. The king made me a present to the value of about two hundred pounds English, and my protector, his kinsman, as much more, together with a letter of recommendation to a friend of his in Lagado, the metropolis. The island being then hovering over a mountain about two miles from it, I was let down from the lowest gallery, in the same manner as I had been taken up.

The continent, as far as it is subject to the monarch of the flying island, passes under the general name of *Balnibarbi*; and the metropolis, as I said before, is called *Lagado*. I felt some little satisfaction in finding myself on firm ground. I walked to the city without any concern, being clad like one of the natives, and sufficiently instructed to converse with them. I soon found out the person's house to whom I was recommended, presented my letter from his friend the grandee in the island, and was received with much kindness. This great lord, whose name was Munodi, ordered me an apartment in his own house, where I continued during my stay, and was entertained in a most hospitable manner.

The next morning after my arrival, he took me in his chariot to see the town, which is about half the bigness of London; but the houses very strangely built, and most of them out of repair. The people in the streets walked fast, looked wild, their eyes fixed, and were generally in rags. We passed through one of the town gates, and went about three miles into the country, where I saw many labourers working with several sorts of tools in the ground, but was not able to conjecture what they were about: neither did observe any expectation either of corn or grass, although the soil appeared to be excellent. I could not forbear admiring at these odd appearances, both in town and country; and I made bold to desire my conductor, that he would be pleased to explain to me, what could be meant by so many busy heads, hands, and faces, both in the streets and the fields, because I did not discover any good effects they produced; but, on the contrary, I never knew a soil so unhappily cultivated, houses so ill contrived and so ruinous, or a people whose countenances and habit expressed so much misery and want.

This lord Munodi was a person of the first rank, and had been some years governor of Lagado; but, by a cabal of ministers, was discharged for insufficiency. However, the king treated him with tenderness, as a well-meaning man, but of a low contemptible understanding.

When I gave that free censure of the country and its inhabitants, he made no further answer than by telling me, "that I had not been long enough among them to form a judgment; and that the different nations of the world had different customs;" with other common topics to the same purpose. But, when we returned to his palace, he asked me "how I liked the building, what absurdities I observed, and what quarrel I had with the dress or looks of his domestics?" This he might safely do; because every thing about him was magnificent, regular, and polite. I answered, "that his excellency's prudence, quality, and fortune, had exempted him from those defects, which folly and beggary had produced in others." He said, "if I would go with him to his country-house, about twenty miles distant, where his estate lay, there would be more leisure for this kind of conversation." I told his excellency "that I was entirely at his disposal;" and accordingly we set out next morning.

During our journey he made me observe the several methods used by farmers in managing their lands, which to me were wholly unaccountable; for, except in some very few places, I could not discover one ear of corn or blade of grass. But, in three hours travelling, the scene was wholly altered; we came into a most beautiful country; farmers' houses, at small distances, neatly built; the fields enclosed, containing vineyards, corn-grounds, and meadows. Neither do I remember to have seen a more delightful prospect. His excellency observed my countenance to clear up; he told me, with a sigh, "that there his estate began, and would continue the same, till we should come to his house: that his countrymen ridiculed and despised him, for managing his affairs no better, and for setting so ill an example to the kingdom; which, however, was followed by very few, such as were old, and wilful, and weak like himself."

We came at length to the house, which was indeed a noble structure, built according to the best rules of ancient architecture. The fountains, gardens, walks, avenues, and groves, were all disposed with exact judgment and taste. I gave due praises to every thing I saw, whereof his excellency took not the least notice till after supper; when, there being no third companion, he told me with a very melancholy air "that he doubted he must throw down his houses in town and country, to rebuild them after the present mode; destroy all his plantations, and cast others into such a form as modern usage required, and give the same directions to all his tenants, unless he would submit to incur the censure of pride, singularity, affectation, ignorance, caprice, and perhaps increase his majesty's displeasure; that the admiration I appeared to be under would cease or diminish, when he had informed me of some particulars which, probably, I never heard of at court, the people there being too much taken up in their own speculations, to have regard to what passed here below."

The sum of his discourse was to this effect: "That about forty years ago, certain persons went up to Laputa, either upon business or diversion, and, after five months continuance, came back with a very little smattering in mathematics, but full of volatile spirits acquired in that airy region: that these persons, upon their return, began to dislike the management of every thing below, and fell into schemes of putting all arts, sciences, languages, and mechanics, upon a new foot. To this end, they procured a royal patent for erecting an academy of projectors in Lagado; and the humour prevailed so strongly among the people, that there is not a town of any consequence in the kingdom without such an academy. In these colleges the professors contrive new rules and methods of agriculture and building, and new instruments, and tools for all trades and manufactures; whereby, as they undertake, one man shall do the work of ten; a palace may be built in a week, of materials so durable as to last for ever without repairing. All the fruits of the earth shall come to maturity at whatever season we think fit to choose, and increase a hundred fold more than they do at present; with innumerable other happy proposals. The only inconvenience is, that none of these projects are yet brought to perfection; and in the mean time, the whole country lies miserably waste, the houses in ruins, and the people without food or clothes. By all which, instead of being discouraged, they are fifty times more violently bent upon prosecuting their schemes, driven equally on by hope and despair: that as for himself, being not of an enterprising spirit, he was content to go on in the old forms, to live in the houses his ancestors had built, and act as they did, in every part of life, without innovation: that some few other persons of quality and gentry had done the same, but were looked on with an eye of contempt and ill-will, as enemies to art, ignorant, and ill common-wealth's men, preferring their own ease and sloth before the general improvement of their country."

His lordship added, "That he would not, by any further particulars, prevent the pleasure I should certainly take in viewing the grand academy, whither he was resolved I should go." He only desired me to observe a ruined building, upon the side of a mountain about three miles distant, of which he gave me this account: "That he had a very convenient mill within half a mile of his house, turned by a current from a large river, and sufficient for his own family, as well as a great number of his tenants; that about seven years ago, a club of those projectors came to him with proposals to destroy this mill, and build another on the side of that mountain, on the long ridge whereof a long canal must be cut, for a repository of water, to be conveyed up by pipes and engines to supply the mill, because the wind and air upon a height agitated the water, and thereby made it fitter for motion, and because the water, descending down a declivity, would turn the mill with half the current of a river whose course is more upon a level." He said, "that being then not very well with the court, and pressed by many of his friends, he complied with the proposal; and after employing a hundred men for two years, the work miscarried, the projectors went off, laying the blame entirely upon him, railing at him ever since, and putting others upon the same experiment, with equal assurance of success, as well as equal disappointment."

In a few days we came back to town; and his excellency, considering the bad character he had in the academy, would not go with me himself, but recommended me to a friend of his, to bear me company thither. My lord was pleased to represent me as a great admirer of projects, and a person of much curiosity and easy belief; which, indeed, was not without truth; for I had myself been a sort of projector in my younger days.

CHAPTER 5: THE AUTHOR PERMITTED TO SEE THE GRAND ACADEMY OF LAGADO. THE ACADEMY LARGELY DESCRIBED. THE ARTS WHEREIN THE PROFESSORS EMPLOY THEMSELVES.

This academy is not an entire single building, but a continuation of several houses on both sides of a street, which growing waste, was purchased and applied to that use.

I was received very kindly by the warden, and went for many days to the academy. Every room has in it one or more projectors; and I believe I could not be in fewer than five hundred rooms.

The first man I saw was of a meagre aspect, with sooty hands and face, his hair and beard long, ragged, and singed in several places. His clothes, shirt, and skin, were all of the same colour. He has been eight years upon a project for extracting sunbeams out of cucumbers, which were to be put in phials hermetically sealed, and let out to warm the air in raw inclement summers. He told me, he did not doubt, that, in eight years more, he should be able to supply the governor's gardens with sunshine, at a reasonable rate: but he complained that his stock was low, and entreated me "to give him something as an encouragement to ingenuity, especially since this had been a very dear season for cucumbers." I made him a small present, for my lord had furnished me with money on purpose, because he knew their practice of begging from all who go to see them.

I went into another chamber, but was ready to hasten back, being almost overcome with a horrible stink. My conductor pressed me forward, conjuring me in a whisper "to give no offence, which would be highly resented;" and therefore I durst not so much as stop my nose. The projector of this cell was the most ancient student of the academy; his face and beard were of a pale yellow; his hands and clothes daubed over with filth. When I was presented to him, he gave me a close embrace, a compliment I could well have excused. His employment, from his first coming into the academy, was an operation to reduce human excrement to its original food, by separating the several parts, removing the tincture which it receives from the gall, making the odour exhale, and scumming off the saliva. He had a weekly allowance, from the society, of a vessel filled with human ordure, about the bigness of a Bristol barrel.

I saw another at work to calcine ice into gunpowder; who likewise showed me a treatise he had written concerning the malleability of fire, which he intended to publish.

There was a most ingenious architect, who had contrived a new method for building houses, by beginning at the roof, and working downward to the foundation; which he justified to me, by the like practice of those two prudent insects, the bee and the spider.

There was a man born blind, who had several apprentices in his own condition: their employment was to mix colours for painters, which their master taught them to distinguish by feeling and smelling. It was indeed my misfortune to find them at that time not very perfect in their lessons, and the professor himself happened to be generally mistaken. This artist is much encouraged and esteemed by the whole fraternity.

In another apartment I was highly pleased with a projector who had found a device of ploughing the ground with hogs, to save the charges of ploughs, cattle, and labour. The method is this: in an acre of ground you bury, at six inches distance and eight deep, a quantity of acorns, dates, chestnuts, and other mast or vegetables, whereof these animals are fondest; then you drive six hundred or more of them into the field, where, in a few days, they will root up the whole ground in search of their food, and make it fit for sowing, at the same time manuring it with their dung: it is true, upon experiment, they found the charge and trouble very great, and they had little or no crop. However it is not doubted, that this invention may be capable of great improvement.

I went into another room, where the walls and ceiling were all hung round with cobwebs, except a narrow passage for the artist to go in and out. At my entrance, he called aloud to me, "not to disturb his webs." He lamented "the fatal mistake the world had been so long in, of using silkworms, while we had such plenty of domestic insects who infinitely excelled the former, because they understood how to weave, as well as spin." And he proposed further, "that by employing spiders, the charge of dyeing silks should be wholly saved;" whereof I was fully convinced, when he showed me a vast number of flies most beautifully coloured, wherewith he fed his spiders, assuring us "that the webs would take a tincture from them; and as he had them of all hues, he hoped to fit everybody's fancy, as soon as he could find proper food for the flies, of certain gums, oils, and other glutinous matter, to give a strength and consistence to the threads."

There was an astronomer, who had undertaken to place a sun-dial upon the great weathercock on the town-house, by adjusting the annual and diurnal motions of the earth and sun, so as to answer and coincide with all accidental turnings of the wind.

I was complaining of a small fit of the colic, upon which my conductor led me into a room where a great physician resided, who was famous for curing that disease, by contrary operations from the same instrument. He had a large pair of bellows, with a long slender muzzle of ivory: this he conveyed eight inches up the anus, and drawing in the wind, he affirmed he could make the guts as lank as a dried bladder. But when the disease was more stubborn and violent, he let in the muzzle while the bellows were full of wind, which he discharged into the body of the patient; then withdrew the instrument to replenish it, clapping his thumb strongly against the orifice of then fundament; and this being repeated three or four times, the adventitious wind would rush out, bringing the noxious along with it, (like water put into a pump), and the patient recovered. I saw him try both experiments upon a dog, but could not discern any effect from the former. After the latter the animal was ready to burst, and made so violent a discharge as was very offensive to me and my companion. The dog died on the spot, and we left the doctor endeavouring to recover him, by the same operation.

I visited many other apartments, but shall not trouble my reader with all the curiosities I observed, being studious of brevity.

I had hitherto seen only one side of the academy, the other being appropriated to the advancers of speculative learning, of whom I shall say something, when I have mentioned one illustrious person more, who is called among them "the universal artist." He told us "he had been thirty years employing his thoughts for the improvement of human life." He had two large rooms full of wonderful curiosities, and fifty men at work. Some were condensing air into a dry tangible substance, by extracting the nitre, and letting the aqueous or fluid particles percolate; others softening marble, for pillows and pin-cushions; others petrifying the hoofs of a living horse, to preserve them from foundering. The artist himself was at that time busy upon two great designs; the first, to sow land with chaff, wherein he affirmed the true seminal virtue to be contained, as he demonstrated by several experiments, which I was not skilful enough to comprehend. The other was, by a certain composition of gums, minerals, and vegetables, outwardly applied, to prevent the growth of wool upon two young lambs; and he hoped, in a reasonable time to propagate the breed of naked sheep, all over the kingdom.

We crossed a walk to the other part of the academy, where, as I have already said, the projectors in speculative learning resided.

The first professor I saw, was in a very large room, with forty pupils about him. After salutation, observing me to look earnestly upon a frame, which took up the greatest part of both the length and breadth of the room, he said, "Perhaps I might wonder to see him employed in a project for improving speculative knowledge, by practical and mechanical operations. But the world would soon be sensible of its usefulness; and he flattered himself, that a more noble, exalted thought never sprang in any other man's head. Every one knew how laborious the usual method is of attaining to arts and sciences; whereas, by his contrivance, the most ignorant person, at a reasonable charge, and with a little bodily labour, might write books in philosophy, poetry, politics, laws, mathematics, and theology, without the least assistance from genius or study." He then led me to the frame, about the sides, whereof all his pupils stood in ranks. It was twenty feet square, placed in the middle of the room. The superfices was composed of several bits of wood, about the bigness of a die, but some larger than others. They were all linked together by slender wires. These bits of wood were covered, on every square, with paper pasted on them; and on these papers were written all the words of their language, in their several moods, tenses, and declensions; but without any order. The professor then desired me "to observe; for he was going to set his engine at work." The pupils, at his command, took each of them hold of an iron handle, whereof there were forty fixed round the edges of the frame; and giving them a sudden turn, the whole disposition of the words was entirely changed. He then commanded six-and-thirty of the lads, to read the several lines softly, as they appeared upon the frame; and where they found three or four words together that might make part of a sentence, they dictated to the four remaining boys, who were scribes. This work was repeated three or four times, and at every turn, the engine was so contrived, that the words shifted into new places, as the square bits of wood moved upside down.

Six hours a day the young students were employed in this labour; and the professor showed me several volumes in large folio, already collected, of broken sentences, which he intended to piece together, and out of those rich materials, to give the world a complete body of all arts and sciences; which, however, might be still improved, and much expedited, if the public would raise a fund for making and employing five hundred such frames in Lagado, and oblige the managers to contribute in common their several collections.

He assured me "that this invention had employed all his thoughts from his youth; that he had emptied the whole vocabulary into his frame, and made the strictest computation of the general proportion there is in books between the numbers of particles, nouns, and verbs, and other parts of speech."

I made my humblest acknowledgment to this illustrious person, for his great communicativeness; and promised, "if ever I had the good fortune to return to my native country, that I would do him justice, as the sole inventor of this wonderful machine;" the form and contrivance of which I desired leave to delineate on paper, as in the figure here annexed. I told him, "although it were the custom of our learned in Europe to steal inventions from each other, who had thereby at least this advantage, that it became a controversy which was the right owner; yet I would take such caution, that he should have the honour entire, without a rival."

We next went to the school of languages, where three professors sat in consultation upon improving that of their own country.

The first project was, to shorten discourse, by cutting polysyllables into one, and leaving out verbs and participles, because, in reality, all things imaginable are but norms.

The other project was, a scheme for entirely abolishing all words whatsoever; and this was urged as a great advantage in point of health, as well as brevity. For it is plain, that every word we speak is, in some degree, a diminution of our lungs by corrosion, and, consequently, contributes to the shortening of our lives. An expedient was therefore offered, "that since words are only names for things, it would be more convenient for all men to carry about them such things as were necessary to express a particular business they are to discourse on." And this invention would certainly have taken place, to the great ease as well as health of the subject, if the women, in conjunction with the vulgar and illiterate, had not threatened to raise a rebellion unless they might be allowed the liberty to speak with their tongues, after the manner of their forefathers; such constant irreconcilable enemies to science are the common people. However, many of the most learned and wise adhere to the new scheme of expressing themselves by things; which has only this inconvenience attending it, that if a man's business be very great, and of various kinds, he must be obliged, in proportion, to carry a greater bundle of things upon his back, unless he can afford one or two strong servants to attend him. I have often beheld two of those sages almost sinking under the weight of their packs, like pedlars among us, who, when they met in the street, would lay down their loads, open their sacks, and hold conversation for an hour together; then put up their implements, help each other to resume their burdens, and take their leave.

But for short conversations, a man may carry implements in his pockets, and under his arms, enough to supply him; and in his house, he cannot be at a loss. Therefore the room where company meet who practise this art, is full of all things, ready at hand, requisite to furnish matter for this kind of artificial converse.

Another great advantage proposed by this invention was, that it would serve as a universal language, to be understood in all civilised nations, whose goods and utensils are generally of the same kind, or nearly resembling, so that their uses might easily be comprehended. And thus ambassadors would be qualified to treat with foreign princes, or ministers of state, to whose tongues they were utter strangers.

I was at the mathematical school, where the master taught his pupils after a method scarce imaginable to us in Europe. The proposition, and demonstration, were fairly written on a thin wafer, with ink composed of a cephalic tincture. This, the student was to swallow upon a fasting stomach, and for three days following, eat nothing but bread and water. As the wafer digested, the tincture mounted to his brain, bearing the proposition along with it. But the success has not hitherto been answerable, partly by some error in the *quantum* or composition, and partly by the perverseness of lads, to whom this bolus is so nauseous, that they generally steal aside, and discharge it upwards, before it can operate; neither have they been yet persuaded to use so long an abstinence, as the prescription requires.

CHAPTER 6: A FURTHER ACCOUNT OF THE ACADEMY. THE AUTHOR PROPOSES SOME IMPROVEMENTS, WHICH ARE HONOURABLY RECEIVED.

In the school of political projectors, I was but ill entertained; the professors appearing, in my judgment, wholly out of their senses, which is a scene that never fails to make me melancholy. These unhappy people were proposing schemes for persuading monarchs to choose favourites upon the score of their wisdom, capacity, and virtue; of teaching ministers to consult the public good; of rewarding merit, great abilities, eminent services; of instructing princes to know their true interest, by placing it on the same foundation with that of their people;

of choosing for employments persons qualified to exercise them, with many other wild, impossible chimeras, that never entered before into the heart of man to conceive; and confirmed in me the old observation, "that there is nothing so extravagant and irrational, which some philosophers have not maintained for truth."

But, however, I shall so far do justice to this part of the Academy, as to acknowledge that all of them were not so visionary. There was a most ingenious doctor, who seemed to be perfectly versed in the whole nature and system of government. This illustrious person had very usefully employed his studies, in finding out effectual remedies for all diseases and corruptions to which the several kinds of public administration are subject, by the vices or infirmities of those who govern, as well as by the licentiousness of those who are to obey. For instance: whereas all writers and reasoners have agreed, that there is a strict universal resemblance between the natural and the political body; can there be any thing more evident, than that the health of both must be preserved, and the diseases cured, by the same prescriptions? It is allowed, that senates and great councils are often troubled with redundant, ebullient, and other peccant humours; with many diseases of the head, and more of the heart; with strong convulsions, with grievous contractions of the nerves and sinews in both hands, but especially the right; with spleen, flatus, vertigos, and deliriums; with scrofulous tumours, full of fetid purulent matter; with sour frothy ructations: with canine appetites, and crudeness of digestion, besides many others, needless to mention. This doctor therefore proposed, "that upon the meeting of the senate, certain physicians should attend it the three first days of their sitting, and at the close of each day's debate feel the pulses of every senator; after which, having maturely considered and consulted upon the nature of the several maladies, and the methods of cure, they should on the fourth day return to the senate house, attended by their apothecaries stored with proper medicines; and before the members sat, administer to each of them lenitives, aperitives, abstersives, corrosives, restringents, palliatives, laxatives, cephalalgics, icterics, apophlegmatics, acoustics, as their several cases required; and, according as these medicines should operate, repeat, alter, or omit them, at the next meeting."

This project could not be of any great expense to the public; and might in my poor opinion, be of much use for the despatch of business, in those countries where senates have any share in the legislative power; beget unanimity, shorten debates, open a few mouths which are now closed, and close many more which are now open; curb the petulancy of the young, and correct the positiveness of the old; rouse the stupid, and damp the pert.

Again: because it is a general complaint, that the favourites of princes are troubled with short and weak memories; the same doctor proposed, "that whoever attended a first minister, after having told his business, with the utmost brevity and in the plainest words, should, at his departure, give the said minister a tweak by the nose, or a kick in the belly, or tread on his corns, or lug him thrice by both ears, or run a pin into his breech; or pinch his arm black and blue, to prevent forgetfulness; and at every levee day, repeat the same operation, till the business were done, or absolutely refused."

He likewise directed, "that every senator in the great council of a nation, after he had delivered his opinion, and argued in the defence of it, should be obliged to give his vote directly contrary; because if that were done, the result would infallibly terminate in the good of the public."

When parties in a state are violent, he offered a wonderful contrivance to reconcile them. The method is this: You take a hundred leaders of each party; you dispose them into couples of such whose heads are nearest of a size; then let two nice operators saw off the occiput of each couple at the same time, in such a manner that the brain may be equally divided. Let the occiputs, thus cut off, be interchanged, applying each to the head of his opposite party-man. It seems indeed to be a work that requires some exactness, but the professor assured us, "that if it were dexterously performed, the cure would be infallible." For he argued thus: "that the two half brains being left to debate the matter between themselves within the space of one skull, would soon come to a good understanding, and produce that moderation, as well as regularity of thinking, so much to be wished for in the heads of those, who imagine they come into the world only to watch and govern its motion: and as to the difference of brains, in quantity or quality, among those who are directors in faction, the doctor assured us, from his own knowledge, that it was a perfect trifle."

I heard a very warm debate between two professors, about the most commodious and effectual ways and means of raising money, without grieving the subject. The first affirmed, "the justest method would be, to lay a certain tax upon vices and folly; and the sum fixed upon every man to be rated, after the fairest manner, by a jury of his neighbours." The second was of an opinion directly contrary; "to tax those qualities of body and mind, for which men chiefly value themselves; the rate to be more or less, according to the degrees of excelling; the decision whereof should be left entirely to their own breast." The highest tax was upon men who are the greatest favourites of the other sex, and the assessments, according to the number and nature of the favours they have received; for which, they are allowed to be their own vouchers. Wit, valour, and politeness, were likewise proposed to be largely taxed, and collected in the same manner, by every person's giving his own word for the quantum of what he possessed. But as to honour, justice, wisdom, and learning, they should not be taxed at all; because they are qualifications of so singular a kind, that no man will either allow them in his neighbour or value them in himself.

The women were proposed to be taxed according to their beauty and skill in dressing, wherein they had the same privilege with the men, to be determined by their own judgment. But constancy, chastity, good sense, and good nature, were not rated, because they would not bear the charge of collecting.

To keep senators in the interest of the crown, it was proposed that the members should raffle for employment; every man first taking an oath, and giving security, that he would vote for the court, whether he won or not; after which, the losers had, in their turn, the liberty of raffling upon the next vacancy. Thus, hope and expectation would be kept alive; none would complain of broken promises, but impute their disappointments wholly to fortune, whose shoulders are broader and stronger than those of a ministry.

Another professor showed me a large paper of instructions for discovering plots and conspiracies against the government. He advised great statesmen to examine into the diet of all suspected persons; their times of eating; upon which side they lay in bed; with which hand they wipe their posteriors; take a strict view of their excrements, and, from the colour, the odour, the taste, the consistence, the crudeness or maturity of digestion, form a judgment of their thoughts and designs; because men are never so serious, thoughtful, and intent, as when they are at stool, which he found by frequent experiment; for, in such conjunctures, when he used, merely as a trial, to consider which was the best way of murdering the king, his ordure would have a tincture of green; but quite different, when he thought only of raising an insurrection, or burning the metropolis.

The whole discourse was written with great acuteness, containing many observations, both curious and useful for politicians; but, as I conceived, not altogether complete. This I ventured to tell the author, and offered, if he pleased, to supply him with some additions. He received my proposition with more compliance than is usual among writers, especially those of the projecting species, professing "he would be glad to receive further information."

I told him, "that in the kingdom of Tribnia,[1] by the natives called Langdon,[2] where I had sojourned some time in my travels, the bulk of the people consist in a manner wholly of discoverers, witnesses, informers, accusers, prosecutors, evidences, swearers, together with their several subservient and subaltern instruments, all under the colours, the conduct, and the pay of ministers of state, and their deputies. The plots, in that kingdom, are usually the workmanship of those persons who desire to raise their own characters of profound politicians; to restore new vigour to a crazy administration; to stifle or divert general discontents; to fill their coffers with forfeitures; and raise, or sink the opinion of public credit, as either shall best answer their private advantage. It is first agreed and settled among them, what suspected persons shall be accused of a plot; then, effectual care is taken to secure all their letters and papers, and put the owners in chains. These papers are delivered to a set of artists, very dexterous in finding out the mysterious meanings of words, syllables, and letters: for instance, they can discover a close stool, to signify a privy council; a flock of geese, a senate; a lame dog, an invader; the plague, a standing army; a buzzard, a prime minister; the gout, a high priest; a gibbet, a secretary of state; a chamber pot, a committee of grandees; a sieve, a court lady; a broom, a revolution; a mouse-trap, an employment; a bottomless pit, a treasury; a sink, a court; a cap and bells, a favourite; a broken reed, a court of justice; an empty tun, a general; a running sore, the administration.[3]

"When this method fails, they have two others more effectual, which the learned among them call acrostics and anagrams. First, they can decipher all initial letters into political meanings. Thus N, shall signify a plot; B, a regiment of horse; L, a fleet at sea; or, secondly, by transposing the letters of the alphabet in any suspected paper, they can lay open the deepest designs of a discontented party. So, for example, if I should say, in a letter to a friend, 'Our brother Tom has just got the piles,' a skilful decipherer would discover, that the same letters which compose that sentence, may be analysed into the following words, 'Resist —, a plot is brought home—The tour.' And this is the anagrammatic method."

The professor made me great acknowledgments for communicating these observations, and promised to make honourable mention of me in his treatise.

I saw nothing in this country that could invite me to a longer continuance, and began to think of returning home to England.

CHAPTER 7: THE AUTHOR LEAVES LAGADO: ARRIVES AT MALDONADA. NO SHIP READY. HE TAKES A SHORT VOYAGE TO GLUBBDUBDRIB. HIS RECEPTION BY THE GOVERNOR.

The continent, of which this kingdom is apart, extends itself, as I have reason to believe, eastward, to that unknown tract of America westward of California; and north, to the Pacific Ocean, which is not above a hundred and fifty miles from Lagado; where there is a good port, and much commerce with the great island of Luggnagg, situated to the north-west about 29 degrees north latitude, and 140 longitude. This island of Luggnagg stands south-eastward of Japan, about a hundred leagues distant. There is a strict alliance between the Japanese emperor and the king of Luggnagg; which affords frequent opportunities of sailing from one island to the other. I determined therefore to direct my course this way, in order to my return to Europe. I hired two mules, with a guide, to show me the way, and carry my small baggage. I took leave of my noble protector, who had shown me so much favour, and made me a generous present at my departure.

My journey was without any accident or adventure worth relating. When I arrived at the port of Maldonada (for so it is called) there was no ship in the harbour bound for Luggnagg, nor likely to be in some time. The town is about as large as Portsmouth. I soon fell into some acquaintance, and was very hospitably received. A gentleman of distinction said to me, "that since the ships bound for Luggnagg could not be ready in less than a month, it might be no disagreeable amusement for me to take a trip to the little island of Glubbdubdrib, about five leagues off to the south-west." He offered himself and a friend to accompany me, and that I should be provided with a small convenient bark for the voyage.

Glubbdubdrib, as nearly as I can interpret the word, signifies the island of sorcerers or magicians. It is about one third as large as the Isle of Wight, and extremely fruitful: it is governed by the head of a certain tribe, who are all magicians. This tribe marries only among each other, and the eldest in succession is prince or governor. He has a noble palace, and a park of about three thousand acres, surrounded by a wall of hewn stone twenty feet high. In this park are several small enclosures for cattle, corn, and gardening.

The governor and his family are served and attended by domestics of a kind somewhat unusual. By his skill in necromancy he has a power of calling whom he pleases from the dead, and commanding their service for twenty-four hours, but no longer; nor can he call the same persons up again in less than three months, except upon very extraordinary occasions.

When we arrived at the island, which was about eleven in the morning, one of the gentlemen who accompanied me went to the governor, and desired admittance for a stranger, who came on purpose to have the honour of attending on his highness. This was immediately granted, and we all three entered the gate of the palace between two rows of guards, armed and dressed after a very antic manner, and with something in their countenances that made my flesh creep with a horror I cannot express. We passed through several apartments, between servants of the same sort, ranked on each side as before, till we came to the chamber of presence; where, after three profound obeisances, and a few general questions, we were permitted to sit on three stools, near the lowest step of his highness's throne. He understood the language of Balnibarbi, although it was different from that of this island. He desired me to give him some account of my travels; and, to let me see that I should be treated without ceremony, he dismissed all his attendants with a turn of his finger; at which, to my great astonishment, they vanished in an instant, like visions in a dream when we awake on a sudden. I could not recover myself in some time, till the governor assured me, "that I should receive no hurt:" and observing my two companions to be under no concern, who had been often entertained in the same manner, I began to take courage, and related to his highness a short history of my several adventures; yet not without some hesitation, and frequently looking behind me to the place where I had seen those domestic spectres. I had the honour to dine with the governor, where a new set of ghosts served up the meat, and waited at table. I now observed myself to be less terrified than I had been in the morning. I stayed till sunset, but humbly desired his highness to excuse me for not accepting his invitation of lodging in the palace. My two friends and I lay at a private house in the town adjoining, which is the capital of this little island; and the next morning we returned to pay our duty to the governor, as he was pleased to command us.

After this manner we continued in the island for ten days, most part of every day with the governor, and at night in our lodging. I soon grew so familiarized to the sight of spirits, that after the third or fourth time they gave me no emotion at all: or, if I had any apprehensions left, my curiosity prevailed over them. For his highness the governor ordered me "to call up whatever persons I would choose to name, and in whatever numbers, among all the dead from the beginning of the world to the present time, and command them to answer any questions I should think fit to ask; with this condition, that my questions must be confined within the compass of the times they lived in. And one thing I might depend upon, that they would certainly tell me the truth, for lying was a talent of no use in the lower world."

I made my humble acknowledgments to his highness for so great a favour. We were in a chamber, from whence there was a fair prospect into the park. And because my first inclination was to be entertained with scenes of pomp and magnificence, I desired to see Alexander the Great at the head of his army, just after the battle of Arbela: which, upon a motion of the governor's finger, immediately appeared in a large field, under the window where we stood. Alexander was called up into the room: it was with great difficulty that I understood his Greek, and had but little of my own. He assured me upon his honour "that he was not poisoned, but died of a bad fever by excessive drinking."

Next, I saw Hannibal passing the Alps, who told me "he had not a drop of vinegar in his camp."

I saw Cæsar and Pompey at the head of their troops, just ready to engage. I saw the former, in his last great triumph. I desired that the senate of Rome might appear before me, in one large chamber, and an assembly of somewhat a later age in counterview, in another. The first seemed to be an assembly of heroes and demigods; the other, a knot of pedlars, pick-pockets, highwayman, and bullies.

The governor, at my request, gave the sign for Cæsar and Brutus to advance towards us. I was struck with a profound veneration at the sight of Brutus, and could easily discover the most consummate virtue, the greatest intrepidity and firmness of mind, the truest love of his country, and general benevolence for mankind, in every lineament of his countenance. I observed, with much pleasure, that these two persons were in good intelligence with each other; and Cæsar freely confessed to me, "that the greatest actions of his own life were not equal, by many degrees, to the glory of taking it away." I had the honour to have much conversation with Brutus; and was told, "that his ancestor Junius, Socrates, Epaminondas, Cato the younger, Sir Thomas More, and himself were perpetually together:" a sextumvirate, to which all the ages of the world cannot add a seventh.

It would be tedious to trouble the reader with relating what vast numbers of illustrious persons were called up to gratify that insatiable desire I had to see the world in every period of antiquity placed before me. I chiefly fed mine eyes with beholding the destroyers of tyrants and usurpers, and the restorers of liberty to oppressed and injured nations. But it is impossible to express the satisfaction I received in my own mind, after such a manner as to make it a suitable entertainment to the reader.

CHAPTER 8: A FURTHER ACCOUNT OF GLUBBDUBDRIB. ANCIENT AND MODERN HISTORY CORRECTED.

Having a desire to see those ancients who were most renowned for wit and learning, I set apart one day on purpose. I proposed that Homer and Aristotle might appear at the head of all their commentators; but these were so numerous, that some hundreds were forced to attend in the court, and outward rooms of the palace. I knew, and could distinguish those two heroes, at first sight, not only from the crowd, but from each other. Homer was the taller and comelier person of the two, walked very erect for one of his age, and his eyes were the most quick and piercing I ever beheld. Aristotle stooped much, and made use of a staff. His visage was meagre, his hair lank and thin, and his voice hollow. I soon discovered that both of them were perfect strangers to the rest of the company, and had never seen or heard of them before; and I had a whisper from a ghost who shall be nameless, "that these commentators always kept in the most distant quarters from their principals, in the lower world, through a consciousness of shame and guilt, because they had so horribly misrepresented the meaning of those authors to posterity." I introduced Didymus and Eustathius to Homer, and prevailed on him to treat them better than perhaps they deserved, for he soon found they wanted a genius to enter into the spirit of a poet. But Aristotle was out of all patience with the account I gave him of Scotus and Ramus, as I presented them to him; and he asked them, "whether the rest of the tribe were as great dunces as themselves?"

I then desired the governor to call up Descartes and Gassendi, with whom I prevailed to explain their systems to Aristotle. This great philosopher freely acknowledged his own mistakes in natural philosophy, because he proceeded in many things upon conjecture, as all men must do; and he found that Gassendi, who had made the doctrine of Epicurus as palatable as he could, and the vortices of Descartes, were equally to be exploded. He predicted the same fate to *attraction*, whereof the present learned are such zealous asserters. He said, "that new systems of nature were but new fashions, which would vary in every age; and even those, who pretend to demonstrate them from mathematical principles, would flourish but a short period of time, and be out of vogue when that was determined."

I spent five days in conversing with many others of the ancient learned. I saw most of the first Roman emperors. I prevailed on the governor to call up Heliogabalus's cooks to dress us a dinner, but they could not show us much of their skill, for want of materials. A helot of Agesilaus made us a dish of Spartan broth, but I was not able to get down a second spoonful.

The two gentlemen, who conducted me to the island, were pressed by their private affairs to return in three days, which I employed in seeing some of the modern dead, who had made the greatest figure, for two or three hundred years past, in our own and other countries of Europe; and having been always a great admirer of old illustrious families, I desired the governor would call up a dozen or two of kings, with their ancestors in order for eight or nine generations. But my disappointment was grievous and unexpected. For, instead of a long train with royal diadems, I saw in one family two fiddlers, three spruce courtiers, and an Italian prelate. In another, a barber, an abbot, and two cardinals. I have too great a veneration for crowned heads, to dwell any longer on so nice a subject. But as to counts, marquises, dukes, earls, and the like, I was not so scrupulous. And I confess, it was not without some pleasure, that I found myself able to trace the particular features, by which certain families are distinguished, up to their originals. I could plainly discover whence one family derives a long chin; why a second has abounded with knaves for two generations, and fools for two more; why a third happened to be crack-brained, and a fourth to be sharpers; whence it came, what Polydore Virgil says of a certain great house, *Nec vir fortis, nec foemina casta*; how cruelty, falsehood, and cowardice, grew to be characteristics by which certain families are distinguished as much as by their coats of arms; who first brought the pox into a noble house, which has lineally descended scrofulous tumours to their posterity. Neither could I wonder at all this, when I saw such an interruption of lineages, by pages, lackeys, valets, coachmen, gamesters, fiddlers, players, captains, and pickpockets.

I was chiefly disgusted with modern history. For having strictly examined all the persons of greatest name in the courts of princes, for a hundred years past, I found how the world had been misled by prostitute writers, to ascribe the greatest exploits in war, to cowards; the wisest counsel, to fools; sincerity, to flatterers; Roman virtue, to betrayers of their country; piety, to atheists; chastity, to sodomites; truth, to informers: how many innocent and excellent persons had been condemned to death or banishment by the practising of great ministers upon the corruption of judges, and the malice of factions: how many villains had been exalted to the highest places of trust, power, dignity, and profit: how great a share in the motions and events of courts, councils, and senates might be challenged by bawds, whores, pimps, parasites, and buffoons. How low an opinion I had of human wisdom and integrity, when I was truly informed of the springs and motives of great enterprises and revolutions in the world, and of the contemptible accidents to which they owed their success.

Here I discovered the roguery and ignorance of those who pretend to write anecdotes, or secret history; who send so many kings to their graves with a cup of poison; will repeat the discourse between a prince and chief minister, where no witness was by; unlock the thoughts and cabinets of ambassadors and secretaries of state; and have the perpetual misfortune to be mistaken. Here I discovered the true causes of many great events that have surprised the world; how a whore can govern the back-stairs, the back-stairs a council, and the council a senate. A general confessed, in my presence, "that he got a victory purely by the force of cowardice and ill conduct;" and an admiral, "that, for want of proper intelligence, he beat the enemy, to whom he intended to betray the fleet." Three kings protested to me, "that in their whole reigns they never did once prefer any person of merit, unless by mistake, or treachery of some minister in whom they confided; neither would they do it if they were to live again:" and they showed, with great strength of reason, "that the royal throne could not be supported without corruption, because that positive, confident, restiff temper, which virtue infused into a man, was a perpetual clog to public business."

I had the curiosity to inquire in a particular manner, by what methods great numbers had procured to themselves high titles of honour, and prodigious estates; and I confined my inquiry to a very modern period: however, without grating upon present times, because I would be sure to give no offence even to foreigners (for I hope the reader need not be told, that I do not in the least intend my own country, in what I say upon this occasion,) a great number of persons concerned were called up; and, upon a very slight examination, discovered such a scene of infamy, that I cannot reflect upon it without some seriousness. Perjury, oppression, subornation, fraud, pandarism, and the like infirmities, were among the most excusable arts they had to mention; and for these I gave, as it was reasonable, great allowance. But when some confessed they owed their greatness and wealth to sodomy, or incest; others, to the prostituting of their own wives and daughters; others, to the betraying of their country or their prince; some, to poisoning; more to the perverting of justice, in order to destroy the innocent, I hope I may be pardoned, if these discoveries inclined me a little to abate of that profound veneration, which I am naturally apt to pay to persons of high rank, who ought to be treated with the utmost respect due to their sublime dignity, by us their inferiors.

I had often read of some great services done to princes and states, and desired to see the persons by whom those services were performed. Upon inquiry I was told, "that their names were to be found on no record, except a few of them, whom history has represented as the vilest of rogues and traitors." As to the rest, I had never once heard of them. They all appeared with dejected looks, and in the meanest habit; most of them telling me, "they died in poverty and disgrace, and the rest on a scaffold or a gibbet."

Among others, there was one person, whose case appeared a little singular. He had a youth about eighteen years old standing by his side. He told me, "he had for many years been commander of a ship; and in the sea fight at Actium had the good fortune to break through the enemy's great line of battle, sink three of their capital ships, and take a fourth, which was the sole cause of Antony's flight, and of the victory that ensued; that the youth standing by him, his only son, was killed in the action." He added, "that upon the confidence of some merit, the war being at an end, he went to Rome, and solicited at the court of Augustus to be preferred to a greater ship, whose commander had been killed; but, without any regard to his pretensions, it was given to a boy who had never seen the sea, the son of Libertina, who waited on one of the emperor's mistresses. Returning back to his own vessel, he was charged with neglect of duty, and the ship given to a favourite page of Publicola, the vice-admiral; whereupon he retired to a poor farm at a great distance from Rome, and there ended his life." I was so curious to know the truth of this story, that I desired Agrippa might be called, who was admiral in that fight. He appeared, and confirmed the whole account: but with much more advantage to the captain, whose modesty had extenuated or concealed a great part of his merit.

I was surprised to find corruption grown so high and so quick in that empire, by the force of luxury so lately introduced; which made me less wonder at many parallel cases in other countries, where vices of all kinds have reigned so much longer, and where the whole praise, as well as pillage, has been engrossed by the chief commander, who perhaps had the least title to either.

As every person called up made exactly the same appearance he had done in the world, it gave me melancholy reflections to observe how much the race of human kind was degenerated among us within these hundred years past; how the pox, under all its consequences and denominations had altered every lineament of an English countenance; shortened the size of bodies, unbraced the nerves, relaxed the sinews and muscles, introduced a sallow complexion, and rendered the flesh loose and rancid.

I descended so low, as to desire some English yeoman of the old stamp might be summoned to appear; once so famous for the simplicity of their manners, diet, and dress; for justice in their dealings; for their true spirit of liberty; for their valour, and love of their country. Neither could I be wholly unmoved, after comparing the living with the dead, when I considered how all these pure native virtues were prostituted for a piece of money by their grand-children; who, in selling their votes and managing at elections, have acquired every vice and corruption that can possibly be learned in a court.

CHAPTER 9: THE AUTHOR RETURNS TO MALDONADA. SAILS TO THE KINGDOM OF LUGGNAGG. THE AUTHOR CONFINED. HE IS SENT FOR TO COURT. THE MANNER OF HIS ADMITTANCE. THE KING'S GREAT LENITY TO HIS SUBJECTS.

The day of our departure being come, I took leave of his highness, the Governor of Glubbdubdrib, and returned with my two companions to Maldonada, where, after a fortnight's waiting, a ship was ready to sail for Luggnagg. The two gentlemen, and some others, were so generous and kind as to furnish me with provisions, and see me on board. I was a month in this voyage. We had one violent storm, and were under a necessity of steering westward to get into the trade wind, which holds for above sixty leagues. On the 21st of April, 1708, we sailed into the river of Clumegnig, which is a seaport town, at the south-east point of Luggnagg. We cast anchor within a league of the town, and made a signal for a pilot. Two of them came on board in less than half an hour, by whom we were guided between certain shoals and rocks, which are very dangerous in the passage, to a large basin, where a fleet may ride in safety within a cable's length of the town-wall.

Some of our sailors, whether out of treachery or inadvertence, had informed the pilots "that I was a stranger, and great traveller;" whereof these gave notice to a custom-house officer, by whom I was examined very strictly upon my landing. This officer spoke to me in the language of Balnibarbi, which, by the force of much commerce, is generally understood in that town, especially by seamen and those employed in the customs. I gave him a short account of some particulars, and made my story as plausible and consistent as I could; but I thought it necessary to disguise my country, and call myself a Hollander; because my intentions were for Japan, and I knew the Dutch were the only Europeans permitted to enter into that kingdom. I therefore told the officer, "that having been shipwrecked on the coast of Balnibarbi, and cast on a rock, I was received up into Laputa, or the flying island (of which he had often heard), and was now endeavouring to get to Japan, whence I might find a convenience of returning to my own country." The officer said, "I must be confined till he could receive orders from court, for which he would write immediately, and hoped to receive an answer in a fortnight." I was carried to a convenient lodging with a sentry placed at the door; however, I had the liberty of a large garden, and was treated with humanity enough, being maintained all the time at the king's charge. I was invited by several persons, chiefly out of curiosity, because it was reported that I came from countries very remote, of which they had never heard.

I hired a young man, who came in the same ship, to be an interpreter; he was a native of Luggnagg, but had lived some years at Maldonada, and was a perfect master of both languages. By his assistance, I was able to hold a conversation with those who came to visit me; but this consisted only of their questions, and my answers.

The despatch came from court about the time we expected. It contained a warrant for conducting me and my retinue to *Traldragdubh*, or *Trildrogdrib* (for it is pronounced both ways as near as I can remember), by a party of ten horse. All my retinue was that poor lad for an interpreter, whom I persuaded into my service, and, at my humble request, we had each of us a mule to ride on. A messenger was despatched half a day's journey before us, to give the king notice of my approach, and to desire, "that his majesty would please to appoint a day and hour, when it would by his gracious pleasure that I might have the honour to lick the dust before his footstool." This is the court style, and I found it to be more than matter of form: for, upon my admittance two days after my arrival, I was commanded to crawl upon my belly, and lick the floor as I advanced; but, on account of my being a stranger, care was taken to have it made so clean, that the dust was not offensive. However, this was a peculiar grace, not allowed to any but persons of the highest rank, when they desire an admittance. Nay, sometimes the floor is strewed with dust on purpose, when the person to be admitted happens to have powerful enemies at court; and I have seen a great lord with his mouth so crammed, that when he had crept to the proper distance from the throne; he was not able to speak a word. Neither is there any remedy; because it is capital for those, who receive an audience to spit or wipe their mouths in his majesty's presence. There is indeed another custom, which I cannot altogether approve of: when the king has a mind to put any of his nobles to death in a gentle indulgent manner, he commands the floor to be strewed with a certain brown powder of a deadly composition, which being licked up, infallibly kills him in twenty-four hours. But in justice to this prince's great clemency, and the care he has of his subjects' lives (wherein it were much to be wished that the Monarchs of Europe would imitate him), it must be mentioned for his honour, that strict orders are given to have the infected parts of the floor well washed after every such execution, which, if his domestics neglect, they are in danger of incurring his royal displeasure. I myself heard him give directions, that one of his pages should be whipped, whose turn it was to give notice about washing the floor after an execution, but maliciously had omitted it; by which neglect a young lord of great hopes, coming to an audience, was unfortunately poisoned, although the king at that time had no design against his life. But this good prince was so gracious as to forgive the poor page his whipping, upon promise that he would do so no more, without special orders.

To return from this digression. When I had crept within four yards of the throne, I raised myself gently upon my knees, and then striking my forehead seven times against the ground, I pronounced the following words, as they had been taught me the night before, *Inckpling gloffthrobb squut serummblhiop mlashnalt zwin tnodbalkuffh slhiophad gurdlubh asht*. This is the compliment, established by the laws of the land, for all persons admitted to the king's presence. It may be rendered into English thus: "May your celestial majesty outlive the sun, eleven moons and a half!" To this the king returned some answer, which, although I could not understand, yet I replied as I had been directed: *Fluft drin yalerick dwuldom prastrad mirpush*, which properly signifies, "My tongue is in the mouth of my friend;" and by this expression was meant, that I desired leave to bring my interpreter; whereupon the young man already mentioned was accordingly introduced, by whose intervention I answered as many questions as his majesty could put in above an hour. I spoke in the Balnibarbian tongue, and my interpreter delivered my meaning in that of Luggnagg.

The king was much delighted with my company, and ordered his *bliffmarklub*, or high-chamberlain, to appoint a lodging in the court for me and my interpreter; with a daily allowance for my table, and a large purse of gold for my common expenses.

I staid three months in this country, out of perfect obedience to his majesty; who was pleased highly to favour me, and made me very honourable offers. But I thought it more consistent with prudence and justice to pass the remainder of my days with my wife and family.

CHAPTER 10: THE LUGGNAGGIANS COMMENDED. A PARTICULAR DESCRIPTION OF THE STRULDBRUGS, WITH MANY CONVERSATIONS BETWEEN THE AUTHOR AND SOME EMINENT PERSONS UPON THAT SUBJECT.

The Luggnaggians are a polite and generous people; and although they are not without some share of that pride which is peculiar to all Eastern countries, yet they show themselves courteous to strangers, especially such who are countenanced by the court. I had many acquaintance, and among persons of the best fashion; and being always attended by my interpreter, the conversation we had was not disagreeable.

One day, in much good company, I was asked by a person of quality, "whether I had seen any of their *struldbrugs*, or immortals?" I said, "I had not;" and desired he would explain to me "what he meant by such an appellation, applied to a mortal creature." He told me "that sometimes, though very rarely, a child happened to be born in a family, with a red circular spot in the forehead, directly over the left eyebrow, which was an infallible mark that it should never die." The spot, as he described it, "was about the compass of a silver threepence, but in the course of time grew larger, and changed its colour; for at twelve years old it became green, so continued till five and twenty, then turned to a deep blue: at five and forty it grew coal black, and as large as an English shilling; but never admitted any further alteration." He said, "these births were so rare, that he did not believe there could be above eleven hundred struldbrugs, of both sexes, in the whole kingdom; of which he computed about fifty in the metropolis, and, among the rest, a young girl born; about three years ago: that these productions were not peculiar to any family, but a mere effect of chance; and the children of the *struldbrugs* themselves were equally mortal with the rest of the people."

I freely own myself to have been struck with inexpressible delight, upon hearing this account: and the person who gave it me happening to understand the Balnibarbian language, which I spoke very well, I could not forbear breaking out into expressions, perhaps a little too extravagant. I cried out, as in a rapture, "Happy nation, where every child hath at least a chance for being immortal! Happy people, who enjoy so many living examples of ancient virtue, and have masters ready to instruct them in the wisdom of all former ages! but happiest, beyond all comparison, are those excellent *struldbrugs*, who, being born exempt from that universal calamity of human nature, have their minds free and disengaged, without the weight and depression of spirits caused by the continual apprehensions of death!" I discovered my admiration, "that I had not observed any of these illustrious persons at court; the black spot on the forehead being so remarkable a distinction, that I could not have easily overlooked it: and it was impossible that his majesty, a most judicious prince, should not provide himself with a good number of such wise and able counsellors. Yet perhaps the virtue of those reverend sages was too strict for the corrupt and libertine manners of a court: and we often find by experience, that young men are too opinionated and volatile to be guided by the sober dictates of their seniors. However, since the king was pleased to allow me access to his royal person, I was resolved, upon the very first occasion, to deliver my opinion to him on this matter freely and at large, by the help of my interpreter; and whether he would please to take my advice or not, yet in one thing I was determined, that his majesty having frequently offered me an establishment in this country, I would, with great thankfulness, accept the favour, and pass my life here in the conversation of those superior beings the *struldbrugs*, if they would please to admit me."

The gentleman to whom I addressed my discourse, because (as I have already observed) he spoke the language of Balnibarbi, said to me, with a sort of a smile which usually arises from pity to the ignorant, "that he was glad of any occasion to keep me among them, and desired my permission to explain to the company what I had spoke." He did so, and they talked together for some time in their own language, whereof I understood not a syllable, neither could I observe by their countenances, what impression my discourse had made on them. After a short silence, the same person told me, "that his friends and mine (so he thought fit to express himself) were very much pleased with the judicious remarks I had made on the great happiness and advantages of immortal life, and they were desirous to know, in a particular manner, what scheme of living I should have formed to myself, if it had fallen to my lot to have been born a *struldbrug*."

I answered, "it was easy to be eloquent on so copious and delightful a subject, especially to me, who had been often apt to amuse myself with visions of what I should do, if I were a king, a general, or a great lord: and upon this very case, I had frequently run over the whole system how I should employ myself, and pass the time, if I were sure to live for ever.

"That, if it had been my good fortune to come into the world a *struldbrug*, as soon as I could discover my own happiness, by understanding the difference between life and death, I would first resolve, by all arts and methods, whatsoever, to procure myself riches. In the pursuit of which, by thrift and management, I might reasonably expect, in about two hundred years, to be the wealthiest man in the kingdom. In the second place, I would, from my earliest youth, apply myself to the study of arts and sciences, by which I should arrive in time to excel all others in learning. Lastly, I would carefully record every action and event of consequence, that happened in the public, impartially draw the characters of the several successions of princes and great ministers of state, with my own observations on every point. I would exactly set down the several changes in customs, language, fashions of dress, diet, and diversions. By all which acquirements, I should be a living treasure of knowledge and wisdom, and certainly become the oracle of the nation.

"I would never marry after threescore, but live in a hospitable manner, yet still on the saving side. I would entertain myself in forming and directing the minds of hopeful young men, by convincing them, from my own remembrance, experience, and observation, fortified by numerous examples, of the usefulness of virtue in public and private life. But my choice and constant companions should be a set of my own immortal brotherhood; among whom, I would elect a dozen from the most ancient, down to my own contemporaries. Where any of these wanted fortunes, I would provide them with convenient lodges round my own estate, and have some of them always at my table; only mingling a few of the most valuable among you mortals, whom length of time would harden me to lose with little or no reluctance, and treat your posterity after the same manner; just as a man diverts himself with the annual succession of pinks and tulips in his garden, without regretting the loss of those which withered the preceding year.

"These *struldbrugs* and I would mutually communicate our observations and memorials, through the course of time; remark the several gradations by which corruption steals into the world, and oppose it in every step, by giving perpetual warning and instruction to mankind; which, added to the strong influence of our own example, would probably prevent that continual degeneracy of human nature so justly complained of in all ages.

"Add to this, the pleasure of seeing the various revolutions of states and empires; the changes in the lower and upper world; ancient cities in ruins, and obscure villages become the seats of kings; famous rivers lessening into shallow brooks; the ocean leaving one coast dry, and overwhelming another; the discovery of many countries yet unknown; barbarity overrunning the politest nations, and the most barbarous become civilized. I should then see the discovery of the longitude, the perpetual motion, the universal medicine, and many other great inventions, brought to the utmost perfection.

"What wonderful discoveries should we make in astronomy, by outliving and confirming our own predictions; by observing the progress and return of comets, with the changes of motion in the sun, moon, and stars!"

I enlarged upon many other topics, which the natural desire of endless life, and sublunary happiness, could easily furnish me with. When I had ended, and the sum of my discourse had been interpreted, as before, to the rest of the company, there was a good deal of talk among them in the language of the country, not without some laughter at my expense. At last, the same gentleman who had been my interpreter, said, "he was desired by the rest to set me right in a few mistakes, which I had fallen into through the common imbecility of human nature, and upon that allowance was less answerable for them. That this breed of *struldbrugs* was peculiar to their country, for there were no such people either in Balnibarbi or Japan, where he had the honour to be ambassador from his majesty, and found the natives in both those kingdoms very hard to believe that the fact was possible: and it appeared from my astonishment when he first mentioned the matter to me, that I received it as a thing wholly new, and scarcely to be credited. That in the two kingdoms above mentioned, where, during his residence, he had conversed very much, he observed long life to be the universal desire and wish of mankind. That whoever had one foot in the grave was sure to hold back the other as strongly as he could. That the oldest had still hopes of living one day longer, and looked on death as the greatest evil, from which nature always prompted him to retreat. Only in this island of Luggnagg the appetite for living was not so eager, from the continual example of the *struldbrugs* before their eyes.

"That the system of living contrived by me, was unreasonable and unjust; because it supposed a perpetuity of youth, health, and vigour, which no man could be so foolish to hope, however extravagant he may be in his wishes. That the question therefore was not, whether a man would choose to be always in the prime of youth, attended with prosperity and health; but how he would pass a perpetual life under all the usual disadvantages which old age brings along with it. For although few men will avow their desires of being immortal, upon such hard conditions, yet in the two kingdoms before mentioned, of Balnibarbi and Japan, he observed that every man desired to put off death some time longer, let it approach ever so late: and he rarely heard of any man who died willingly, except he were incited by the extremity of grief or torture. And he appealed to me, whether in those countries I had travelled, as well as my own, I had not observed the same general disposition."

After this preface, he gave me a particular account of the *struldbrugs* among them. He said, "they commonly acted like mortals till about thirty years old; after which, by degrees, they grew melancholy and dejected, increasing in both till they came to fourscore. This he learned from their own confession: for otherwise, there not being above two or three of that species born in an age, they were too few to form a general observation by. When they came to fourscore years, which is reckoned the extremity of living in this country, they had not only all the follies and infirmities of other old men, but many more which arose from the dreadful prospect of never dying. They were not only opinionative, peevish, covetous, morose, vain, talkative, but incapable of friendship, and dead to all natural affection, which never descended below their grandchildren. Envy and impotent desires are their prevailing passions. But those objects against which their envy seems principally directed, are the vices of the younger sort and the deaths of the old. By reflecting on the former, they find themselves cut off from all possibility of pleasure; and whenever they see a funeral, they lament and repine that others have gone to a harbour of rest to which they themselves never can hope to arrive. They have no remembrance of anything but what they learned and observed in their youth and middle-age, and even that is very imperfect; and for the truth or particulars of any fact, it is safer to depend on common tradition, than upon their best recollections. The least miserable among them appear to be those who turn to dotage, and entirely lose their memories; these meet with more pity and assistance, because they want many bad qualities which abound in others.

"If a *struldbrug* happen to marry one of his own kind, the marriage is dissolved of course, by the courtesy of the kingdom, as soon as the younger of the two comes to be fourscore; for the law thinks it a reasonable indulgence, that those who are condemned, without any fault of their own, to a perpetual continuance in the world, should not have their misery doubled by the load of a wife.

"As soon as they have completed the term of eighty years, they are looked on as dead in law; their heirs immediately succeed to their estates; only a small pittance is reserved for their support; and the poor ones are maintained at the public charge. After that period, they are held incapable of any employment of trust or profit; they cannot purchase lands, or take leases; neither are they allowed to be witnesses in any cause, either civil or criminal, not even for the decision of meers and bounds.

"At ninety, they lose their teeth and hair; they have at that age no distinction of taste, but eat and drink whatever they can get, without relish or appetite. The diseases they were subject to still continue, without increasing or diminishing. In talking, they forget the common appellation of things, and the names of persons, even of those who are their nearest friends and relations. For the same reason, they never can amuse themselves with reading, because their memory will not serve to carry them from the beginning of a sentence to the end; and by this defect, they are deprived of the only entertainment whereof they might otherwise be capable.

"The language of this country being always upon the flux, the *struldbrugs* of one age do not understand those of another; neither are they able, after two hundred years, to hold any conversation (farther than by a few general words) with their neighbours the mortals; and thus they lie under the disadvantage of living like foreigners in their own country."

This was the account given me of the *struldbrugs*, as near as I can remember. I afterwards saw five or six of different ages, the youngest not above two hundred years old, who were brought to me at several times by some of my friends; but although they were told, "that I was a great traveller, and had seen all the world," they had not the least curiosity to ask me a question; only desired "I would give them *slumskudask*," or a token of remembrance; which is a modest way of begging, to avoid the law, that strictly forbids it, because they are provided for by the public, although indeed with a very scanty allowance.

They are despised and hated by all sorts of people. When one of them is born, it is reckoned ominous, and their birth is recorded very particularly so that you may know their age by consulting the register, which, however, has not been kept above a thousand years past, or at least has been destroyed by time or public disturbances. But the usual way of computing how old they are, is by asking them what kings or great persons they can remember, and then consulting history; for infallibly the last prince in their mind did not begin his reign after they were fourscore years old.

They were the most mortifying sight I ever beheld; and the women more horrible than the men. Besides the usual deformities in extreme old age, they acquired an additional ghastliness, in proportion to their number of years, which is not to be described; and among half a dozen, I soon distinguished which was the eldest, although there was not above a century or two between them.

The reader will easily believe, that from what I had hear and seen, my keen appetite for perpetuity of life was much abated. I grew heartily ashamed of the pleasing visions I had formed; and thought no tyrant could invent a death into which I would not run with pleasure, from such a life. The king heard of all that had passed between me and my friends upon this occasion, and rallied me very pleasantly; wishing I could send a couple of *struldbrugs* to my own country, to arm our people against the fear of death; but this, it seems, is forbidden by the fundamental laws of the kingdom, or else I should have been well content with the trouble and expense of transporting them.

I could not but agree, that the laws of this kingdom relative to the *struldbrugs* were founded upon the strongest reasons, and such as any other country would be under the necessity of enacting, in the like circumstances. Otherwise, as avarice is the necessary consequence of old age, those immortals would in time become proprietors of the whole nation, and engross the civil power, which, for want of abilities to manage, must end in the ruin of the public.

CHAPTER 11: THE AUTHOR LEAVES LUGGNAGG, AND SAILS TO JAPAN. FROM THENCE HE RETURNS IN A DUTCH SHIP TO AMSTERDAM, AND FROM AMSTERDAM TO ENGLAND.

I thought this account of the *struldbrugs* might be some entertainment to the reader, because it seems to be a little out of the common way; at least I do not remember to have met the like in any book of travels that has come to my hands: and if I am deceived, my excuse must be, that it is necessary for travellers who describe the same country, very often to agree in dwelling on the same particulars, without deserving the censure of having borrowed or transcribed from those who wrote before them.

There is indeed a perpetual commerce between this kingdom and the great empire of Japan; and it is very probable, that the Japanese authors may have given some account of the *struldbrugs*; but my stay in Japan was so short, and I was so entirely a stranger to the language, that I was not qualified to make any inquiries. But I hope the Dutch, upon this notice, will be curious and able enough to supply my defects.

His majesty having often pressed me to accept some employment in his court, and finding me absolutely determined to return to my native country, was pleased to give me his license to depart; and honoured me with a letter of recommendation, under his own hand, to the Emperor of Japan. He likewise presented me with four hundred and forty-four large pieces of gold (this nation delighting in even numbers), and a red diamond, which I sold in England for eleven hundred pounds.

On the 6th of May, 1709, I took a solemn leave of his majesty, and all my friends. This prince was so gracious as to order a guard to conduct me to Glanguenstald, which is a royal port to the south-west part of the island. In six days I found a vessel ready to carry me to Japan, and spent fifteen days in the voyage. We landed at a small port-town called Xamoschi, situated on the south-east part of Japan; the town lies on the western point, where there is a narrow strait leading northward into along arm of the sea, upon the north-west part of which, Yedo, the metropolis, stands. At landing, I showed the custom-house officers my letter from the king of Luggnagg to his imperial majesty. They knew the seal perfectly well; it was as broad as the palm of my hand. The impression was, *A king lifting up a lame beggar from the earth.* The magistrates of the town, hearing of my letter, received me as a public minister. They provided me with carriages and servants, and bore my charges to Yedo; where I was admitted to an audience, and delivered my letter, which was opened with great ceremony, and explained to the Emperor by an interpreter, who then gave me notice, by his majesty's order, "that I should signify my request, and, whatever it were, it should be granted, for the sake of his royal brother of Luggnagg." This interpreter was a person employed to transact affairs with the Hollanders. He soon conjectured, by my countenance, that I was a European, and therefore repeated his majesty's commands in Low Dutch, which he spoke perfectly well. I answered, as I had before determined, "that I was a Dutch merchant, shipwrecked in a very remote country, whence I had travelled by sea and land to Luggnagg, and then took shipping for Japan; where I knew my countrymen often traded, and with some of these I hoped to get an opportunity of returning into Europe: I therefore most humbly entreated his royal favour, to give order that I should be conducted in safety to Nangasac." To this I added another petition, "that for the sake of my patron the king of Luggnagg, his majesty would condescend to excuse my performing the ceremony imposed on my countrymen, of trampling upon the crucifix: because I had been thrown into his kingdom by my misfortunes, without any intention of trading." When this latter petition was interpreted to the Emperor, he seemed a little surprised; and said, "he believed I was the first of my countrymen who ever made any scruple in this point; and that he began to doubt, whether I was a real Hollander, or not; but rather suspected I must be a Christian. However, for the reasons I had offered, but chiefly to gratify the king of Luggnagg by an uncommon mark of his favour, he would comply with the singularity of my humour; but the affair must be managed with dexterity, and his officers should be commanded to let me pass, as it were by forgetfulness. For he assured me, that if the secret should be discovered by my countrymen the Dutch, they would cut my throat in the voyage." I returned my thanks, by the interpreter, for so unusual a favour; and some troops being at that time on their march to Nangasac, the commanding officer had orders to convey me safe thither, with particular instructions about the business of the crucifix.

On the 9th day of June, 1709, I arrived at Nangasac, after a very long and troublesome journey. I soon fell into the company of some Dutch sailors belonging to the Amboyna, of Amsterdam, a stout ship of 450 tons. I had lived long in Holland, pursuing my studies at Leyden, and I spoke Dutch well. The seamen soon knew whence I came last: they were curious to inquire into my voyages and course of life. I made up a story as short and probable as I could, but concealed the greatest part. I knew many persons in Holland. I was able to invent names for my parents, whom I pretended to be obscure people in the province of Gelderland. I would have given the captain (one Theodorus Vangrult) what he pleased to ask for my voyage to Holland; but understanding I was a surgeon, he was contented to take half the usual rate, on condition that I would serve him in the way of my calling. Before we took shipping, I was often asked by some of the crew, whether I had performed the ceremony above mentioned? I evaded the question by general answers; "that I had satisfied the Emperor and court in all particulars." However, a malicious rogue of a skipper went to an officer, and pointing to me, told him, "I had not yet trampled on the crucifix;" but the other, who had received instructions to let me pass, gave the rascal twenty strokes on the shoulders with a bamboo; after which I was no more troubled with such questions.

Nothing happened worth mentioning in this voyage. We sailed with a fair wind to the Cape of Good Hope, where we staid only to take in fresh water. On the 10th of April, 1710, we arrived safe at Amsterdam, having lost only three men by sickness in the voyage, and a fourth, who fell from the foremast into the sea, not far from the coast of Guinea. From Amsterdam I soon after set sail for England, in a small vessel belonging to that city.

On the 16th of April we put in at the Downs. I landed next morning, and saw once more my native country, after an absence of five years and six months complete. I went straight to Redriff, where I arrived the same day at two in the afternoon, and found my wife and family in good health.

---

1. Britannia.—*Sir W. Scott.*
2. *London.—Sir W. Scott.*
3. This is the revised text adopted by Dr. Hawksworth (1766). The above paragraph in the original editions (1726) takes another form, commencing:—"I told him that should I happen to live in a kingdom where lots were in vogue," &c. The names Tribnia and Langdon are not mentioned, and the "close stool" and its signification do not occur.

A VOYAGE TO THE COUNTRY OF
THE HOUYHNHNMS

CHAPTER 1: THE AUTHOR SETS OUT AS CAPTAIN OF A SHIP. HIS MEN CONSPIRE AGAINST HIM, CONFINE HIM A LONG TIME TO HIS CABIN, AND SET HIM ON SHORE IN AN UNKNOWN LAND. HE TRAVELS UP INTO THE COUNTRY. THE YAHOOS, A STRANGE SORT OF ANIMAL, DESCRIBED. THE AUTHOR MEETS TWO HOUYHNHNMS.

I continued at home with my wife and children about five months, in a very happy condition, if I could have learned the lesson of knowing when I was well. I left my poor wife big with child, and accepted an advantageous offer made me to be captain of the Adventurer, a stout merchantman of 350 tons: for I understood navigation well, and being grown weary of a surgeon's employment at sea, which, however, I could exercise upon occasion, I took a skilful young man of that calling, one Robert Purefoy, into my ship. We set sail from Portsmouth upon the 7th day of September, 1710; on the 14th we met with Captain Pocock, of Bristol, at Teneriffe, who was going to the bay of Campechy to cut logwood. On the 16th, he was parted from us by a storm; I heard since my return, that his ship foundered, and none escaped but one cabin boy. He was an honest man, and a good sailor, but a little too positive in his own opinions, which was the cause of his destruction, as it has been with several others; for if he had followed my advice, he might have been safe at home with his family at this time, as well as myself.

I had several men who died in my ship of calentures, so that I was forced to get recruits out of Barbadoes and the Leeward Islands, where I touched, by the direction of the merchants who employed me; which I had soon too much cause to repent: for I found afterwards, that most of them had been buccaneers. I had fifty hands onboard; and my orders were, that I should trade with the Indians in the South-Sea, and make what discoveries I could. These rogues, whom I had picked up, debauched my other men, and they all formed a conspiracy to seize the ship, and secure me; which they did one morning, rushing into my cabin, and binding me hand and foot, threatening to throw me overboard, if I offered to stir. I told them, "I was their prisoner, and would submit." This they made me swear to do, and then they unbound me, only fastening one of my legs with a chain, near my bed, and placed a sentry at my door with his piece charged, who was commanded to shoot me dead if I attempted my liberty. They sent me own victuals and drink, and took the government of the ship to themselves. Their design was to turn pirates and, plunder the Spaniards, which they could not do till they got more men. But first they resolved to sell the goods in the ship, and then go to Madagascar for recruits, several among them having died since my confinement. They sailed many weeks, and traded with the Indians; but I knew not what course they took, being kept a close prisoner in my cabin, and expecting nothing less than to be murdered, as they often threatened me.

Upon the 9th day of May, 1711, one James Welch came down to my cabin, and said, "he had orders from the captain to set me ashore." I expostulated with him, but in vain; neither would he so much as tell me who their new captain was. They forced me into the long-boat, letting me put on my best suit of clothes, which were as good as new, and take a small bundle of linen, but no arms, except my hanger; and they were so civil as not to search my pockets, into which I conveyed what money I had, with some other little necessaries. They rowed about a league, and then set me down on a strand. I desired them to tell me what country it was. They all swore, "they knew no more than myself;" but said, "that the captain" (as they called him) "was resolved, after they had sold the lading, to get rid of me in the first place where they could discover land." They pushed off immediately, advising me to make haste for fear of being overtaken by the tide, and so bade me farewell.

In this desolate condition I advanced forward, and soon got upon firm ground, where I sat down on a bank to rest myself, and consider what I had best do. When I was a little refreshed, I went up into the country, resolving to deliver myself to the first savages I should meet, and purchase my life from them by some bracelets, glass rings, and other toys, which sailors usually provide themselves with in those voyages, and whereof I had some about me. The land was divided by long rows of trees, not regularly planted, but naturally growing; there was great plenty of grass, and several fields of oats. I walked very circumspectly, for fear of being surprised, or suddenly shot with an arrow from behind, or on either side. I fell into a beaten road, where I saw many tracts of human feet, and some of cows, but most of horses. At last I beheld several animals in a field, and one or two of the same kind sitting in trees. Their shape was very singular and deformed, which a little discomposed me, so that I lay down behind a thicket to observe them better. Some of them coming forward near the place where I lay, gave me an opportunity of distinctly marking their form. Their heads and breasts were covered with a thick hair, some frizzled, and others lank; they had beards like goats, and a long ridge of hair down their backs, and the fore parts of their legs and feet; but the rest of their bodies was bare, so that I might see their skins, which were of a brown buff colour. They had no tails, nor any hair at all on their buttocks, except about the anus, which, I presume, nature had placed there to defend them as they sat on the ground, for this posture they used, as well as lying down, and often stood on their hind feet. They climbed high trees as nimbly as a squirrel, for they had strong extended claws before and behind, terminating in sharp points, and hooked. They would often spring, and bound, and leap, with prodigious agility. The females were not so large as the males; they had long lank hair on their heads, but none on their faces, nor any thing more than a sort of down on the rest of their bodies, except about the anus and pudenda. The dugs hung between their fore feet, and often reached almost to the ground as they walked. The hair of both sexes was of several colours, brown, red, black, and yellow. Upon the whole, I never beheld, in all my travels, so disagreeable an animal, or one against which I naturally conceived so strong an antipathy. So that, thinking I had seen enough, full of contempt and aversion, I got up, and pursued the beaten road, hoping it might direct me to the cabin of some Indian. I had not got far, when I met one of these creatures full in my way, and coming up directly to me. The ugly monster, when he saw me, distorted several ways, every feature of his visage, and stared, as at an object he had never seen before; then approaching nearer, lifted up his fore-paw, whether out of curiosity or mischief I could not tell; but I drew my hanger, and gave him a good blow with the flat side of it, for I durst not strike with the edge, fearing the inhabitants might be provoked against me, if they should come to know that I had killed or maimed any of their cattle. When the beast felt the smart, he drew back, and roared so loud, that a herd of at least forty came flocking about me from the next field, howling and making odious faces; but I ran to the body of a tree, and leaning my back against it, kept them off by waving my hanger. Several of this cursed brood, getting hold of the branches behind, leaped up into the tree, whence they began to discharge their excrements on my head; however, I escaped pretty well by sticking close to the stem of the tree, but was almost stifled with the filth, which fell about me on every side.

In the midst of this distress, I observed them all to run away on a sudden as fast as they could; at which I ventured to leave the tree and pursue the road, wondering what it was that could put them into this fright. But looking on my left hand, I saw a horse walking softly in the field; which my persecutors having sooner discovered, was the cause of their flight. The horse started a little, when he came near me, but soon recovering himself, looked full in my face with manifest tokens of wonder; he viewed my hands and feet, walking round me several times. I would have pursued my journey, but he placed himself directly in the way, yet looking with a very mild aspect, never offering the least violence. We stood gazing at each other for some time; at last I took the boldness to reach my hand towards his neck with a design to stroke it, using the common style and whistle of jockeys, when they are going to handle a strange horse. But this animal seemed to receive my civilities with disdain, shook his head, and bent his brows, softly raising up his right fore-foot to remove my hand. Then he neighed three or four times, but in so different a cadence, that I almost began to think he was speaking to himself, in some language of his own.

While he and I were thus employed, another horse came up; who applying himself to the first in a very formal manner, they gently struck each other's right hoof before, neighing several times by turns, and varying the sound, which seemed to be almost articulate. They went some paces off, as if it were to confer together, walking side by side, backward and forward, like persons deliberating upon some affair of weight, but often turning their eyes towards me, as it were to watch that I might not escape. I was amazed to see such actions and behaviour in brute beasts; and concluded with myself, that if the inhabitants of this country were endued with a proportionable degree of reason, they must needs be the wisest people upon earth. This thought gave me so much comfort, that I resolved to go forward, until I could discover some house or village, or meet with any of the natives, leaving the two horses to discourse together as they pleased. But the first, who was a dapple gray, observing me to steal off, neighed after me in so expressive a tone, that I fancied myself to understand what he meant; whereupon I turned back, and came near to him to expect his farther commands: but concealing my fear as much as I could, for I began to be in some pain how this adventure might terminate; and the reader will easily believe I did not much like my present situation.

The two horses came up close to me, looking with great earnestness upon my face and hands. The gray steed rubbed my hat all round with his right fore-hoof, and discomposed it so much that I was forced to adjust it better by taking it off and settling it again; whereat, both he and his companion (who was a brown bay) appeared to be much surprised: the latter felt the lappet of my coat, and finding it to hang loose about me, they both looked with new signs of wonder. He stroked my right hand, seeming to admire the softness and colour; but he squeezed it so hard between his hoof and his pastern, that I was forced to roar; after which they both touched me with all possible tenderness. They were under great perplexity about my shoes and stockings, which they felt very often, neighing to each other, and using various gestures, not unlike those of a philosopher, when he would attempt to solve some new and difficult phenomenon.

Upon the whole, the behaviour of these animals was so orderly and rational, so acute and judicious, that I at last concluded they must needs be magicians, who had thus metamorphosed themselves upon some design, and seeing a stranger in the way, resolved to divert themselves with him; or, perhaps, were really amazed at the sight of a man so very different in habit, feature, and complexion, from those who might probably live in so remote a climate. Upon the strength of this reasoning, I ventured to address them in the following manner: "Gentlemen, if you be conjurers, as I have good cause to believe, you can understand my language; therefore I make bold to let your worships know that I am a poor distressed Englishman, driven by his misfortunes upon your coast; and I entreat one of you to let me ride upon his back, as if he were a real horse, to some house or village where I can be relieved. In return of which favour, I will make you a present of this knife and bracelet," taking them out of my pocket. The two creatures stood silent while I spoke, seeming to listen with great attention, and when I had ended, they neighed frequently towards each other, as if they were engaged in serious conversation. I plainly observed that their language expressed the passions very well, and the words might, with little pains, be resolved into an alphabet more easily than the Chinese.

I could frequently distinguish the word *Yahoo*, which was repeated by each of them several times: and although it was impossible for me to conjecture what it meant, yet while the two horses were busy in conversation, I endeavoured to practise this word upon my tongue; and as soon as they were silent, I boldly pronounced *Yahoo* in a loud voice, imitating at the same time, as near as I could, the neighing of a horse; at which they were both visibly surprised; and the gray repeated the same word twice, as if he meant to teach me the right accent; wherein I spoke after him as well as I could, and found myself perceivably to improve every time, though very far from any degree of perfection. Then the bay tried me with a second word, much harder to be pronounced; but reducing it to the English orthography, may be spelt thus, *Houyhnhnm*. I did not succeed in this so well as in the former; but after two or three farther trials, I had better fortune; and they both appeared amazed at my capacity.

After some further discourse, which I then conjectured might relate to me, the two friends took their leaves, with the same compliment of striking each other's hoof; and the gray made me signs that I should walk before him; wherein I thought it prudent to comply, till I could find a better director. When I offered to slacken my pace, he would cry *hhuun hhuun*: I guessed his meaning, and gave him to understand, as well as I could, "that I was weary, and not able to walk faster;" upon which he would stand awhile to let me rest.

CHAPTER 2: THE AUTHOR CONDUCTED BY A HOUYHNHNM TO HIS HOUSE. THE HOUSE DESCRIBED. THE AUTHOR'S RECEPTION. THE FOOD OF THE HOUYHNHNMS. THE AUTHOR IN DISTRESS FOR WANT OF MEAT. IS AT LAST RELIEVED. HIS MANNER OF FEEDING IN THIS COUNTRY.

Having travelled about three miles, we came to a long kind of building, made of timber stuck in the ground, and wattled across; the roof was low and covered with straw. I now began to be a little comforted; and took out some toys, which travellers usually carry for presents to the savage Indians of America, and other parts, in hopes the people of the house would be thereby encouraged to receive me kindly. The horse made me a sign to go in first; it was a large room with a smooth clay floor, and a rack and manger, extending the whole length on one side. There were three nags and two mares, not eating, but some of them sitting down upon their hams, which I very much wondered at; but wondered more to see the rest employed in domestic business; these seemed but ordinary cattle. However, this confirmed my first opinion, that a people who could so far civilise brute animals, must needs excel in wisdom all the nations of the world. The gray came in just after, and thereby prevented any ill treatment which the others might have given me. He neighed to them several times in a style of authority, and received answers.

Beyond this room there were three others, reaching the length of the house, to which you passed through three doors, opposite to each other, in the manner of a vista. We went through the second room towards the third. Here the gray walked in first, beckoning me to attend: I waited in the second room, and got ready my presents for the master and mistress of the house; they were two knives, three bracelets of false pearls, a small looking-glass, and a bead necklace. The horse neighed three or four times, and I waited to hear some answers in a human voice, but I heard no other returns than in the same dialect, only one or two a little shriller than his. I began to think that this house must belong to some person of great note among them, because there appeared so much ceremony before I could gain admittance. But, that a man of quality should be served all by horses, was beyond my comprehension. I feared my brain was disturbed by my sufferings and misfortunes. I roused myself, and looked about me in the room where I was left alone: this was furnished like the first, only after a more elegant manner. I rubbed my eyes often, but the same objects still occurred. I pinched my arms and sides to awake myself, hoping I might be in a dream. I then absolutely concluded, that all these appearances could be nothing else but necromancy and magic. But I had no time to pursue these reflections; for the gray horse came to the door, and made me a sign to follow him into the third room where I saw a very comely mare, together with a colt and foal, sitting on their haunches upon mats of straw, not unartfully made, and perfectly neat and clean.

The mare soon after my entrance rose from her mat, and coming up close, after having nicely observed my hands and face, gave me a most contemptuous look; and turning to the horse, I heard the word *Yahoo* often repeated betwixt them; the meaning of which word I could not then comprehend, although it was the first I had learned to pronounce. But I was soon better informed, to my everlasting mortification; for the horse, beckoning to me with his head, and repeating the *hhuun, hhuun*, as he did upon the road, which I understood was to attend him, led me out into a kind of court, where was another building, at some distance from the house. Here we entered, and I saw three of those detestable creatures, which I first met after my landing, feeding upon roots, and the flesh of some animals, which I afterwards found to be that of asses and dogs, and now and then a cow, dead by accident or disease. They were all tied by the neck with strong withes fastened to a beam; they held their food between the claws of their fore feet, and tore it with their teeth.

The master horse ordered a sorrel nag, one of his servants, to untie the largest of these animals, and take him into the yard. The beast and I were brought close together, and by our countenances diligently compared both by master and servant, who thereupon repeated several times the word *Yahoo*. My horror and astonishment are not to be described, when I observed in this abominable animal, a perfect human figure: the face of it indeed was flat and broad, the nose depressed, the lips large, and the mouth wide; but these differences are common to all savage nations, where the lineaments of the countenance are distorted, by the natives suffering their infants to lie grovelling on the earth, or by carrying them on their backs, nuzzling with their face against the mothers' shoulders. The fore-feet of the *Yahoo* differed from my hands in nothing else but the length of the nails, the coarseness and brownness of the palms, and the hairiness on the backs. There was the same resemblance between our feet, with the same differences; which I knew very well, though the horses did not, because of my shoes and stockings; the same in every part of our bodies except as to hairiness and colour, which I have already described.

The great difficulty that seemed to stick with the two horses, was to see the rest of my body so very different from that of a *Yahoo*, for which I was obliged to my clothes, whereof they had no conception. The sorrel nag offered me a root, which he held (after their manner, as we shall describe in its proper place) between his hoof and pastern; I took it in my hand, and, having smelt it, returned it to him again as civilly as I could. He brought out of the *Yahoos'* kennel a piece of ass's flesh; but it smelt so offensively that I turned from it with loathing: he then threw it to the *Yahoo*, by whom it was greedily devoured. He afterwards showed me a wisp of hay, and a fetlock full of oats; but I shook my head, to signify that neither of these were food for me. And indeed I now apprehended that I must absolutely starve, if I did not get to some of my own species; for as to those filthy *Yahoos*, although there were few greater lovers of mankind at that time than myself, yet I confess I never saw any sensitive being so detestable on all accounts; and the more I came near them the more hateful they grew, while I stayed in that country. This the master horse observed by my behaviour, and therefore sent the *Yahoo* back to his kennel. He then put his fore-hoof to his mouth, at which I was much surprised, although he did it with ease, and with a motion that appeared perfectly natural, and made other signs, to know what I would eat; but I could not return him such an answer as he was able to apprehend; and if he had understood me, I did not see how it was possible to contrive any way for finding myself nourishment. While we were thus engaged, I observed a cow passing by, whereupon I pointed to her, and expressed a desire to go and milk her. This had its effect; for he led me back into the house, and ordered a mare-servant to open a room, where a good store of milk lay in earthen and wooden vessels, after a very orderly and cleanly manner. She gave me a large bowlful, of which I drank very heartily, and found myself well refreshed.

About noon, I saw coming towards the house a kind of vehicle drawn like a sledge by four *Yahoos*. There was in it an old steed, who seemed to be of quality; he alighted with his hind-feet forward, having by accident got a hurt in his left fore-foot. He came to dine with our horse, who received him with great civility. They dined in the best room, and had oats boiled in milk for the second course, which the old horse ate warm, but the rest cold. Their mangers were placed circular in the middle of the room, and divided into several partitions, round which they sat on their haunches, upon bosses of straw. In the middle was a large rack, with angles answering to every partition of the manger; so that each horse and mare ate their own hay, and their own mash of oats and milk, with much decency and regularity. The behaviour of the young colt and foal appeared very modest, and that of the master and mistress extremely cheerful and complaisant to their guest. The gray ordered me to stand by him; and much discourse passed between him and his friend concerning me, as I found by the stranger's often looking on me, and the frequent repetition of the word *Yahoo*.

I happened to wear my gloves, which the master gray observing, seemed perplexed, discovering signs of wonder what I had done to my fore-feet. He put his hoof three or four times to them, as if he would signify, that I should reduce them to their former shape, which I presently did, pulling off both my gloves, and putting them into my pocket. This occasioned farther talk; and I saw the company was pleased with my behaviour, whereof I soon found the good effects. I was ordered to speak the few words I understood; and while they were at dinner, the master taught me the names for oats, milk, fire, water, and some others, which I could readily pronounce after him, having from my youth a great facility in learning languages.

When dinner was done, the master horse took me aside, and by signs and words made me understand the concern he was in that I had nothing to eat. Oats in their tongue are called *hlunnh*. This word I pronounced two or three times; for although I had refused them at first, yet, upon second thoughts, I considered that I could contrive to make of them a kind of bread, which might be sufficient, with milk, to keep me alive, till I could make my escape to some other country, and to creatures of my own species. The horse immediately ordered a white mare servant of his family to bring me a good quantity of oats in a sort of wooden tray. These I heated before the fire, as well as I could, and rubbed them till the husks came off, which I made a shift to winnow from the grain. I ground and beat them between two stones; then took water, and made them into a paste or cake, which I toasted at the fire and eat warm with milk. It was at first a very insipid diet, though common enough in many parts of Europe, but grew tolerable by time; and having been often reduced to hard fare in my life, this was not the first experiment I had made how easily nature is satisfied. And I cannot but observe, that I never had one hours sickness while I stayed in this island. It is true, I sometimes made a shift to catch a rabbit, or bird, by springs made of *Yahoo's* hairs; and I often gathered wholesome herbs, which I boiled, and ate as salads with my bread; and now and then, for a rarity, I made a little butter, and drank the whey. I was at first at a great loss for salt, but custom soon reconciled me to the want of it; and I am confident that the frequent use of salt among us is an effect of luxury, and was first introduced only as a provocative to drink, except where it is necessary for preserving flesh in long voyages, or in places remote from great markets; for we observe no animal to be fond of it but man, and as to myself, when I left this country, it was a great while before I could endure the taste of it in anything that I ate.

This is enough to say upon the subject of my diet, wherewith other travellers fill their books, as if the readers were personally concerned whether we fare well or ill. However, it was necessary to mention this matter, lest the world should think it impossible that I could find sustenance for three years in such a country, and among such inhabitants.

When it grew towards evening, the master horse ordered a place for me to lodge in; it was but six yards from the house and separated from the stable of the *Yahoos*. Here I got some straw, and covering myself with my own clothes, slept very sound. But I was in a short time better accommodated, as the reader shall know hereafter, when I come to treat more particularly about my way of living.

CHAPTER 3: THE AUTHOR STUDIES TO LEARN THE LANGUAGE. THE HOUYHNHNM, HIS MASTER, ASSISTS IN TEACHING HIM. THE LANGUAGE DESCRIBED. SEVERAL HOUYHNHNMS OF QUALITY COME OUT OF CURIOSITY TO SEE THE AUTHOR. HE GIVES HIS MASTER A SHORT ACCOUNT OF HIS VOYAGE.

My principal endeavour was to learn the language, which my master (for so I shall henceforth call him), and his children, and every servant of his house, were desirous to teach me; for they looked upon it as a prodigy, that a brute animal should discover such marks of a rational creature. I pointed to every thing, and inquired the name of it, which I wrote down in my journal-book when I was alone, and corrected my bad accent by desiring those of the family to pronounce it often. In this employment, a sorrel nag, one of the under-servants, was very ready to assist me.

In speaking, they pronounced through the nose and throat, and their language approaches nearest to the High-Dutch, or German, of any I know in Europe; but is much more graceful and significant. The emperor Charles V. made almost the same observation, when he said "that if he were to speak to his horse, it should be in High-Dutch."

The curiosity and impatience of my master were so great, that he spent many hours of his leisure to instruct me. He was convinced (as he afterwards told me) that I must be a *Yahoo*; but my teachableness, civility, and cleanliness, astonished him; which were qualities altogether opposite to those animals. He was most perplexed about my clothes, reasoning sometimes with himself, whether they were a part of my body: for I never pulled them off till the family were asleep, and got them on before they waked in the morning. My master was eager to learn "whence I came; how I acquired those appearances of reason, which I discovered in all my actions; and to know my story from my own mouth, which he hoped he should soon do by the great proficiency I made in learning and pronouncing their words and sentences." To help my memory, I formed all I learned into the English alphabet, and writ the words down, with the translations. This last, after some time, I ventured to do in my master's presence. It cost me much trouble to explain to him what I was doing; for the inhabitants have not the least idea of books or literature.

In about ten weeks time, I was able to understand most of his questions; and in three months, could give him some tolerable answers. He was extremely curious to know "from what part of the country I came, and how I was taught to imitate a rational creature; because the *Yahoos* (whom he saw I exactly resembled in my head, hands, and face, that were only visible), with some appearance of cunning, and the strongest disposition to mischief, were observed to be the most unteachable of all brutes." I answered, "that I came over the sea, from a far place, with many others of my own kind, in a great hollow vessel made of the bodies of trees: that my companions forced me to land on this coast, and then left me to shift for myself." It was with some difficulty, and by the help of many signs, that I brought him to understand me. He replied, "that I must needs be mistaken, or that I said the thing which was not;" for they have no word in their language to express lying or falsehood. "He knew it was impossible that there could be a country beyond the sea, or that a parcel of brutes could move a wooden vessel whither they pleased upon water. He was sure no *Houyhnhnm* alive could make such a vessel, nor would trust *Yahoos* to manage it."

The word *Houyhnhnm*, in their tongue, signifies a *horse*, and, in its etymology, the *perfection of nature*. I told my master, "that I was at a loss for expression, but would improve as fast as I could; and hoped, in a short time, I should be able to tell him wonders." He was pleased to direct his own mare, his colt, and foal, and the servants of the family, to take all opportunities of instructing me; and every day, for two or three hours, he was at the same pains himself. Several horses and mares of quality in the neighbourhood came often to our house, upon the report spread of "a wonderful *Yahoo*, that could speak like a *Houyhnhnm*, and seemed, in his words and actions, to discover some glimmerings of reason." These delighted to converse with me: they put many questions, and received such answers as I was able to return. By all these advantages I made so great a progress, that, in five months from my arrival I understood whatever was spoken, and could express myself tolerably well.

The *Houyhnhnms*, who came to visit my master out of a design of seeing and talking with me, could hardly believe me to be a right *Yahoo*, because my body had a different covering from others of my kind. They were astonished to observe me without the usual hair or skin, except on my head, face, and hands; but I discovered that secret to my master upon an accident which happened about a fortnight before.

I have already told the reader, that every night, when the family were gone to bed, it was my custom to strip, and cover myself with my clothes. It happened, one morning early, that my master sent for me by the sorrel nag, who was his valet. When he came I was fast asleep, my clothes fallen off on one side, and my shirt above my waist. I awaked at the noise he made, and observed him to deliver his message in some disorder; after which he went to my master, and in a great fright gave him a very confused account of what he had seen. This I presently discovered, for, going as soon as I was dressed to pay my attendance upon his honour, he asked me "the meaning of what his servant had reported, that I was not the same thing when I slept, as I appeared to be at other times; that his vale assured him, some part of me was white, some yellow, at least not so white, and some brown."

I had hitherto concealed the secret of my dress, in order to distinguish myself, as much as possible, from that cursed race of *Yahoos*; but now I found it in vain to do so any longer. Besides, I considered that my clothes and shoes would soon wear out, which already were in a declining condition, and must be supplied by some contrivance from the hides of *Yahoos*, or other brutes; whereby the whole secret would be known. I therefore told my master, "that in the country whence I came, those of my kind always covered their bodies with the hairs of certain animals prepared by art, as well for decency as to avoid the inclemencies of air, both hot and cold; of which, as to my own person, I would give him immediate conviction, if he pleased to command me: only desiring his excuse, if I did not expose those parts that nature taught us to conceal." He said, "my discourse was all very strange, but especially the last part; for he could not understand, why nature should teach us to conceal what nature had given; that neither himself nor family were ashamed of any parts of their bodies; but, however, I might do as I pleased." Whereupon I first unbuttoned my coat, and pulled it off. I did the same with my waistcoat. I drew off my shoes, stockings, and breeches. I let my shirt down to my waist, and drew up the bottom; fastening it like a girdle about my middle, to hide my nakedness.

My master observed the whole performance with great signs of curiosity and admiration. He took up all my clothes in his pastern, one piece after another, and examined them diligently; he then stroked my body very gently, and looked round me several times; after which, he said, it was plain I must be a perfect *Yahoo*; but that I differed very much from the rest of my species in the softness, whiteness, and smoothness of my skin; my want of hair in several parts of my body; the shape and shortness of my claws behind and before; and my affectation of walking continually on my two hinder feet. He desired to see no more; and gave me leave to put on my clothes again, for I was shuddering with cold.

I expressed my uneasiness at his giving me so often the appellation of *Yahoo*, an odious animal, for which I had so utter a hatred and contempt: I begged he would forbear applying that word to me, and make the same order in his family and among his friends whom he suffered to see me. I requested likewise, "that the secret of my having a false covering to my body, might be known to none but himself, at least as long as my present clothing should last; for as to what the sorrel nag, his valet, had observed, his honour might command him to conceal it."

All this my master very graciously consented to; and thus the secret was kept till my clothes began to wear out, which I was forced to supply by several contrivances that shall hereafter be mentioned. In the meantime, he desired "I would go on with my utmost diligence to learn their language, because he was more astonished at my capacity for speech and reason, than at the figure of my body, whether it were covered or not;" adding, "that he waited with some impatience to hear the wonders which I promised to tell him."

Thenceforward he doubled the pains he had been at to instruct me: he brought me into all company, and made them treat me with civility; "because," as he told them, privately, "this would put me into good humour, and make me more diverting."

Every day, when I waited on him, beside the trouble he was at in teaching, he would ask me several questions concerning myself, which I answered as well as I could, and by these means he had already received some general ideas, though very imperfect. It would be tedious to relate the several steps by which I advanced to a more regular conversation; but the first account I gave of myself in any order and length was to this purpose:

"That I came from a very far country, as I already had attempted to tell him, with about fifty more of my own species; that we travelled upon the seas in a great hollow vessel made of wood, and larger than his honour's house. I described the ship to him in the best terms I could, and explained, by the help of my handkerchief displayed, how it was driven forward by the wind. That upon a quarrel among us, I was set on shore on this coast, where I walked forward, without knowing whither, till he delivered me from the persecution of those execrable *Yahoos*." He asked me, "who made the ship, and how it was possible that the *Houyhnhnms* of my country would leave it to the management of brutes?" My answer was, "that I durst proceed no further in my relation, unless he would give me his word and honour that he would not be offended, and then I would tell him the wonders I had so often promised." He agreed; and I went on by assuring him, that the ship was made by creatures like myself; who, in all the countries I had travelled, as well as in my own, were the only governing rational animals; and that upon my arrival hither, I was as much astonished to see the *Houyhnhnms* act like rational beings, as he, or his friends, could be, in finding some marks of reason in a creature he was pleased to call a *Yahoo*; to which I owned my resemblance in every part, but could not account for their degenerate and brutal nature. I said farther, "that if good fortune ever restored me to my native country, to relate my travels hither, as I resolved to do, everybody would believe, that I said the thing that was not, that I invented the story out of my own head; and (with all possible respect to himself, his family, and friends, and under his promise of not being offended) our countrymen would hardly think it probable that a *Houyhnhnm* should be the presiding creature of a nation, and a *Yahoo* the brute."

CHAPTER 4: THE HOUYHNHNM'S NOTION OF TRUTH AND
FALSEHOOD. THE AUTHOR'S DISCOURSE DISAPPROVED BY
HIS MASTER. THE AUTHOR GIVES A MORE PARTICULAR
ACCOUNT OF HIMSELF, AND THE ACCIDENTS OF HIS
VOYAGE.

My master heard me with great appearances of uneasiness in his countenance;
because doubting, or not believing, are so little known in this country, that the
inhabitants cannot tell how to behave themselves under such circumstances. And
I remember, in frequent discourses with my master concerning the nature of
manhood in other parts of the world, having occasion to talk of lying and false
representation, it was with much difficulty that he comprehended what I meant,
although he had otherwise a most acute judgment. For he argued thus: "that the
use of speech was to make us understand one another, and to receive information
of facts; now, if any one said the thing which was not, these ends were defeated,
because I cannot properly be said to understand him; and I am so far from
receiving information, that he leaves me worse than in ignorance; for I am led to
believe a thing black, when it is white, and short, when it is long." And these were
all the notions he had concerning that faculty of lying, so perfectly well
understood, and so universally practised, among human creatures.

To return from this digression. When I asserted that the *Yahoos* were the only
governing animals in my country, which my master said was altogether past his
conception, he desired to know, "whether we had *Houyhnhnms* among us, and
what was their employment?" I told him, "we had great numbers; that in summer
they grazed in the fields, and in winter were kept in houses with hay and oats,
where *Yahoo* servants were employed to rub their skins smooth, comb their manes,
pick their feet, serve them with food, and make their beds." "I understand you
well," said my master: "it is now very plain, from all you have spoken, that
whatever share of reason the *Yahoos* pretend to, the *Houyhnhnms* are your masters;
I heartily wish our *Yahoos* would be so tractable." I begged "his honour would
please to excuse me from proceeding any further, because I was very certain that
the account he expected from me would be highly displeasing." But he insisted in
commanding me to let him know the best and the worst. I told him "he should be
obeyed." I owned "that the *Houyhnhnms* among us, whom we called horses, were
the most generous and comely animals we had; that they excelled in strength and
swiftness; and when they belonged to persons of quality, were employed in
travelling, racing, or drawing chariots; they were treated with much kindness and
care, till they fell into diseases, or became foundered in the feet; but then they were
sold, and used to all kind of drudgery till they died; after which their skins were
stripped, and sold for what they were worth, and their bodies left to be devoured

by dogs and birds of prey. But the common race of horses had not so good fortune, being kept by farmers and carriers, and other mean people, who put them to greater labour, and fed them worse." I described, as well as I could, our way of riding; the shape and use of a bridle, a saddle, a spur, and a whip; of harness and wheels. I added, "that we fastened plates of a certain hard substance, called iron, at the bottom of their feet, to preserve their hoofs from being broken by the stony ways, on which we often travelled."

My master, after some expressions of great indignation, wondered "how we dared to venture upon a *Houyhnhnm's* back; for he was sure, that the weakest servant in his house would be able to shake off the strongest *Yahoo*; or by lying down and rolling on his back, squeeze the brute to death." I answered "that our horses were trained up, from three or four years old, to the several uses we intended them for; that if any of them proved intolerably vicious, they were employed for carriages; that they were severely beaten, while they were young, for any mischievous tricks; that the males, designed for the common use of riding or draught, were generally castrated about two years after their birth, to take down their spirits, and make them more tame and gentle; that they were indeed sensible of rewards and punishments; but his honour would please to consider, that they had not the least tincture of reason, any more than the *Yahoos* in this country."

It put me to the pains of many circumlocutions, to give my master a right idea of what I spoke; for their language does not abound in variety of words, because their wants and passions are fewer than among us. But it is impossible to express his noble resentment at our savage treatment of the *Houyhnhnm* race; particularly after I had explained the manner and use of castrating horses among us, to hinder them from propagating their kind, and to render them more servile. He said, "if it were possible there could be any country where *Yahoos* alone were endued with reason, they certainly must be the governing animal; because reason in time will always prevail against brutal strength. But, considering the frame of our bodies, and especially of mine, he thought no creature of equal bulk was so ill-contrived for employing that reason in the common offices of life;" whereupon he desired to know "whether those among whom I lived resembled me, or the *Yahoos* of his country?" I assured him, "that I was as well shaped as most of my age; but the younger, and the females, were much more soft and tender, and the skins of the latter generally as white as milk." He said, "I differed indeed from other *Yahoos*, being much more cleanly, and not altogether so deformed; but, in point of real advantage, he thought I differed for the worse: that my nails were of no use either to my fore or hinder feet; as to my fore feet, he could not properly call them by that name, for he never observed me to walk upon them; that they were too soft to bear the ground; that I generally went with them uncovered; neither was the covering I sometimes wore on them of the same shape, or so strong as that on my feet behind: that I could not walk with any security, for if either of my hinder feet slipped, I must inevitably fall." He then began to find fault with other parts of my body: "the flatness of my face, the prominence of my nose, mine eyes placed directly in front, so that I could not look on either side without turning my head: that I was not able to feed myself, without lifting one of my fore-feet to my mouth: and therefore nature had placed those joints to answer that necessity. He knew not what could be the use of those several clefts and divisions in my feet behind; that these were too soft to bear the hardness and sharpness of stones, without a covering made from the skin of some other brute; that my whole body wanted a fence against heat and cold, which I was forced to put on and off every day, with tediousness and trouble: and lastly, that he observed every animal in this country naturally to abhor the *Yahoos*, whom the weaker avoided, and the stronger drove from them. So that, supposing us to have the gift of reason, he could not see how it were possible to cure that natural antipathy, which every creature discovered against us; nor consequently how we could tame and render them serviceable. However, he would," as he said, "debate the matter no farther, because he was more desirous to know my own story, the country where I was born, and the several actions and events of my life, before I came hither."

I assured him, "how extremely desirous I was that he should be satisfied on every point; but I doubted much, whether it would be possible for me to explain myself on several subjects, whereof his honour could have no conception; because I saw nothing in his country to which I could resemble them; that, however, I would do my best, and strive to express myself by similitudes, humbly desiring his assistance when I wanted proper words;" which he was pleased to promise me.

I said, "my birth was of honest parents, in an island called England; which was remote from his country, as many days' journey as the strongest of his honour's servants could travel in the annual course of the sun; that I was bred a surgeon, whose trade it is to cure wounds and hurts in the body, gotten by accident or violence; that my country was governed by a female man, whom we called queen; that I left it to get riches, whereby I might maintain myself and family, when I should return; that, in my last voyage, I was commander of the ship, and had about fifty *Yahoos* under me, many of which died at sea, and I was forced to supply them by others picked out from several nations; that our ship was twice in danger of being sunk, the first time by a great storm, and the second by striking against a rock." Here my master interposed, by asking me, "how I could persuade strangers, out of different countries, to venture with me, after the losses I had sustained, and the hazards I had run?" I said, "they were fellows of desperate fortunes, forced to fly from the places of their birth on account of their poverty or their crimes. Some were undone by lawsuits; others spent all they had in drinking, whoring, and gaming; others fled for treason; many for murder, theft, poisoning, robbery, perjury, forgery, coining false money, for committing rapes, or sodomy; for flying from their colours, or deserting to the enemy; and most of them had broken prison; none of these durst return to their native countries, for fear of being hanged, or of starving in a jail; and therefore they were under the necessity of seeking a livelihood in other places."

During this discourse, my master was pleased to interrupt me several times. I had made use of many circumlocutions in describing to him the nature of the several crimes for which most of our crew had been forced to fly their country. This labour took up several days' conversation, before he was able to comprehend me. He was wholly at a loss to know what could be the use or necessity of practising those vices. To clear up which, I endeavoured to give some ideas of the desire of power and riches; of the terrible effects of lust, intemperance, malice, and envy. All this I was forced to define and describe by putting cases and making suppositions. After which, like one whose imagination was struck with something never seen or heard of before, he would lift up his eyes with amazement and indignation. Power, government, war, law, punishment, and a thousand other things, had no terms wherein that language could express them, which made the difficulty almost insuperable, to give my master any conception of what I meant. But being of an excellent understanding, much improved by contemplation and converse, he at last arrived at a competent knowledge of what human nature, in our parts of the world, is capable to perform, and desired I would give him some particular account of that land which we call Europe, but especially of my own country.

CHAPTER 5: THE AUTHOR AT HIS MASTER'S COMMAND, INFORMS HIM OF THE STATE OF ENGLAND. THE CAUSES OF WAR AMONG THE PRINCES OF EUROPE. THE AUTHOR BEGINS TO EXPLAIN THE ENGLISH CONSTITUTION.

The reader may please to observe, that the following extract of many conversations I had with my master, contains a summary of the most material points which were discoursed at several times for above two years; his honour often desiring fuller satisfaction, as I farther improved in the *Houyhnhnm* tongue. I laid before him, as well as I could, the whole state of Europe; I discoursed of trade and manufactures, of arts and sciences; and the answers I gave to all the questions he made, as they arose upon several subjects, were a fund of conversation not to be exhausted. But I shall here only set down the substance of what passed between us concerning my own country, reducing it in order as well as I can, without any regard to time or other circumstances, while I strictly adhere to truth. My only concern is, that I shall hardly be able to do justice to my master's arguments and expressions, which must needs suffer by my want of capacity, as well as by a translation into our barbarous English.

In obedience, therefore, to his honour's commands, I related to him the Revolution under the Prince of Orange; the long war with France, entered into by the said prince, and renewed by his successor, the present queen, wherein the greatest powers of Christendom were engaged, and which still continued: I computed, at his request, "that about a million of *Yahoos* might have been killed in the whole progress of it; and perhaps a hundred or more cities taken, and five times as many ships burnt or sunk."

He asked me, "what were the usual causes or motives that made one country go to war with another?" I answered "they were innumerable; but I should only mention a few of the chief. Sometimes the ambition of princes, who never think they have land or people enough to govern; sometimes the corruption of ministers, who engage their master in a war, in order to stifle or divert the clamour of the subjects against their evil administration. Difference in opinions has cost many millions of lives: for instance, whether flesh be bread, or bread be flesh; whether the juice of a certain berry be blood or wine; whether whistling be a vice or a virtue; whether it be better to kiss a post, or throw it into the fire; what is the best colour for a coat, whether black, white, red, or gray; and whether it should be long or short, narrow or wide, dirty or clean; with many more. Neither are any wars so furious and bloody, or of so long a continuance, as those occasioned by difference in opinion, especially if it be in things indifferent.

"Sometimes the quarrel between two princes is to decide which of them shall dispossess a third of his dominions, where neither of them pretend to any right. Sometimes one prince quarrels with another for fear the other should quarrel with him. Sometimes a war is entered upon, because the enemy is too strong; and sometimes, because he is too weak. Sometimes our neighbours want the things which we have, or have the things which we want, and we both fight, till they take ours, or give us theirs. It is a very justifiable cause of a war, to invade a country after the people have been wasted by famine, destroyed by pestilence, or embroiled by factions among themselves. It is justifiable to enter into war against our nearest ally, when one of his towns lies convenient for us, or a territory of land, that would render our dominions round and complete. If a prince sends forces into a nation, where the people are poor and ignorant, he may lawfully put half of them to death, and make slaves of the rest, in order to civilize and reduce them from their barbarous way of living. It is a very kingly, honourable, and frequent practice, when one prince desires the assistance of another, to secure him against an invasion, that the assistant, when he has driven out the invader, should seize on the dominions himself, and kill, imprison, or banish, the prince he came to relieve. Alliance by blood, or marriage, is a frequent cause of war between princes;

and the nearer the kindred is, the greater their disposition to quarrel; poor nations are hungry, and rich nations are proud; and pride and hunger will ever be at variance. For these reasons, the trade of a soldier is held the most honourable of all others; because a soldier is a *Yahoo* hired to kill, in cold blood, as many of his own species, who have never offended him, as possibly he can.

"There is likewise a kind of beggarly princes in Europe, not able to make war by themselves, who hire out their troops to richer nations, for so much a day to each man; of which they keep three-fourths to themselves, and it is the best part of their maintenance: such are those in many northern parts of Europe."

"What you have told me," said my master, "upon the subject of war, does indeed discover most admirably the effects of that reason you pretend to: however, it is happy that the shame is greater than the danger; and that nature has left you utterly incapable of doing much mischief. For, your mouths lying flat with your faces, you can hardly bite each other to any purpose, unless by consent. Then as to the claws upon your feet before and behind, they are so short and tender, that one of our *Yahoos* would drive a dozen of yours before him. And therefore, in recounting the numbers of those who have been killed in battle, I cannot but think you have said the thing which is not."

I could not forbear shaking my head, and smiling a little at his ignorance. And being no stranger to the art of war, I gave him a description of cannons, culverins, muskets, carabines, pistols, bullets, powder, swords, bayonets, battles, sieges, retreats, attacks, undermines, countermines, bombardments, sea fights, ships sunk with a thousand men, twenty thousand killed on each side, dying groans, limbs flying in the air, smoke, noise, confusion, trampling to death under horses' feet, flight, pursuit, victory; fields strewed with carcases, left for food to dogs and wolves and birds of prey; plundering, stripping, ravishing, burning, and destroying. And to set forth the valour of my own dear countrymen, I assured him, "that I had seen them blow up a hundred enemies at once in a siege, and as many in a ship, and beheld the dead bodies drop down in pieces from the clouds, to the great diversion of the spectators."

I was going on to more particulars, when my master commanded me silence. He said, "whoever understood the nature of *Yahoos*, might easily believe it possible for so vile an animal to be capable of every action I had named, if their strength and cunning equalled their malice. But as my discourse had increased his abhorrence of the whole species, so he found it gave him a disturbance in his mind to which he was wholly a stranger before. He thought his ears, being used to such abominable words, might, by degrees, admit them with less detestation: that although he hated the *Yahoos* of this country, yet he no more blamed them for their odious qualities, than he did a *gnnayh* (a bird of prey) for its cruelty, or a sharp stone for cutting his hoof. But when a creature pretending to reason could be capable of such enormities, he dreaded lest the corruption of that faculty might be worse than brutality itself. He seemed therefore confident, that, instead of reason we were only possessed of some quality fitted to increase our natural vices; as the reflection from a troubled stream returns the image of an ill shapen body, not only larger but more distorted."

He added, "that he had heard too much upon the subject of war, both in this and some former discourses. There was another point, which a little perplexed him at present. I had informed him, that some of our crew left their country on account of being ruined by law; that I had already explained the meaning of the word; but he was at a loss how it should come to pass, that the law, which was intended for every man's preservation, should be any man's ruin. Therefore he desired to be further satisfied what I meant by law, and the dispensers thereof, according to the present practice in my own country; because he thought nature and reason were sufficient guides for a reasonable animal, as we pretended to be, in showing us what he ought to do, and what to avoid."

I assured his honour, "that the law was a science in which I had not much conversed, further than by employing advocates, in vain, upon some injustices that had been done me: however, I would give him all the satisfaction I was able."

I said, "there was a society of men among us, bred up from their youth in the art of proving, by words multiplied for the purpose, that white is black, and black is white, according as they are paid. To this society all the rest of the people are slaves. For example, if my neighbour has a mind to my cow, he has a lawyer to prove that he ought to have my cow from me. I must then hire another to defend my right, it being against all rules of law that any man should be allowed to speak for himself. Now, in this case, I, who am the right owner, lie under two great disadvantages: first, my lawyer, being practised almost from his cradle in defending falsehood, is quite out of his element when he would be an advocate for justice, which is an unnatural office he always attempts with great awkwardness, if not with ill-will. The second disadvantage is, that my lawyer must proceed with great caution, or else he will be reprimanded by the judges, and abhorred by his brethren, as one that would lessen the practice of the law. And therefore I have but two methods to preserve my cow. The first is, to gain over my adversary's lawyer with a double fee, who will then betray his client by insinuating that he hath justice on his side. The second way is for my lawyer to make my cause appear as unjust as he can, by allowing the cow to belong to my adversary: and this, if it be skilfully done, will certainly bespeak the favour of the bench. Now your honour is to know, that these judges are persons appointed to decide all controversies of property, as well as for the trial of criminals, and picked out from the most dexterous lawyers, who are grown old or lazy; and having been biassed all their lives against truth and equity, lie under such a fatal necessity of favouring fraud, perjury, and oppression, that I have known some of them refuse a large bribe from the side where justice lay, rather than injure the faculty, by doing any thing unbecoming their nature or their office.

"It is a maxim among these lawyers that whatever has been done before, may legally be done again: and therefore they take special care to record all the decisions formerly made against common justice, and the general reason of mankind. These, under the name of precedents, they produce as authorities to justify the most iniquitous opinions; and the judges never fail of directing accordingly.

"In pleading, they studiously avoid entering into the merits of the cause; but are loud, violent, and tedious, in dwelling upon all circumstances which are not to the purpose. For instance, in the case already mentioned; they never desire to know what claim or title my adversary has to my cow; but whether the said cow were red or black; her horns long or short; whether the field I graze her in be round or square; whether she was milked at home or abroad; what diseases she is subject to, and the like; after which they consult precedents, adjourn the cause from time to time, and in ten, twenty, or thirty years, come to an issue.

"It is likewise to be observed, that this society has a peculiar cant and jargon of their own, that no other mortal can understand, and wherein all their laws are written, which they take special care to multiply; whereby they have wholly confounded the very essence of truth and falsehood, of right and wrong; so that it will take thirty years to decide, whether the field left me by my ancestors for six generations belongs to me, or to a stranger three hundred miles off.

"In the trial of persons accused for crimes against the state, the method is much more short and commendable: the judge first sends to sound the disposition of those in power, after which he can easily hang or save a criminal, strictly preserving all due forms of law."

Here my master interposing, said, "it was a pity, that creatures endowed with such prodigious abilities of mind, as these lawyers, by the description I gave of them, must certainly be, were not rather encouraged to be instructors of others in wisdom and knowledge." In answer to which I assured his honour, "that in all points out of their own trade, they were usually the most ignorant and stupid generation among us, the most despicable in common conversation, avowed enemies to all knowledge and learning, and equally disposed to pervert the general reason of mankind in every other subject of discourse as in that of their own profession."

CHAPTER 6: A CONTINUATION OF THE STATE OF ENGLAND UNDER QUEEN ANNE. THE CHARACTER OF A FIRST MINISTER OF STATE IN EUROPEAN COURTS.

My master was yet wholly at a loss to understand what motives could incite this race of lawyers to perplex, disquiet, and weary themselves, and engage in a confederacy of injustice, merely for the sake of injuring their fellow-animals; neither could he comprehend what I meant in saying, they did it for hire. Whereupon I was at much pains to describe to him the use of money, the materials it was made of, and the value of the metals; "that when a *Yahoo* had got a great store of this precious substance, he was able to purchase whatever he had a mind to; the finest clothing, the noblest houses, great tracts of land, the most costly meats and drinks, and have his choice of the most beautiful females. Therefore since money alone was able to perform all these feats, our *Yahoos* thought they could never have enough of it to spend, or to save, as they found themselves inclined, from their natural bent either to profusion or avarice; that the rich man enjoyed the fruit of the poor man's labour, and the latter were a thousand to one in proportion to the former; that the bulk of our people were forced to live miserably, by labouring every day for small wages, to make a few live plentifully."

I enlarged myself much on these, and many other particulars to the same purpose; but his honour was still to seek; for he went upon a supposition, that all animals had a title to their share in the productions of the earth, and especially those who presided over the rest. Therefore he desired I would let him know, "what these costly meats were, and how any of us happened to want them?" Whereupon I enumerated as many sorts as came into my head, with the various methods of dressing them, which could not be done without sending vessels by sea to every part of the world, as well for liquors to drink as for sauces and innumerable other conveniences. I assured him "that this whole globe of earth must be at least three times gone round before one of our better female *Yahoos* could get her breakfast, or a cup to put it in." He said "that must needs be a miserable country which cannot furnish food for its own inhabitants. But what he chiefly wondered at was, how such vast tracts of ground as I described should be wholly without fresh water, and the people put to the necessity of sending over the sea for drink." I replied "that England (the dear place of my nativity) was computed to produce three times the quantity of food more than its inhabitants are able to consume, as well as liquors extracted from grain, or pressed out of the fruit of certain trees, which made excellent drink, and the same proportion in every other convenience of life. But, in order to feed the luxury and intemperance of the males, and the vanity of the females, we sent away the greatest part of our necessary things to other countries, whence, in return, we brought the materials of diseases, folly, and vice, to spend among ourselves. Hence it follows of necessity, that vast numbers of our people are compelled to seek their livelihood by begging, robbing, stealing, cheating, pimping, flattering, suborning, forswearing, forging, gaming, lying, fawning, hectoring, voting, scribbling, star-gazing, poisoning, whoring, canting, libelling, freethinking, and the like occupations:" every one of which terms I was at much pains to make him understand.

"That wine was not imported among us from foreign countries to supply the want of water or other drinks, but because it was a sort of liquid which made us merry by putting us out of our senses, diverted all melancholy thoughts, begat wild extravagant imaginations in the brain, raised our hopes and banished our fears, suspended every office of reason for a time, and deprived us of the use of our limbs, till we fell into a profound sleep; although it must be confessed, that we always awaked sick and dispirited; and that the use of this liquor filled us with diseases which made our lives uncomfortable and short.

"But beside all this, the bulk of our people supported themselves by furnishing the necessities or conveniences of life to the rich and to each other. For instance, when I am at home, and dressed as I ought to be, I carry on my body the workmanship of a hundred tradesmen; the building and furniture of my house employ as many more, and five times the number to adorn my wife."

I was going on to tell him of another sort of people, who get their livelihood by attending the sick, having, upon some occasions, informed his honour that many of my crew had died of diseases. But here it was with the utmost difficulty that I brought him to apprehend what I meant. "He could easily conceive, that a *Houyhnhnm*, grew weak and heavy a few days before his death, or by some accident might hurt a limb; but that nature, who works all things to perfection, should suffer any pains to breed in our bodies, he thought impossible, and desired to know the reason of so unaccountable an evil."

I told him "we fed on a thousand things which operated contrary to each other; that we ate when we were not hungry, and drank without the provocation of thirst; that we sat whole nights drinking strong liquors, without eating a bit, which disposed us to sloth, inflamed our bodies, and precipitated or prevented digestion; that prostitute female *Yahoos* acquired a certain malady, which bred rottenness in the bones of those who fell into their embraces; that this, and many other diseases, were propagated from father to son; so that great numbers came into the world with complicated maladies upon them; that it would be endless to give him a catalogue of all diseases incident to human bodies, for they would not be fewer than five or six hundred, spread over every limb and joint—in short, every part, external and intestine, having diseases appropriated to itself. To remedy which, there was a sort of people bred up among us in the profession, or pretence, of curing the sick. And because I had some skill in the faculty, I would, in gratitude to his honour, let him know the whole mystery and method by which they proceed.

"Their fundamental is, that all diseases arise from repletion; whence they conclude, that a great evacuation of the body is necessary, either through the natural passage or upwards at the mouth. Their next business is from herbs, minerals, gums, oils, shells, salts, juices, sea-weed, excrements, barks of trees, serpents, toads, frogs, spiders, dead men's flesh and bones, birds, beasts, and fishes, to form a composition, for smell and taste, the most abominable, nauseous, and detestable, they can possibly contrive, which the stomach immediately rejects with loathing, and this they call a vomit; or else, from the same store-house, with some other poisonous additions, they command us to take in at the orifice above or below (just as the physician then happens to be disposed) a medicine equally annoying and disgustful to the bowels; which, relaxing the belly, drives down all before it; and this they call a purge, or a clyster. For nature (as the physicians allege) having intended the superior anterior orifice only for the intromission of solids and liquids, and the inferior posterior for ejection, these artists ingeniously considering that in all diseases nature is forced out of her seat, therefore, to replace her in it, the body must be treated in a manner directly contrary, by interchanging the use of each orifice; forcing solids and liquids in at the anus, and making evacuations at the mouth.

"But, besides real diseases, we are subject to many that are only imaginary, for which the physicians have invented imaginary cures; these have their several names, and so have the drugs that are proper for them; and with these our female *Yahoos* are always infested.

"One great excellency in this tribe, is their skill at prognostics, wherein they seldom fail; their predictions in real diseases, when they rise to any degree of malignity, generally portending death, which is always in their power, when recovery is not: and therefore, upon any unexpected signs of amendment, after they have pronounced their sentence, rather than be accused as false prophets, they know how to approve their sagacity to the world, by a seasonable dose.

"They are likewise of special use to husbands and wives who are grown weary of their mates; to eldest sons, to great ministers of state, and often to princes."

I had formerly, upon occasion, discoursed with my master upon the nature of government in general, and particularly of our own excellent constitution, deservedly the wonder and envy of the whole world. But having here accidentally mentioned a minister of state, he commanded me, some time after, to inform him, "what species of *Yahoo* I particularly meant by that appellation."

I told him, "that a first or chief minister of state, who was the person I intended to describe, was the creature wholly exempt from joy and grief, love and hatred, pity and anger; at least, makes use of no other passions, but a violent desire of wealth, power, and titles; that he applies his words to all uses, except to the indication of his mind; that he never tells a truth but with an intent that you should take it for a lie; nor a lie, but with a design that you should take it for a truth; that those he speaks worst of behind their backs are in the surest way of preferment; and whenever he begins to praise you to others, or to yourself, you are from that day forlorn. The worst mark you can receive is a promise, especially when it is confirmed with an oath; after which, every wise man retires, and gives over all hopes.

"There are three methods, by which a man may rise to be chief minister. The first is, by knowing how, with prudence, to dispose of a wife, a daughter, or a sister; the second, by betraying or undermining his predecessor; and the third is, by a furious zeal, in public assemblies, against the corruptions of the court. But a wise prince would rather choose to employ those who practise the last of these methods; because such zealots prove always the most obsequious and subservient to the will and passions of their master. That these ministers, having all employments at their disposal, preserve themselves in power, by bribing the majority of a senate or great council; and at last, by an expedient, called an act of indemnity" (whereof I described the nature to him), "they secure themselves from after-reckonings, and retire from the public laden with the spoils of the nation.

"The palace of a chief minister is a seminary to breed up others in his own trade: the pages, lackeys, and porters, by imitating their master, become ministers of state in their several districts, and learn to excel in the three principal ingredients, of insolence, lying, and bribery. Accordingly, they have a subaltern court paid to them by persons of the best rank; and sometimes by the force of dexterity and impudence, arrive, through several gradations, to be successors to their lord.

"He is usually governed by a decayed wench, or favourite footman, who are the tunnels through which all graces are conveyed, and may properly be called, in the last resort, the governors of the kingdom."

One day, in discourse, my master, having heard me mention the nobility of my country, was pleased to make me a compliment which I could not pretend to deserve: "that he was sure I must have been born of some noble family, because I far exceeded in shape, colour, and cleanliness, all the *Yahoos* of his nation, although I seemed to fail in strength and agility, which must be imputed to my different way of living from those other brutes; and besides I was not only endowed with the faculty of speech, but likewise with some rudiments of reason, to a degree that, with all his acquaintance, I passed for a prodigy."

He made me observe, "that among the *Houyhnhnms*, the white, the sorrel, and the iron-gray, were not so exactly shaped as the bay, the dapple-gray, and the black;

nor born with equal talents of mind, or a capacity to improve them; and therefore continued always in the condition of servants, without ever aspiring to match out of their own race, which in that country would be reckoned monstrous and unnatural."

I made his honour my most humble acknowledgments for the good opinion he was pleased to conceive of me, but assured him at the same time, "that my birth was of the lower sort, having been born of plain honest parents, who were just able to give me a tolerable education; that nobility, among us, was altogether a different thing from the idea he had of it; that our young noblemen are bred from their childhood in idleness and luxury; that, as soon as years will permit, they consume their vigour, and contract odious diseases among lewd females; and when their fortunes are almost ruined, they marry some woman of mean birth, disagreeable person, and unsound constitution (merely for the sake of money), whom they hate and despise. That the productions of such marriages are generally scrofulous, rickety, or deformed children; by which means the family seldom continues above three generations, unless the wife takes care to provide a healthy father, among her neighbours or domestics, in order to improve and continue the breed. That a weak diseased body, a meagre countenance, and sallow complexion, are the true marks of noble blood; and a healthy robust appearance is so disgraceful in a man of quality, that the world concludes his real father to have been a groom or a coachman. The imperfections of his mind run parallel with those of his body, being a composition of spleen, dullness, ignorance, caprice, sensuality, and pride.

"Without the consent of this illustrious body, no law can be enacted, repealed, or altered: and these nobles have likewise the decision of all our possessions, without appeal."[1]

CHAPTER 7: THE AUTHOR'S GREAT LOVE OF HIS NATIVE COUNTRY. HIS MASTER'S OBSERVATIONS UPON THE CONSTITUTION AND ADMINISTRATION OF ENGLAND, AS DESCRIBED BY THE AUTHOR, WITH PARALLEL CASES AND COMPARISONS. HIS MASTER'S OBSERVATIONS UPON HUMAN NATURE.

The reader may be disposed to wonder how I could prevail on myself to give so free a representation of my own species, among a race of mortals who are already too apt to conceive the vilest opinion of humankind, from that entire congruity between me and their *Yahoos*. But I must freely confess, that the many virtues of those excellent quadrupeds, placed in opposite view to human corruptions, had so far opened my eyes and enlarged my understanding, that I began to view the actions and passions of man in a very different light, and to think the honour of my own kind not worth managing; which, besides, it was impossible for me to do, before a person of so acute a judgment as my master, who daily convinced me of a thousand faults in myself, whereof I had not the least perception before, and which, with us, would never be numbered even among human infirmities. I had likewise learned, from his example, an utter detestation of all falsehood or disguise; and truth appeared so amiable to me, that I determined upon sacrificing every thing to it.

Let me deal so candidly with the reader as to confess that there was yet a much stronger motive for the freedom I took in my representation of things. I had not yet been a year in this country before I contracted such a love and veneration for the inhabitants, that I entered on a firm resolution never to return to humankind, but to pass the rest of my life among these admirable *Houyhnhnms*, in the contemplation and practice of every virtue, where I could have no example or incitement to vice. But it was decreed by fortune, my perpetual enemy, that so great a felicity should not fall to my share. However, it is now some comfort to reflect, that in what I said of my countrymen, I extenuated their faults as much as I durst before so strict an examiner; and upon every article gave as favourable a turn as the matter would bear. For, indeed, who is there alive that will not be swayed by his bias and partiality to the place of his birth?

I have related the substance of several conversations I had with my master during the greatest part of the time I had the honour to be in his service; but have, indeed, for brevity sake, omitted much more than is here set down.

When I had answered all his questions, and his curiosity seemed to be fully satisfied, he sent for me one morning early, and commanded me to sit down at some distance (an honour which he had never before conferred upon me). He said, "he had been very seriously considering my whole story, as far as it related both to myself and my country; that he looked upon us as a sort of animals, to whose share, by what accident he could not conjecture, some small pittance of reason had fallen, whereof we made no other use, than by its assistance, to aggravate our natural corruptions, and to acquire new ones, which nature had not given us; that we disarmed ourselves of the few abilities she had bestowed; had been very successful in multiplying our original wants, and seemed to spend our whole lives in vain endeavours to supply them by our own inventions; that, as to myself, it was manifest I had neither the strength nor agility of a common *Yahoo*; that I walked infirmly on my hinder feet; had found out a contrivance to make my claws of no use or defence, and to remove the hair from my chin, which was intended as a shelter from the sun and the weather: lastly, that I could neither run with speed, nor climb trees like my brethren," as he called them, "the *Yahoos* in his country.

"That our institutions of government and law were plainly owing to our gross defects in reason, and by consequence in virtue; because reason alone is sufficient to govern a rational creature; which was, therefore, a character we had no pretence to challenge, even from the account I had given of my own people; although he manifestly perceived, that, in order to favour them, I had concealed many particulars, and often said the thing which was not.

"He was the more confirmed in this opinion, because, he observed, that as I agreed in every feature of my body with other *Yahoos*, except where it was to my real disadvantage in point of strength, speed, and activity, the shortness of my claws, and some other particulars where nature had no part; so from the representation I had given him of our lives, our manners, and our actions, he found as near a resemblance in the disposition of our minds." He said, "the *Yahoos* were known to hate one another, more than they did any different species of animals; and the reason usually assigned was, the odiousness of their own shapes, which all could see in the rest, but not in themselves. He had therefore begun to think it not unwise in us to cover our bodies, and by that invention conceal many of our deformities from each other, which would else be hardly supportable. But he now found he had been mistaken, and that the dissensions of those brutes in his country were owing to the same cause with ours, as I had described them. For if," said he, "you throw among five *Yahoos* as much food as would be sufficient for fifty, they will, instead of eating peaceably, fall together by the ears, each single one impatient to have all to itself; and therefore a servant was usually employed to stand by while they were feeding abroad, and those kept at home were tied at a distance from each other: that if a cow died of age or accident, before a *Houyhnhnm* could secure it for his own *Yahoos*, those in the neighbourhood would come in herds to seize it, and then would ensue such a battle as I had described, with terrible wounds made by their claws on both sides, although they seldom were able to kill one another, for want of such convenient instruments of death as we had invented. At other times, the like battles have been fought between the *Yahoos* of several neighbourhoods, without any visible cause; those of one district watching all opportunities to surprise the next, before they are prepared. But if they find their project has miscarried, they return home, and, for want of enemies, engage in what I call a civil war among themselves.

"That in some fields of his country there are certain shining stones of several colours, whereof the *Yahoos* are violently fond: and when part of these stones is fixed in the earth, as it sometimes happens, they will dig with their claws for whole days to get them out; then carry them away, and hide them by heaps in their kennels; but still looking round with great caution, for fear their comrades should find out their treasure." My master said, "he could never discover the reason of this unnatural appetite, or how these stones could be of any use to a *Yahoo*; but now he believed it might proceed from the same principle of avarice which I had ascribed to mankind. That he had once, by way of experiment, privately removed a heap of these stones from the place where one of his *Yahoos* had buried it; whereupon the sordid animal, missing his treasure, by his loud lamenting brought the whole herd to the place, there miserably howled, then fell to biting and tearing the rest, began to pine away, would neither eat, nor sleep, nor work, till he ordered a servant privately to convey the stones into the same hole, and hide them as before; which, when his *Yahoo* had found, he presently recovered his spirits and good humour, but took good care to remove them to a better hiding place, and has ever since been a very serviceable brute."

My master further assured me, which I also observed myself, "that in the fields where the shining stones abound, the fiercest and most frequent battles are fought, occasioned by perpetual inroads of the neighbouring *Yahoos*."

He said, "it was common, when two *Yahoos* discovered such a stone in a field, and were contending which of them should be the proprietor, a third would take the advantage, and carry it away from them both;" which my master would needs contend to have some kind of resemblance with our suits at law; wherein I thought it for our credit not to undeceive him; since the decision he mentioned was much more equitable than many decrees among us; because the plaintiff and defendant there lost nothing beside the stone they contended for: whereas our courts of equity would never have dismissed the cause, while either of them had any thing left.

My master, continuing his discourse, said, "there was nothing that rendered the *Yahoos* more odious, than their undistinguishing appetite to devour every thing that came in their way, whether herbs, roots, berries, the corrupted flesh of animals, or all mingled together: and it was peculiar in their temper, that they were fonder of what they could get by rapine or stealth, at a greater distance, than much better food provided for them at home. If their prey held out, they would eat till they were ready to burst; after which, nature had pointed out to them a certain root that gave them a general evacuation.

"There was also another kind of root, very juicy, but somewhat rare and difficult to be found, which the *Yahoos* sought for with much eagerness, and would suck it with great delight; it produced in them the same effects that wine has upon us. It would make them sometimes hug, and sometimes tear one another; they would howl, and grin, and chatter, and reel, and tumble, and then fall asleep in the mud."

I did indeed observe that the *Yahoos* were the only animals in this country subject to any diseases; which, however, were much fewer than horses have among us, and contracted, not by any ill-treatment they meet with, but by the nastiness and greediness of that sordid brute. Neither has their language any more than a general appellation for those maladies, which is borrowed from the name of the beast, and called *hnea-yahoo*, or *Yahoo's evil*; and the cure prescribed is a mixture of their own dung and urine, forcibly put down the *Yahoo's* throat. This I have since often known to have been taken with success, and do here freely recommend it to my countrymen for the public good, as an admirable specific against all diseases produced by repletion.

"As to learning, government, arts, manufactures, and the like," my master confessed, "he could find little or no resemblance between the *Yahoos* of that country and those in ours; for he only meant to observe what parity there was in our natures. He had heard, indeed, some curious *Houyhnhnms* observe, that in most herds there was a sort of ruling *Yahoo* (as among us there is generally some leading or principal stag in a park), who was always more deformed in body, and mischievous in disposition, than any of the rest; that this leader had usually a favourite as like himself as he could get, whose employment was to lick his master's feet and posteriors, and drive the female *Yahoos* to his kennel; for which he was now and then rewarded with a piece of ass's flesh. This favourite is hated by the whole herd, and therefore, to protect himself, keeps always near the person of his leader. He usually continues in office till a worse can be found; but the very moment he is discarded, his successor, at the head of all the *Yahoos* in that district, young and old, male and female, come in a body, and discharge their excrements upon him from head to foot. But how far this might be applicable to our courts, and favourites, and ministers of state, my master said I could best determine."

I durst make no return to this malicious insinuation, which debased human understanding below the sagacity of a common hound, who has judgment enough to distinguish and follow the cry of the ablest dog in the pack, without being ever mistaken.

My master told me, "there were some qualities remarkable in the *Yahoos*, which he had not observed me to mention, or at least very slightly, in the accounts I had given of humankind." He said, "those animals, like other brutes, had their females in common; but in this they differed, that the she *Yahoo* would admit the males while she was pregnant; and that the hes would quarrel and fight with the females, as fiercely as with each other; both which practices were such degrees of infamous brutality, as no other sensitive creature ever arrived at.

"Another thing he wondered at in the *Yahoos*, was their strange disposition to nastiness and dirt; whereas there appears to be a natural love of cleanliness in all other animals." As to the two former accusations, I was glad to let them pass without any reply, because I had not a word to offer upon them in defence of my species, which otherwise I certainly had done from my own inclinations. But I could have easily vindicated humankind from the imputation of singularity upon the last article, if there had been any swine in that country (as unluckily for me there were not), which, although it may be a sweeter quadruped than a *Yahoo*, cannot, I humbly conceive, in justice, pretend to more cleanliness; and so his honour himself must have owned, if he had seen their filthy way of feeding, and their custom of wallowing and sleeping in the mud.

My master likewise mentioned another quality which his servants had discovered in several Yahoos, and to him was wholly unaccountable. He said, "a fancy would sometimes take a *Yahoo* to retire into a corner, to lie down, and howl, and groan, and spurn away all that came near him, although he were young and fat, wanted neither food nor water, nor did the servant imagine what could possibly ail him. And the only remedy they found was, to set him to hard work, after which he would infallibly come to himself." To this I was silent out of partiality to my own kind; yet here I could plainly discover the true seeds of spleen, which only seizes on the lazy, the luxurious, and the rich; who, if they were forced to undergo the same regimen, I would undertake for the cure.

His honour had further observed, "that a female *Yahoo* would often stand behind a bank or a bush, to gaze on the young males passing by, and then appear, and hide, using many antic gestures and grimaces, at which time it was observed that she had a most offensive smell; and when any of the males advanced, would slowly retire, looking often back, and with a counterfeit show of fear, run off into some convenient place, where she knew the male would follow her.

"At other times, if a female stranger came among them, three or four of her own sex would get about her, and stare, and chatter, and grin, and smell her all over; and then turn off with gestures, that seemed to express contempt and disdain."

Perhaps my master might refine a little in these speculations, which he had drawn from what he observed himself, or had been told him by others; however, I could not reflect without some amazement, and much sorrow, that the rudiments of lewdness, coquetry, censure, and scandal, should have place by instinct in womankind.

I expected every moment that my master would accuse the *Yahoos* of those unnatural appetites in both sexes, so common among us. But nature, it seems, has not been so expert a school-mistress; and these politer pleasures are entirely the productions of art and reason on our side of the globe.

CHAPTER 8: THE AUTHOR RELATES SEVERAL PARTICULARS OF THE YAHOOS. THE GREAT VIRTUES OF THE HOUYHNHNMS. THE EDUCATION AND EXERCISE OF THEIR YOUTH. THEIR GENERAL ASSEMBLY.

As I ought to have understood human nature much better than I supposed it possible for my master to do, so it was easy to apply the character he gave of the

Yahoos to myself and my countrymen; and I believed I could yet make further discoveries, from my own observation. I therefore often begged his honour to let me go among the herds of *Yahoos* in the neighbourhood; to which he always very graciously consented, being perfectly convinced that the hatred I bore these brutes would never suffer me to be corrupted by them; and his honour ordered one of his servants, a strong sorrel nag, very honest and good-natured, to be my guard; without whose protection I durst not undertake such adventures. For I have already told the reader how much I was pestered by these odious animals, upon my first arrival; and I afterwards failed very narrowly, three or four times, of falling into their clutches, when I happened to stray at any distance without my hanger. And I have reason to believe they had some imagination that I was of their own species, which I often assisted myself by stripping up my sleeves, and showing my naked arms and breasts in their sight, when my protector was with me. At which times they would approach as near as they durst, and imitate my actions after the manner of monkeys, but ever with great signs of hatred; as a tame jackdaw with cap and stockings is always persecuted by the wild ones, when he happens to be got among them.

They are prodigiously nimble from their infancy. However, I once caught a young male of three years old, and endeavoured, by all marks of tenderness, to make it quiet; but the little imp fell a squalling, and scratching, and biting with such violence, that I was forced to let it go; and it was high time, for a whole troop of old ones came about us at the noise, but finding the cub was safe (for away it ran), and my sorrel nag being by, they durst not venture near us. I observed the young animal's flesh to smell very rank, and the stink was somewhat between a weasel and a fox, but much more disagreeable. I forgot another circumstance (and perhaps I might have the reader's pardon if it were wholly omitted), that while I held the odious vermin in my hands, it voided its filthy excrements of a yellow liquid substance all over my clothes; but by good fortune there was a small brook hard by, where I washed myself as clean as I could; although I durst not come into my master's presence until I were sufficiently aired.

By what I could discover, the *Yahoos* appear to be the most unteachable of all animals: their capacity never reaching higher than to draw or carry burdens. Yet I am of opinion, this defect arises chiefly from a perverse, restive disposition; for they are cunning, malicious, treacherous, and revengeful. They are strong and hardy, but of a cowardly spirit, and, by consequence, insolent, abject, and cruel. It is observed, that the red haired of both sexes are more libidinous and mischievous than the rest, whom yet they much exceed in strength and activity.

The *Houyhnhnms* keep the *Yahoos* for present use in huts not far from the house; but the rest are sent abroad to certain fields, where they dig up roots, eat several kinds of herbs, and search about for carrion, or sometimes catch weasels and *luhimuhs* (a sort of wild rat), which they greedily devour. Nature has taught them to dig deep holes with their nails on the side of a rising ground, wherein they lie by themselves; only the kennels of the females are larger, sufficient to hold two or three cubs.

They swim from their infancy like frogs, and are able to continue long under water, where they often take fish, which the females carry home to their young. And, upon this occasion, I hope the reader will pardon my relating an odd adventure.

Being one day abroad with my protector the sorrel nag, and the weather exceeding hot, I entreated him to let me bathe in a river that was near. He consented, and I immediately stripped myself stark naked, and went down softly into the stream. It happened that a young female *Yahoo*, standing behind a bank, saw the whole proceeding, and inflamed by desire, as the nag and I conjectured, came running with all speed, and leaped into the water, within five yards of the place where I bathed. I was never in my life so terribly frightened. The nag was grazing at some distance, not suspecting any harm. She embraced me after a most fulsome manner. I roared as loud as I could, and the nag came galloping towards me, whereupon she quitted her grasp, with the utmost reluctancy, and leaped upon the opposite bank, where she stood gazing and howling all the time I was putting on my clothes.

This was a matter of diversion to my master and his family, as well as of mortification to myself. For now I could no longer deny that I was a real *Yahoo* in every limb and feature, since the females had a natural propensity to me, as one of their own species. Neither was the hair of this brute of a red colour (which might have been some excuse for an appetite a little irregular), but black as a sloe, and her countenance did not make an appearance altogether so hideous as the rest of her kind; for I think she could not be above eleven years old.

Having lived three years in this country, the reader, I suppose, will expect that I should, like other travellers, give him some account of the manners and customs of its inhabitants, which it was indeed my principal study to learn.

As these noble *Houyhnhnms* are endowed by nature with a general disposition to all virtues, and have no conceptions or ideas of what is evil in a rational creature, so their grand maxim is, to cultivate reason, and to be wholly governed by it. Neither is reason among them a point problematical, as with us, where men can argue with plausibility on both sides of the question, but strikes you with immediate conviction; as it must needs do, where it is not mingled, obscured, or discoloured, by passion and interest. I remember it was with extreme difficulty that I could bring my master to understand the meaning of the word opinion, or how a point could be disputable; because reason taught us to affirm or deny only where we are certain; and beyond our knowledge we cannot do either. So that controversies, wranglings, disputes, and positiveness, in false or dubious propositions, are evils unknown among the *Houyhnhnms*. In the like manner, when I used to explain to him our several systems of natural philosophy, he would laugh, "that a creature pretending to reason, should value itself upon the knowledge of other people's conjectures, and in things where that knowledge, if it were certain, could be of no use." Wherein he agreed entirely with the sentiments of Socrates, as Plato delivers them; which I mention as the highest honour I can do that prince of philosophers. I have often since reflected, what destruction such doctrine would make in the libraries of Europe; and how many paths of fame would be then shut up in the learned world.

Friendship and benevolence are the two principal virtues among the *Houyhnhnms*; and these not confined to particular objects, but universal to the whole race; for a stranger from the remotest part is equally treated with the nearest neighbour, and wherever he goes, looks upon himself as at home. They preserve decency and civility in the highest degrees, but are altogether ignorant of ceremony. They have no fondness for their colts or foals, but the care they take in educating them proceeds entirely from the dictates of reason. And I observed my master to show the same affection to his neighbour's issue, that he had for his own. They will have it that nature teaches them to love the whole species, and it is reason only that makes a distinction of persons, where there is a superior degree of virtue.

When the matron *Houyhnhnms* have produced one of each sex, they no longer accompany with their consorts, except they lose one of their issue by some casualty, which very seldom happens; but in such a case they meet again; or when the like accident befalls a person whose wife is past bearing, some other couple bestow on him one of their own colts, and then go together again until the mother is pregnant. This caution is necessary, to prevent the country from being overburdened with numbers. But the race of inferior *Houyhnhnms*, bred up to be servants, is not so strictly limited upon this article: these are allowed to produce three of each sex, to be domestics in the noble families.

In their marriages, they are exactly careful to choose such colours as will not make any disagreeable mixture in the breed. Strength is chiefly valued in the male, and comeliness in the female; not upon the account of love, but to preserve the race from degenerating; for where a female happens to excel in strength, a consort is chosen, with regard to comeliness.

Courtship, love, presents, jointures, settlements have no place in their thoughts, or terms whereby to express them in their language. The young couple meet, and are joined, merely because it is the determination of their parents and friends; it is what they see done every day, and they look upon it as one of the necessary actions of a reasonable being. But the violation of marriage, or any other unchastity, was never heard of; and the married pair pass their lives with the same friendship and mutual benevolence, that they bear to all others of the same species who come in their way, without jealousy, fondness, quarrelling, or discontent.

In educating the youth of both sexes, their method is admirable, and highly deserves our imitation. These are not suffered to taste a grain of oats, except upon certain days, till eighteen years old; nor milk, but very rarely; and in summer they graze two hours in the morning, and as many in the evening, which their parents likewise observe; but the servants are not allowed above half that time, and a great part of their grass is brought home, which they eat at the most convenient hours, when they can be best spared from work.

Temperance, industry, exercise, and cleanliness, are the lessons equally enjoined to the young ones of both sexes: and my master thought it monstrous in us, to give the females a different kind of education from the males, except in some articles of domestic management; whereby, as he truly observed, one half of our natives were good for nothing but bringing children into the world; and to trust the care of our children to such useless animals, he said, was yet a greater instance of brutality.

But the *Houyhnhnms* train up their youth to strength, speed, and hardiness, by exercising them in running races up and down steep hills, and over hard stony grounds; and when they are all in a sweat, they are ordered to leap over head and ears into a pond or river. Four times a year the youth of a certain district meet to show their proficiency in running and leaping, and other feats of strength and agility; where the victor is rewarded with a song in his or her praise. On this festival, the servants drive a herd of *Yahoos* into the field, laden with hay, and oats, and milk, for a repast to the *Houyhnhnms*; after which, these brutes are immediately driven back again, for fear of being noisome to the assembly.

Every fourth year, at the vernal equinox, there is a representative council of the whole nation, which meets in a plain about twenty miles from our house, and continues about five or six days. Here they inquire into the state and condition of the several districts; whether they abound or be deficient in hay or oats, or cows, or *Yahoos*; and wherever there is any want (which is but seldom) it is immediately supplied by unanimous consent and contribution. Here likewise the regulation of children is settled: as for instance, if a *Houyhnhnm* has two males, he changes one of them with another that has two females; and when a child has been lost by any casualty, where the mother is past breeding, it is determined what family in the district shall breed another to supply the loss.

CHAPTER 9: A GRAND DEBATE AT THE GENERAL
ASSEMBLY OF THE HOUYHNHNMS, AND HOW IT WAS
DETERMINED. THE LEARNING OF THE HOUYHNHNMS.
THEIR BUILDINGS. THEIR MANNER OF BURIALS. THE
DEFECTIVENESS OF THEIR LANGUAGE.

One of these grand assemblies was held in my time, about three months before my departure, whither my master went as the representative of our district. In this council was resumed their old debate, and indeed the only debate that ever happened in their country; whereof my master, after his return, give me a very particular account.

The question to be debated was, "whether the *Yahoos* should be exterminated from the face of the earth?" One of the members for the affirmative offered several arguments of great strength and weight, alleging, "that as the *Yahoos* were the most filthy, noisome, and deformed animals which nature ever produced, so they were the most restive and indocible, mischievous and malicious; they would privately suck the teats of the *Houyhnhnms'* cows, kill and devour their cats, trample down their oats and grass, if they were not continually watched, and commit a thousand other extravagancies." He took notice of a general tradition, "that *Yahoos* had not been always in their country; but that many ages ago, two of these brutes appeared together upon a mountain; whether produced by the heat of the sun upon corrupted mud and slime, or from the ooze and froth of the sea, was never known; that these *Yahoos* engendered, and their brood, in a short time, grew so numerous as to overrun and infest the whole nation; that the *Houyhnhnms*, to get rid of this evil, made a general hunting, and at last enclosed the whole herd; and destroying the elder, every *Houyhnhnm* kept two young ones in a kennel, and brought them to such a degree of tameness, as an animal, so savage by nature, can be capable of acquiring, using them for draught and carriage; that there seemed to be much truth in this tradition, and that those creatures could not be *yinhniamshy* (or *aborigines* of the land), because of the violent hatred the *Houyhnhnms*, as well as all other animals, bore them, which, although their evil disposition sufficiently deserved, could never have arrived at so high a degree if they had been *aborigines*, or else they would have long since been rooted out; that the inhabitants, taking a fancy to use the service of the *Yahoos*, had, very imprudently, neglected to cultivate the breed of asses, which are a comely animal, easily kept, more tame and orderly, without any offensive smell, strong enough for labour, although they yield to the other in agility of body, and if their braying be no agreeable sound, it is far preferable to the horrible howlings of the *Yahoos.*"

Several others declared their sentiments to the same purpose, when my master proposed an expedient to the assembly, whereof he had indeed borrowed the hint from me. "He approved of the tradition mentioned by the honourable member who spoke before, and affirmed, that the two *Yahoos* said to be seen first among them, had been driven thither over the sea; that coming to land, and being forsaken by their companions, they retired to the mountains, and degenerating by degrees, became in process of time much more savage than those of their own species in the country whence these two originals came. The reason of this assertion was, that he had now in his possession a certain wonderful *Yahoo* (meaning myself) which most of them had heard of, and many of them had seen. He then related to them how he first found me; that my body was all covered with an artificial composure of the skins and hairs of other animals; that I spoke in a language of my own, and had thoroughly learned theirs; that I had related to him the accidents which brought me thither; that when he saw me without my covering, I was an exact *Yahoo* in every part, only of a whiter colour, less hairy, and with shorter claws. He added, how I had endeavoured to persuade him, that in my own and other countries, the *Yahoos* acted as the governing, rational animal, and held the *Houyhnhnms* in servitude; that he observed in me all the qualities of a *Yahoo*, only a little more civilized by some tincture of reason, which, however, was in a degree as far inferior to the *Houyhnhnm* race, as the *Yahoos* of their country were to me; that, among other things, I mentioned a custom we had of castrating *Houyhnhnms* when they were young, in order to render them tame; that the operation was easy and safe; that it was no shame to learn wisdom from brutes, as industry is taught by the ant, and building by the swallow (for so I translate the word *lyhannh*, although it be a much larger fowl); that this invention might be practised upon the younger *Yahoos* here, which besides rendering them tractable and fitter for use, would in an age put an end to the whole species, without destroying life; that in the mean time the *Houyhnhnms* should be exhorted to cultivate the breed of asses, which, as they are in all respects more valuable brutes, so they have this advantage, to be fit for service at five years old, which the others are not till twelve."

This was all my master thought fit to tell me, at that time, of what passed in the grand council. But he was pleased to conceal one particular, which related personally to myself, whereof I soon felt the unhappy effect, as the reader will know in its proper place, and whence I date all the succeeding misfortunes of my life.

The *Houyhnhnms* have no letters, and consequently their knowledge is all traditional. But there happening few events of any moment among a people so well united, naturally disposed to every virtue, wholly governed by reason, and cut off from all commerce with other nations, the historical part is easily preserved without burdening their memories. I have already observed that they are subject to no diseases, and therefore can have no need of physicians. However, they have excellent medicines, composed of herbs, to cure accidental bruises and cuts in the pastern or frog of the foot, by sharp stones, as well as other maims and hurts in the several parts of the body.

They calculate the year by the revolution of the sun and moon, but use no subdivisions into weeks. They are well enough acquainted with the motions of those two luminaries, and understand the nature of eclipses; and this is the utmost progress of their astronomy.

In poetry, they must be allowed to excel all other mortals; wherein the justness of their similes, and the minuteness as well as exactness of their descriptions, are indeed inimitable. Their verses abound very much in both of these, and usually contain either some exalted notions of friendship and benevolence or the praises of those who were victors in races and other bodily exercises. Their buildings, although very rude and simple, are not inconvenient, but well contrived to defend them from all injuries of cold and heat. They have a kind of tree, which at forty years old loosens in the root, and falls with the first storm: it grows very straight, and being pointed like stakes with a sharp stone (for the *Houyhnhnms* know not the use of iron), they stick them erect in the ground, about ten inches asunder, and then weave in oat straw, or sometimes wattles, between them. The roof is made after the same manner, and so are the doors.

The *Houyhnhnms* use the hollow part, between the pastern and the hoof of their fore-foot, as we do our hands, and this with greater dexterity than I could at first imagine. I have seen a white mare of our family thread a needle (which I lent her on purpose) with that joint. They milk their cows, reap their oats, and do all the work which requires hands, in the same manner. They have a kind of hard flints, which, by grinding against other stones, they form into instruments, that serve instead of wedges, axes, and hammers. With tools made of these flints, they likewise cut their hay, and reap their oats, which there grow naturally in several fields; the *Yahoos* draw home the sheaves in carriages, and the servants tread them in certain covered huts to get out the grain, which is kept in stores. They make a rude kind of earthen and wooden vessels, and bake the former in the sun.

If they can avoid casualties, they die only of old age, and are buried in the obscurest places that can be found, their friends and relations expressing neither joy nor grief at their departure; nor does the dying person discover the least regret that he is leaving the world, any more than if he were upon returning home from a visit to one of his neighbours. I remember my master having once made an appointment with a friend and his family to come to his house, upon some affair of importance: on the day fixed, the mistress and her two children came very late; she made two excuses, first for her husband, who, as she said, happened that very morning to *shnuwnh*. The word is strongly expressive in their language, but not easily rendered into English; it signifies, "to retire to his first mother." Her excuse for not coming sooner, was, that her husband dying late in the morning, she was a good while consulting her servants about a convenient place where his body should be laid; and I observed, she behaved herself at our house as cheerfully as the rest. She died about three months after.

They live generally to seventy, or seventy-five years, very seldom to fourscore. Some weeks before their death, they feel a gradual decay; but without pain. During this time they are much visited by their friends, because they cannot go abroad with their usual ease and satisfaction. However, about ten days before their death, which they seldom fail in computing, they return the visits that have been made them by those who are nearest in the neighbourhood, being carried in a convenient sledge drawn by *Yahoos*; which vehicle they use, not only upon this occasion, but when they grow old, upon long journeys, or when they are lamed by any accident: and therefore when the dying *Houyhnhnms* return those visits, they take a solemn leave of their friends, as if they were going to some remote part of the country, where they designed to pass the rest of their lives.

I know not whether it may be worth observing, that the *Houyhnhnms* have no word in their language to express any thing that is evil, except what they borrow from the deformities or ill qualities of the *Yahoos*. Thus they denote the folly of a servant, an omission of a child, a stone that cuts their feet, a continuance of foul or unseasonable weather, and the like, by adding to each the epithet of *Yahoo*. For instance, *hhnm Yahoo*, *whnaholm Yahoo*, *ynlhmndwihlma Yahoo*, and an ill-contrived house *ynholmhnmrohlnw Yahoo*.

I could, with great pleasure, enlarge further upon the manners and virtues of this excellent people; but intending in a short time to publish a volume by itself, expressly upon that subject, I refer the reader thither; and, in the mean time, proceed to relate my own sad catastrophe.

CHAPTER 10

The author's economy, and happy life, among the Houyhnhnms. His great improvement in virtue by conversing with them. Their conversations. The author has notice given him by his master, that he must depart from the country. He falls into a swoon for grief; but submits. He contrives and finishes a canoe by the help of a fellow-servant, and puts to sea at a venture.

I had settled my little economy to my own heart's content. My master had ordered a room to be made for me, after their manner, about six yards from the house: the sides and floors of which I plastered with clay, and covered with rush-mats of my own contriving. I had beaten hemp, which there grows wild, and made of it a sort of ticking; this I filled with the feathers of several birds I had taken with springes made of *Yahoos'* hairs, and were excellent food. I had worked two chairs with my knife, the sorrel nag helping me in the grosser and more laborious part. When my clothes were worn to rags, I made myself others with the skins of rabbits, and of a certain beautiful animal, about the same size, called *nnuhnoh*, the skin of which is covered with a fine down. Of these I also made very tolerable stockings. I soled my shoes with wood, which I cut from a tree, and fitted to the upper-leather; and when this was worn out, I supplied it with the skins of *Yahoos* dried in the sun. I often got honey out of hollow trees, which I mingled with water, or ate with my bread. No man could more verify the truth of these two maxims, "That nature is very easily satisfied;" and, "That necessity is the mother of invention." I enjoyed perfect health of body, and tranquillity of mind; I did not feel the treachery or inconstancy of a friend, nor the injuries of a secret or open enemy. I had no occasion of bribing, flattering, or pimping, to procure the favour of any great man, or of his minion; I wanted no fence against fraud or oppression: here was neither physician to destroy my body, nor lawyer to ruin my fortune; no informer to watch my words and actions, or forge accusations against me for hire: here were no gibers, censurers, backbiters, pickpockets, highwaymen, housebreakers, attorneys, bawds, buffoons, gamesters, politicians, wits, splenetics, tedious talkers, controvertists, ravishers, murderers, robbers, virtuosos; no leaders, or followers, of party and faction; no encouragers to vice, by seducement or examples; no dungeon, axes, gibbets, whipping-posts, or pillories; no cheating shopkeepers or mechanics; no pride, vanity, or affectation; no fops, bullies, drunkards, strolling whores, or poxes; no ranting, lewd, expensive wives; no stupid, proud pedants; no importunate, overbearing, quarrelsome, noisy, roaring, empty, conceited, swearing companions; no scoundrels raised from the dust upon the merit of their vices, or nobility thrown into it on account of their virtues; no lords, fiddlers, judges, or dancing-masters.

I had the favour of being admitted to several *Houyhnhnms*, who came to visit or dine with my master; where his honour graciously suffered me to wait in the room, and listen to their discourse. Both he and his company would often descend to ask me questions, and receive my answers. I had also sometimes the honour of attending my master in his visits to others. I never presumed to speak, except in answer to a question; and then I did it with inward regret, because it was a loss of so much time for improving myself; but I was infinitely delighted with the station of an humble auditor in such conversations, where nothing passed but what was useful, expressed in the fewest and most significant words; where, as I have already said, the greatest decency was observed, without the least degree of ceremony; where no person spoke without being pleased himself, and pleasing his companions; where there was no interruption, tediousness, heat, or difference of sentiments. They have a notion, that when people are met together, a short silence does much improve conversation: this I found to be true; for during those little intermissions of talk, new ideas would arise in their minds, which very much enlivened the discourse. Their subjects are, generally on friendship and benevolence, on order and economy; sometimes upon the visible operations of nature, or ancient traditions; upon the bounds and limits of virtue; upon the unerring rules of reason, or upon some determinations to be taken at the next great assembly: and often upon the various excellences of poetry. I may add, without vanity, that my presence often gave them sufficient matter for discourse, because it afforded my master an occasion of letting his friends into the history of me and my country, upon which they were all pleased to descant, in a manner not very advantageous to humankind: and for that reason I shall not repeat what they said; only I may be allowed to observe, that his honour, to my great admiration, appeared to understand the nature of *Yahoos* much better than myself. He went through all our vices and follies, and discovered many, which I had never mentioned to him, by only supposing what qualities a *Yahoo* of their country, with a small proportion of reason, might be capable of exerting; and concluded, with too much probability, "how vile, as well as miserable, such a creature must be."

I freely confess, that all the little knowledge I have of any value, was acquired by the lectures I received from my master, and from hearing the discourses of him and his friends; to which I should be prouder to listen, than to dictate to the greatest and wisest assembly in Europe. I admired the strength, comeliness, and speed of the inhabitants; and such a constellation of virtues, in such amiable persons, produced in me the highest veneration. At first, indeed, I did not feel that natural awe, which the *Yahoos* and all other animals bear toward them; but it grew upon me by decrees, much sooner than I imagined, and was mingled with a respectful love and gratitude, that they would condescend to distinguish me from the rest of my species.

When I thought of my family, my friends, my countrymen, or the human race in general, I considered them, as they really were, *Yahoos* in shape and disposition, perhaps a little more civilized, and qualified with the gift of speech; but making no other use of reason, than to improve and multiply those vices whereof their brethren in this country had only the share that nature allotted them. When I happened to behold the reflection of my own form in a lake or fountain, I turned away my face in horror and detestation of myself, and could better endure the sight of a common *Yahoo* than of my own person. By conversing with the *Houyhnhnms*, and looking upon them with delight, I fell to imitate their gait and gesture, which is now grown into a habit; and my friends often tell me, in a blunt way, "that I trot like a horse;" which, however, I take for a great compliment. Neither shall I disown, that in speaking I am apt to fall into the voice and manner of the *Houyhnhnms*, and hear myself ridiculed on that account, without the least mortification.

In the midst of all this happiness, and when I looked upon myself to be fully settled for life, my master sent for me one morning a little earlier than his usual hour. I observed by his countenance that he was in some perplexity, and at a loss how to begin what he had to speak. After a short silence, he told me, "he did not know how I would take what he was going to say: that in the last general assembly, when the affair of the *Yahoos* was entered upon, the representatives had taken offence at his keeping a *Yahoo* (meaning myself) in his family, more like a *Houyhnhnm* than a brute animal; that he was known frequently to converse with me, as if he could receive some advantage or pleasure in my company; that such a practice was not agreeable to reason or nature, or a thing ever heard of before among them; the assembly did therefore exhort him either to employ me like the rest of my species, or command me to swim back to the place whence I came: that the first of these expedients was utterly rejected by all the *Houyhnhnms* who had ever seen me at his house or their own; for they alleged, that because I had some rudiments of reason, added to the natural pravity of those animals, it was to be feared I might be able to seduce them into the woody and mountainous parts of the country, and bring them in troops by night to destroy the *Houyhnhnms'* cattle, as being naturally of the ravenous kind, and averse from labour."

My master added, "that he was daily pressed by the *Houyhnhnms* of the neighbourhood to have the assembly's exhortation executed, which he could not put off much longer. He doubted it would be impossible for me to swim to another country; and therefore wished I would contrive some sort of vehicle, resembling those I had described to him, that might carry me on the sea; in which work I should have the assistance of his own servants, as well as those of his neighbours." He concluded, "that for his own part, he could have been content to keep me in his service as long as I lived; because he found I had cured myself of some bad habits and dispositions, by endeavouring, as far as my inferior nature was capable, to imitate the *Houyhnhnms*."

I should here observe to the reader, that a decree of the general assembly in this country is expressed by the word *hnhloayn*, which signifies an exhortation, as near as I can render it; for they have no conception how a rational creature can be compelled, but only advised, or exhorted; because no person can disobey reason, without giving up his claim to be a rational creature.

I was struck with the utmost grief and despair at my master's discourse; and being unable to support the agonies I was under, I fell into a swoon at his feet. When I came to myself, he told me "that he concluded I had been dead;" for these people are subject to no such imbecilities of nature. I answered in a faint voice, "that death would have been too great a happiness; that although I could not blame the assembly's exhortation, or the urgency of his friends; yet, in my weak and corrupt judgment, I thought it might consist with reason to have been less rigorous; that I could not swim a league, and probably the nearest land to theirs might be distant above a hundred: that many materials, necessary for making a small vessel to carry me off, were wholly wanting in this country; which, however, I would attempt, in obedience and gratitude to his honour, although I concluded the thing to be impossible, and therefore looked on myself as already devoted to destruction; that the certain prospect of an unnatural death was the least of my evils; for, supposing I should escape with life by some strange adventure, how could I think with temper of passing my days among *Yahoos*, and relapsing into my old corruptions, for want of examples to lead and keep me within the paths of virtue? that I knew too well upon what solid reasons all the determinations of the wise *Houyhnhnms* were founded, not to be shaken by arguments of mine, a miserable *Yahoo*; and therefore, after presenting him with my humble thanks for the offer of his servants' assistance in making a vessel, and desiring a reasonable time for so difficult a work, I told him I would endeavour to preserve a wretched being; and if ever I returned to England, was not without hopes of being useful to my own species, by celebrating the praises of the renowned *Houyhnhnms*, and proposing their virtues to the imitation of mankind."

My master, in a few words, made me a very gracious reply; allowed me the space of two months to finish my boat; and ordered the sorrel nag, my fellow-servant (for so, at this distance, I may presume to call him), to follow my instruction; because I told my master, "that his help would be sufficient, and I knew he had a tenderness for me."

In his company, my first business was to go to that part of the coast where my rebellious crew had ordered me to be set on shore. I got upon a height, and looking on every side into the sea; fancied I saw a small island toward the north-east. I took out my pocket glass, and could then clearly distinguish it above five leagues off, as I computed; but it appeared to the sorrel nag to be only a blue cloud: for as he had no conception of any country beside his own, so he could not be as expert in distinguishing remote objects at sea, as we who so much converse in that element.

After I had discovered this island, I considered no further; but resolved it should if possible, be the first place of my banishment, leaving the consequence to fortune.

I returned home, and consulting with the sorrel nag, we went into a copse at some distance, where I with my knife, and he with a sharp flint, fastened very artificially after their manner, to a wooden handle, cut down several oak wattles, about the thickness of a walking-staff, and some larger pieces. But I shall not trouble the reader with a particular description of my own mechanics; let it suffice to say, that in six weeks time with the help of the sorrel nag, who performed the parts that required most labour, I finished a sort of Indian canoe, but much larger, covering it with the skins of *Yahoos*, well stitched together with hempen threads of my own making. My sail was likewise composed of the skins of the same animal; but I made use of the youngest I could get, the older being too tough and thick; and I likewise provided myself with four paddles. I laid in a stock of boiled flesh, of rabbits and fowls, and took with me two vessels, one filled with milk and the other with water.

I tried my canoe in a large pond, near my master's house, and then corrected in it what was amiss; stopping all the chinks with *Yahoos'* tallow, till I found it staunch, and able to bear me and my freight; and, when it was as complete as I could possibly make it, I had it drawn on a carriage very gently by *Yahoos* to the sea-side, under the conduct of the sorrel nag and another servant.

When all was ready, and the day came for my departure, I took leave of my master and lady and the whole family, my eyes flowing with tears, and my heart quite sunk with grief. But his honour, out of curiosity, and, perhaps, (if I may speak without vanity,) partly out of kindness, was determined to see me in my canoe, and got several of his neighbouring friends to accompany him. I was forced to wait above an hour for the tide; and then observing the wind very fortunately bearing toward the island to which I intended to steer my course, I took a second leave of my master: but as I was going to prostrate myself to kiss his hoof, he did me the honour to raise it gently to my mouth. I am not ignorant how much I have been censured for mentioning this last particular. Detractors are pleased to think it improbable, that so illustrious a person should descend to give so great a mark of distinction to a creature so inferior as I. Neither have I forgotten how apt some travellers are to boast of extraordinary favours they have received. But, if these censurers were better acquainted with the noble and courteous disposition of the *Houyhnhnms*, they would soon change their opinion.

I paid my respects to the rest of the *Houyhnhnms* in his honour's company; then getting into my canoe, I pushed off from shore.

CHAPTER 11: THE AUTHOR'S DANGEROUS VOYAGE. HE ARRIVES AT NEW HOLLAND, HOPING TO SETTLE THERE. IS WOUNDED WITH AN ARROW BY ONE OF THE NATIVES. IS SEIZED AND CARRIED BY FORCE INTO A PORTUGUESE SHIP. THE GREAT CIVILITIES OF THE CAPTAIN. THE AUTHOR ARRIVES AT ENGLAND.

I began this desperate voyage on February 15, 1714–15, at nine o'clock in the morning. The wind was very favourable; however, I made use at first only of my paddles; but considering I should soon be weary, and that the wind might chop about, I ventured to set up my little sail; and thus, with the help of the tide, I went at the rate of a league and a half an hour, as near as I could guess. My master and his friends continued on the shore till I was almost out of sight; and I often heard the sorrel nag (who always loved me) crying out, "*Hnuy illa nyha, majah Yahoo*;" "Take care of thyself, gentle *Yahoo*."

My design was, if possible, to discover some small island uninhabited, yet sufficient, by my labour, to furnish me with the necessaries of life, which I would have thought a greater happiness, than to be first minister in the politest court of Europe; so horrible was the idea I conceived of returning to live in the society, and under the government of *Yahoos*. For in such a solitude as I desired, I could at least enjoy my own thoughts, and reflect with delight on the virtues of those inimitable *Houyhnhnms*, without an opportunity of degenerating into the vices and corruptions of my own species.

The reader may remember what I related, when my crew conspired against me, and confined me to my cabin; how I continued there several weeks without knowing what course we took; and when I was put ashore in the long-boat, how the sailors told me, with oaths, whether true or false, "that they knew not in what part of the world we were." However, I did then believe us to be about 10 degrees southward of the Cape of Good Hope, or about 45 degrees southern latitude, as I gathered from some general words I overheard among them, being I supposed to the south-east in their intended voyage to Madagascar. And although this were little better than conjecture, yet I resolved to steer my course eastward, hoping to reach the south-west coast of New Holland, and perhaps some such island as I desired lying westward of it. The wind was full west, and by six in the evening I computed I had gone eastward at least eighteen leagues; when I spied a very small island about half a league off, which I soon reached. It was nothing but a rock, with one creek naturally arched by the force of tempests. Here I put in my canoe, and climbing a part of the rock, I could plainly discover land to the east, extending from south to north. I lay all night in my canoe; and repeating my voyage early in the morning, I arrived in seven hours to the south-east point of New Holland. This confirmed me in the opinion I have long entertained, that the maps and charts place this country at least three degrees more to the east than it really is; which thought I communicated many years ago to my worthy friend, Mr. Herman Moll, and gave him my reasons for it, although he has rather chosen to follow other authors.

I saw no inhabitants in the place where I landed, and being unarmed, I was afraid of venturing far into the country. I found some shellfish on the shore, and ate them raw, not daring to kindle a fire, for fear of being discovered by the natives. I continued three days feeding on oysters and limpets, to save my own provisions; and I fortunately found a brook of excellent water, which gave me great relief.

On the fourth day, venturing out early a little too far, I saw twenty or thirty natives upon a height not above five hundred yards from me. They were stark naked, men, women, and children, round a fire, as I could discover by the smoke. One of them spied me, and gave notice to the rest; five of them advanced toward me, leaving the women and children at the fire. I made what haste I could to the shore, and, getting into my canoe, shoved off: the savages, observing me retreat, ran after me: and before I could get far enough into the sea, discharged an arrow which wounded me deeply on the inside of my left knee: I shall carry the mark to my grave. I apprehended the arrow might be poisoned, and paddling out of the reach of their darts (being a calm day), I made a shift to suck the wound, and dress it as well as I could.

I was at a loss what to do, for I durst not return to the same landing-place, but stood to the north, and was forced to paddle, for the wind, though very gentle, was against me, blowing north-west. As I was looking about for a secure landing-place, I saw a sail to the north-north-east, which appearing every minute more visible, I was in some doubt whether I should wait for them or not; but at last my detestation of the *Yahoo* race prevailed: and turning my canoe, I sailed and paddled together to the south, and got into the same creek whence I set out in the morning, choosing rather to trust myself among these barbarians, than live with European *Yahoos*. I drew up my canoe as close as I could to the shore, and hid myself behind a stone by the little brook, which, as I have already said, was excellent water.

The ship came within half a league of this creek, and sent her long boat with vessels to take in fresh water (for the place, it seems, was very well known); but I did not observe it, till the boat was almost on shore; and it was too late to seek another hiding-place. The seamen at their landing observed my canoe, and rummaging it all over, easily conjectured that the owner could not be far off. Four of them, well armed, searched every cranny and lurking-hole, till at last they found me flat on my face behind the stone. They gazed awhile in admiration at my strange uncouth dress; my coat made of skins, my wooden-soled shoes, and my furred stockings; whence, however, they concluded, I was not a native of the place, who all go naked. One of the seamen, in Portuguese, bid me rise, and asked who I was. I understood that language very well, and getting upon my feet, said, "I was a poor *Yahoo* banished from the *Houyhnhnms*, and desired they would please to let me depart." They admired to hear me answer them in their own tongue, and saw by my complexion I must be a European; but were at a loss to know what I meant by *Yahoos* and *Houyhnhnms*; and at the same time fell a-laughing at my strange tone in speaking, which resembled the neighing of a horse. I trembled all the while betwixt fear and hatred. I again desired leave to depart, and was gently moving to my canoe; but they laid hold of me, desiring to know, "what country I was of? whence I came?" with many other questions. I told them "I was born in England, whence I came about five years ago, and then their country and ours were at peace. I therefore hoped they would not treat me as an enemy, since I meant them no harm, but was a poor *Yahoo* seeking some desolate place where to pass the remainder of his unfortunate life."

When they began to talk, I thought I never heard or saw any thing more unnatural; for it appeared to me as monstrous as if a dog or a cow should speak in England, or a *Yahoo* in *Houyhnhnmland*. The honest Portuguese were equally amazed at my strange dress, and the odd manner of delivering my words, which, however, they understood very well. They spoke to me with great humanity, and said, "they were sure the captain would carry me *gratis* to Lisbon, whence I might return to my own country; that two of the seamen would go back to the ship, inform the captain of what they had seen, and receive his orders; in the mean time, unless I would give my solemn oath not to fly, they would secure me by force." I thought it best to comply with their proposal. They were very curious to know my story, but I gave them very little satisfaction, and they all conjectured that my misfortunes had impaired my reason. In two hours the boat, which went laden with vessels of water, returned, with the captain's command to fetch me on board. I fell on my knees to preserve my liberty; but all was in vain; and the men, having tied me with cords, heaved me into the boat, whence I was taken into the ship, and thence into the captain's cabin.

His name was Pedro de Mendez; he was a very courteous and generous person. He entreated me to give some account of myself, and desired to know what I would eat or drink; said, "I should be used as well as himself;" and spoke so many obliging things, that I wondered to find such civilities from a *Yahoo*. However, I remained silent and sullen; I was ready to faint at the very smell of him and his men. At last I desired something to eat out of my own canoe; but he ordered me a chicken, and some excellent wine, and then directed that I should be put to bed in a very clean cabin. I would not undress myself, but lay on the bed-clothes, and in half an hour stole out, when I thought the crew was at dinner, and getting to the side of the ship, was going to leap into the sea, and swim for my life, rather than continue among *Yahoos*. But one of the seamen prevented me, and having informed the captain, I was chained to my cabin.

After dinner, Don Pedro came to me, and desired to know my reason for so desperate an attempt; assured me, "he only meant to do me all the service he was able;" and spoke so very movingly, that at last I descended to treat him like an animal which had some little portion of reason. I gave him a very short relation of my voyage; of the conspiracy against me by my own men; of the country where they set me on shore, and of my five years residence there. All which he looked upon as if it were a dream or a vision; whereat I took great offence; for I had quite forgot the faculty of lying, so peculiar to *Yahoos*, in all countries where they preside, and, consequently, their disposition of suspecting truth in others of their own species. I asked him, "whether it were the custom in his country to say the thing which was not?" I assured him, "I had almost forgot what he meant by falsehood, and if I had lived a thousand years in *Houyhnhnmland*, I should never have heard a lie from the meanest servant; that I was altogether indifferent whether he believed me or not; but, however, in return for his favours, I would give so much allowance to the corruption of his nature, as to answer any objection he would please to make, and then he might easily discover the truth."

The captain, a wise man, after many endeavours to catch me tripping in some part of my story, at last began to have a better opinion of my veracity. But he added, "that since I professed so inviolable an attachment to truth, I must give him my word and honour to bear him company in this voyage, without attempting any thing against my life; or else he would continue me a prisoner till we arrived at Lisbon." I gave him the promise he required; but at the same time protested, "that I would suffer the greatest hardships, rather than return to live among *Yahoos*."

Our voyage passed without any considerable accident. In gratitude to the captain, I sometimes sat with him, at his earnest request, and strove to conceal my antipathy against human kind, although it often broke out; which he suffered to pass without observation. But the greatest part of the day I confined myself to my cabin, to avoid seeing any of the crew. The captain had often entreated me to strip myself of my savage dress, and offered to lend me the best suit of clothes he had. This I would not be prevailed on to accept, abhorring to cover myself with any thing that had been on the back of a *Yahoo*. I only desired he would lend me two clean shirts, which, having been washed since he wore them, I believed would not so much defile me. These I changed every second day, and washed them myself.

We arrived at Lisbon, Nov. 5, 1715. At our landing, the captain forced me to cover myself with his cloak, to prevent the rabble from crowding about me. I was conveyed to his own house; and at my earnest request he led me up to the highest room backwards. I conjured him "to conceal from all persons what I had told him of the *Houyhnhnms*; because the least hint of such a story would not only draw numbers of people to see me, but probably put me in danger of being imprisoned, or burnt by the Inquisition." The captain persuaded me to accept a suit of clothes newly made; but I would not suffer the tailor to take my measure; however, Don Pedro being almost of my size, they fitted me well enough. He accoutred me with other necessaries, all new, which I aired for twenty-four hours before I would use them.

The captain had no wife, nor above three servants, none of which were suffered to attend at meals; and his whole deportment was so obliging, added to very good human understanding, that I really began to tolerate his company. He gained so far upon me, that I ventured to look out of the back window. By degrees I was brought into another room, whence I peeped into the street, but drew my head back in a fright. In a week's time he seduced me down to the door. I found my terror gradually lessened, but my hatred and contempt seemed to increase. I was at last bold enough to walk the street in his company, but kept my nose well stopped with rue, or sometimes with tobacco.

In ten days, Don Pedro, to whom I had given some account of my domestic affairs, put it upon me, as a matter of honour and conscience, "that I ought to return to my native country, and live at home with my wife and children." He told me, "there was an English ship in the port just ready to sail, and he would furnish me with all things necessary." It would be tedious to repeat his arguments, and my contradictions. He said, "it was altogether impossible to find such a solitary island as I desired to live in; but I might command in my own house, and pass my time in a manner as recluse as I pleased."

I complied at last, finding I could not do better. I left Lisbon the 24th day of November, in an English merchantman, but who was the master I never inquired. Don Pedro accompanied me to the ship, and lent me twenty pounds. He took kind leave of me, and embraced me at parting, which I bore as well as I could. During this last voyage I had no commerce with the master or any of his men; but, pretending I was sick, kept close in my cabin. On the fifth of December, 1715, we cast anchor in the Downs, about nine in the morning, and at three in the afternoon I got safe to my house at Rotherhith.[2]

My wife and family received me with great surprise and joy, because they concluded me certainly dead; but I must freely confess the sight of them filled me only with hatred, disgust, and contempt; and the more, by reflecting on the near alliance I had to them. For although, since my unfortunate exile from the *Houyhnhnm* country, I had compelled myself to tolerate the sight of *Yahoos*, and to converse with Don Pedro de Mendez, yet my memory and imagination were perpetually filled with the virtues and ideas of those exalted *Houyhnhnms*. And when I began to consider that, by copulating with one of the *Yahoo* species I had become a parent of more, it struck me with the utmost shame, confusion, and horror.

As soon as I entered the house, my wife took me in her arms, and kissed me; at which, having not been used to the touch of that odious animal for so many years, I fell into a swoon for almost an hour. At the time I am writing, it is five years since my last return to England. During the first year, I could not endure my wife or children in my presence; the very smell of them was intolerable; much less could I suffer them to eat in the same room. To this hour they dare not presume to touch my bread, or drink out of the same cup, neither was I ever able to let one of them take me by the hand. The first money I laid out was to buy two young stone-horses, which I keep in a good stable; and next to them, the groom is my greatest favourite, for I feel my spirits revived by the smell he contracts in the stable. My horses understand me tolerably well; I converse with them at least four hours every day. They are strangers to bridle or saddle; they live in great amity with me and friendship to each other.

CHAPTER 12: THE AUTHOR'S VERACITY. HIS DESIGN IN PUBLISHING THIS WORK. HIS CENSURE OF THOSE TRAVELLERS WHO SWERVE FROM THE TRUTH. THE AUTHOR CLEARS HIMSELF FROM ANY SINISTER ENDS IN WRITING. AN OBJECTION ANSWERED. THE METHOD OF PLANTING COLONIES. HIS NATIVE COUNTRY COMMENDED. THE RIGHT OF THE CROWN TO THOSE COUNTRIES DESCRIBED BY THE AUTHOR IS JUSTIFIED. THE DIFFICULTY OF CONQUERING THEM. THE AUTHOR TAKES HIS LAST LEAVE OF THE READER; PROPOSES HIS MANNER OF LIVING FOR THE FUTURE; GIVES GOOD ADVICE, AND CONCLUDES.

Thus, gentle reader, I have given thee a faithful history of my travels for sixteen years and above seven months: wherein I have not been so studious of ornament as of truth. I could, perhaps, like others, have astonished thee with strange improbable tales; but I rather chose to relate plain matter of fact, in the simplest manner and style; because my principal design was to inform, and not to amuse thee.

It is easy for us who travel into remote countries, which are seldom visited by Englishmen or other Europeans, to form descriptions of wonderful animals both at sea and land. Whereas a traveller's chief aim should be to make men wiser and better, and to improve their minds by the bad, as well as good, example of what they deliver concerning foreign places.

I could heartily wish a law was enacted, that every traveller, before he were permitted to publish his voyages, should be obliged to make oath before the Lord High Chancellor, that all he intended to print was absolutely true to the best of his knowledge; for then the world would no longer be deceived, as it usually is, while some writers, to make their works pass the better upon the public, impose the grossest falsities on the unwary reader. I have perused several books of travels with great delight in my younger days; but having since gone over most parts of the globe, and been able to contradict many fabulous accounts from my own observation, it has given me a great disgust against this part of reading, and some indignation to see the credulity of mankind so impudently abused. Therefore, since my acquaintance were pleased to think my poor endeavours might not be unacceptable to my country, I imposed on myself, as a maxim never to be swerved from, that I would strictly adhere to truth; neither indeed can I be ever under the least temptation to vary from it, while I retain in my mind the lectures and example of my noble master and the other illustrious *Houyhnhnms* of whom I had so long the honour to be an humble hearer.

—*Nec si miserum Fortuna Sinonem*
Finxit, vanum etiam, mendacemque improba finget.

I know very well, how little reputation is to be got by writings which require neither genius nor learning, nor indeed any other talent, except a good memory, or an exact journal. I know likewise, that writers of travels, like dictionary-makers, are sunk into oblivion by the weight and bulk of those who come last, and therefore lie uppermost. And it is highly probable, that such travellers, who shall hereafter visit the countries described in this work of mine, may, by detecting my errors (if there be any), and adding many new discoveries of their own, justle me out of vogue, and stand in my place, making the world forget that ever I was an author. This indeed would be too great a mortification, if I wrote for fame: but as my sole intention was the public good, I cannot be altogether disappointed. For who can read of the virtues I have mentioned in the glorious *Houyhnhnms*, without being ashamed of his own vices, when he considers himself as the reasoning, governing animal of his country? I shall say nothing of those remote nations where *Yahoos* preside; among which the least corrupted are the *Brobdingnagians*; whose wise maxims in morality and government it would be our happiness to observe. But I forbear descanting further, and rather leave the judicious reader to his own remarks and application.

I am not a little pleased that this work of mine can possibly meet with no censurers: for what objections can be made against a writer, who relates only plain facts, that happened in such distant countries, where we have not the least interest, with respect either to trade or negotiations? I have carefully avoided every fault with which common writers of travels are often too justly charged. Besides, I meddle not the least with any party, but write without passion, prejudice, or ill-will against any man, or number of men, whatsoever. I write for the noblest end, to inform and instruct mankind; over whom I may, without breach of modesty, pretend to some superiority, from the advantages I received by conversing so long among the most accomplished *Houyhnhnms*. I write without any view to profit or praise. I never suffer a word to pass that may look like reflection, or possibly give the least offence, even to those who are most ready to take it. So that I hope I may with justice pronounce myself an author perfectly blameless; against whom the tribes of Answerers, Considerers, Observers, Reflectors, Detectors, Remarkers, will never be able to find matter for exercising their talents.

I confess, it was whispered to me, "that I was bound in duty, as a subject of England, to have given in a memorial to a secretary of state at my first coming over; because, whatever lands are discovered by a subject belong to the crown." But I doubt whether our conquests in the countries I treat of would be as easy as those of Ferdinando Cortez over the naked Americans. The *Lilliputians*, I think, are hardly worth the charge of a fleet and army to reduce them; and I question whether it might be prudent or safe to attempt the *Brobdingnagians*; or whether an English army would be much at their ease with the Flying Island over their heads. The *Houyhnhnms* indeed appear not to be so well prepared for war, a science to which they are perfect strangers, and especially against missive weapons. However, supposing myself to be a minister of state, I could never give my advice for invading them. Their prudence, unanimity, unacquaintedness with fear, and their love of their country, would amply supply all defects in the military art. Imagine twenty thousand of them breaking into the midst of an European army, confounding the ranks, overturning the carriages, battering the warriors' faces into mummy by terrible yerks from their hinder hoofs; for they would well deserve the character given to Augustus, *Recalcitrat undique tutus*. But, instead of proposals for conquering that magnanimous nation, I rather wish they were in a capacity, or disposition, to send a sufficient number of their inhabitants for civilizing Europe, by teaching us the first principles of honour, justice, truth, temperance, public spirit, fortitude, chastity, friendship, benevolence, and fidelity. The names of all which virtues are still retained among us in most languages, and are to be met with in modern, as well as ancient authors; which I am able to assert from my own small reading.

But I had another reason, which made me less forward to enlarge his majesty's dominions by my discoveries. To say the truth, I had conceived a few scruples with relation to the distributive justice of princes upon those occasions. For instance, a crew of pirates are driven by a storm they know not whither; at length a boy discovers land from the top-mast; they go on shore to rob and plunder, they see a harmless people, are entertained with kindness; they give the country a new name; they take formal possession of it for their king; they set up a rotten plank, or a stone, for a memorial; they murder two or three dozen of the natives, bring away a couple more, by force, for a sample; return home, and get their pardon. Here commences a new dominion acquired with a title by divine right. Ships are sent with the first opportunity; the natives driven out or destroyed; their princes tortured to discover their gold; a free license given to all acts of inhumanity and lust, the earth reeking with the blood of its inhabitants: and this execrable crew of butchers, employed in so pious an expedition, is a modern colony, sent to convert and civilize an idolatrous and barbarous people!

But this description, I confess, does by no means affect the British nation, who may be an example to the whole world for their wisdom, care, and justice in planting colonies; their liberal endowments for the advancement of religion and learning; their choice of devout and able pastors to propagate Christianity; their caution in stocking their provinces with people of sober lives and conversations from this the mother kingdom; their strict regard to the distribution of justice, in supplying the civil administration through all their colonies with officers of the greatest abilities, utter strangers to corruption; and, to crown all, by sending the most vigilant and virtuous governors, who have no other views than the happiness of the people over whom they preside, and the honour of the king their master.

But as those countries which I have described do not appear to have any desire of being conquered and enslaved, murdered or driven out by colonies, nor abound either in gold, silver, sugar, or tobacco, I did humbly conceive, they were by no means proper objects of our zeal, our valour, or our interest. However, if those whom it more concerns think fit to be of another opinion, I am ready to depose, when I shall be lawfully called, that no European did ever visit those countries before me. I mean, if the inhabitants ought to be believed, unless a dispute may arise concerning the two *Yahoos*, said to have been seen many years ago upon a mountain in *Houyhnhnmland*.

But, as to the formality of taking possession in my sovereign's name, it never came once into my thoughts; and if it had, yet, as my affairs then stood, I should perhaps, in point of prudence and self-preservation, have put it off to a better opportunity.

Having thus answered the only objection that can ever be raised against me as a traveller, I here take a final leave of all my courteous readers, and return to enjoy my own speculations in my little garden at Redriff; to apply those excellent lessons of virtue which I learned among the *Houyhnhnms*; to instruct the *Yahoos* of my own family, is far as I shall find them docible animals; to behold my figure often in a glass, and thus, if possible, habituate myself by time to tolerate the sight of a human creature; to lament the brutality to *Houyhnhnms* in my own country, but always treat their persons with respect, for the sake of my noble master, his family, his friends, and the whole *Houyhnhnm* race, whom these of ours have the honour to resemble in all their lineaments, however their intellectuals came to degenerate.

I began last week to permit my wife to sit at dinner with me, at the farthest end of a long table; and to answer (but with the utmost brevity) the few questions I asked her. Yet, the smell of a *Yahoo* continuing very offensive, I always keep my nose well stopped with rue, lavender, or tobacco leaves. And, although it be hard for a man late in life to remove old habits, I am not altogether out of hopes, in some time, to suffer a neighbour *Yahoo* in my company, without the apprehensions I am yet under of his teeth or his claws.

My reconcilement to the *Yahoo* kind in general might not be so difficult, if they would be content with those vices and follies only which nature has entitled them to. I am not in the least provoked at the sight of a lawyer, a pickpocket, a colonel, a fool, a lord, a gamester, a politician, a whoremonger, a physician, an evidence, a suborner, an attorney, a traitor, or the like; this is all according to the due course of things: but when I behold a lump of deformity and diseases, both in body and mind, smitten with pride, it immediately breaks all the measures of my patience; neither shall I be ever able to comprehend how such an animal, and such a vice, could tally together. The wise and virtuous *Houyhnhnms*, who abound in all excellences that can adorn a rational creature, have no name for this vice in their language, which has no terms to express any thing that is evil, except those whereby they describe the detestable qualities of their *Yahoos*, among which they were not able to distinguish this of pride, for want of thoroughly understanding human nature, as it shows itself in other countries where that animal presides. But I, who had more experience, could plainly observe some rudiments of it among the wild *Yahoos*.

But the *Houyhnhnms*, who live under the government of reason, are no more proud of the good qualities they possess, than I should be for not wanting a leg or an arm; which no man in his wits would boast of, although he must be miserable without them. I dwell the longer upon this subject from the desire I have to make the society of an English *Yahoo* by any means not insupportable; and therefore I here entreat those who have any tincture of this absurd vice, that they will not presume to come in my sight.

---

1. This paragraph is not in the original editions.
2. The original editions and Hawksworth's have Rotherhith here, though earlier in the work, Redriff is said to have been Gulliver's home in England.

A MODEST PROPOSAL

A MODEST PROPOSAL

A MODEST PROPOSAL FOR PREVENTING THE CHILDREN OF POOR PEOPLE IN IRELAND, FROM BEING A BURDEN ON THEIR PARENTS OR COUNTRY, AND FOR MAKING THEM BENEFICIAL TO THE PUBLIC.

It is a melancholy object to those, who walk through this great town, or travel in the country, when they see the streets, the roads, and cabin-doors crowded with beggars of the female sex, followed by three, four, or six children, all in rags, and importuning every passenger for an alms. These mothers, instead of being able to work for their honest livelihood, are forced to employ all their time in strolling to beg sustenance for their helpless infants who, as they grow up, either turn thieves for want of work, or leave their dear native country, to fight for the Pretender in Spain, or sell themselves to the Barbados.

I think it is agreed by all parties, that this prodigious number of children in the arms, or on the backs, or at the heels of their mothers, and frequently of their fathers, is in the present deplorable state of the kingdom, a very great additional grievance; and therefore whoever could find out a fair, cheap and easy method of making these children sound and useful members of the commonwealth, would deserve so well of the public, as to have his statue set up for a preserver of the nation.

But my intention is very far from being confined to provide only for the children of professed beggars: it is of a much greater extent, and shall take in the whole number of infants at a certain age, who are born of parents in effect as little able to support them, as those who demand our charity in the streets.

As to my own part, having turned my thoughts for many years upon this important subject, and maturely weighed the several schemes of our projectors, I have always found them grossly mistaken in their computation. It is true, a child just dropped from its dam, may be supported by her milk, for a solar year, with little other nourishment: at most not above the value of two shillings, which the mother may certainly get, or the value in scraps, by her lawful occupation of begging; and it is exactly at one year old that I propose to provide for them in such a manner, as, instead of being a charge upon their parents, or the parish, or wanting food and raiment for the rest of their lives, they shall, on the contrary, contribute to the feeding, and partly to the clothing of many thousands.

There is likewise another great advantage in my scheme, that it will prevent those voluntary abortions, and that horrid practice of women murdering their bastard children, alas! too frequent among us, sacrificing the poor innocent babes, I doubt, more to avoid the expense than the shame, which would move tears and pity in the most savage and inhuman breast.

The number of souls in this kingdom being usually reckoned one million and a half, of these I calculate there may be about two hundred thousand couple, whose wives are breeders; from which number I subtract thirty thousand couple, who are able to maintain their own children, (although I apprehend there cannot be so many under the present distresses of the kingdom) but this being granted, there will remain a hundred and seventy thousand breeders. I again subtract fifty thousand, for those women who miscarry, or whose children die by accident or disease within the year. There only remain a hundred and twenty thousand children of poor parents annually born. The question therefore is, How this number shall be reared and provided for? which, as I have already said, under the present situation of affairs, is utterly impossible by all the methods hitherto proposed. For we can neither employ them in handicraft or agriculture; they neither build houses, (I mean in the country) nor cultivate land: they can very seldom pick up a livelihood by stealing till they arrive at six years old; except where they are of towardly parts, although I confess they learn the rudiments much earlier; during which time they can however be properly looked upon only as probationers; as I have been informed by a principal gentleman in the county of Cavan, who protested to me, that he never knew above one or two instances under the age of six, even in a part of the kingdom so renowned for the quickest proficiency in that art.

I am assured by our merchants, that a boy or a girl, before twelve years old, is no sale-able commodity, and even when they come to this age, they will not yield above three pounds, or three pounds and half a crown at most, on the exchange; which cannot turn to account either to the parents or kingdom, the charge of nutriments and rags having been at least four times that value.

I shall now therefore humbly propose my own thoughts, which I hope will not be liable to the least objection.

I have been assured by a very knowing American of my acquaintance in London, that a young healthy child well nursed, is, at a year old, a most delicious nourishing and wholesome food, whether stewed, roasted, baked, or boiled; and I make no doubt that it will equally serve in a fricassee, or a ragout.

I do therefore humbly offer it to public consideration, that of the hundred and twenty thousand children, already computed, twenty thousand may be reserved for breed, whereof only one fourth part to be males; which is more than we allow to sheep, black cattle, or swine, and my reason is, that these children are seldom the fruits of marriage, a circumstance not much regarded by our savages, therefore, one male will be sufficient to serve four females. That the remaining hundred thousand may, at a year old, be offered in sale to the persons of quality and fortune, through the kingdom, always advising the mother to let them suck plentifully in the last month, so as to render them plump, and fat for a good table. A child will make two dishes at an entertainment for friends, and when the family dines alone, the fore or hind quarter will make a reasonable dish, and seasoned with a little pepper or salt, will be very good boiled on the fourth day, especially in winter.

I have reckoned upon a medium, that a child just born will weigh 12 pounds, and in a solar year, if tolerably nursed, increase to 28 pounds.

I grant this food will be somewhat dear, and therefore very proper for landlords, who, as they have already devoured most of the parents, seem to have the best title to the children.

Infant's flesh will be in season throughout the year, but more plentiful in March, and a little before and after; for we are told by a grave author, an eminent French physician, that fish being a prolific diet, there are more children born in Roman Catholic countries about nine months after Lent, than at any other season; therefore, reckoning a year after Lent, the markets will be more glutted than usual, because the number of Popish infants, is at least three to one in this kingdom, and therefore it will have one other collateral advantage, by lessening the number of Papists among us.

I have already computed the charge of nursing a beggar's child (in which list I reckon all cottagers, laborers, and four-fifths of the farmers) to be about two shillings per annum, rags included; and I believe no gentleman would repine to give ten shillings for the carcass of a good fat child, which, as I have said, will make four dishes of excellent nutritive meat, when he hath only some particular friend, or his own family to dine with him. Thus the squire will learn to be a good landlord, and grow popular among his tenants, the mother will have eight shillings neat profit, and be fit for work till she produces another child.

Those who are more thrifty (as I must confess the times require) may flay the carcass; the skin of which, artificially dressed, will make admirable gloves for ladies, and summer boots for fine gentlemen.

As to our City of Dublin, shambles may be appointed for this purpose, in the most convenient parts of it, and butchers we may be assured will not be wanting; although I rather recommend buying the children alive, and dressing them hot from the knife, as we do roasting pigs.

A very worthy person, a true lover of his country, and whose virtues I highly esteem, was lately pleased in discoursing on this matter, to offer a refinement upon my scheme. He said, that many gentlemen of this kingdom, having of late destroyed their deer, he conceived that the want of venison might be well supplied by the bodies of young lads and maidens, not exceeding fourteen years of age, nor under twelve; so great a number of both sexes in every county being now ready to starve for want of work and service: and these to be disposed of by their parents if alive, or otherwise by their nearest relations. But with due deference to so excellent a friend, and so deserving a patriot, I cannot be altogether in his sentiments; for as to the males, my American acquaintance assured me from frequent experience, that their flesh was generally tough and lean, like that of our schoolboys, by continual exercise, and their taste disagreeable, and to fatten them would not answer the charge. Then as to the females, it would, I think, with humble submission, be a loss to the public, because they soon would become breeders themselves: and besides, it is not improbable that some scrupulous people might be apt to censure such a practice, (although indeed very unjustly) as a little bordering upon cruelty, which, I confess, hath always been with me the strongest objection against any project, how well soever intended.

But in order to justify my friend, he confessed, that this expedient was put into his head by the famous Psalmanaazor, a native of the island Formosa, who came from thence to London, above twenty years ago, and in conversation told my friend, that in his country, when any young person happened to be put to death, the executioner sold the carcass to persons of quality, as a prime dainty; and that, in his time, the body of a plump girl of fifteen, who was crucified for an attempt to poison the Emperor, was sold to his imperial majesty's prime minister of state, and other great mandarins of the court in joints from the gibbet, at four hundred crowns. Neither indeed can I deny, that if the same use were made of several plump young girls in this town, who without one single groat to their fortunes, cannot stir abroad without a chair, and appear at a playhouse and assemblies in foreign fineries which they never will pay for, the kingdom would not be the worse.

Some persons of a desponding spirit are in great concern about that vast number of poor people, who are aged, diseased, or maimed; and I have been desired to employ my thoughts what course may be taken, to ease the nation of so grievous an incumbrance. But I am not in the least pain upon that matter, because it is very well known, that they are every day dying, and rotting, by cold and famine, and filth, and vermin, as fast as can be reasonably expected. And as to the young laborers, they are now in almost as hopeful a condition. They cannot get work, and consequently pine away from want of nourishment, to a degree, that if at any time they are accidentally hired to common labour, they have not strength to perform it, and thus the country and themselves are happily delivered from the evils to come.

I have too long digressed, and therefore shall return to my subject. I think the advantages by the proposal which I have made are obvious and many, as well as of the highest importance.

For first, as I have already observed, it would greatly lessen the number of Papists, with whom we are yearly overrun, being the principal breeders of the nation, as well as our most dangerous enemies, and who stay at home on purpose with a design to deliver the kingdom to the Pretender, hoping to take their advantage by the absence of so many good Protestants, who have chosen rather to leave their country, than stay at home and pay tithes against their conscience to an episcopal curate.

Secondly, The poorer tenants will have something valuable of their own, which by law may be made liable to a distress, and help to pay their landlord's rent, their corn and cattle being already seized, and money a thing unknown.

Thirdly, Whereas the maintenance of a hundred thousand children, from two years old, and upwards, cannot be computed at less than ten shillings a piece per annum, the nation's stock will be thereby increased fifty thousand pounds per annum, besides the profit of a new dish, introduced to the tables of all gentlemen of fortune in the kingdom, who have any refinement in taste. And the money will circulate among our selves, the goods being entirely of our own growth and manufacture.

Fourthly, The constant breeders, besides the gain of eight shillings sterling per annum by the sale of their children, will be rid of the charge of maintaining them after the first year.

Fifthly, This food would likewise bring great custom to taverns, where the vintners will certainly be so prudent as to procure the best receipts for dressing it to perfection; and consequently have their houses frequented by all the fine gentlemen, who justly value themselves upon their knowledge in good eating; and a skillful cook, who understands how to oblige his guests, will contrive to make it as expensive as they please.

Sixthly, This would be a great inducement to marriage, which all wise nations have either encouraged by rewards, or enforced by laws and penalties. It would increase the care and tenderness of mothers towards their children, when they were sure of a settlement for life to the poor babes, provided in some sort by the public, to their annual profit instead of expense. We should soon see an honest emulation among the married women, which of them could bring the fattest child to the market. Men would become as fond of their wives, during the time of their pregnancy, as they are now of their mares in foal, their cows in calf, or sows when they are ready to farrow; nor offer to beat or kick them (as is too frequent a practice) for fear of a miscarriage.

Many other advantages might be enumerated. For instance, the addition of some thousand carcasses in our exportation of barrel'd beef: the propagation of swine's flesh, and improvement in the art of making good bacon, so much wanted among us by the great destruction of pigs, too frequent at our tables; which are no way comparable in taste or magnificence to a well grown, fat yearling child, which roasted whole will make a considerable figure at a Lord Mayor's feast, or any other public entertainment. But this, and many others, I omit, being studious of brevity.

Supposing that one thousand families in this city, would be constant customers for infants flesh, besides others who might have it at merry meetings, particularly at weddings and christenings, I compute that Dublin would take off annually about twenty thousand carcasses; and the rest of the kingdom (where probably they will be sold somewhat cheaper) the remaining eighty thousand.

I can think of no one objection, that will possibly be raised against this proposal, unless it should be urged, that the number of people will be thereby much lessened in the kingdom. This I freely own, and was indeed one principal design in offering it to the world. I desire the reader will observe, that I calculate my remedy for this one individual Kingdom of Ireland, and for no other that ever was, is, or, I think, ever can be upon Earth. Therefore let no man talk to me of other expedients: Of taxing our absentees at five shillings a pound: Of using neither clothes, nor household furniture, except what is of our own growth and manufacture: Of utterly rejecting the materials and instruments that promote foreign luxury: Of curing the expensiveness of pride, vanity, idleness, and gaming in our women: Of introducing a vein of parsimony, prudence and temperance: Of learning to love our country, wherein we differ even from Laplanders, and the inhabitants of Topinamboo: Of quitting our animosities and factions, nor acting any longer like the Jews, who were murdering one another at the very moment their city was taken: Of being a little cautious not to sell our country and consciences for nothing: Of teaching landlords to have at least one degree of mercy towards their tenants. Lastly, of putting a spirit of honesty, industry, and skill into our shopkeepers, who, if a resolution could now be taken to buy only our native goods, would immediately unite to cheat and exact upon us in the price, the measure, and the goodness, nor could ever yet be brought to make one fair proposal of just dealing, though often and earnestly invited to it.

Therefore I repeat, let no man talk to me of these and the like expedients, till he hath at least some glimpse of hope, that there will ever be some hearty and sincere attempt to put them into practice.

But, as to myself, having been wearied out for many years with offering vain, idle, visionary thoughts, and at length utterly despairing of success, I fortunately fell upon this proposal, which, as it is wholly new, so it hath something solid and real, of no expense and little trouble, full in our own power, and whereby we can incur no danger in disobliging England. For this kind of commodity will not bear exportation, and flesh being of too tender a consistency, to admit a long continuance in salt, although perhaps I could name a country, which would be glad to eat up our whole nation without it.

After all, I am not so violently bent upon my own opinion, as to reject any offer, proposed by wise men, which shall be found equally innocent, cheap, easy, and effectual. But before something of that kind shall be advanced in contradiction to my scheme, and offering a better, I desire the author or authors will be pleased maturely to consider two points. First, As things now stand, how they will be able to find food and raiment for a hundred thousand useless mouths and backs. And secondly, There being a round million of creatures in humane figure throughout this kingdom, whose whole subsistence put into a common stock, would leave them in debt two million of pounds sterling, adding those who are beggars by profession, to the bulk of farmers, cottagers and laborers, with their wives and children, who are beggars in effect; I desire those politicians who dislike my overture, and may perhaps be so bold to attempt an answer, that they will first ask the parents of these mortals, whether they would not at this day think it a great happiness to have been sold for food at a year old, in the manner I prescribe, and thereby have avoided such a perpetual scene of misfortunes, as they have since gone through, by the oppression of landlords, the impossibility of paying rent without money or trade, the want of common sustenance, with neither house nor clothes to cover them from the inclemencies of the weather, and the most inevitable prospect of entailing the like, or greater miseries, upon their breed for ever.

I profess in the sincerity of my heart, that I have not the least personal interest in endeavoring to promote this necessary work, having no other motive than the public good of my country, by advancing our trade, providing for infants, relieving the poor, and giving some pleasure to the rich. I have no children, by which I can propose to get a single penny; the youngest being nine years old, and my wife past child-bearing.

THE BATTLE OF THE BOOKS
& OTHER SHORT PIECES

THE BATTLE OF THE BOOKS &
OTHER SHORT PIECES

THE BATTLE OF THE BOOKS: A FULL AND TRUE ACCOUNT OF THE BATTLE FOUGHT LAST FRIDAY BETWEEN THE ANCIENT AND THE MODERN BOOKS IN SAINT JAMES'S LIBRARY.

Whoever examines, with due circumspection, into the annual records of time, will find it remarked that War is the child of Pride, and Pride the daughter of Riches: —the former of which assertions may be soon granted, but one cannot so easily subscribe to the latter; for Pride is nearly related to Beggary and Want, either by father or mother, and sometimes by both: and, to speak naturally, it very seldom happens among men to fall out when all have enough; invasions usually traveling from north to south, that is to say, from poverty to plenty. The most ancient and natural grounds of quarrels are lust and avarice; which, though we may allow to be brethren, or collateral branches of pride, are certainly the issues of want. For, to speak in the phrase of writers upon politics, we may observe in the republic of dogs, which in its original seems to be an institution of the many, that the whole state is ever in the profoundest peace after a full meal; and that civil broils arise among them when it happens for one great bone to be seized on by some leading dog, who either divides it among the few, and then it falls to an oligarchy, or keeps it to himself, and then it runs up to a tyranny. The same reasoning also holds place among them in those dissensions we behold upon a turgescenncy in any of their females. For the right of possession lying in common (it being impossible to establish a property in so delicate a case), jealousies and suspicions do so abound, that the whole commonwealth of that street is reduced to a manifest state of war, of every citizen against every citizen, till some one of more courage, conduct, or fortune than the rest seizes and enjoys the prize: upon which naturally arises plenty of heart-burning, and envy, and snarling against the happy dog. Again, if we look upon any of these republics engaged in a foreign war, either of invasion or defense, we shall find the same reasoning will serve as to the grounds and occasions of each; and that poverty or want, in some degree or other (whether real or in opinion, which makes no alteration in the case), has a great share, as well as pride, on the part of the aggressor.

Now whoever will please to take this scheme, and either reduce or adapt it to an intellectual state or commonwealth of learning, will soon discover the first ground of disagreement between the two great parties at this time in arms, and may form just conclusions upon the merits of either cause. But the issue or events of this war are not so easy to conjecture at; for the present quarrel is so inflamed by the warm heads of either faction, and the pretensions somewhere or other so exorbitant, as not to admit the least overtures of accommodation. This quarrel first began, as I have heard it affirmed by an old dweller in the neighborhood, about a small spot of ground, lying and being upon one of the two tops of the hill Parnassus; the highest and largest of which had, it seems, been time out of mind in quiet possession of certain tenants, called the Ancients; and the other was held by the Moderns. But these disliking their present station, sent certain ambassadors to the Ancients, complaining of a great nuisance; how the height of that part of Parnassus quite spoiled the prospect of theirs, especially towards the east; and therefore, to avoid a war, offered them the choice of this alternative, either that the Ancients would please to remove themselves and their effects down to the lower summit, which the Moderns would graciously surrender to them, and advance into their place; or else the said Ancients will give leave to the Moderns to come with shovels and mattocks, and level the said hill as low as they shall think it convenient. To which the Ancients made answer, how little they expected such a message as this from a colony whom they had admitted, out of their own free grace, to so near a neighborhood. That, as to their own seat, they were aborigines of it, and therefore to talk with them of a removal or surrender was a language they did not understand. That if the height of the hill on their side shortened the prospect of the Moderns, it was a disadvantage they could not help; but desired them to consider whether that injury (if it be any) were not largely recompensed by the shade and shelter it afforded them. That as to the leveling or digging down, it was either folly or ignorance to propose it if they did or did not know how that side of the hill was an entire rock, which would break their tools and hearts, without any damage to itself. That they would therefore advise the Moderns rather to raise their own side of the hill than dream of pulling down that of the

Ancients; to the former of which they would not only give license, but also largely contribute. All this was rejected by the Moderns with much indignation, who still insisted upon one of the two expedients; and so this difference broke out into a long and obstinate war, maintained on the one part by resolution, and by the courage of certain leaders and allies; but, on the other, by the greatness of their number, upon all defeats affording continual recruits. In this quarrel whole rivulets of ink have been exhausted, and the virulence of both parties enormously augmented. Now, it must be here understood, that ink is the great missive weapon in all battles of the learned, which, conveyed through a sort of engine called a quill, infinite numbers of these are darted at the enemy by the valiant on each side, with equal skill and violence, as if it were an engagement of porcupines. This malignant liquor was compounded, by the engineer who invented it, of two ingredients, which are, gall and copperas; by its bitterness and venom to suit, in some degree, as well as to foment, the genius of the combatants. And as the Grecians, after an engagement, when they could not agree about the victory, were wont to set up trophies on both sides, the beaten party being content to be at the same expense, to keep itself in countenance (a laudable and ancient custom, happily revived of late in the art of war), so the learned, after a sharp and bloody dispute, do, on both sides, hang out their trophies too, whichever comes by the worst. These trophies have largely inscribed on them the merits of the cause; a full impartial account of such a Battle, and how the victory fell clearly to the party that set them up. They are known to the world under several names; as disputes, arguments, rejoinders, brief considerations, answers, replies, remarks, reflections, objections, confutations. For a very few days they are fixed up all in public places, either by themselves or their representatives, for passengers to gaze at; whence the chiefest and largest are removed to certain magazines they call libraries, there to remain in a quarter purposely assigned them, and thenceforth begin to be called books of controversy.

In these books is wonderfully instilled and preserved the spirit of each warrior while he is alive; and after his death his soul transmigrates thither to inform them. This, at least, is the more common opinion; but I believe it is with libraries as with other cemeteries, where some philosophers affirm that a certain spirit, which they call *brutum hominis*, hovers over the monument, till the body is corrupted and turns to dust or to worms, but then vanishes or dissolves; so, we may say, a restless spirit haunts over every book, till dust or worms have seized upon it—which to some may happen in a few days, but to others later—and therefore, books of controversy being, of all others, haunted by the most disorderly spirits, have always been confined in a separate lodge from the rest, and for fear of a mutual violence against each other, it was thought prudent by our ancestors to bind them to the peace with strong iron chains. Of which invention the original occasion was this: When the works of Scotus first came out, they were carried to a certain library, and had lodgings appointed them; but this author was no sooner settled than he went to visit his master Aristotle, and there both concerted together to seize Plato by main force, and turn him out from his ancient station among the divines, where he had peaceably dwelt near eight hundred years. The attempt succeeded, and the two usurpers have reigned ever since in his stead; but, to maintain quiet for the future, it was decreed that all polemics of the larger size should be hold fast with a chain.

By this expedient, the public peace of libraries might certainly have been preserved if a new species of controversial books had not arisen of late years, instinct with a more malignant spirit, from the war above mentioned between the learned about the higher summit of Parnassus.

When these books were first admitted into the public libraries, I remember to have said, upon occasion, to several persons concerned, how I was sure they would create broils wherever they came, unless a world of care were taken; and therefore I advised that the champions of each side should be coupled together, or otherwise mixed, that, like the blending of contrary poisons, their malignity might be employed among themselves. And it seems I was neither an ill prophet nor an ill counsellor; for it was nothing else but the neglect of this caution which gave occasion to the terrible fight that happened on Friday last between the Ancient and Modern Books in the King's library. Now, because the talk of this battle is so fresh in everybody's mouth, and the expectation of the town so great to be informed in the particulars, I, being possessed of all qualifications requisite in an historian, and retained by neither party, have resolved to comply with the urgent importunity of my friends, by writing down a full impartial account thereof.

The guardian of the regal library, a person of great valor, but chiefly renowned for his humanity, had been a fierce champion for the Moderns, and, in an engagement upon Parnassus, had vowed with his own hands to knock down two of the ancient chiefs who guarded a small pass on the superior rock, but, endeavoring to climb up, was cruelly obstructed by his own unhappy weight and tendency towards his centre, a quality to which those of the Modern party are extremely subject; for, being light-headed, they have, in speculation, a wonderful agility, and conceive nothing too high for them to mount, but, in reducing to practice, discover a mighty pressure about their posteriors and their heels. Having thus failed in his design, the disappointed champion bore a cruel rancor to the Ancients, which he resolved to gratify by showing all marks of his favor to the books of their adversaries, and lodging them in the fairest apartments; when, at the same time, whatever book had the boldness to own itself for an advocate of the Ancients was buried alive in some obscure corner, and threatened, upon the least displeasure, to be turned out of doors. Besides, it so happened that about this time there was a strange confusion of place among all the books in the library, for which several reasons were assigned. Some imputed it to a great heap of learned dust, which a perverse wind blew off from a shelf of Moderns into the keeper's eyes. Others affirmed he had a humor to pick the worms out of the schoolmen, and swallow them fresh and fasting, whereof some fell upon his spleen, and some climbed up into his head, to the great perturbation of both. And lastly, others maintained that, by walking much in the dark about the library, he had quite lost the situation of it out of his head; and therefore, in replacing his books, he was apt to mistake and clap Descartes next to Aristotle, poor Plato had got between Hobbes and the Seven Wise Masters, and Virgil was hemmed in with Dryden on one side and Wither on the other.

Meanwhile, those books that were advocates for the Moderns, chose out one from among them to make a progress through the whole library, examine the number and strength of their party, and concert their affairs. This messenger performed all things very industriously, and brought back with him a list of their forces, in all, fifty thousand, consisting chiefly of light-horse, heavy-armed foot, and mercenaries; whereof the foot were in general but sorrily armed and worse clad; their horses large, but extremely out of case and heart; however, some few, by trading among the Ancients, had furnished themselves tolerably enough.

While things were in this ferment, discord grew extremely high; hot words passed on both sides, and ill blood was plentifully bred. Here a solitary Ancient, squeezed up among a whole shelf of Moderns, offered fairly to dispute the case, and to prove by manifest reason that the priority was due to them from long possession, and in regard of their prudence, antiquity, and, above all, their great merits toward the Moderns. But these denied the premises, and seemed very much to wonder how the Ancients could pretend to insist upon their antiquity, when it was so plain (if they went to that) that the Moderns were much the more ancient of the two. As for any obligations they owed to the Ancients, they renounced them all. "It is true," said they, "we are informed some few of our party have been so mean as to borrow their subsistence from you, but the rest, infinitely the greater number (and especially we French and English), were so far from stooping to so base an example, that there never passed, till this very hour, six words between us. For our horses were of our own breeding, our arms of our own forging, and our clothes of our own cutting out and sewing." Plato was by chance up on the next shelf, and observing those that spoke to be in the ragged plight mentioned a while ago, their jades lean and foundered, their weapons of rotten wood, their armour rusty, and nothing but rags underneath, he laughed loud, and in his pleasant way swore, by ---, he believed them.

Now, the Moderns had not proceeded in their late negotiation with secrecy enough to escape the notice of the enemy. For those advocates who had begun the quarrel, by setting first on foot the dispute of precedency, talked so loud of coming to a battle, that Sir William Temple happened to overhear them, and gave immediate intelligence to the Ancients, who thereupon drew up their scattered troops together, resolving to act upon the defensive; upon which, several of the Moderns fled over to their party, and among the rest Temple himself. This Temple, having been educated and long conversed among the Ancients, was, of all the Moderns, their greatest favorite, and became their greatest champion.

Things were at this crisis when a material accident fell out. For upon the highest corner of a large window, there dwelt a certain spider, swollen up to the first magnitude by the destruction of infinite numbers of flies, whose spoils lay scattered before the gates of his palace, like human bones before the cave of some giant. The avenues to his castle were guarded with turnpikes and palisades, all after the modern way of fortification. After you had passed several courts you came to the centre, wherein you might behold the constable himself in his own lodgings, which had windows fronting to each avenue, and ports to sally out upon all occasions of prey or defense. In this mansion he had for some time dwelt in peace and plenty, without danger to his person by swallows from above, or to his palace by brooms from below; when it was the pleasure of fortune to conduct thither a wandering bee, to whose curiosity a broken pane in the glass had discovered itself, and in he went, where, expatiating a while, he at last happened to alight upon one of the outward walls of the spider's citadel; which, yielding to the unequal weight, sunk down to the very foundation. Thrice he endeavored to force his passage, and thrice the centre shook. The spider within, feeling the terrible convulsion, supposed at first that nature was approaching to her final dissolution, or else that Beelzebub, with all his legions, was come to revenge the death of many thousands of his subjects whom his enemy had slain and devoured. However, he at length valiantly resolved to issue forth and meet his fate. Meanwhile the bee had acquitted himself of his toils, and, posted securely at some distance, was employed in cleansing his wings, and disengaging them from the ragged remnants of the cobweb. By this time the spider was adventured out, when, beholding the chasms, the ruins, and dilapidations of his fortress, he was very near at his wit's end; he stormed and swore like a madman, and swelled till he was ready to burst. At length, casting his eye upon the bee, and wisely gathering causes from events (for they know each other by sight), "A plague split you," said he; "is it you, with a vengeance, that have made this litter here; could not you look before you, and be d---d? Do you think I have nothing else to do (in the devil's name) but to mend and repair after you?" "Good words, friend," said the bee, having now pruned himself, and being disposed to droll; "I'll give you my hand and word to come near your kennel no more; I was never in such a confounded pickle since I was born." "Sirrah," replied the spider, "if it were not for breaking an old custom in our family, never to stir abroad against an enemy, I should come and teach you better manners." "I pray have patience," said the bee, "or you'll spend your substance, and, for aught I see, you may stand in need of it all, towards the repair of your house." "Rogue, rogue," replied the spider, "yet methinks you should have more respect to a person whom all the world allows to be so much your betters." "By my troth," said the bee, "the comparison will amount to a very good jest, and you will do me a favor to let me know the reasons that all the world is pleased to use in so hopeful a dispute." At this the spider, having swelled himself into the size and posture of a disputant, began his argument in the true spirit of controversy, with resolution to be heartily scurrilous and angry, to urge on his own reasons without the least regard to the answers or objections of his opposite, and fully predetermined in his mind against all conviction.

"Not to disparage myself," said he, "by the comparison with such a rascal, what art thou but a vagabond without house or home, without stock or inheritance? born to no possession of your own, but a pair of wings and a drone-pipe. Your livelihood is a universal plunder upon nature; a freebooter over fields and gardens; and, for the sake of stealing, will rob a nettle as easily as a violet. Whereas I am a domestic animal, furnished with a native stock within myself. This large castle (to show my improvements in the mathematics) is all built with my own hands, and the materials extracted altogether out of my own person."

"I am glad," answered the bee, "to hear you grant at least that I am come honestly by my wings and my voice; for then, it seems, I am obliged to Heaven alone for my flights and my music; and Providence would never have bestowed on me two such gifts without designing them for the noblest ends. I visit, indeed, all the flowers and blossoms of the field and garden, but whatever I collect thence enriches myself without the least injury to their beauty, their smell, or their taste. Now, for you and your skill in architecture and other mathematics, I have little to say: in that building of yours there might, for aught I know, have been labour and method enough; but, by woeful experience for us both, it is too plain the materials are naught; and I hope you will henceforth take warning, and consider duration and matter, as well as method and art. You boast, indeed, of being obliged to no other creature, but of drawing and spinning out all from yourself; that is to say, if we may judge of the liquor in the vessel by what issues out, you possess a good plentiful store of dirt and poison in your breast; and, though I would by no means lesson or disparage your genuine stock of either, yet I doubt you are somewhat obliged, for an increase of both, to a little foreign assistance. Your inherent portion of dirt does not fall of acquisitions, by sweepings exhaled from below; and one insect furnishes you with a share of poison to destroy another. So that, in short, the question comes all to this: whether is the nobler being of the two, that which, by a lazy contemplation of four inches round, by an overweening pride, feeding, and engendering on itself, turns all into excrement and venom, producing nothing at all but flybane and a cobweb; or that which, by a universal range, with long search, much study, true judgment, and distinction of things, brings home honey and wax."

This dispute was managed with such eagerness, clamor, and warmth, that the two parties of books, in arms below, stood silent a while, waiting in suspense what would be the issue; which was not long undetermined: for the bee, grown impatient at so much loss of time, fled straight away to a bed of roses, without looking for a reply, and left the spider, like an orator, collected in himself, and just prepared to burst out.

It happened upon this emergency that Aesop broke silence first. He had been of late most barbarously treated by a strange effect of the regent's humanity, who had torn off his title-page, sorely defaced one half of his leaves, and chained him fast among a shelf of Moderns. Where, soon discovering how high the quarrel was likely to proceed, he tried all his arts, and turned himself to a thousand forms. At length, in the borrowed shape of an ass, the regent mistook him for a Modern; by which means he had time and opportunity to escape to the Ancients, just when the spider and the bee were entering into their contest; to which he gave his attention with a world of pleasure, and, when it was ended, swore in the loudest key that in all his life he had never known two cases, so parallel and adapt to each other as that in the window and this upon the shelves. "The disputants," said he, "have admirably managed the dispute between them, have taken in the full strength of all that is to be said on both sides, and exhausted the substance of every argument *pro* and *con*. It is but to adjust the reasonings of both to the present quarrel, then to compare and apply the labors and fruits of each, as the bee has learnedly deduced them, and we shall find the conclusion fall plain and close upon the Moderns and us. For pray, gentlemen, was ever anything so modern as the spider in his air, his turns, and his paradoxes? he argues in the behalf of you, his brethren, and himself, with many boastings of his native stock and great genius; that he spins and spits wholly from himself, and scorns to own any obligation or assistance from without. Then he displays to you his great skill in architecture and improvement in the mathematics. To all this the bee, as an advocate retained by us, the Ancients, thinks fit to answer, that, if one may judge of the great genius or inventions of the Moderns by what they have produced, you will hardly have countenance to bear you out in boasting of either. Erect your schemes with as much method and skill as you please; yet, if the materials be nothing but dirt, spun out of your own entrails (the guts of modern brains), the edifice will conclude at last in a cobweb; the duration of which, like that of other spiders' webs, may be imputed to their being forgotten, or neglected, or hid in a corner. For anything else of genuine that the Moderns may pretend to, I cannot recollect;

unless it be a large vein of wrangling and satire, much of a nature and substance with the spiders' poison; which, however they pretend to spit wholly out of themselves, is improved by the same arts, by feeding upon the insects and vermin of the age. As for us, the Ancients, we are content with the bee, to pretend to nothing of our own beyond our wings and our voice: that is to say, our flights and our language. For the rest, whatever we have got has been by infinite labour and search, and ranging through every corner of nature; the difference is, that, instead of dirt and poison, we have rather chosen to till our hives with honey and wax; thus furnishing mankind with the two noblest of things, which are sweetness and light."

It is wonderful to conceive the tumult arisen among the books upon the close of this long descant of Aesop: both parties took the hint, and heightened their animosities so on a sudden, that they resolved it should come to a battle. Immediately the two main bodies withdrew, under their several ensigns, to the farther parts of the library, and there entered into cabals and consults upon the present emergency. The Moderns were in very warm debates upon the choice of their leaders; and nothing less than the fear impending from their enemies could have kept them from mutinies upon this occasion. The difference was greatest among the horse, where every private trooper pretended to the chief command, from Tasso and Milton to Dryden and Wither. The light-horse were commanded by Cowley and Despreaux. There came the bowmen under their valiant leaders, Descartes, Gassendi, and Hobbes; whose strength was such that they could shoot their arrows beyond the atmosphere, never to fall down again, but turn, like that of Evander, into meteors; or, like the cannon-ball, into stars. Paracelsus brought a squadron of stinkpot-flingers from the snowy mountains of Rhætia. There came a vast body of dragoons, of different nations, under the leading of Harvey, their great aga: part armed with scythes, the weapons of death; part with lances and long knives, all steeped in poison; part shot bullets of a most malignant nature, and used white powder, which infallibly killed without report. There came several bodies of heavy-armed foot, all mercenaries, under the ensigns of Guicciardini, Davila, Polydore Vergil, Buchanan, Mariana, Camden, and others. The engineers were commanded by Regiomontanus and Wilkins. The rest was a confused multitude, led by Scotus, Aquinas, and Bellarmine; of mighty bulk and stature, but without either arms, courage, or discipline. In the last place came infinite swarms of calones, a disorderly rout led by L'Estrange; rogues and ragamuffins, that follow the camp for nothing but the plunder, all without coats to cover them.

The army of the Ancients was much fewer in number; Homer led the horse, and Pindar the light-horse; Euclid was chief engineer; Plato and Aristotle commanded the bowmen; Herodotus and Livy the foot; Hippocrates, the dragoons; the allies, led by Vossius and Temple, brought up the rear.

All things violently tending to a decisive battle, Fame, who much frequented, and had a large apartment formerly assigned her in the regal library, fled up straight to Jupiter, to whom she delivered a faithful account of all that passed between the two parties below; for among the gods she always tells truth. Jove, in great concern, convokes a council in the Milky Way. The senate assembled, he declares the occasion of convening them; a bloody battle just impendent between two mighty armies of ancient and modern creatures, called books, wherein the celestial interest was but too deeply concerned. Momus, the patron of the Moderns, made an excellent speech in their favor, which was answered by Pallas, the protectress of the Ancients. The assembly was divided in their affections; when Jupiter commanded the Book of Fate to be laid before him. Immediately were brought by Mercury three large volumes in folio, containing memoirs of all things past, present, and to come. The clasps were of silver double gilt, the covers of celestial turkey leather, and the paper such as here on earth might pass almost for vellum. Jupiter, having silently read the decree, would communicate the import to none, but presently shut up the book.

Without the doors of this assembly there attended a vast number of light, nimble gods, menial servants to Jupiter: those are his ministering instruments in all affairs below. They travel in a caravan, more or less together, and are fastened to each other like a link of galley-slaves, by a light chain, which passes from them to Jupiter's great toe: and yet, in receiving or delivering a message, they may never approach above the lowest step of his throne, where he and they whisper to each other through a large hollow trunk. These deities are called by mortal men accidents or events; but the gods call them second causes. Jupiter having delivered his message to a certain number of these divinities, they flew immediately down to the pinnacle of the regal library, and consulting a few minutes, entered unseen, and disposed the parties according to their orders.

Meanwhile Momus, fearing the worst, and calling to mind an ancient prophecy which bore no very good face to his children the Moderns, bent his flight to the region of a malignant deity called Criticism. She dwelt on the top of a snowy mountain in Nova Zembla; there Momus found her extended in her den, upon the spoils of numberless volumes, half devoured. At her right hand sat Ignorance, her father and husband, blind with age; at her left, Pride, her mother, dressing her up in the scraps of paper herself had torn. There was Opinion, her sister, light of foot, hood-winked, and head-strong, yet giddy and perpetually turning. About her played her children, Noise and Impudence, Dulness and Vanity, Positiveness, Pedantry, and Ill-manners. The goddess herself had claws like a cat; her head, and ears, and voice resembled those of an ass; her teeth fallen out before, her eyes turned inward, as if she looked only upon herself; her diet was the overflowing of her own gall; her spleen was so large as to stand prominent, like a dug of the first rate; nor wanted excrescences in form of teats, at which a crew of ugly monsters were greedily sucking; and, what is wonderful to conceive, the bulk of spleen increased faster than the sucking could diminish it. "Goddess," said Momus, "can you sit idly here while our devout worshippers, the Moderns, are this minute entering into a cruel battle, and perhaps now lying under the swords of their enemies? who then hereafter will ever sacrifice or build altars to our divinities? Haste, therefore, to the British Isle, and, if possible, prevent their destruction; while I make factions among the gods, and gain them over to our party."

Momus, having thus delivered himself, stayed not for an answer, but left the goddess to her own resentment. Up she rose in a rage, and, as it is the form on such occasions, began a soliloquy: "It is I" (said she) "who give wisdom to infants and idiots; by me children grow wiser than their parents, by me beaux become politicians, and schoolboys judges of philosophy; by me sophisters debate and conclude upon the depths of knowledge; and coffee-house wits, instinct by me, can correct an author's style, and display his minutest errors, without understanding a syllable of his matter or his language; by me striplings spend their judgment, as they do their estate, before it comes into their hands. It is I who have deposed wit and knowledge from their empire over poetry, and advanced myself in their stead. And shall a few upstart Ancients dare to oppose me? But come, my aged parent, and you, my children dear, and thou, my beauteous sister; let us ascend my chariot, and haste to assist our devout Moderns, who are now sacrificing to us a hecatomb, as I perceive by that grateful smell which from thence reaches my nostrils."

The goddess and her train, having mounted the chariot, which was drawn by tame geese, flew over infinite regions, shedding her influence in due places, till at length she arrived at her beloved island of Britain; but in hovering over its metropolis, what blessings did she not let fall upon her seminaries of Gresham and Covent-garden! And now she reached the fatal plain of St. James's library, at what time the two armies were upon the point to engage; where, entering with all her caravan unseen, and landing upon a case of shelves, now desert, but once inhabited by a colony of virtuosos, she stayed awhile to observe the posture of both armies.

But here the tender cares of a mother began to fill her thoughts and move in her breast: for at the head of a troop of Modern bowmen she cast her eyes upon her son Wotton, to whom the fates had assigned a very short thread. Wotton, a young hero, whom an unknown father of mortal race begot by stolen embraces with this goddess. He was the darling of his mother above all her children, and she resolved to go and comfort him. But first, according to the good old custom of deities, she cast about to change her shape, for fear the divinity of her countenance might dazzle his mortal sight and overcharge the rest of his senses. She therefore gathered up her person into an octavo compass: her body grow white and arid, and split in pieces with dryness; the thick turned into pasteboard, and the thin into paper; upon which her parents and children artfully strewed a black juice, or decoction of gall and soot, in form of letters: her head, and voice, and spleen, kept their primitive form; and that which before was a cover of skin did still continue so. In this guise she marched on towards the Moderns, indistinguishable in shape and dress from the divine Bentley, Wotton's dearest friend. "Brave Wotton," said the goddess, "why do our troops stand idle here, to spend their present vigor and opportunity of the day? away, let us haste to the generals, and advise to give the onset immediately." Having spoke thus, she took the ugliest of her monsters, full glutted from her spleen, and flung it invisibly into his mouth, which, flying straight up into his head, squeezed out his eye-balls, gave him a distorted look, and half-overturned his brain. Then she privately ordered two of her beloved children, Dulness and Ill-manners, closely to attend his person in all encounters. Having thus accoutered him, she vanished in a mist, and the hero perceived it was the goddess his mother.

The destined hour of fate being now arrived, the fight began; whereof, before I dare adventure to make a particular description, I must, after the example of other authors, petition for a hundred tongues, and mouths, and hands, and pens, which would all be too little to perform so immense a work. Say, goddess, that presides over history, who it was that first advanced in the field of battle! Paracelsus, at the head of his dragoons, observing Galen in the adverse wing, darted his javelin with a mighty force, which the brave Ancient received upon his shield, the point breaking in the second fold . . .

Hic pauca
. . . . desunt

They bore the wounded aga on their shields to his

chariot . . .
Desunt . . .
nonnulla. . . .

Then Aristotle, observing Bacon advance with a furious mien, drew his bow to the head, and let fly his arrow, which missed the valiant Modern and went whizzing over his head; but Descartes it hit; the steel point quickly found a defect in his head-piece; it pierced the leather and the pasteboard, and went in at his right eye. The torture of the pain whirled the valiant bow-man round till death, like a star of superior influence, drew him into his own vortex

Ingens hiatus . . . .
hic in MS. . . . .

. . . . when Homer appeared at the head of the cavalry, mounted on a furious horse, with difficulty managed by the rider himself, but which no other mortal durst approach; he rode among the enemy's ranks, and bore down all before him. Say, goddess, whom he slew first and whom he slew last! First, Gondibert advanced against him, clad in heavy armor and mounted on a staid sober gelding, not so famed for his speed as his docility in kneeling whenever his rider would mount or alight. He had made a vow to Pallas that he would never leave the field till he had spoiled Homer of his armor: madman, who had never once seen the wearer, nor understood his strength! Him Homer overthrew, horse and man, to the ground, there to be trampled and choked in the dirt. Then with a long spear he slew Denham, a stout Modern, who from his father's side derived his lineage from Apollo, but his mother was of mortal race. He fell, and bit the earth. The celestial part Apollo took, and made it a star; but the terrestrial lay wallowing upon the ground. Then Homer slew Sam Wesley with a kick of his horse's heel; he took Perrault by mighty force out of his saddle, then hurled him at Fontenelle, with the same blow dashing out both their brains.

On the left wing of the horse Virgil appeared, in shining armor, completely fitted to his body; he was mounted on a dapple-grey steed, the slowness of whose pace was an effect of the highest mettle and vigor. He cast his eye on the adverse wing, with a desire to find an object worthy of his valor, when behold upon a sorrel gelding of a monstrous size appeared a foe, issuing from among the thickest of the enemy's squadrons; but his speed was less than his noise; for his horse, old and lean, spent the dregs of his strength in a high trot, which, though it made slow advances, yet caused a loud clashing of his armor, terrible to hear. The two cavaliers had now approached within the throw of a lance, when the stranger desired a parley, and, lifting up the visor of his helmet, a face hardly appeared from within which, after a pause, was known for that of the renowned Dryden. The brave Ancient suddenly started, as one possessed with surprise and disappointment together; for the helmet was nine times too large for the head, which appeared situate far in the hinder part, even like the lady in a lobster, or like a mouse under a canopy of state, or like a shriveled beau from within the penthouse of a modern periwig; and the voice was suited to the visage, sounding weak and remote. Dryden, in a long harangue, soothed up the good Ancient; called him father, and, by a large deduction of genealogies, made it plainly appear that they were nearly related. Then he humbly proposed an exchange of armor, as a lasting mark of hospitality between them. Virgil consented (for the goddess Diffidence came unseen, and cast a mist before his eyes), though his was of gold and cost a hundred beeves, the other's but of rusty iron. However, this glittering armor became the Modern yet worsen than his own. Then they agreed to exchange horses; but, when it came to the trial, Dryden was afraid and utterly unable to mount...

Alter hiatus
.... in MS.

Lucan appeared upon a fiery horse of admirable shape, but headstrong, bearing the rider where he list over the field; he made a mighty slaughter among the enemy's horse; which destruction to stop, Blackmore, a famous Modern (but one of the mercenaries), strenuously opposed himself, and darted his javelin with a strong hand, which, falling short of its mark, struck deep in the earth. Then Lucan threw a lance; but Æsculapius came unseen and turned off the point. "Brave Modern," said Lucan, "I perceive some god protects you, for never did my arm so deceive me before: but what mortal can contend with a god? Therefore, let us fight no longer, but present gifts to each other." Lucan then bestowed on the Modern a pair of spurs, and Blackmore gave Lucan a bridle....

Pauca desunt....
....

Creech: but the goddess Dulness took a cloud, formed into the shape of Horace, armed and mounted, and placed in a flying posture before him. Glad was the cavalier to begin a combat with a flying foe, and pursued the image, threatening aloud; till at last it led him to the peaceful bower of his father, Ogleby, by whom he was disarmed and assigned to his repose.

Then Pindar slew ---, and --- and Oldham, and ---, and Afra the Amazon, light of foot; never advancing in a direct line, but wheeling with incredible agility and force, he made a terrible slaughter among the enemy's light-horse. Him when Cowley observed, his generous heart burnt within him, and he advanced against the fierce Ancient, imitating his address, his pace, and career, as well as the vigor of his horse and his own skill would allow. When the two cavaliers had approached within the length of three javelins, first Cowley threw a lance, which missed Pindar, and, passing into the enemy's ranks, fell ineffectual to the ground. Then Pindar darted a javelin so large and weighty, that scarce a dozen Cavaliers, as cavaliers are in our degenerate days, could raise it from the ground; yet he threw it with ease, and it went, by an unerring hand, singing through the air; nor could the Modern have avoided present death if he had not luckily opposed the shield that had been given him by Venus. And now both heroes drew their swords; but the Modern was so aghast and disordered that he knew not where he was; his shield dropped from his hands; thrice he fled, and thrice he could not escape. At last he turned, and lifting up his hand in the posture of a suppliant, "Godlike Pindar," said he, "spare my life, and possess my horse, with these arms, beside the ransom which my friends will give when they hear I am alive and your prisoner." "Dog!" said Pindar, "let your ransom stay with your friends; but your carcass shall be left for the fowls of the air and the beasts of the field." With that he raised his sword, and, with a mighty stroke, cleft the wretched Modern in twain, the sword pursuing the blow; and one half lay panting on the ground, to be trod in pieces by the horses' feet; the other half was borne by the frighted steed through the field. This Venus took, washed it seven times in ambrosia, then struck it thrice with a sprig of amaranth; upon which the leather grow round and soft, and the leaves turned into feathers, and, being gilded before, continued gilded still; so it became a dove, and she harnessed it to her chariot. . . .

. . . . Hiatus valde de-
. . . . flendus in MS.

THE EPISODE OF BENTLEY AND WOTTON

Day being far spent, and the numerous forces of the Moderns half inclining to a retreat, there issued forth, from a squadron of their heavy-armed foot, a captain whose name was Bentley, the most deformed of all the Moderns; tall, but without shape or comeliness; large, but without strength or proportion. His armor was patched up of a thousand incoherent pieces, and the sound of it, as he marched, was loud and dry, like that made by the fall of a sheet of lead, which an Etesian wind blows suddenly down from the roof of some steeple. His helmet was of old rusty iron, but the vizor was brass, which, tainted by his breath, corrupted into copperas, nor wanted gall from the same fountain, so that, whenever provoked by anger or labour, an atramentous quality, of most malignant nature, was seen to distill from his lips. In his right hand he grasped a flail, and (that he might never be unprovided of an offensive weapon) a vessel full of ordure in his left. Thus completely armed, he advanced with a slow and heavy pace where the Modern chiefs were holding a consult upon the sum of things, who, as he came onwards, laughed to behold his crooked leg and humped shoulder, which his boot and armor, vainly endeavoring to hide, were forced to comply with and expose. The generals made use of him for his talent of railing, which, kept within government, proved frequently of great service to their cause, but, at other times, did more mischief than good; for, at the least touch of offense, and often without any at all, he would, like a wounded elephant, convert it against his leaders. Such, at this juncture, was the disposition of Bentley, grieved to see the enemy prevail, and dissatisfied with everybody's conduct but his own. He humbly gave the Modern generals to understand that he conceived, with great submission, they were all a pack of rogues, and fools, and confounded logger-heads, and illiterate whelps, and nonsensical scoundrels; that, if himself had been constituted general, those presumptuous dogs, the Ancients, would long before this have been beaten out of the field. "You," said he, "sit here idle, but when I, or any other valiant Modern kill an enemy, you are sure to seize the spoil. But I will not march one foot against the foe till you all swear to me that whomever I take or kill, his arms I shall quietly possess." Bentley having spoken thus, Scaliger, bestowing him a sour look, "Miscreant prater!" said he, "eloquent only in thine own eyes, thou railest without wit, or truth, or discretion. The malignity of thy temper perverteth nature; thy learning makes thee more barbarous; thy study of humanity more inhuman; thy converse among poets more groveling, miry, and dull. All arts of civilizing others render thee rude and intractable; courts have taught thee ill manners, and polite conversation has finished thee a pedant. Besides, a greater coward burdeneth not the army. But never despond; I pass my word, whatever spoil thou takest shall certainly be thy own; though I hope that vile carcass will first become a prey to kites and worms."

Bentley durst not reply, but, half choked with spleen and rage, withdrew, in full resolution of performing some great achievement. With him, for his aid and companion, he took his beloved Wotton, resolving by policy or surprise to attempt some neglected quarter of the Ancients' army. They began their march over carcasses of their slaughtered friends; then to the right of their own forces; then wheeled northward, till they came to Aldrovandus's tomb, which they passed on the side of the declining sun. And now they arrived, with fear, toward the enemy's out-guards, looking about, if haply they might spy the quarters of the wounded, or some straggling sleepers, unarmed and remote from the rest. As when two mongrel curs, whom native greediness and domestic want provoke and join in partnership, though fearful, nightly to invade the folds of some rich grazier, they, with tails depressed and lolling tongues, creep soft and slow. Meanwhile the conscious moon, now in her zenith, on their guilty heads darts perpendicular rays; nor dare they bark, though much provoked at her refulgent visage, whether seen in puddle by reflection or in sphere direct; but one surveys the region round, while the other scouts the plain, if haply to discover, at distance from the flock, some carcass half devoured, the refuse of gorged wolves or ominous ravens. So marched this lovely, loving pair of friends, nor with less fear and circumspection, when at a distance they might perceive two shining suits of armor hanging upon an oak, and the owners not far off in a profound sleep. The two friends drew lots, and the pursuing of this adventure fell to Bentley; on he went, and in his van Confusion and Amaze, while Horror and Affright brought up the rear. As he came near, behold two heroes of the Ancient army, Phalaris and Aesop, lay fast asleep. Bentley would fain have despatched them both, and, stealing close, aimed his flail at Phalaris's breast; but then the goddess Affright, interposing, caught the Modern in her icy arms, and dragged him from the danger she foresaw; both the dormant heroes happened to turn at the same instant, though soundly sleeping, and busy in a dream. For Phalaris was just that minute dreaming how a most vile poetaster had lampooned him, and how he had got him roaring in his bull. And Æsop dreamed that as he and the Ancient were lying on the ground, a wild ass broke loose, ran about, trampling and kicking in their faces. Bentley, leaving the two heroes asleep, seized on both their armors, and withdrew in quest of his darling Wotton.

He, in the meantime, had wandered long in search of some enterprise, till at length he arrived at a small rivulet that issued from a fountain hard by, called, in the language of mortal men, Helicon. Here he stopped, and, parched with thirst, resolved to allay it in this limpid stream. Thrice with profane hands he essayed to raise the water to his lips, and thrice it slipped all through his fingers. Then he stopped prone on his breast, but, ere his mouth had kissed the liquid crystal, Apollo came, and in the channel held his shield betwixt the Modern and the fountain, so that he drew up nothing but mud. For, although no fountain on earth can compare with the clearness of Helicon, yet there lies at bottom a thick sediment of slime and mud; for so Apollo begged of Jupiter, as a punishment to those who durst attempt to taste it with unhallowed lips, and for a lesson to all not to draw too deep or far from the spring.

At the fountain-head Wotton discerned two heroes; the one he could not distinguish, but the other was soon known for Temple, general of the allies to the Ancients. His back was turned, and he was employed in drinking large draughts in his helmet from the fountain, where he had withdrawn himself to rest from the toils of the war. Wotton, observing him, with quaking knees and trembling hands, spoke thus to himself: O that I could kill this destroyer of our army, what renown should I purchase among the chiefs! but to issue out against him, man against man, shield against shield, and lance against lance, what Modern of us dare? for he fights like a god, and Pallas or Apollo are ever at his elbow. But, O mother! if what Fame reports be true, that I am the son of so great a goddess, grant me to hit Temple with this lance, that the stroke may send him to hell, and that I may return in safety and triumph, laden with his spoils. The first part of this prayer the gods granted at the intercession of his mother and of Momus; but the rest, by a perverse wind sent from Fate, was scattered in the air. Then Wotton grasped his lance, and, brandishing it thrice over his head, darted it with all his might; the goddess, his mother, at the same time adding strength to his arm. Away the lance went hizzing, and reached even to the belt of the averted Ancient, upon which, lightly grazing, it fell to the ground. Temple neither felt the weapon touch him nor heard it fall: and Wotton might have escaped to his army, with the honor of having remitted his lance against so great a leader unrevenged; but Apollo, enraged that a javelin flung by the assistance of so foul a goddess should pollute his fountain, put on the shape of ---, and softly came to young Boyle, who then accompanied Temple: he pointed first to the lance, then to the distant Modern that flung it, and commanded the young hero to take immediate revenge. Boyle, clad in a suit of armor which had been given him by all the gods, immediately advanced against the trembling foe, who now fled before him. As a young lion in the Libyan plains, or Araby desert, sent by his aged sire to hunt for prey, or health, or exercise, he scours along, wishing to meet some tiger from the mountains, or a furious boar; if chance a wild ass, with brayings importune, affronts his ear, the generous beast, though loathing to distain his claws with blood so vile, yet, much provoked at the offensive noise, which Echo, foolish nymph, like her ill-judging sex, repeats much louder, and with more delight than Philomela's song, he vindicates the honor of the forest, and hunts the noisy long-eared animal. So Wotton fled, so Boyle pursued. But Wotton, heavy-armed, and slow of foot, began to slack his course, when his lover Bentley appeared, returning laden with the spoils of the two sleeping Ancients. Boyle observed him well, and soon discovering the helmet and shield of Phalaris his friend, both which he had lately with his own hands new polished and gilt, rage sparkled in his eyes, and, leaving his pursuit after Wotton, he furiously rushed on against this new approacher. Fain would he be revenged on both; but both now fled different ways: and, as a woman in a little house that gets a painful livelihood by spinning, if chance her geese be scattered o'er the common, she courses round the plain from side to side, compelling here and there the stragglers to the flock; they cackle loud, and flutter o'er the champaign; so Boyle pursued, so fled this pair of friends: finding at length their flight was vain, they bravely joined, and drew themselves in phalanx. First Bentley threw a spear with all his force, hoping to pierce the enemy's breast; but Pallas came unseen, and in the air took off the point, and clapped on one of lead, which, after a dead bang against the enemy's shield, fell blunted to the ground. Then Boyle, observing well his time, took up a lance of wondrous length and sharpness; and, as this pair of friends compacted, stood close side by side, he wheeled him to the right, and, with unusual force, darted the weapon. Bentley saw his fate approach, and flanking down his arms close to his ribs, hoping to save his body, in went the point, passing through arm and side, nor stopped or spent its force till it had also pierced the valiant Wotton, who, going to sustain his dying friend, shared his fate. As when a skillful cook has trussed a brace of woodcocks, he with iron skewer pierces the tender sides of both, their legs and wings close pinioned to the rib; so was this pair of friends transfixed, till down they fell, joined in their lives, joined in their deaths; so closely joined that Charon would mistake them both for one, and waft them over Styx for half his fare. Farewell, beloved, loving pair; few equals have you left behind: and happy and immortal shall you be, if all my wit and eloquence can make you.

And now....

Desunt cætera.

PREDICTIONS FOR THE YEAR 1708

According to the Style and Manner of the Hon. Robert Boyle's Meditations.

This single stick, which you now behold ingloriously lying in that neglected corner, I once knew in a flourishing state in a forest. It was full of sap, full of leaves, and full of boughs; but now in vain does the busy art of man pretend to vie with nature, by tying that withered bundle of twigs to its sapless trunk; it is now at best but the reverse of what it was, a tree turned upside-down, the branches on the earth, and the root in the air; it is now handled by every dirty wench, condemned to do her drudgery, and, by a capricious kind of fate, destined to make other things clean, and be nasty itself; at length, worn to the stumps in the service of the maids, it is either thrown out of doors or condemned to the last use—of kindling a fire. When I behold this I sighed, and said within myself, "Surely mortal man is a broomstick!" Nature sent him into the world strong and lusty, in a thriving condition, wearing his own hair on his head, the proper branches of this reasoning vegetable, till the axe of intemperance has lopped off his green boughs, and left him a withered trunk; he then flies to art, and puts on a periwig, valuing himself upon an unnatural bundle of hairs, all covered with powder, that never grew on his head; but now should this our broomstick pretend to enter the scene, proud of those birchen spoils it never bore, and all covered with dust, through the sweepings of the finest lady's chamber, we should be apt to ridicule and despise its vanity. Partial judges that we are of our own excellencies, and other men's defaults!

But a broomstick, perhaps you will say, is an emblem of a tree standing on its head; and pray what is a man but a topsy-turvy creature, his animal faculties perpetually mounted on his rational, his head where his heels should be, groveling on the earth? And yet, with all his faults, he sets up to be a universal reformer and corrector of abuses, a remover of grievances, rakes into every slut's corner of nature, bringing hidden corruptions to the light, and raises a mighty dust where there was none before, sharing deeply all the while in the very same pollutions he pretends to sweep away. His last days are spent in slavery to women, and generally the least deserving; till, worn to the stumps, like his brother besom, he is either kicked out of doors, or made use of to kindle flames for others to warm themselves by.

PREDICTIONS FOR THE YEAR 1708

Wherein the Month, and Day of the Month are set down, the Persons named, and the great Actions and Events of next Year particularly related as will come to pass.
Written to prevent the people of England from being farther imposed on by vulgar Almanack-makers.
By Isaac Bickerstaff, Esq.

I have long considered the gross abuse of astrology in this kingdom, and upon debating the matter with myself, I could not possibly lay the fault upon the art, but upon those gross impostors who set up to be the artists. I know several learned men have contended that the whole is a cheat; that it is absurd and ridiculous to imagine the stars can have any influence at all upon human actions, thoughts, or inclinations; and whoever has not bent his studies that way may be excused for thinking so, when he sees in how wretched a manner that noble art is treated by a few mean illiterate traders between us and the stars, who import a yearly stock of nonsense, lies, folly, and impertinence, which they offer to the world as genuine from the planets, though they descend from no greater a height than their own brains.

I intend in a short time to publish a large and rational defense of this art, and therefore shall say no more in its justification at present than that it hath been in all ages defended by many learned men, and among the rest by Socrates himself, whom I look upon as undoubtedly the wisest of uninspired mortals: to which if we add that those who have condemned this art, though otherwise learned, having been such as either did not apply their studies this way, or at least did not succeed in their applications, their testimony will not be of much weight to its disadvantage, since they are liable to the common objection of condemning what they did not understand.

Nor am I at all offended, or think it an injury to the art, when I see the common dealers in it, the students in astrology, the Philomaths, and the rest of that tribe, treated by wise men with the utmost scorn and contempt; but rather wonder, when I observe gentlemen in the country, rich enough to serve the nation in Parliament, poring in Partridge's Almanack to find out the events of the year at home and abroad, not daring to propose a hunting-match till Gadbury or he have fixed the weather.

I will allow either of the two I have mentioned, or any other of the fraternity, to be not only astrologers, but conjurers too, if I do not produce a hundred instances in all their almanacks to convince any reasonable man that they do not so much as understand common grammar and syntax; that they are not able to spell any word out of the usual road, nor even in their prefaces write common sense or intelligible English. Then for their observations and predictions, they are such as will equally suit any age or country in the world. "This month a certain great person will be threatened with death or sickness." This the newspapers will tell them; for there we find at the end of the year that no month passes without the death of some person of note; and it would be hard if it should be otherwise, when there are at least two thousand persons of note in this kingdom, many of them old, and the almanack-maker has the liberty of choosing the sickliest season of the year where he may fix his prediction. Again, "This month an eminent clergyman will be preferred;" of which there may be some hundreds, half of them with one foot in the grave. Then "such a planet in such a house shows great machinations, plots, and conspiracies, that may in time be brought to light:" after which, if we hear of any discovery, the astrologer gets the honor; if not, his prediction still stands good. And at last, "God preserve King William from all his open and secret enemies, Amen." When if the King should happen to have died, the astrologer plainly foretold it; otherwise it passes but for the pious ejaculation of a loyal subject; though it unluckily happened in some of their almanacks that poor King William was prayed for many months after he was dead, because it fell out that he died about the beginning of the year.

To mention no more of their impertinent predictions: what have we to do with their advertisements about pills and drink for disease? or their mutual quarrels in verse and prose of Whig and Tory, wherewith the stars have little to do?

Having long observed and lamented these, and a hundred other abuses of this art, too tedious to repeat, I resolved to proceed in a new way, which I doubt not will be to the general satisfaction of the kingdom. I can this year produce but a specimen of what I design for the future, having employed most part of my time in adjusting and correcting the calculations I made some years past, because I would offer nothing to the world of which I am not as fully satisfied as that I am now alive. For these two last years I have not failed in above one or two particulars, and those of no very great moment. I exactly foretold the miscarriage at Toulon, with all its particulars, and the loss of Admiral Shovel, though I was mistaken as to the day, placing that accident about thirty-six hours sooner than it happened; but upon reviewing my schemes, I quickly found the cause of that error. I likewise foretold the Battle of Almanza to the very day and hour, with the loss on both sides, and the consequences thereof. All which I showed to some friends many months before they happened—that is, I gave them papers sealed up, to open at such a time, after which they were at liberty to read them; and there they found my predictions true in every article, except one or two very minute.

As for the few following predictions I now offer the world, I forbore to publish them till I had perused the several almanacks for the year we are now entered on. I find them all in the usual strain, and I beg the reader will compare their manner with mine. And here I make bold to tell the world that I lay the whole credit of my art upon the truth of these predictions; and I will be content that Partridge, and the rest of his clan, may hoot me for a cheat and impostor if I fail in any single particular of moment. I believe any man who reads this paper will look upon me to be at least a person of as much honesty and understanding as a common maker of almanacks. I do not lurk in the dark; I am not wholly unknown in the world; I have set my name at length, to be a mark of infamy to mankind, if they shall find I deceive them.

In one thing I must desire to be forgiven, that I talk more sparingly of home affairs. As it will be imprudence to discover secrets of State, so it would be dangerous to my person; but in smaller matters, and that are not of public consequence, I shall be very free; and the truth of my conjectures will as much appear from those as the others. As for the most signal events abroad, in France, Flanders, Italy, and Spain, I shall make no scruple to predict them in plain terms. Some of them are of importance, and I hope I shall seldom mistake the day they will happen; therefore I think good to inform the reader that I all along make use of the Old Style observed in England, which I desire he will compare with that of the newspapers at the time they relate the actions I mention.

I must add one word more. I know it hath been the opinion of several of the learned, who think well enough of the true art of astrology, that the stars do only incline, and not force the actions or wills of men, and therefore, however I may proceed by right rules, yet I cannot in prudence so confidently assure the events will follow exactly as I predict them.

I hope I have maturely considered this objection, which in some cases is of no little weight. For example: a man may, by the influence of an over-ruling planet, be disposed or inclined to lust, rage, or avarice, and yet by the force of reason overcome that bad influence; and this was the case of Socrates. But as the great events of the world usually depend upon numbers of men, it cannot be expected they should all unite to cross their inclinations from pursuing a general design wherein they unanimously agree. Besides, the influence of the stars reaches to many actions and events which are not any way in the power of reason, as sickness, death, and what we commonly call accidents, with many more, needless to repeat.

But now it is time to proceed to my predictions, which I have begun to calculate from the time that the sun enters into Aries. And this I take to be properly the beginning of the natural year. I pursue them to the time that he enters Libra, or somewhat more, which is the busy period of the year. The remainder I have not yet adjusted, upon account of several impediments needless here to mention. Besides, I must remind the reader again that this is but a specimen of what I design in succeeding years to treat more at large, if I may have liberty and encouragement.

My first prediction is but a trifle, yet I will mention it, to show how ignorant those sottish pretenders to astrology are in their own concerns. It relates to Partridge, the almanack-maker. I have consulted the stars of his nativity by my own rules, and find he will infallibly die upon the 29th of March next, about eleven at night, of a raging fever; therefore I advise him to consider of it, and settle his affairs in time.

The month of *April* will be observable for the death of many great persons. On the 4th will die the Cardinal de Noailles, Archbishop of Paris; on the 11th, the young Prince of Asturias, son to the Duke of Anjou; on the 14th, a great peer of this realm will die at his country house; on the 19th, an old layman of great fame for learning, and on the 23rd, an eminent goldsmith in Lombard Street. I could mention others, both at home and abroad, if I did not consider it is of very little use or instruction to the reader, or to the world.

As to public affairs: On the 7th of this month there will be an insurrection in Dauphiny, occasioned by the oppressions of the people, which will not be quieted in some months.

On the 15th will be a violent storm on the south-east coast of France, which will destroy many of their ships, and some in the very harbor.

The 11th will be famous for the revolt of a whole province or kingdom, excepting one city, by which the affairs of a certain prince in the Alliance will take a better face.

May, against common conjectures, will be no very busy month in Europe, but very signal for the death of the Dauphin, which will happen on the 7th, after a short fit of sickness, and grievous torments with the strangury. He dies less lamented by the Court than the kingdom.

On the 9th a Marshal of France will break his leg by a fall from his horse. I have not been able to discover whether he will then die or not.

On the 11th will begin a most important siege, which the eyes of all Europe will be upon: I cannot be more particular, for in relating affairs that so nearly concern the Confederates, and consequently this kingdom, I am forced to confine myself for several reasons very obvious to the reader.

On the 15th news will arrive of a very surprising event, than which nothing could be more unexpected.

On the 19th three noble ladies of this kingdom will, against all expectation, prove with child, to the great joy of their husbands.

On the 23rd a famous buffoon of the playhouse will die a ridiculous death, suitable to his vocation.

June. This month will be distinguished at home by the utter dispersing of those ridiculous deluded enthusiasts commonly called the Prophets, occasioned chiefly by seeing the time come that many of their prophecies should be fulfilled, and then finding themselves deceived by contrary events. It is indeed to be admired how any deceiver can be so weak to foretell things near at hand, when a very few months must of necessity discover the impostor to all the world; in this point less prudent than common almanack-makers, who are so wise to wonder in generals, and talk dubiously, and leave to the reader the business of interpreting.

On the 1st of this month a French general will be killed by a random shot of a cannon-ball.

On the 6th a fire will break out in the suburbs of Paris, which will destroy above a thousand houses, and seems to be the foreboding of what will happen, to the surprise of all Europe, about the end of the following month.

On the 10th a great battle will be fought, which will begin at four of the clock in the afternoon, and last till nine at night with great obstinacy, but no very decisive event. I shall not name the place, for the reasons aforesaid, but the commanders on each left wing will be killed. I see bonfires and hear the noise of guns for a victory.

On the 14th there will be a false report of the French king's death.

On the 20th Cardinal Portocarero will die of a dysentery, with great suspicion of poison, but the report of his intention to revolt to King Charles will prove false.

July. The 6th of this month a certain general will, by a glorious action, recover the reputation he lost by former misfortunes.

On the 12th a great commander will die a prisoner in the hands of his enemies.

On the 14th a shameful discovery will be made of a French Jesuit giving poison to a great foreign general; and when he is put to the torture, will make wonderful discoveries.

In short, this will prove a month of great action, if I might have liberty to relate the particulars.

At home, the death of an old famous senator will happen on the 15th at his country house, worn with age and diseases.

But that which will make this month memorable to all posterity is the death of the French king, Louis the Fourteenth, after a week's sickness at Marli, which will happen on the 29th, about six o'clock in the evening. It seems to be an effect of the gout in his stomach, followed by a flux. And in three days after Monsieur Chamillard will follow his master, dying suddenly of an apoplexy.

In this month likewise an ambassador will die in London, but I cannot assign the day.

August. The affairs of France will seem to suffer no change for a while under the Duke of Burgundy's administration; but the genius that animated the whole machine being gone, will be the cause of mighty turns and revolutions in the following year. The new king makes yet little change either in the army or the Ministry, but the libels against his grandfather, that fly about his very Court, give him uneasiness.

I see an express in mighty haste, with joy and wonder in his looks, arriving by break of day on the 26th of this month, having travelled in three days a prodigious journey by land and sea. In the evening I hear bells and guns, and see the blazing of a thousand bonfires.

A young admiral of noble birth does likewise this month gain immortal honor by a great achievement.

The affairs of Poland are this month entirely settled; Augustus resigns his pretensions which he had again taken up for some time: Stanislaus is peaceably possessed of the throne, and the King of Sweden declares for the emperor.

I cannot omit one particular accident here at home: that near the end of this month much mischief will be done at Bartholomew Fair by the fall of a booth.

September. This month begins with a very surprising fit of frosty weather, which will last near twelve days.

The Pope, having long languished last month, the swellings in his legs breaking, and the flesh mortifying, will die on the 11th instant; and in three weeks' time, after a mighty contest, be succeeded by a cardinal of the Imperial faction, but native of Tuscany, who is now about sixty-one years old.

The French army acts now wholly on the defensive, strongly fortified in their trenches, and the young French king sends overtures for a treaty of peace by the Duke of Mantua; which, because it is a matter of State that concerns us here at home, I shall speak no farther of it.

I shall add but one prediction more, and that in mystical terms, which shall be included in a verse out of Virgil—

Alter erit jam Tethys, et altera quæ vehat Argo
Delectos Heroas.

Upon the 25th day of this month, the fulfilling of this prediction will be manifest to everybody.

This is the farthest I have proceeded in my calculations for the present year. I do not pretend that these are all the great events which will happen in this period, but that those I have set down will infallibly come to pass. It will perhaps still be objected why I have not spoken more particularly of affairs at home, or of the success of our armies abroad, which I might, and could very largely have done; but those in power have wisely discouraged men from meddling in public concerns, and I was resolved by no means to give the least offense. This I will venture to say, that it will be a glorious campaign for the Allies, wherein the English forces, both by sea and land, will have their full share of honor; that Her Majesty Queen Anne will continue in health and prosperity; and that no ill accident will arrive to any in the chief Ministry.

As to the particular events I have mentioned, the readers may judge by the fulfilling of them, whether I am on the level with common astrologers, who, with an old paltry cant, and a few pothooks for planets, to amuse the vulgar, have, in my opinion, too long been suffered to abuse the world. But an honest physician ought not to be despised because there are such things as mountebanks. I hope I have some share of reputation, which I would not willingly forfeit for a frolic or humor; and I believe no gentleman who reads this paper will look upon it to be of the same cast or mould with the common scribblers that are every day hawked about. My fortune has placed me above the little regard of scribbling for a few pence, which I neither value nor want; therefore, let no wise man too hastily condemn this essay, intended for a good design, to cultivate and improve an ancient art long in disgrace, by having fallen into mean and unskilful hands. A little time will determine whether I have deceived others or myself; and I think it is no very unreasonable request that men would please to suspend their judgments till then. I was once of the opinion with those who despise all predictions from the stars, till in the year 1686 a man of quality showed me, written in his album, that the most learned astronomer, Captain H---, assured him, he would never believe anything of the stars' influence if there were not a great revolution in England in the year 1688. Since that time I began to have other thoughts, and after eighteen years' diligent study and application, I think I have no reason to repent of my pains. I shall detain the reader no longer than to let him know that the account I design to give of next year's events shall take in the principal affairs that happen in Europe; and if I be denied the liberty of offering it to my own country, I shall appeal to the learned world, by publishing it in Latin, and giving order to have it printed in Holland.

THE ACCOMPLISHMENT OF THE FIRST OF MR. BICKERSTAFF'S PREDICTIONS

THE ACCOMPLISHMENT OF THE FIRST OF MR. BICKERSTAFF'S PREDICTIONS; BEING AN ACCOUNT OF THE DEATH OF MR. PARTRIDGE THE ALMANACK-MAKER, UPON THE 29TH INSTANT.

In a Letter to a Person of Honor; Written in the Year 1708.

My Lord,—In obedience to your lordship's commands, as well as to satisfy my own curiosity, I have for some days past inquired constantly after Partridge the almanack-maker, of whom it was foretold in Mr. Bickerstaff's predictions, published about a month ago, that he should die the 29th instant, about eleven at night, of a raging fever. I had some sort of knowledge of him when I was employed in the Revenue, because he used every year to present me with his almanack, as he did other gentlemen, upon the score of some little gratuity we gave him. I saw him accidentally once or twice about ten days before he died, and observed he began very much to droop and languish, though I hear his friends did not seem to apprehend him in any danger. About two or three days ago he grew ill, was confined first to his chamber, and in a few hours after to his bed, where Dr. Case and Mrs. Kirleus were sent for, to visit and to prescribe to him. Upon this intelligence I sent thrice every day one servant or other to inquire after his health; and yesterday, about four in the afternoon, word was brought me that he was past hopes; upon which, I prevailed with myself to go and see him, partly out of commiseration, and I confess, partly out of curiosity. He knew me very well, seemed surprised at my condescension, and made me compliments upon it as well as he could in the condition he was. The people about him said he had been for some time delirious; but when I saw him, he had his understanding as well as ever I knew, and spoke strong and hearty, without any seeming uneasiness or constraint. After I had told him how sorry I was to see him in those melancholy circumstances, and said some other civilities suitable to the occasion, I desired him to tell me freely and ingenuously, whether the predictions Mr. Bickerstaff had published relating to his death had not too much affected and worked on his imagination. He confessed he had often had it in his head, but never with much apprehension, till about a fortnight before; since which time it had the perpetual possession of his mind and thoughts, and he did verily believe was the true natural cause of his present distemper: "For," said he, "I am thoroughly persuaded, and I think I have very good reasons, that Mr. Bickerstaff spoke altogether by guess, and knew no more what will happen this year than I did myself." I told him his discourse surprised me, and I would be glad he were in a state of health to be able to tell me what reason he had to be convinced of Mr. Bickerstaff's ignorance. He replied, "I am a poor, ignorant follow, bred to a mean trade, yet I have sense enough to know that all pretenses of foretelling by astrology are deceits, for this manifest reason, because the wise and the learned, who can only know whether there be any truth in this science, do all unanimously agree to laugh at and despise it; and none but the poor ignorant vulgar give it any credit, and that only upon the word of such silly wretches as I and my fellows, who can hardly write or read." I then asked him why he had not calculated his own nativity, to see whether it agreed with Bickerstaff's prediction, at which he shook his head and said, "Oh, sir, this is no time for jesting, but for repenting those fooleries, as I do now from the very bottom of my heart." "By what I can gather from you," said I, "the observations and predictions you printed with your almanacks were mere impositions on the people." He replied, "If it were otherwise I should have the less to answer for. We have a common form for all those things; as to foretelling the weather, we never meddle with that, but leave it to the printer, who takes it out of any old almanack as he thinks fit; the rest was my own invention, to make my almanack sell, having a wife to maintain, and no other way to get my bread; for mending old shoes is a poor livelihood; and," added he, sighing, "I wish I may not have done more mischief by my physic than my astrology; though I had some good receipts from my grandmother, and my own compositions were such as I thought could at least do no hurt."

I had some other discourse with him, which now I cannot call to mind; and I fear I have already tired your lordship. I shall only add one circumstance, that on his death-bed he declared himself a Nonconformist, and had a fanatic preacher to be his spiritual guide. After half an hour's conversation I took my leave, being half stifled by the closeness of the room. I imagined he could not hold out long, and therefore withdrew to a little coffee-house hard by, leaving a servant at the house with orders to come immediately and tell me, as nearly as he could, the minute when Partridge should expire, which was not above two hours after, when, looking upon my watch, I found it to be above five minutes after seven; by which it is clear that Mr. Bickerstaff was mistaken almost four hours in his calculation. In the other circumstances he was exact enough. But, whether he has not been the cause of this poor man's death, as well as the predictor, may be very reasonably disputed. However, it must be confessed the matter is odd enough, whether we should endeavor to account for it by chance, or the effect of imagination. For my own part, though I believe no man has less faith in these matters, yet I shall wait with some impatience, and not without some expectation, the fulfilling of Mr. Bickerstaff's second prediction, that the Cardinal do Noailles is to die upon the 4th of April, and if that should be verified as exactly as this of poor Partridge, I must own I should be wholly surprised, and at a loss, and should infallibly expect the accomplishment of all the rest.

AN ARGUMENT AGAINST ABOLISHING CHRISTIANITY

AN ARGUMENT TO PROVE THAT THE ABOLISHING OF CHRISTIANITY IN ENGLAND MAY, AS THINGS NOW STAND, BE ATTENDED WITH SOME INCONVENIENCES, AND PERHAPS NOT PRODUCE THOSE MANY GOOD EFFECTS PROPOSED THEREBY.

Written in the year 1708.

I am very sensible what a weakness and presumption it is to reason against the general humor and disposition of the world. I remember it was with great justice, and a due regard to the freedom, both of the public and the press, forbidden upon several penalties to write, or discourse, or lay wagers against the --- even before it was confirmed by Parliament; because that was looked upon as a design to oppose the current of the people, which, besides the folly of it, is a manifest breach of the fundamental law, that makes this majority of opinions the voice of God. In like manner, and for the very same reasons, it may perhaps be neither safe nor prudent to argue against the abolishing of Christianity, at a juncture when all parties seem so unanimously determined upon the point, as we cannot but allow from their actions, their discourses, and their writings. However, I know not how, whether from the affectation of singularity, or the perverseness of human nature, but so it unhappily falls out, that I cannot be entirely of this opinion. Nay, though I were sure an order were issued for my immediate prosecution by the Attorney-General, I should still confess, that in the present posture of our affairs at home or abroad, I do not yet see the absolute necessity of extirpating the Christian religion from among us.

This perhaps may appear too great a paradox even for our wise and parodoxical age to endure; therefore I shall handle it with all tenderness, and with the utmost deference to that great and profound majority which is of another sentiment.

And yet the curious may please to observe, how much the genius of a nation is liable to alter in half an age. I have heard it affirmed for certain by some very odd people, that the contrary opinion was even in their memories as much in vogue as the other is now; and that a project for the abolishing of Christianity would then have appeared as singular, and been thought as absurd, as it would be at this time to write or discourse in its defense.

Therefore I freely own, that all appearances are against me. The system of the

Gospel, after the fate of other systems, is generally antiquated and exploded, and the mass or body of the common people, among whom it seems to have had its latest credit, are now grown as much ashamed of it as their betters; opinions, like fashions, always descending from those of quality to the middle sort, and thence to the vulgar, where at length they are dropped and vanish.

But here I would not be mistaken, and must therefore be so bold as to borrow a distinction from the writers on the other side, when they make a difference betwixt nominal and real Trinitarians. I hope no reader imagines me so weak to stand up in the defense of real Christianity, such as used in primitive times (if we may believe the authors of those ages) to have an influence upon men's belief and actions. To offer at the restoring of that, would indeed be a wild project: it would be to dig up foundations; to destroy at one blow all the wit, and half the learning of the kingdom; to break the entire frame and constitution of things; to ruin trade, extinguish arts and sciences, with the professors of them; in short, to turn our courts, exchanges, and shops into deserts; and would be full as absurd as the proposal of Horace, where he advises the Romans, all in a body, to leave their city, and seek a new seat in some remote part of the world, by way of a cure for the corruption of their manners.

Therefore I think this caution was in itself altogether unnecessary (which I have inserted only to prevent all possibility of caviling), since every candid reader will easily understand my discourse to be intended only in defense of nominal Christianity, the other having been for some time wholly laid aside by general consent, as utterly inconsistent with all our present schemes of wealth and power.

But why we should therefore cut off the name and title of Christians, although the general opinion and resolution be so violent for it, I confess I cannot (with submission) apprehend the consequence necessary. However, since the undertakers propose such wonderful advantages to the nation by this project, and advance many plausible objections against the system of Christianity, I shall briefly consider the strength of both, fairly allow them their greatest weight, and offer such answers as I think most reasonable. After which I will beg leave to show what inconveniences may possibly happen by such an innovation, in the present posture of our affairs.

First, one great advantage proposed by the abolishing of Christianity is, that it would very much enlarge and establish liberty of conscience, that great bulwark of our nation, and of the Protestant religion, which is still too much limited by priestcraft, notwithstanding all the good intentions of the legislature, as we have lately found by a severe instance. For it is confidently reported, that two young gentlemen of real hopes, bright wit, and profound judgment, who, upon a thorough examination of causes and effects, and by the mere force of natural abilities, without the least tincture of learning, having made a discovery that there was no God, and generously communicating their thoughts for the good of the public, were some time ago, by an unparalleled severity, and upon I know not what obsolete law, broke for blasphemy. And as it has been wisely observed, if persecution once begins, no man alive knows how far it may reach, or where it will end.

In answer to all which, with deference to wiser judgments, I think this rather shows the necessity of a nominal religion among us. Great wits love to be free with the highest objects; and if they cannot be allowed a god to revile or renounce, they will speak evil of dignities, abuse the government, and reflect upon the ministry, which I am sure few will deny to be of much more pernicious consequence, according to the saying of Tiberius, *deorum offensa diis curæ*. As to the particular fact related, I think it is not fair to argue from one instance, perhaps another cannot be produced: yet (to the comfort of all those who may be apprehensive of persecution) blasphemy we know is freely spoke a million of times in every coffee-house and tavern, or wherever else good company meet. It must be allowed, indeed, that to break an English free-born officer only for blasphemy was, to speak the gentlest of such an action, a very high strain of absolute power. Little can be said in excuse for the general; perhaps he was afraid it might give offense to the allies, among whom, for aught we know, it may be the custom of the country to believe a God. But if he argued, as some have done, upon a mistaken principle, that an officer who is guilty of speaking blasphemy may, some time or other, proceed so far as to raise a mutiny, the consequence is by no means to be admitted: for surely the commander of an English army is like to be but ill obeyed whose soldiers fear and reverence him as little as they do a Deity.

It is further objected against the Gospel system that it obliges men to the belief of things too difficult for Freethinkers, and such who have shook off the prejudices that usually cling to a confined education. To which I answer, that men should be cautious how they raise objections which reflect upon the wisdom of the nation. Is not everybody freely allowed to believe whatever he pleases, and to publish his belief to the world whenever he thinks fit, especially if it serves to strengthen the party which is in the right? Would any indifferent foreigner, who should read the trumpery lately written by Asgil, Tindal, Toland, Coward, and forty more, imagine the Gospel to be our rule of faith, and to be confirmed by Parliaments? Does any man either believe, or say he believes, or desire to have it thought that he says he believes, one syllable of the matter? And is any man worse received upon that score, or does he find his want of nominal faith a disadvantage to him in the pursuit of any civil or military employment? What if there be an old dormant statute or two against him, are they not now obsolete, to a degree, that Empson and Dudley themselves, if they were now alive, would find it impossible to put them in execution?

It is likewise urged, that there are, by computation, in this kingdom, above ten thousand parsons, whose revenues, added to those of my lords the bishops, would suffice to maintain at least two hundred young gentlemen of wit and pleasure, and free-thinking, enemies to priestcraft, narrow principles, pedantry, and prejudices, who might be an ornament to the court and town: and then again, so a great number of able [bodied] divines might be a recruit to our fleet and armies. This indeed appears to be a consideration of some weight; but then, on the other side, several things deserve to be considered likewise: as, first, whether it may not be thought necessary that in certain tracts of country, like what we call parishes, there should be one man at least of abilities to read and write. Then it seems a wrong computation that the revenues of the Church throughout this island would be large enough to maintain two hundred young gentlemen, or even half that number, after the present refined way of living, that is, to allow each of them such a rent as, in the modern form of speech, would make them easy. But still there is in this project a greater mischief behind; and we ought to beware of the woman's folly, who killed the hen that every morning laid her a golden egg. For, pray what would become of the race of men in the next age, if we had nothing to trust to beside the scrofulous consumptive production furnished by our men of wit and pleasure, when, having squandered away their vigor, health, and estates, they are forced, by some disagreeable marriage, to piece up their broken fortunes, and entail rottenness and politeness on their posterity? Now, here are ten thousand persons reduced, by the wise regulations of Henry VIII., to the necessity of a low diet, and moderate exercise, who are the only great restorers of our breed, without which the nation would in an age or two become one great hospital.

Another advantage proposed by the abolishing of Christianity is the clear gain of one day in seven, which is now entirely lost, and consequently the kingdom one seventh less considerable in trade, business, and pleasure; besides the loss to the public of so many stately structures now in the hands of the clergy, which might be converted into play-houses, exchanges, market-houses, common dormitories, and other public edifices.

I hope I shall be forgiven a hard word if I call this a perfect cavil. I readily own there hath been an old custom, time out of mind, for people to assemble in the churches every Sunday, and that shops are still frequently shut, in order, as it is conceived, to preserve the memory of that ancient practice; but how this can prove a hindrance to business or pleasure is hard to imagine. What if the men of pleasure are forced, one day in the week, to game at home instead of the chocolate-house? Are not the taverns and coffee-houses open? Can there be a more convenient season for taking a dose of physic? Is not that the chief day for traders to sum up the accounts of the week, and for lawyers to prepare their briefs? But I would fain know how it can be pretended that the churches are misapplied?

Where are more appointments and rendezvouses of gallantry? Where more care to appear in the foremost box, with greater advantage of dress? Where more meetings for business? Where more bargains driven of all sorts? And where so many conveniences or incitements to sleep?

There is one advantage greater than any of the foregoing, proposed by the abolishing of Christianity, that it will utterly extinguish parties among us, by removing those factious distinctions of high and low church, of Whig and Tory, Presbyterian and Church of England, which are now so many mutual clogs upon public proceedings, and are apt to prefer the gratifying themselves or depressing their adversaries before the most important interest of the State.

I confess, if it were certain that so great an advantage would redound to the nation by this expedient, I would submit, and be silent; but will any man say, that if the words, whoring, drinking, cheating, lying, stealing, were, by Act of Parliament, ejected out of the English tongue and dictionaries, we should all awake next morning chaste and temperate, honest and just, and lovers of truth? Is this a fair consequence? Or if the physicians would forbid us to pronounce the words pox, gout, rheumatism, and stone, would that expedient serve like so many talismen to destroy the diseases themselves? Are party and faction rooted in men's hearts no deeper than phrases borrowed from religion, or founded upon no firmer principles? And is our language so poor that we cannot find other terms to express them? Are envy, pride, avarice, and ambition such ill nomenclators, that they cannot furnish appellations for their owners? Will not heydukes and mamalukes, mandarins and patshaws, or any other words formed at pleasure, serve to distinguish those who are in the ministry from others who would be in it if they could? What, for instance, is easier than to vary the form of speech, and instead of the word church, make it a question in politics, whether the monument be in danger? Because religion was nearest at hand to furnish a few convenient phrases, is our invention so barren we can find no other? Suppose, for argument sake, that the Tories favored Margarita, the Whigs, Mrs. Tofts, and the Trimmers, Valentini, would not Margaritians, Toftians, and Valentinians be very tolerable marks of distinction? The Prasini and Veniti, two most virulent factions in Italy, began, if I remember right, by a distinction of colors in ribbons, which we might do with as good a grace about the dignity of the blue and the green, and serve as properly to divide the Court, the Parliament, and the kingdom between them, as any terms of art whatsoever, borrowed from religion. And therefore I think there is little force in this objection against Christianity, or prospect of so great an advantage as is proposed in the abolishing of it.

It is again objected, as a very absurd, ridiculous custom, that a set of men should be suffered, much less employed and hired, to bawl one day in seven against the lawfulness of those methods most in use towards the pursuit of greatness, riches, and pleasure, which are the constant practice of all men alive on the other six. But this objection is, I think, a little unworthy so refined an age as ours. Let us argue this matter calmly. I appeal to the breast of any polite Free-thinker, whether, in the pursuit of gratifying a pre-dominant passion, he hath not always felt a wonderful incitement, by reflecting it was a thing forbidden; and therefore we see, in order to cultivate this test, the wisdom of the nation hath taken special care that the ladies should be furnished with prohibited silks, and the men with prohibited wine. And indeed it were to be wished that some other prohibitions were promoted, in order to improve the pleasures of the town, which, for want of such expedients, begin already, as I am told, to flag and grow languid, giving way daily to cruel inroads from the spleen.

'Tis likewise proposed, as a great advantage to the public, that if we once discard the system of the Gospel, all religion will of course be banished for ever, and consequently along with it those grievous prejudices of education which, under the names of conscience, honor, justice, and the like, are so apt to disturb the peace of human minds, and the notions whereof are so hard to be eradicated by right reason or free-thinking, sometimes during the whole course of our lives.

Here first I observe how difficult it is to get rid of a phrase which the world has once grown fond of, though the occasion that first produced it be entirely taken away. For some years past, if a man had but an ill-favored nose, the deep thinkers of the age would, some way or other contrive to impute the cause to the prejudice of his education. From this fountain were said to be derived all our foolish notions of justice, piety, love of our country; all our opinions of God or a future state, heaven, hell, and the like; and there might formerly perhaps have been some pretense for this charge. But so effectual care hath been since taken to remove those prejudices, by an entire change in the methods of education, that (with honor I mention it to our polite innovators) the young gentlemen, who are now on the scene, seem to have not the least tincture left of those infusions, or string of those weeds, and by consequence the reason for abolishing nominal Christianity upon that pretext is wholly ceased.

For the rest, it may perhaps admit a controversy, whether the banishing all notions of religion whatsoever would be inconvenient for the vulgar. Not that I am in the least of opinion with those who hold religion to have been the invention of politicians, to keep the lower part of the world in awe by the fear of invisible powers; unless mankind were then very different from what it is now; for I look upon the mass or body of our people here in England to be as Freethinkers, that is to say, as staunch unbelievers, as any of the highest rank. But I conceive some scattered notions about a superior power to be of singular use for the common people, as furnishing excellent materials to keep children quiet when they grow peevish, and providing topics of amusement in a tedious winter night.

Lastly, it is proposed, as a singular advantage, that the abolishing of Christianity will very much contribute to the uniting of Protestants, by enlarging the terms of communion, so as to take in all sorts of Dissenters, who are now shut out of the pale upon account of a few ceremonies, which all sides confess to be things indifferent. That this alone will effectually answer the great ends of a scheme for comprehension, by opening a large noble gate, at which all bodies may enter; whereas the chaffering with Dissenters, and dodging about this or t'other ceremony, is but like opening a few wickets, and leaving them at jar, by which no more than one can get in at a time, and that not without stooping, and sidling, and squeezing his body.

To all this I answer, that there is one darling inclination of mankind which usually affects to be a retainer to religion, though she be neither its parent, its godmother, nor its friend. I mean the spirit of opposition, that lived long before Christianity, and can easily subsist without it. Let us, for instance, examine wherein the opposition of sectaries among us consists. We shall find Christianity to have no share in it at all. Does the Gospel anywhere prescribe a starched, squeezed countenance, a stiff formal gait, a singularity of manners and habit, or any affected forms and modes of speech different from the reasonable part of mankind? Yet, if Christianity did not lend its name to stand in the gap, and to employ or divert these humors, they must of necessity be spent in contraventions to the laws of the land, and disturbance of the public peace. There is a portion of enthusiasm assigned to every nation, which, if it hath not proper objects to work on, will burst out, and set all into a flame. If the quiet of a State can be bought by only flinging men a few ceremonies to devour, it is a purchase no wise man would refuse. Let the mastiffs amuse themselves about a sheep's skin stuffed with hay, provided it will keep them from worrying the flock. The institution of convents abroad seems in one point a strain of great wisdom, there being few irregularities in human passions which may not have recourse to vent themselves in some of those orders, which are so many retreats for the speculative, the melancholy, the proud, the silent, the politic, and the morose, to spend themselves, and evaporate the noxious particles; for each of whom we in this island are forced to provide a several sect of religion to keep them quiet; and whenever Christianity shall be abolished, the Legislature must find some other expedient to employ and entertain them. For what imports it how large a gate you open, if there will be always left a number who place a pride and a merit in not coming in?

Having thus considered the most important objections against Christianity, and the chief advantages proposed by the abolishing thereof, I shall now, with equal deference and submission to wiser judgments, as before, proceed to mention a few inconveniences that may happen if the Gospel should be repealed, which, perhaps, the projectors may not have sufficiently considered.

And first, I am very sensible how much the gentlemen of wit and pleasure are apt to murmur, and be choked at the sight of so many daggle-tailed parsons that happen to fall in their way, and offend their eyes; but at the same time, these wise reformers do not consider what an advantage and felicity it is for great wits to be always provided with objects of scorn and contempt, in order to exercise and improve their talents, and divert their spleen from falling on each other, or on themselves, especially when all this may be done without the least imaginable danger to their persons.

And to urge another argument of a parallel nature: if Christianity were once abolished, how could the Freethinkers, the strong reasoners, and the men of profound learning be able to find another subject so calculated in all points whereon to display their abilities? What wonderful productions of wit should we be deprived of from those whose genius, by continual practice, hath been wholly turned upon raillery and invectives against religion, and would therefore never be able to shine or distinguish themselves upon any other subject? We are daily complaining of the great decline of wit among as, and would we take away the greatest, perhaps the only topic we have left? Who would ever have suspected Asgil for a wit, or Toland for a philosopher, if the inexhaustible stock of Christianity had not been at hand to provide them with materials? What other subject through all art or nature could have produced Tindal for a profound author, or furnished him with readers? It is the wise choice of the subject that alone adorns and distinguishes the writer. For had a hundred such pens as these been employed on the side of religion, they would have immediately sunk into silence and oblivion.

Nor do I think it wholly groundless, or my fears altogether imaginary, that the abolishing of Christianity may perhaps bring the Church in danger, or at least put the Senate to the trouble of another securing vote. I desire I may not be mistaken; I am far from presuming to affirm or think that the Church is in danger at present, or as things now stand; but we know not how soon it may be so when the Christian religion is repealed. As plausible as this project seems, there may be a dangerous design lurk under it. Nothing can be more notorious than that the Atheists, Deists, Socinians, Anti-Trinitarians, and other subdivisions of Freethinkers, are persons of little zeal for the present ecclesiastical establishment: their declared opinion is for repealing the sacramental test; they are very indifferent with regard to ceremonies; nor do they hold the *Jus Divinum* of episcopacy: therefore they may be intended as one politic step towards altering the constitution of the Church established, and setting up Presbytery in the stead, which I leave to be further considered by those at the helm.

In the last place, I think nothing can be more plain, than that by this expedient we shall run into the evil we chiefly pretend to avoid; and that the abolishment of the Christian religion will be the readiest course we can take to introduce Popery. And I am the more inclined to this opinion because we know it has been the constant practice of the Jesuits to send over emissaries, with instructions to personate themselves members of the several prevailing sects amongst us. So it is recorded that they have at sundry times appeared in the guise of Presbyterians, Anabaptists, Independents, and Quakers, according as any of these were most in credit; so, since the fashion hath been taken up of exploding religion, the Popish missionaries have not been wanting to mix with the Freethinkers; among whom Toland, the great oracle of the Anti-Christians, is an Irish priest, the son of an Irish priest; and the most learned and ingenious author of a book called the "Rights of the Christian Church," was in a proper juncture reconciled to the Romish faith, whose true son, as appears by a hundred passages in his treatise, he still continues. Perhaps I could add some others to the number; but the fact is beyond dispute, and the reasoning they proceed by is right: for supposing Christianity to be extinguished the people will never he at ease till they find out some other method of worship, which will as infallibly produce superstition as this will end in Popery.

And therefore, if, notwithstanding all I have said, it still be thought necessary to have a Bill brought in for repealing Christianity, I would humbly offer an amendment, that instead of the word Christianity may be put religion in general, which I conceive will much better answer all the good ends proposed by the projectors of it. For as long as we leave in being a God and His Providence, with all the necessary consequences which curious and inquisitive men will be apt to draw from such promises, we do not strike at the root of the evil, though we should ever so effectually annihilate the present scheme of the Gospel; for of what use is freedom of thought if it will not produce freedom of action, which is the sole end, how remote soever in appearance, of all objections against Christianity? and therefore, the Freethinkers consider it as a sort of edifice, wherein all the parts have such a mutual dependence on each other, that if you happen to pull out one single nail, the whole fabric must fall to the ground. This was happily expressed by him who had heard of a text brought for proof of the Trinity, which in an ancient manuscript was differently read; he thereupon immediately took the hint, and by a sudden deduction of a long Sorites, most logically concluded: why, if it be as you say, I may safely drink on, and defy the parson. From which, and many the like instances easy to be produced, I think nothing can be more manifest than that the quarrel is not against any particular points of hard digestion in the Christian system, but against religion in general, which, by laying restraints on human nature, is supposed the great enemy to the freedom of thought and action.

Upon the whole, if it shall still be thought for the benefit of Church and State that Christianity be abolished, I conceive, however, it may be more convenient to defer the execution to a time of peace, and not venture in this conjuncture to disoblige our allies, who, as it falls out, are all Christians, and many of them, by the prejudices of their education, so bigoted as to place a sort of pride in the appellation. If, upon being rejected by them, we are to trust to an alliance with the Turk, we shall find ourselves much deceived; for, as he is too remote, and generally engaged in war with the Persian emperor, so his people would be more scandalized at our infidelity than our Christian neighbors. For they are not only strict observers of religions worship, but what is worse, believe a God; which is more than is required of us, even while we preserve the name of Christians.

To conclude, whatever some may think of the great advantages to trade by this favorite scheme, I do very much apprehend that in six months' time after the Act is passed for the extirpation of the Gospel, the Bank and East India stock may fall at least one per cent. And since that is fifty times more than ever the wisdom of our age thought fit to venture for the preservation of Christianity, there is no reason we should be at so great a loss merely for the sake of destroying it.

HINTS TOWARDS AN ESSAY ON CONVERSATION

I have observed few obvious subjects to have been so seldom, or at least so slightly, handled as this; and, indeed, I know few so difficult to be treated as it ought, nor yet upon which there seemeth so much to be said.

Most things pursued by men for the happiness of public or private life our wit or folly have so refined, that they seldom subsist but in idea; a true friend, a good marriage, a perfect form of government, with some others, require so many ingredients, so good in their several kinds, and so much niceness in mixing them, that for some thousands of years men have despaired of reducing their schemes to perfection. But in conversation it is or might be otherwise; for here we are only to avoid a multitude of errors, which, although a matter of some difficulty, may be in every man's power, for want of which it remaineth as mere an idea as the other. Therefore it seemeth to me that the truest way to understand conversation is to know the faults and errors to which it is subject, and from thence every man to form maxims to himself whereby it may be regulated, because it requireth few talents to which most men are not born, or at least may not acquire without any great genius or study. For nature bath left every man a capacity of being agreeable, though not of shining in company; and there are a hundred men sufficiently qualified for both, who, by a very few faults that they might correct in half an hour, are not so much as tolerable.

I was prompted to write my thoughts upon this subject by mere indignation, to reflect that so useful and innocent a pleasure, so fitted for every period and condition of life, and so much in all men's power, should be so much neglected and abused.

And in this discourse it will be necessary to note those errors that are obvious, as well as others which are seldomer observed, since there are few so obvious or acknowledged into which most men, some time or other, are not apt to run.

For instance, nothing is more generally exploded than the folly of talking too much; yet I rarely remember to have seen five people together where some one among them hath not been predominant in that kind, to the great constraint and disgust of all the rest. But among such as deal in multitudes of words, none are comparable to the sober deliberate talker, who proceedeth with much thought and caution, maketh his preface, brancheth out into several digressions, findeth a hint that putteth him in mind of another story, which he promiseth to tell you when this is done; cometh back regularly to his subject, cannot readily call to mind some person's name, holdeth his head, complaineth of his memory; the whole company all this while in suspense; at length, says he, it is no matter, and so goes on. And, to crown the business, it perhaps proveth at last a story the company hath heard fifty times before; or, at best, some insipid adventure of the relater.

Another general fault in conversation is that of those who affect to talk of themselves. Some, without any ceremony, will run over the history of their lives; will relate the annals of their diseases, with the several symptoms and circumstances of them; will enumerate the hardships and injustice they have suffered in court, in parliament, in love, or in law. Others are more dexterous, and with great art will lie on the watch to hook in their own praise. They will call a witness to remember they always foretold what would happen in such a case, but none would believe them; they advised such a man from the beginning, and told him the consequences just as they happened, but he would have his own way. Others make a vanity of telling their faults. They are the strangest men in the world; they cannot dissemble; they own it is a folly; they have lost abundance of advantages by it; but, if you would give them the world, they cannot help it; there is something in their nature that abhors insincerity and constraint; with many other insufferable topics of the same altitude.

Of such mighty importance every man is to himself, and ready to think he is so to others, without once making this easy and obvious reflection, that his affairs can have no more weight with other men than theirs have with him; and how little that is he is sensible enough.

Where company hath met, I often have observed two persons discover by some accident that they were bred together at the same school or university, after which the rest are condemned to silence, and to listen while these two are refreshing each other's memory with the arch tricks and passages of themselves and their comrades.

I know a great officer of the army, who will sit for some time with a supercilious and impatient silence, full of anger and contempt for those who are talking; at length of a sudden demand audience; decide the matter in a short dogmatical way; then withdraw within himself again, and vouchsafe to talk no more, until his spirits circulate again to the same point.

There are some faults in conversation which none are so subject to as the men of wit, nor ever so much as when they are with each other. If they have opened their mouths without endeavoring to say a witty thing, they think it is so many words lost. It is a torment to the hearers, as much as to themselves, to see them upon the rack for invention, and in perpetual constraint, with so little success. They must do something extraordinary, in order to acquit themselves, and answer their character, else the standers by may be disappointed and be apt to think them only like the rest of mortals. I have known two men of wit industriously brought together, in order to entertain the company, where they have made a very ridiculous figure, and provided all the mirth at their own expense.

I know a man of wit, who is never easy but where he can be allowed to dictate and preside; he neither expecteth to be informed or entertained, but to display his own talents. His business is to be good company, and not good conversation, and therefore he chooseth to frequent those who are content to listen, and profess themselves his admirers. And, indeed, the worst conversation I ever remember to have heard in my life was that at Will's coffee-house, where the wits, as they were called, used formerly to assemble; that is to say, five or six men who had written plays, or at least prologues, or had share in a miscellany, came thither, and entertained one another with their trifling composures in so important an air, as if they had been the noblest efforts of human nature, or that the fate of kingdoms depended on them; and they were usually attended with a humble audience of young students from the inns of courts, or the universities, who, at due distance, listened to these oracles, and returned home with great contempt for their law and philosophy, their heads filled with trash under the name of politeness, criticism, and belles lettres.

By these means the poets, for many years past, were all overrun with pedantry. For, as I take it, the word is not properly used; because pedantry is the too front or unseasonable obtruding our own knowledge in common discourse, and placing too great a value upon it; by which definition men of the court or the army may be as guilty of pedantry as a philosopher or a divine; and it is the same vice in women when they are over copious upon the subject of their petticoats, or their fans, or their china. For which reason, although it be a piece of prudence, as well as good manners, to put men upon talking on subjects they are best versed in, yet that is a liberty a wise man could hardly take; because, beside the imputation of pedantry, it is what he would never improve by.

This great town is usually provided with some player, mimic, or buffoon, who hath a general reception at the good tables; familiar and domestic with persons of the first quality, and usually sent for at every meeting to divert the company, against which I have no objection. You go there as to a farce or a puppet-show; your business is only to laugh in season, either out of inclination or civility, while this merry companion is acting his part. It is a business he hath undertaken, and we are to suppose he is paid for his day's work. I only quarrel when in select and private meetings, where men of wit and learning are invited to pass an evening, this jester should be admitted to run over his circle of tricks, and make the whole company unfit for any other conversation, besides the indignity of confounding men's talents at so shameful a rate.

Raillery is the finest part of conversation; but, as it is our usual custom to counterfeit and adulterate whatever is too dear for us, so we have done with this, and turned it all into what is generally called repartee, or being smart; just as when an expensive fashion cometh up, those who are not able to reach it content themselves with some paltry imitation. It now passeth for raillery to run a man down in discourse, to put him out of countenance, and make him ridiculous, sometimes to expose the defects of his person or understanding; on all which occasions he is obliged not to be angry, to avoid the imputation of not being able to take a jest. It is admirable to observe one who is dexterous at this art, singling out a weak adversary, getting the laugh on his side, and then carrying all before him. The French, from whom we borrow the word, have a quite different idea of the thing, and so had we in the politer age of our fathers. Raillery was, to say something that at first appeared a reproach or reflection, but, by some turn of wit unexpected and surprising, ended always in a compliment, and to the advantage of the person it was addressed to. And surely one of the best rules in conversation is, never to say a thing which any of the company can reasonably wish we had rather left unsaid; nor can there anything be well more contrary to the ends for which people meet together, than to part unsatisfied with each other or themselves.

There are two faults in conversation which appear very different, yet arise from the same root, and are equally blamable; I mean, an impatience to interrupt others, and the uneasiness of being interrupted ourselves. The two chief ends of conversation are, to entertain and improve those we are among, or to receive those benefits ourselves; which whoever will consider, cannot easily run into either of those two errors; because, when any man speaketh in company, it is to be supposed he doth it for his hearers' sake, and not his own; so that common discretion will teach us not to force their attention, if they are not willing to lend it; nor, on the other side, to interrupt him who is in possession, because that is in the grossest manner to give the preference to our own good sense.

There are some people whose good manners will not suffer them to interrupt you; but, what is almost as bad, will discover abundance of impatience, and lie upon the watch until you have done, because they have started something in their own thoughts which they long to be delivered of. Meantime, they are so far from regarding what passes, that their imaginations are wholly turned upon what they have in reserve, for fear it should slip out of their memory; and thus they confine their invention, which might otherwise range over a hundred things full as good, and that might be much more naturally introduced.

There is a sort of rude familiarity, which some people, by practicing among their intimates, have introduced into their general conversation, and would have it pass for innocent freedom or humor, which is a dangerous experiment in our northern climate, where all the little decorum and politeness we have are purely forced by art, and are so ready to lapse into barbarity. This, among the Romans, was the raillery of slaves, of which we have many instances in Plautus. It seemeth to have been introduced among us by Cromwell, who, by preferring the scum of the people, made it a court-entertainment, of which I have heard many particulars; and, considering all things were turned upside down, it was reasonable and judicious; although it was a piece of policy found out to ridicule a point of honor in the other extreme, when the smallest word misplaced among gentlemen ended in a duel.

There are some men excellent at telling a story, and provided with a plentiful stock of them, which they can draw out upon occasion in all companies; and considering how low conversation runs now among us, it is not altogether a contemptible talent; however, it is subject to two unavoidable defects: frequent repetition, and being soon exhausted; so that whoever valueth this gift in himself hath need of a good memory, and ought frequently to shift his company, that he may not discover the weakness of his fund; for those who are thus endowed have seldom any other revenue, but live upon the main stock.

Great speakers in public are seldom agreeable in private conversation, whether their faculty be natural, or acquired by practice and often venturing. Natural elocution, although it may seem a paradox, usually springeth from a barrenness of invention and of words, by which men who have only one stock of notions upon every subject, and one set of phrases to express them in, they swim upon the superficies, and offer themselves on every occasion; therefore, men of much learning, and who know the compass of a language, are generally the worst talkers on a sudden, until much practice hath inured and emboldened them; because they are confounded with plenty of matter, variety of notions, and of words, which they cannot readily choose, but are perplexed and entangled by too great a choice, which is no disadvantage in private conversation; where, on the other side, the talent of haranguing is, of all others, most insupportable.

Nothing hath spoiled men more for conversation than the character of being wits; to support which, they never fail of encouraging a number of followers and admirers, who list themselves in their service, wherein they find their accounts on both sides by pleasing their mutual vanity. This hath given the former such an air of superiority, and made the latter so pragmatical, that neither of them are well to be endured. I say nothing here of the itch of dispute and contradiction, telling of lies, or of those who are troubled with the disease called the wandering of the thoughts, that they are never present in mind at what passeth in discourse; for whoever labors under any of these possessions is as unfit for conversation as madmen in Bedlam.

I think I have gone over most of the errors in conversation that have fallen under my notice or memory, except some that are merely personal, and others too gross to need exploding; such as lewd or profane talk; but I pretend only to treat the errors of conversation in general, and not the several subjects of discourse, which would be infinite. Thus we see how human nature is most debased, by the abuse of that faculty, which is held the great distinction between men and brutes; and how little advantage we make of that which might be the greatest, the most lasting, and the most innocent, as well as useful pleasure of life: in default of which, we are forced to take up with those poor amusements of dress and visiting, or the more pernicious ones of play, drink, and vicious amours, whereby the nobility and gentry of both sexes are entirely corrupted both in body and mind, and have lost all notions of love, honour, friendship, and generosity; which, under the name of fopperies, have been for some time laughed out of doors.

This degeneracy of conversation, with the pernicious consequences thereof upon our humors and dispositions, hath been owing, among other causes, to the custom arisen, for some time past, of excluding women from any share in our society, further than in parties at play, or dancing, or in the pursuit of an amour. I take the highest period of politeness in England (and it is of the same date in France) to have been the peaceable part of King Charles I.'s reign; and from what we read of those times, as well as from the accounts I have formerly met with from some who lived in that court, the methods then used for raising and cultivating conversation were altogether different from ours; several ladies, whom we find celebrated by the poets of that age, had assemblies at their houses, where persons of the best understanding, and of both sexes, met to pass the evenings in discoursing upon whatever agreeable subjects were occasionally started; and although we are apt to ridicule the sublime Platonic notions they had, or personated in love and friendship, I conceive their refinements were grounded upon reason, and that a little grain of the romance is no ill ingredient to preserve and exalt the dignity of human nature, without which it is apt to degenerate into everything that is sordid, vicious, and low. If there were no other use in the conversation of ladies, it is sufficient that it would lay a restraint upon those odious topics of immodesty and indecencies, into which the rudeness of our northern genius is so apt to fall. And, therefore, it is observable in those sprightly gentlemen about the town, who are so very dexterous at entertaining a vizard mask in the park or the playhouse, that, in the company of ladies of virtue and honor, they are silent and disconcerted, and out of their element.

There are some people who think they sufficiently acquit themselves and entertain their company with relating of facts of no consequence, nor at all out of the road of such common incidents as happen every day; and this I have observed more frequently among the Scots than any other nation, who are very careful not to omit the minutest circumstances of time or place; which kind of discourse, if it were not a little relieved by the uncouth terms and phrases, as well as accent and gesture peculiar to that country, would be hardly tolerable. It is not a fault in company to talk much; but to continue it long is certainly one; for, if the majority of those who are got together be naturally silent or cautious, the conversation will flag, unless it be often renewed by one among them who can start new subjects, provided he doth not dwell upon them, but leaveth room for answers and replies.

THOUGHTS ON VARIOUS SUBJECTS

We have just enough religion to make us hate, but not enough to make us love one another.

Reflect on things past as wars, negotiations, factions, etc. We enter so little into those interests, that we wonder how men could possibly be so busy and concerned for things so transitory; look on the present times, we find the same humor, yet wonder not at all.

A wise man endeavors, by considering all circumstances, to make conjectures and form conclusions; but the smallest accident intervening (and in the course of affairs it is impossible to foresee all) does often produce such turns and changes, that at last he is just as much in doubt of events as the most ignorant and inexperienced person.

Positiveness is a good quality for preachers and orators, because he that would obtrude his thoughts and reasons upon a multitude, will convince others the more, as he appears convinced himself.

How is it possible to expect that mankind will take advice, when they will not so much as take warning?

I forget whether Advice be among the lost things which Aristo says are to be found in the moon; that and Time ought to have been there.

No preacher is listened to but Time, which gives us the same train and turn of thought that older people have tried in vain to put into our heads before.

When we desire or solicit anything, our minds run wholly on the good side or circumstances of it; when it is obtained, our minds run wholly on the bad ones.

In a glass-house the workmen often fling in a small quantity of fresh coals, which seems to disturb the fire, but very much enlivens it. This seems to allude to a gentle stirring of the passions, that the mind may not languish.

Religion seems to have grown an infant with age, and requires miracles to nurse it, as it had in its infancy.

All fits of pleasure are balanced by an equal degree of pain or languor; it is like spending this year part of the next year's revenue.

The latter part of a wise man's life is taken up in curing the follies, prejudices, and false opinions he had contracted in the former.

Would a writer know how to behave himself with relation to posterity, let him consider in old books what he finds that he is glad to know, and what omissions he most laments.

Whatever the poets pretend, it is plain they give immortality to none but themselves; it is Homer and Virgil we reverence and admire, not Achilles or Aeneas. With historians it is quite the contrary; our thoughts are taken up with the actions, persons, and events we read, and we little regard the authors.

When a true genius appears in the world you may know him by this sign; that the dunces are all in confederacy against him.

Men who possess all the advantages of life, are in a state where there are many accidents to disorder and discompose, but few to please them.

It is unwise to punish cowards with ignominy, for if they had regarded that they would not have been cowards; death is their proper punishment, because they fear it most.

The greatest inventions were produced in the times of ignorance, as the use of the compass, gunpowder, and printing, and by the dullest nation, as the Germans.

One argument to prove that the common relations of ghosts and specters are generally false, may be drawn from the opinion held that spirits are never seen by more than one person at a time; that is to say, it seldom happens to above one person in a company to be possessed with any high degree of spleen or melancholy.

I am apt to think that, in the day of Judgment, there will be small allowance given to the wise for their want of morals, nor to the ignorant for their want of faith, because both are without excuse. This renders the advantages equal of ignorance and knowledge. But, some scruples in the wise, and some vices in the ignorant, will perhaps be forgiven upon the strength of temptation to each.

The value of several circumstances in story lessens very much by distance of time, though some minute circumstances are very valuable; and it requires great judgment in a writer to distinguish.

It is grown a word of course for writers to say, "This critical age," as divines say, "This sinful age."

It is pleasant to observe how free the present age is in laying taxes on the next. *Future ages shall talk of this; this shall be famous to all posterity.* Whereas their time and thoughts will be taken up about present things, as ours are now.

The chameleon, who is said to feed upon nothing but air, hath, of all animals, the nimblest tongue.

When a man is made a spiritual peer he loses his surname; when a temporal, his Christian name.

It is in disputes as in armies, where the weaker side sets up false lights, and makes a great noise, to make the enemy believe them more numerous and strong than they really are.

Some men, under the notions of weeding out prejudices, eradicate virtue, honesty, and religion.

In all well-instituted commonwealths, care has been taken to limit men's possessions; which is done for many reasons, and among the rest, for one which perhaps is not often considered: that when bounds are set to men's desires, after they have acquired as much as the laws will permit them, their private interest is at an end, and they have nothing to do but to take care of the public.

There are but three ways for a man to revenge himself of the censure of the world: to despise it, to return the like, or to endeavor to live so as to avoid it. The first of these is usually pretended, the last is almost impossible; the universal practice is for the second.

I never heard a finer piece of satire against lawyers than that of astrologers, when they pretend by rules of art to tell when a suit will end, and whether to the advantage of the plaintiff or defendant; thus making the matter depend entirely upon the influence of the stars, without the least regard to the merits of the cause.

The expression in Apocrypha about Tobit and his dog following him I have often heard ridiculed, yet Homer has the same words of Telemachus more than once; and Virgil says something like it of Evander. And I take the book of Tobit to be partly poetical.

I have known some men possessed of good qualities, which were very serviceable to others, but useless to themselves; like a sun-dial on the front of a house, to inform the neighbors and passengers, but not the owner within.

If a man would register all his opinions upon love, politics, religion, learning, etc., beginning from his youth and so go on to old age, what a bundle of inconsistencies and contradictions would appear at last!

What they do in heaven we are ignorant of; what they do not we are told expressly: that they neither marry, nor are given in marriage.

It is a miserable thing to live in suspense; it is the life of a spider.

The Stoical scheme of supplying our wants by lopping off our desires, is like cutting off our feet when we want shoes.

Physicians ought not to give their judgment of religion, for the same reason that butchers are not admitted to be jurors upon life and death.

The reason why so few marriages are happy, is, because young ladies spend their time in making nets, not in making cages.

If a man will observe as he walks the streets, I believe he will find the merriest countenances in mourning coaches.

Nothing more unqualifies a man to act with prudence than a misfortune that is attended with shame and guilt.

The power of fortune is confessed only by the miserable; for the happy impute all their success to prudence or merit.

Ambition often puts men upon doing the meanest offices; so climbing is performed in the same posture with creeping.

Censure is the tax a man pays to the public for being eminent.

Although men are accused for not knowing their own weakness, yet perhaps as few know their own strength. It is, in men as in soils, where sometimes there is a vein of gold which the owner knows not of.

Satire is reckoned the easiest of all wit, but I take it to be otherwise in very bad times: for it is as hard to satirize well a man of distinguished vices, as to praise well a man of distinguished virtues. It is easy enough to do either to people of moderate characters.

Invention is the talent of youth, and judgment of age; so that our judgment grows harder to please, when we have fewer things to offer it: this goes through the whole commerce of life. When we are old, our friends find it difficult to please us, and are less concerned whether we be pleased or no.

No wise man ever wished to be younger.

An idle reason lessens the weight of the good ones you gave before.

The motives of the best actions will not bear too strict an inquiry. It is allowed that the cause of most actions, good or bad, may he resolved into the love of ourselves; but the self-love of some men inclines them to please others, and the self-love of others is wholly employed in pleasing themselves. This makes the great distinction between virtue and vice. Religion is the best motive of all actions, yet religion is allowed to be the highest instance of self-love.

Old men view best at a distance with the eyes of their understanding as well as with those of nature.

Some people take more care to hide their wisdom than their folly.

Anthony Henley's farmer, dying of an asthma, said, "Well, if I can get this breath once *out*, I'll take care it never got *in* again."

The humor of exploding many things under the name of trifles, fopperies, and only imaginary goods, is a very false proof either of wisdom or magnanimity, and a great check to virtuous actions. For instance, with regard to fame, there is in most people a reluctance and unwillingness to be forgotten. We observe, even among the vulgar, how fond they are to have an inscription over their grave. It requires but little philosophy to discover and observe that there is no intrinsic value in all this; however, if it be founded in our nature as an incitement to virtue, it ought not to be ridiculed.

Complaint is the largest tribute heaven receives, and the sincerest part of our devotion.

The common fluency of speech in many men, and most women, is owing to a scarcity of matter, and a scarcity of words; for whoever is a master of language, and hath a mind full of ideas, will be apt, in speaking, to hesitate upon the choice of both; whereas common speakers have only one set of ideas, and one set of words to clothe them in, and these are always ready at the mouth. So people come faster out of a church when it is almost empty, than when a crowd is at the door.

Few are qualified to shine in company; but it is in most men's power to be agreeable. The reason, therefore, why conversation runs so low at present, is not the defect of understanding, but pride, vanity, ill-nature, affectation, singularity, positiveness, or some other vice, the effect of a wrong education.

To be vain is rather a mark of humility than pride. Vain men delight in telling what honors have been done them, what great company they have kept, and the like, by which they plainly confess that these honors were more than their due, and such as their friends would not believe if they had not been told: whereas a man truly proud thinks the greatest honors below his merit, and consequently scorns to boast. I therefore deliver it as a maxim, that whoever desires the character of a proud man, ought to conceal his vanity.

Law, in a free country, is, or ought to be, the determination of the majority of those who have property in land.

One argument used to the disadvantage of Providence I take to be a very strong one in its defense. It is objected that storms and tempests, unfruitful seasons, serpents, spiders, flies, and other noxious or troublesome animals, with many more instances of the like kind, discover an imperfection in nature, because human life would be much easier without them; but the design of Providence may clearly be perceived in this proceeding. The motions of the sun and moon—in short, the whole system of the universe, as far as philosophers have been able to discover and observe, are in the utmost degree of regularity and perfection; but wherever God hath left to man the power of interposing a remedy by thought or labour, there he hath placed things in a state of imperfection, on purpose to stir up human industry, without which life would stagnate, or, indeed, rather, could not subsist at all: *Curis accuunt mortalia corda.*

Praise is the daughter of present power.

How inconsistent is man with himself!

I have known several persons of great fame for wisdom in public affairs and counsels governed by foolish servants.

I have known great Ministers, distinguished for wit and learning, who preferred none but dunces.

I have known men of great valor cowards to their wives.

I have known men of the greatest cunning perpetually cheated.

I knew three great Ministers, who could exactly compute and settle the accounts of a kingdom, but were wholly ignorant of their own economy.

The preaching of divines helps to preserve well-inclined men in the course of virtue, but seldom or never reclaims the vicious.

Princes usually make wiser choices than the servants whom they trust for the disposal of places: I have known a prince, more than once, choose an able Minister, but I never observed that Minister to use his credit in the disposal of an employment to a person whom he thought the fittest for it. One of the greatest in this age owned and excused the matter from the violence of parties and the unreasonableness of friends.

Small causes are sufficient to make a man uneasy when great ones are not in the way. For want of a block he will stumble at a straw.

Dignity, high station, or great riches, are in some sort necessary to old men, in order to keep the younger at a distance, who are otherwise too apt to insult them upon the score of their age.

Every man desires to live long; but no man would be old.

Love of flattery in most men proceeds from the mean opinion they have of themselves; in women from the contrary.

If books and laws continue to increase as they have done for fifty years past, I am in some concern for future ages how any man will be learned, or any man a lawyer.

Kings are commonly said to have *long hands*; I wish they had as *long ears*.

Princes in their infancy, childhood, and youth are said to discover prodigious parts and wit, to speak things that surprise and astonish. Strange, so many hopeful princes, and so many shameful kings! If they happen to die young, they would have been prodigies of wisdom and virtue. If they live, they are often prodigies indeed, but of another sort.

Politics, as the word is commonly understood, are nothing but corruptions, and consequently of no use to a good king or a good ministry; for which reason Courts are so overrun with politics.

A nice man is a man of nasty ideas.

Apollo was held the god of physic and sender of diseases. Both were originally the same trade, and still continue.

Old men and comets have been reverenced for the same reason: their long beards, and pretenses to foretell events.

A person was asked at court, what he thought of an ambassador and his train, who were all embroidery and lace, full of bows, cringes, and gestures; he said, it was Solomon's importation, gold and apes.

Most sorts of diversion in men, children, and other animals, is an imitation of fighting.

Augustus meeting an ass with a lucky name foretold himself good fortune. I meet many asses, but none of them have lucky names.

If a man makes me keep my distance, the comfort is he keeps his at the same time.

Who can deny that all men are violent lovers of truth when we see them so positive in their errors, which they will maintain out of their zeal to truth, although they contradict themselves every day of their lives?

That was excellently observed, say I, when I read a passage in an author, where his opinion agrees with mine. When we differ, there I pronounce him to be mistaken.

Very few men, properly speaking, live at present, but are providing to live another time.

Laws penned with the utmost care and exactness, and in the vulgar language, are often perverted to wrong meanings; then why should we wonder that the Bible is so?

Although men are accused for not knowing their weakness, yet perhaps as few know their own strength.

A man seeing a wasp creeping into a vial filled with honey, that was hung on a fruit tree, said thus: "Why, thou sottish animal, art thou mad to go into that vial, where you see many hundred of your kind there dying in it before you?" "The reproach is just," answered the wasp, "but not from you men, who are so far from taking example by other people's follies, that you will not take warning by your own. If after falling several times into this vial, and escaping by chance, I should fall in again, I should then but resemble you."

An old miser kept a tame jackdaw, that used to steal pieces of money, and hide them in a hole, which the cat observing, asked why he would hoard up those round shining things that he could make no use of? "Why," said the jackdaw, "my master has a whole chest full, and makes no more use of them than I."

Men are content to be laughed at for their wit, but not for their folly.

If the men of wit and genius would resolve never to complain in their works of critics and detractors, the next age would not know that they ever had any.

After all the maxims and systems of trade and commerce, a stander-by would think the affairs of the world were most ridiculously contrived.

There are few countries which, if well cultivated, would not support double the number of their inhabitants, and yet fewer where one-third of the people are not extremely stinted even in the necessaries of life. I send out twenty barrels of corn, which would maintain a family in bread for a year, and I bring back in return a vessel of wine, which half a dozen good follows would drink in less than a month, at the expense of their health and reason.

A man would have but few spectators, if he offered to show for threepence how he could thrust a red-hot iron into a barrel of gunpowder, and it should not take fire.

A TALE OF A TUB

A TALE OF A TUB

TO THE RIGHT HONOURABLE JOHN LORD SOMERS

My Lord,

Though the author has written a large Dedication, yet that being addressed to a Prince whom I am never likely to have the honour of being known to; a person, besides, as far as I can observe, not at all regarded or thought on by any of our present writers; and I being wholly free from that slavery which booksellers usually lie under to the caprices of authors, I think it a wise piece of presumption to inscribe these papers to your Lordship, and to implore your Lordship's protection of them. God and your Lordship know their faults and their merits; for as to my own particular, I am altogether a stranger to the matter; and though everybody else should be equally ignorant, I do not fear the sale of the book at all the worse upon that score. Your Lordship's name on the front in capital letters will at any time get off one edition: neither would I desire any other help to grow an alderman than a patent for the sole privilege of dedicating to your Lordship.

I should now, in right of a dedicator, give your Lordship a list of your own virtues, and at the same time be very unwilling to offend your modesty; but chiefly I should celebrate your liberality towards men of great parts and small fortunes, and give you broad hints that I mean myself. And I was just going on in the usual method to peruse a hundred or two of dedications, and transcribe an abstract to be applied to your Lordship, but I was diverted by a certain accident. For upon the covers of these papers I casually observed written in large letters the two following words, DETUR DIGNISSIMO, which, for aught I knew, might contain some important meaning. But it unluckily fell out that none of the Authors I employ understood Latin (though I have them often in pay to translate out of that language). I was therefore compelled to have recourse to the Curate of our Parish, who Englished it thus, *Let it be given to the worthiest*; and his comment was that the Author meant his work should be dedicated to the sublimest genius of the age for wit, learning, judgment, eloquence, and wisdom. I called at a poet's chamber (who works for my shop) in an alley hard by, showed him the translation, and desired his opinion who it was that the Author could mean. He told me, after some consideration, that vanity was a thing he abhorred, but by the description he thought himself to be the person aimed at; and at the same time he very kindly offered his own assistance gratis towards penning a dedication to himself. I desired him, however, to give a second guess. Why then, said he, it must be I, or my Lord Somers. From thence I went to several other wits of my acquaintance, with no small hazard and weariness to my person, from a prodigious number of dark winding stairs; but found them all in the same story, both of your Lordship and themselves. Now your Lordship is to understand that this proceeding was not of my own invention; for I have somewhere heard it is a maxim that those to whom everybody allows the second place have an undoubted title to the first.

This infallibly convinced me that your Lordship was the person intended by the Author. But being very unacquainted in the style and form of dedications, I employed those wits aforesaid to furnish me with hints and materials towards a panegyric upon your Lordship's virtues.

In two days they brought me ten sheets of paper filled up on every side. They swore to me that they had ransacked whatever could be found in the characters of Socrates, Aristides, Epaminondas, Cato, Tully, Atticus, and other hard names which I cannot now recollect. However, I have reason to believe they imposed upon my ignorance, because when I came to read over their collections, there was not a syllable there but what I and everybody else knew as well as themselves: therefore I grievously suspect a cheat; and that these Authors of mine stole and transcribed every word from the universal report of mankind. So that I took upon myself as fifty shillings out of pocket to no manner of purpose.

If by altering the title I could make the same materials serve for another dedication (as my betters have done), it would help to make up my loss; but I have made several persons dip here and there in those papers, and before they read three lines they have all assured me plainly that they cannot possibly be applied to any person besides your Lordship.

I expected, indeed, to have heard of your Lordship's bravery at the head of an army; of your undaunted courage in mounting a breach or scaling a wall; or to have had your pedigree traced in a lineal descent from the House of Austria; or of your wonderful talent at dress and dancing; or your profound knowledge in algebra, metaphysics, and the Oriental tongues: but to ply the world with an old beaten story of your wit, and eloquence, and learning, and wisdom, and justice, and politeness, and candour, and evenness of temper in all scenes of life; of that great discernment in discovering and readiness in favouring deserving men; with forty other common topics; I confess I have neither conscience nor countenance to do it. Because there is no virtue either of a public or private life which some circumstances of your own have not often produced upon the stage of the world; and those few which for want of occasions to exert them might otherwise have passed unseen or unobserved by your friends, your enemies have at length brought to light.

It is true I should be very loth the bright example of your Lordship's virtues should be lost to after-ages, both for their sake and your own; but chiefly because they will be so very necessary to adorn the history of a late reign; and that is another reason why I would forbear to make a recital of them here; because I have been told by wise men that as dedications have run for some years past, a good historian will not be apt to have recourse thither in search of characters.

There is one point wherein I think we dedicators would do well to change our measures; I mean, instead of running on so far upon the praise of our patron's liberality, to spend a word or two in admiring their patience. I can put no greater compliment on your Lordship's than by giving you so ample an occasion to exercise it at present. Though perhaps I shall not be apt to reckon much merit to your Lordship upon that score, who having been formerly used to tedious harangues, and sometimes to as little purpose, will be the readier to pardon this, especially when it is offered by one who is, with all respect and veneration,

My Lord,

Your Lordship's most obedient
and most faithful Servant,
THE BOOKSELLER.

THE BOOKSELLER TO THE READER

It is now six years since these papers came first to my hand, which seems to have been about a twelvemonth after they were written, for the Author tells us in his preface to the first treatise that he had calculated it for the year 1697; and in several passages of that discourse, as well as the second, it appears they were written about that time.

As to the Author, I can give no manner of satisfaction. However, I am credibly informed that this publication is without his knowledge, for he concludes the copy is lost, having lent it to a person since dead, and being never in possession of it after; so that, whether the work received his last hand, or whether he intended to fill up the defective places, is like to remain a secret.

If I should go about to tell the reader by what accident I became master of these papers, it would, in this unbelieving age, pass for little more than the cant or jargon of the trade. I therefore gladly spare both him and myself so unnecessary a trouble. There yet remains a difficult question—why I published them no sooner? I forbore upon two accounts. First, because I thought I had better work upon my hands; and secondly, because I was not without some hope of hearing from the Author and receiving his directions. But I have been lately alarmed with intelligence of a surreptitious copy which a certain great wit had new polished and refined, or, as our present writers express themselves, "fitted to the humour of the age," as they have already done with great felicity to Don Quixote, Boccalini, La Bruyère, and other authors. However, I thought it fairer dealing to offer the whole work in its naturals. If any gentleman will please to furnish me with a key, in order to explain the more difficult parts, I shall very gratefully acknowledge the favour, and print it by itself.

THE EPISTLE DEDICATORY TO HIS ROYAL HIGHNESS PRINCE POSTERITY

Sir,

I here present your Highness with the fruits of a very few leisure hours, stolen from the short intervals of a world of business, and of an employment quite alien from such amusements as this; the poor production of that refuse of time which has lain heavy upon my hands during a long prorogation of Parliament, a great dearth of foreign news, and a tedious fit of rainy weather. For which, and other reasons, it cannot choose extremely to deserve such a patronage as that of your Highness, whose numberless virtues in so few years, make the world look upon you as the future example to all princes. For although your Highness is hardly got clear of infancy, yet has the universal learned world already resolved upon appealing to your future dictates with the lowest and most resigned submission, fate having decreed you sole arbiter of the productions of human wit in this polite and most accomplished age. Methinks the number of appellants were enough to shock and startle any judge of a genius less unlimited than yours; but in order to prevent such glorious trials, the person, it seems, to whose care the education of your Highness is committed, has resolved, as I am told, to keep you in almost an universal ignorance of our studies, which it is your inherent birthright to inspect.

It is amazing to me that this person should have assurance, in the face of the sun, to go about persuading your Highness that our age is almost wholly illiterate and has hardly produced one writer upon any subject. I know very well that when your Highness shall come to riper years, and have gone through the learning of antiquity, you will be too curious to neglect inquiring into the authors of the very age before you; and to think that this insolent, in the account he is preparing for your view, designs to reduce them to a number so insignificant as I am ashamed to mention; it moves my zeal and my spleen for the honour and interest of our vast flourishing body, as well as of myself, for whom I know by long experience he has professed, and still continues, a peculiar malice.

It is not unlikely that, when your Highness will one day peruse what I am now writing, you may be ready to expostulate with your governor upon the credit of what I here affirm, and command him to show you some of our productions. To which he will answer—for I am well informed of his designs—by asking your Highness where they are, and what is become of them? and pretend it a demonstration that there never were any, because they are not then to be found. Not to be found! Who has mislaid them? Are they sunk in the abyss of things? It is certain that in their own nature they were light enough to swim upon the surface for all eternity; therefore, the fault is in him who tied weights so heavy to their heels as to depress them to the centre. Is their very essence destroyed? Who has annihilated them? Were they drowned by purges or martyred by pipes? Who administered them to the posteriors of —. But that it may no longer be a doubt with your Highness who is to be the author of this universal ruin, I beseech you to observe that large and terrible scythe which your governor affects to bear continually about him. Be pleased to remark the length and strength, the sharpness and hardness, of his nails and teeth; consider his baneful, abominable breath, enemy to life and matter, infectious and corrupting, and then reflect whether it be possible for any mortal ink and paper of this generation to make a suitable resistance. Oh, that your Highness would one day resolve to disarm this usurping *maître de palais* of his furious engines, and bring your empire *hors du page*.

It were endless to recount the several methods of tyranny and destruction which your governor is pleased to practise upon this occasion. His inveterate malice is such to the writings of our age, that, of several thousands produced yearly from this renowned city, before the next revolution of the sun there is not one to be heard of. Unhappy infants! many of them barbarously destroyed before they have so much as learnt their mother-tongue to beg for pity. Some he stifles in their cradles, others he frights into convulsions, whereof they suddenly die, some he flays alive, others he tears limb from limb, great numbers are offered to Moloch, and the rest, tainted by his breath, die of a languishing consumption.

But the concern I have most at heart is for our Corporation of Poets, from whom I am preparing a petition to your Highness, to be subscribed with the names of one hundred and thirty-six of the first race, but whose immortal productions are never likely to reach your eyes, though each of them is now an humble and an earnest appellant for the laurel, and has large comely volumes ready to show for a support to his pretensions. The never-dying works of these illustrious persons your governor, sir, has devoted to unavoidable death, and your Highness is to be made believe that our age has never arrived at the honour to produce one single poet.

We confess immortality to be a great and powerful goddess, but in vain we offer up to her our devotions and our sacrifices if your Highness's governor, who has usurped the priesthood, must, by an unparalleled ambition and avarice, wholly intercept and devour them.

To affirm that our age is altogether unlearned and devoid of writers in any kind, seems to be an assertion so bold and so false, that I have been sometimes thinking the contrary may almost be proved by uncontrollable demonstration. It is true, indeed, that although their numbers be vast and their productions numerous in proportion, yet are they hurried so hastily off the scene that they escape our memory and delude our sight. When I first thought of this address, I had prepared a copious list of titles to present your Highness as an undisputed argument for what I affirm. The originals were posted fresh upon all gates and corners of streets; but returning in a very few hours to take a review, they were all torn down and fresh ones in their places. I inquired after them among readers and booksellers, but I inquired in vain; the memorial of them was lost among men, their place was no more to be found; and I was laughed to scorn for a clown and a pedant, devoid of all taste and refinement, little versed in the course of present affairs, and that knew nothing of what had passed in the best companies of court and town. So that I can only avow in general to your Highness that we do abound in learning and wit, but to fix upon particulars is a task too slippery for my slender abilities. If I should venture, in a windy day, to affirm to your Highness that there is a large cloud near the horizon in the form of a bear, another in the zenith with the head of an ass, a third to the westward with claws like a dragon; and your Highness should in a few minutes think fit to examine the truth, it is certain they would be all chanced in figure and position, new ones would arise, and all we could agree upon would be, that clouds there were, but that I was grossly mistaken in the zoography and topography of them.

But your governor, perhaps, may still insist, and put the question, What is then become of those immense bales of paper which must needs have been employed in such numbers of books? Can these also be wholly annihilated, and to of a sudden, as I pretend? What shall I say in return of so invidious an objection? It ill befits the distance between your Highness and me to send you for ocular conviction to a jakes or an oven, to the windows of a bawdyhouse, or to a sordid lanthorn. Books, like men their authors, have no more than one way of coming into the world, but there are ten thousand to go out of it and return no more.

I profess to your Highness, in the integrity of my heart, that what I am going to say is literally true this minute I am writing; what revolutions may happen before it shall be ready for your perusal I can by no means warrant; however, I beg you to accept it as a specimen of our learning, our politeness, and our wit. I do therefore affirm, upon the word of a sincere man, that there is now actually in being a certain poet called John Dryden, whose translation of Virgil was lately printed in large folio, well bound, and if diligent search were made, for aught I know, is yet to be seen. There is another called Nahum Tate, who is ready to make oath that he has caused many reams of verse to be published, whereof both himself and his bookseller, if lawfully required, can still produce authentic copies, and therefore wonders why the world is pleased to make such a secret of it. There is a third, known by the name of Tom Durfey, a poet of a vast comprehension, an universal genius, and most profound learning. There are also one Mr. Rymer and one Mr. Dennis, most profound critics. There is a person styled Dr. Bentley, who has wrote near a thousand pages of immense erudition, giving a full and true account of a certain squabble of wonderful importance between himself and a bookseller; he is a writer of infinite wit and humour, no man rallies with a better grace and in more sprightly turns. Further, I avow to your Highness that with these eyes I have beheld the person of William Wotton, B.D., who has written a good-sized volume against a friend of your governor, from whom, alas! he must therefore look for little favour, in a most gentlemanly style, adorned with utmost politeness and civility, replete with discoveries equally valuable for their novelty and use, and embellished with traits of wit so poignant and so apposite, that he is a worthy yoke-mate to his fore-mentioned friend.

Why should I go upon farther particulars, which might fill a volume with the just eulogies of my contemporary brethren? I shall bequeath this piece of justice to a larger work, wherein I intend to write a character of the present set of wits in our nation; their persons I shall describe particularly and at length, their genius and understandings in miniature.

In the meantime, I do here make bold to present your Highness with a faithful abstract drawn from the universal body of all arts and sciences, intended wholly for your service and instruction. Nor do I doubt in the least but your Highness will peruse it as carefully and make as considerable improvements as other young princes have already done by the many volumes of late years written for a help to their studies.

That your Highness may advance in wisdom and virtue, as well as years, and at last outshine all your royal ancestors, shall be the daily prayer of,

Sir,
Your Highness's most devoted, &c.
Decemb. 1697.

THE PREFACE

The wits of the present age being so very numerous and penetrating, it seems the grandees of Church and State begin to fall under horrible apprehensions lest these gentlemen, during the intervals of a long peace, should find leisure to pick holes in the weak sides of religion and government. To prevent which, there has been much thought employed of late upon certain projects for taking off the force and edge of those formidable inquirers from canvassing and reasoning upon such delicate points. They have at length fixed upon one, which will require some time as well as cost to perfect. Meanwhile, the danger hourly increasing, by new levies of wits, all appointed (as there is reason to fear) with pen, ink, and paper, which may at an hour's warning be drawn out into pamphlets and other offensive weapons ready for immediate execution, it was judged of absolute necessity that some present expedient be thought on till the main design can be brought to maturity. To this end, at a grand committee, some days ago, this important discovery was made by a certain curious and refined observer, that seamen have a custom when they meet a Whale to fling him out an empty Tub, by way of amusement, to divert him from laying violent hands upon the Ship. This parable was immediately mythologised; the Whale was interpreted to be Hobbes's "Leviathan," which tosses and plays with all other schemes of religion and government, whereof a great many are hollow, and dry, and empty, and noisy, and wooden, and given to rotation. This is the Leviathan from whence the terrible wits of our age are said to borrow their weapons. The Ship in danger is easily understood to be its old antitype the commonwealth. But how to analyse the Tub was a matter of difficulty, when, after long inquiry and debate, the literal meaning was preserved, and it was decreed that, in order to prevent these Leviathans from tossing and sporting with the commonwealth, which of itself is too apt to fluctuate, they should be diverted from that game by "A Tale of a Tub." And my genius being conceived to lie not unhappily that way, I had the honour done me to be engaged in the performance.

This is the sole design in publishing the following treatise, which I hope will serve for an interim of some months to employ those unquiet spirits till the perfecting of that great work, into the secret of which it is reasonable the courteous reader should have some little light.

It is intended that a large Academy be erected, capable of containing nine thousand seven hundred forty and three persons, which, by modest computation, is reckoned to be pretty near the current number of wits in this island.[1] These are to be disposed into the several schools of this Academy, and there pursue those studies to which their genius most inclines them. The undertaker himself will publish his proposals with all convenient speed, to which I shall refer the curious reader for a more particular account, mentioning at present only a few of the principal schools. There is, first, a large pederastic school, with French and Italian masters; there is also the spelling school, a very spacious building; the school of looking-glasses; the school of swearing; the school of critics; the school of salivation; the school of hobby-horses; the school of poetry; the school of tops; the school of spleen; the school of gaming; with many others too tedious to recount. No person to be admitted member into any of these schools without an attestation under two sufficient persons' hands certifying him to be a wit.

But to return. I am sufficiently instructed in the principal duty of a preface if my genius, were capable of arriving at it. Thrice have I forced my imagination to take the tour of my invention, and thrice it has returned empty, the latter having been wholly drained by the following treatise. Not so my more successful brethren the moderns, who will by no means let slip a preface or dedication without some notable distinguishing stroke to surprise the reader at the entry, and kindle a wonderful expectation of what is to ensue. Such was that of a most ingenious poet, who, soliciting his brain for something new, compared himself to the hangman and his patron to the patient. This was *insigne, recens, indictum ore alio.*[2] When I went through that necessary and noble course of study,[3] I had the happiness to observe many such egregious touches, which I shall not injure the authors by transplanting, because I have remarked that nothing is so very tender as a modern piece of wit, and which is apt to suffer so much in the carriage. Some things are extremely witty to-day, or fasting, or in this place, or at eight o'clock, or over a bottle, or spoke by Mr. Whatdyecall'm, or in a summer's morning, any of which, by the smallest transposal or misapplication, is utterly annihilate. Thus wit has its walks and purlieus, out of which it may not stray the breadth of a hair, upon peril of being lost. The moderns have artfully fixed this Mercury, and reduced it to the circumstances of time, place, and person. Such a jest there is that will not pass out of Covent Garden, and such a one that is nowhere intelligible but at Hyde Park Corner. Now, though it sometimes tenderly affects me to consider that all the towardly passages I shall deliver in the following treatise will grow quite out of date and relish with the first shifting of the present scene, yet I must need subscribe to the justice of this proceeding, because I cannot imagine why we should be at expense to furnish wit for succeeding ages, when the former have made no sort of provision for ours; wherein I speak the sentiment of the very newest, and consequently the most orthodox refiners, as well as my own. However, being extremely solicitous that every accomplished person who has got into the taste of wit calculated for this present month of August 1697 should descend to the very bottom of all the sublime throughout this treatise, I hold it fit to lay down this general maxim. Whatever reader desires to have a thorough comprehension of an author's thoughts, cannot take a better method than by putting himself into the circumstances and posture of life that the writer was in upon every important passage as it flowed from his pen, for this will introduce a parity and strict correspondence of ideas between the reader and the author. Now, to assist the diligent reader in so delicate an affair—as far as brevity will permit—I have recollected that the shrewdest pieces of this treatise were conceived in bed in a garret. At other times (for a reason best known to myself) I thought fit to sharpen my invention with hunger, and in general the whole work was begun, continued, and ended under a long course of physic and a great want of money. Now, I do affirm it will be absolutely impossible for the candid peruser to go along with me in a great many bright passages, unless upon the several difficulties emergent he will please to capacitate and prepare himself by these directions. And this I lay down as my principal *postulatum*.

Because I have professed to be a most devoted servant of all modern forms, I apprehend some curious wit may object against me for proceeding thus far in a preface without declaiming, according to custom, against the multitude of writers whereof the whole multitude of writers most reasonably complain. I am just come from perusing some hundreds of prefaces, wherein the authors do at the very beginning address the gentle reader concerning this enormous grievance. Of these I have preserved a few examples, and shall set them down as near as my memory has been able to retain them.

One begins thus: "For a man to set up for a writer when the press swarms with," &c.

Another: "The tax upon paper does not lessen the number of scribblers who daily pester," &c.

Another: "When every little would-be wit takes pen in hand, 'tis in vain to enter the lists," &c.

Another: "To observe what trash the press swarms with," &c.

Another: "Sir, it is merely in obedience to your commands that I venture into the public, for who upon a less consideration would be of a party with such a rabble of scribblers," &c.

Now, I have two words in my own defence against this objection. First, I am far from granting the number of writers a nuisance to our nation, having strenuously maintained the contrary in several parts of the following discourse; secondly, I do not well understand the justice of this proceeding, because I observe many of these polite prefaces to be not only from the same hand, but from those who are most voluminous in their several productions; upon which I shall tell the reader a short tale.

A mountebank in Leicester Fields had drawn a huge assembly about him. Among the rest, a fat unwieldy fellow, half stifled in the press, would be every fit crying out, "Lord! what a filthy crowd is here. Pray, good people, give way a little. Bless need what a devil has raked this rabble together. Z—ds, what squeezing is this? Honest friend, remove your elbow." At last a weaver that stood next him could hold no longer. "A plague confound you," said he, "for an overgrown sloven; and who in the devil's name, I wonder, helps to make up the crowd half so much as yourself? Don't you consider that you take up more room with that carcass than any five here? Is not the place as free for us as for you? Bring your own guts to a reasonable compass, and then I'll engage we shall have room enough for us all."

There are certain common privileges of a writer, the benefit whereof I hope there will be no reason to doubt; particularly, that where I am not understood, it shall be concluded that something very useful and profound is couched underneath; and again, that whatever word or sentence is printed in a different character shall be judged to contain something extraordinary either of wit or sublime.

As for the liberty I have thought fit to take of praising myself, upon some occasions or none, I am sure it will need no excuse if a multitude of great examples be allowed sufficient authority; for it is here to be noted that praise was originally a pension paid by the world, but the moderns, finding the trouble and charge too great in collecting it, have lately bought out the fee-simple, since which time the right of presentation is wholly in ourselves. For this reason it is that when an author makes his own eulogy, he uses a certain form to declare and insist upon his title, which is commonly in these or the like words, "I speak without vanity," which I think plainly shows it to be a matter of right and justice. Now, I do here once for all declare, that in every encounter of this nature through the following treatise the form aforesaid is implied, which I mention to save the trouble of repeating it on so many occasions.

It is a great ease to my conscience that I have written so elaborate and useful a discourse without one grain of satire intermixed, which is the sole point wherein I have taken leave to dissent from the famous originals of our age and country. I have observed some satirists to use the public much at the rate that pedants do a naughty boy ready horsed for discipline. First expostulate the case, then plead the necessity of the rod from great provocations, and conclude every period with a lash. Now, if I know anything of mankind, these gentlemen might very well spare their reproof and correction, for there is not through all Nature another so callous and insensible a member as the world's posteriors, whether you apply to it the toe or the birch. Besides, most of our late satirists seem to lie under a sort of mistake, that because nettles have the prerogative to sting, therefore all other weeds must do so too. I make not this comparison out of the least design to detract from these worthy writers, for it is well known among mythologists that weeds have the pre-eminence over all other vegetables; and therefore the first monarch of this island whose taste and judgment were so acute and refined, did very wisely root out the roses from the collar of the order and plant the thistles in their stead, as the nobler flower of the two. For which reason it is conjectured by profounder antiquaries that the satirical itch, so prevalent in this part of our island, was first brought among us from beyond the Tweed. Here may it long flourish and abound; may it survive and neglect the scorn of the world with as much ease and contempt as the world is insensible to the lashes of it. May their own dulness, or that of their party, be no discouragement for the authors to proceed; but let them remember it is with wits as with razors, which are never so apt to cut those they are employed on as when they have lost their edge. Besides, those whose teeth are too rotten to bite are best of all others qualified to revenge that defect with their breath.

I am not, like other men, to envy or undervalue the talents I cannot reach, for which reason I must needs bear a true honour to this large eminent sect of our British writers. And I hope this little panegyric will not be offensive to their ears, since it has the advantage of being only designed for themselves. Indeed, Nature herself has taken order that fame and honour should be purchased at a better pennyworth by satire than by any other productions of the brain, the world being soonest provoked to praise by lashes, as men are to love. There is a problem in an ancient author why dedications and other bundles of flattery run all upon stale musty topics, without the smallest tincture of anything new, not only to the torment and nauseating of the Christian reader, but, if not suddenly prevented, to the universal spreading of that pestilent disease the lethargy in this island, whereas there is very little satire which has not something in it untouched before. The defects of the former are usually imputed to the want of invention among those who are dealers in that kind; but I think with a great deal of injustice, the solution being easy and natural, for the materials of panegyric, being very few in number, have been long since exhausted; for as health is but one thing, and has been always the same, whereas diseases are by thousands, besides new and daily additions, so all the virtues that have been ever in mankind are to be counted upon a few fingers, but his follies and vices are innumerable, and time adds hourly to the heap. Now the utmost a poor poet can do is to get by heart a list of the cardinal virtues and deal them with his utmost liberality to his hero or his patron. He may ring the changes as far as it will go, and vary his phrase till he has talked round, but the reader quickly finds it is all pork,[4] with a little variety of sauce, for there is no inventing terms of art beyond our ideas, and when ideas are exhausted, terms of art must be so too.

But though the matter for panegyric were as fruitful as the topics of satire, yet would it not be hard to find out a sufficient reason why the latter will be always better received than the first; for this being bestowed only upon one or a few persons at a time, is sure to raise envy, and consequently ill words, from the rest who have no share in the blessing. But satire, being levelled at all, is never resented for an offence by any, since every individual person makes bold to understand it of others, and very wisely removes his particular part of the burden upon the shoulders of the World, which are broad enough and able to bear it. To this purpose I have sometimes reflected upon the difference between Athens and England with respect to the point before us. In the Attic[5] commonwealth it was the privilege and birthright of every citizen and poet to rail aloud and in public, or to expose upon the stage by name any person they pleased, though of the greatest figure, whether a Creon, an Hyperbolus, an Alcibiades, or a Demosthenes. But, on the other side, the least reflecting word let fall against the people in general was immediately caught up and revenged upon the authors, however considerable for their quality or their merits; whereas in England it is just the reverse of all this. Here you may securely display your utmost rhetoric against mankind in the face of the world; tell them that all are gone astray; that there is none that doeth good, no, not one; that we live in the very dregs of time; that knavery and atheism are epidemic as the pox; that honesty is fled with Astræa; with any other common-places equally new and eloquent, which are furnished by the *splendida bilis*;[6] and when you have done, the whole audience, far from being offended, shall return you thanks as a deliverer of precious and useful truths. Nay, further, it is but to venture your lungs, and you may preach in Covent Garden against foppery and fornication, and something else; against pride, and dissimulation, and bribery at Whitehall. You may expose rapine and injustice in the Inns-of-Court chapel, and in a City pulpit be as fierce as you please against avarice, hypocrisy, and extortion. It is but a ball bandied to and fro, and every man carries a racket about him to strike it from himself among the rest of the company. But, on the other side, whoever should mistake the nature of things so far as to drop but a single hint in public how such a one starved half the fleet, and half poisoned the rest; how such a one, from a true principle of love and honour, pays no debts but for wenches and play; how such a one runs out of his estate; how Paris, bribed by Juno and Venus, loath to offend either party, slept out the whole cause on the bench; or how such an orator makes long speeches in the Senate, with much thought, little sense, and to no purpose;—whoever, I say, should venture to be thus particular, must expect to be imprisoned for *scandalum magnatum*, to have challenges sent him, to be sued for defamation, and to be brought before the bar of the House.

But I forget that I am expatiating on a subject wherein I have no concern, having neither a talent nor an inclination for satire. On the other side, I am so entirely satisfied with the whole present procedure of human things, that I have been for some years preparing material towards "A Panegyric upon the World;" to which I intended to add a second part, entitled "A Modest Defence of the Proceedings of the Rabble in all Ages." Both these I had thoughts to publish by way of appendix to the following treatise; but finding my common-place book fill much slower than I had reason to expect, I have chosen to defer them to another occasion. Besides, I have been unhappily prevented in that design by a certain domestic misfortune, in the particulars whereof, though it would be very seasonable, and much in the modern way, to inform the gentle reader, and would also be of great assistance towards extending this preface into the size now in vogue—which by rule ought to be large in proportion as the subsequent volume is small—yet I shall now dismiss our impatient reader from any further attendance at the porch; and having duly prepared his mind by a preliminary discourse, shall gladly introduce him to the sublime mysteries that ensue.

SECTION I: THE INTRODUCTION

Whoever has an ambition to be heard in a crowd must press, and squeeze, and thrust, and climb with indefatigable pains, till he has exalted himself to a certain degree of altitude above them. Now, in all assemblies, though you wedge them ever so close, we may observe this peculiar property, that over their heads there is room enough; but how to reach it is the difficult point, it being as hard to get quit of number as of hell.

"—Evadere ad auras,
Hoc opus, hic labor est."[7]

To this end the philosopher's way in all ages has been by erecting certain edifices in the air; but whatever practice and reputation these kind of structures have formerly possessed, or may still continue in, not excepting even that of Socrates when he was suspended in a basket to help contemplation, I think, with due submission, they seem to labour under two inconveniences. First, that the foundations being laid too high, they have been often out of sight and ever out of hearing. Secondly, that the materials being very transitory, have suffered much from inclemencies of air, especially in these north-west regions.

Therefore, towards the just performance of this great work there remain but three methods that I can think on; whereof the wisdom of our ancestors being highly sensible, has, to encourage all aspiring adventures, thought fit to erect three wooden machines for the use of those orators who desire to talk much without interruption. These are the Pulpit, the Ladder, and the Stage-itinerant. For as to the Bar, though it be compounded of the same matter and designed for the same use, it cannot, however, be well allowed the honour of a fourth, by reason of its level or inferior situation exposing it to perpetual interruption from collaterals. Neither can the Bench itself, though raised to a proper eminency, put in a better claim, whatever its advocates insist on. For if they please to look into the original design of its erection, and the circumstances or adjuncts subservient to that design, they will soon acknowledge the present practice exactly correspondent to the primitive institution, and both to answer the etymology of the name, which in the Phoenician tongue is a word of great signification, importing, if literally interpreted, "The place of sleep," but in common acceptation, "A seat well bolstered and cushioned, for the repose of old and gouty limbs;" *senes ut in otia tuta recedant.*[8] Fortune being indebted to them this part of retaliation, that as formerly they have long talked whilst others slept, so now they may sleep as long whilst others talk.

But if no other argument could occur to exclude the Bench and the Bar from the list of oratorical machines, it were sufficient that the admission of them would overthrow a number which I was resolved to establish, whatever argument it might cost me; in imitation of that prudent method observed by many other philosophers and great clerks, whose chief art in division has been to grow fond of some proper mystical number, which their imaginations have rendered sacred to a degree that they force common reason to find room for it in every part of Nature, reducing, including, and adjusting, every genus and species within that compass by coupling some against their wills and banishing others at any rate. Now, among all the rest, the profound number THREE[9] is that which has most employed my sublimest speculations, nor ever without wonderful delight. There is now in the press, and will be published next term, a panegyrical essay of mine upon this number, wherein I have, by most convincing proofs, not only reduced the senses and the elements under its banner, but brought over several deserters from its two great rivals, SEVEN and NINE.

Now, the first of these oratorical machines, in place as well as dignity, is the Pulpit. Of pulpits there are in this island several sorts, but I esteem only that made of timber from the Sylva Caledonia, which agrees very well with our climate. If it be upon its decay, it is the better, both for conveyance of sound and for other reasons to be mentioned by and by. The degree of perfection in shape and size I take to consist in being extremely narrow, with little ornament, and, best of all, without a cover; for, by ancient rule, it ought to be the only uncovered vessel in every assembly where it is rightfully used, by which means, from its near resemblance to a pillory, it will ever have a mighty influence on human ears.

Of Ladders I need say nothing. It is observed by foreigners themselves, to the honour of our country, that we excel all nations in our practice and understanding of this machine. The ascending orators do not only oblige their audience in the agreeable delivery, but the whole world in their early publication of their speeches, which I look upon as the choicest treasury of our British eloquence, and whereof I am informed that worthy citizen and bookseller, Mr. John Dunton, has made a faithful and a painful collection, which he shortly designs to publish in twelve volumes in folio, illustrated with copper-plates,—a work highly useful and curious, and altogether worthy of such a hand.

The last engine of orators is the Stage-itinerant, erected with much sagacity, *sub Jove pluvio, in triviis et quadriviis.*[10] It is the great seminary of the two former, and its orators are sometimes preferred to the one and sometimes to the other, in proportion to their deservings, there being a strict and perpetual intercourse between all three.

From this accurate deduction it is manifest that for obtaining attention in public there is of necessity required a superior position of place. But although this point be generally granted, yet the cause is little agreed in; and it seems to me that very few philosophers have fallen into a true natural solution of this phenomenon. The deepest account, and the most fairly digested of any I have yet met with is this, that air being a heavy body, and therefore, according to the system of Epicurus,[11] continually descending, must needs be more so when laden and pressed down by words, which are also bodies of much weight and gravity, as is manifest from those deep impressions they make and leave upon us, and therefore must be delivered from a due altitude, or else they will neither carry a good aim nor fall down with a sufficient force.

"Corpoream quoque enim vocem constare fatendum est,
Et sonitum, quoniam possunt impellere sensus." — Luca. lib. 4[12]

And I am the readier to favour this conjecture from a common observation, that in the several assemblies of these orators Nature itself has instructed the hearers to stand with their mouths open and erected parallel to the horizon, so as they may be intersected by a perpendicular line from the zenith to the centre of the earth. In which position, if the audience be well compact, every one carries home a share, and little or nothing is lost.

I confess there is something yet more refined in the contrivance and structure of our modern theatres. For, first, the pit is sunk below the stage with due regard to the institution above deduced, that whatever weighty matter shall be delivered thence, whether it be lead or gold, may fall plump into the jaws of certain critics, as I think they are called, which stand ready open to devour them. Then the boxes are built round and raised to a level with the scene, in deference to the ladies, because that large portion of wit laid out in raising pruriences and protuberances is observed to run much upon a line, and ever in a circle. The whining passions and little starved conceits are gently wafted up by their own extreme levity to the middle region, and there fix and are frozen by the frigid understandings of the inhabitants. Bombast and buffoonery, by nature lofty and light, soar highest of all, and would be lost in the roof if the prudent architect had not, with much foresight, contrived for them a fourth place, called the twelve-penny gallery, and there planted a suitable colony, who greedily intercept them in their passage.

Now this physico-logical scheme of oratorical receptacles or machines contains a great mystery, being a type, a sign, an emblem, a shadow, a symbol, bearing analogy to the spacious commonwealth of writers and to those methods by which they must exalt themselves to a certain eminency above the inferior world. By the Pulpit are adumbrated the writings of our modern saints in Great Britain, as they have spiritualised and refined them from the dross and grossness of sense and human reason. The matter, as we have said, is of rotten wood, and that upon two considerations: because it is the quality of rotten wood to light in the dark; and secondly, because its cavities are full of worms—which is a type with a pair of handles, having a respect to the two principal qualifications of the orator and the two different fates attending upon his works.[13]

The Ladder is an adequate symbol of faction and of poetry, to both of which so noble a number of authors are indebted for their fame. Of faction, because . . . (Hiatus in MS.) . . . Of poetry, because its orators do *perorare* with a song; and because, climbing up by slow degrees, fate is sure to turn them off before they can reach within many steps of the top; and because it is a preferment attained by transferring of propriety and a confounding of *meum* and *tuum*.

Under the Stage-itinerant are couched those productions designed for the pleasure and delight of mortal man, such as "Six Pennyworth of Wit," "Westminster Drolleries," "Delightful Tales," "Complete Jesters," and the like, by which the writers of and for Grub Street have in these later ages so nobly triumphed over time, have clipped his wings, pared his nails, filed his teeth, turned back his hour-glass, blunted his scythe, and drawn the hobnails out of his shoes. It is under this class I have presumed to list my present treatise, being just come from having the honour conferred upon me to be adopted a member of that illustrious fraternity.

Now, I am not unaware how the productions of the Grub Street brotherhood have of late years fallen under many prejudices, nor how it has been the perpetual employment of two junior start-up societies to ridicule them and their authors as unworthy their established post in the commonwealth of wit and learning. Their own consciences will easily inform them whom I mean; nor has the world been so negligent a looker-on as not to observe the continual efforts made by the societies of Gresham and of Will's,[14] to edify a name and reputation upon the ruin of ours. And this is yet a more feeling grief to us, upon the regards of tenderness as well as of justice, when we reflect on their proceedings not only as unjust, but as ungrateful, undutiful, and unnatural. For how can it be forgot by the world or themselves, to say nothing of our own records, which are full and clear in the point, that they both are seminaries, not only of our planting, but our watering too. I am informed our two rivals have lately made an offer to enter into the lists with united forces and challenge us to a comparison of books, both as to weight and number. In return to which, with license from our president, I humbly offer two answers. First, we say the proposal is like that which Archimedes made upon a smaller affair,[15] including an impossibility in the practice; for where can they find scales of capacity enough for the first, or an arithmetician of capacity enough for the second. Secondly, we are ready to accept the challenge, but with this condition, that a third indifferent person be assigned, to whose impartial judgment it shall be left to decide which society each book, treatise, or pamphlet do most properly belong to. This point, God knows, is very far from being fixed at present, for we are ready to produce a catalogue of some thousands which in all common justice ought to be entitled to our fraternity, but by the revolted and newfangled writers most perfidiously ascribed to the others. Upon all which we think it very unbecoming our prudence that the determination should be remitted to the authors themselves, when our adversaries by briguing and caballing have caused so universal a defection from us, that the greatest part of our society has already deserted to them, and our nearest friends begin to stand aloof, as if they were half ashamed to own us.

This is the utmost I am authorised to say upon so ungrateful and melancholy a subject, because we are extremely unwilling to inflame a controversy whose continuance may be so fatal to the interests of us all, desiring much rather that things be amicably composed; and we shall so far advance on our side as to be ready to receive the two prodigals with open arms whenever they shall think fit to return from their husks and their harlots, which I think, from the present course of their studies,[16] they most properly may be said to be engaged in, and, like an indulgent parent, continue to them our affection and our blessing.

But the greatest maim given to that general reception which the writings of our society have formerly received, next to the transitory state of all sublunary things, has been a superficial vein among many readers of the present age, who will by no means be persuaded to inspect beyond the surface and the rind of things; whereas wisdom is a fox, who, after long hunting, will at last cost you the pains to dig out. It is a cheese which, by how much the richer, has the thicker, the homelier, and the coarser coat, and whereof to a judicious palate the maggots are the best. It is a sack-posset, wherein the deeper you go you will find it the sweeter. Wisdom is a hen whose cackling we must value and consider, because it is attended with an egg. But then, lastly, it is a nut, which, unless you choose with judgment, may cost you a tooth, and pay you with nothing but a worm. In consequence of these momentous truths, the Grubæan sages have always chosen to convey their precepts and their arts shut up within the vehicles of types and fables; which having been perhaps more careful and curious in adorning than was altogether necessary, it has fared with these vehicles after the usual fate of coaches over-finely painted and gilt, that the transitory gazers have so dazzled their eyes and filled their imaginations with the outward lustre, as neither to regard nor consider the person or the parts of the owner within. A misfortune we undergo with somewhat less reluctancy, because it has been common to us with Pythagoras, Æsop, Socrates, and other of our predecessors.

However, that neither the world nor ourselves may any longer suffer by such misunderstandings, I have been prevailed on, after much importunity from my friends, to travail in a complete and laborious dissertation upon the prime productions of our society, which, besides their beautiful externals for the gratification of superficial readers, have darkly and deeply couched under them the most finished and refined systems of all sciences and arts, as I do not doubt to lay open by untwisting or unwinding, and either to draw up by exantlation or display by incision.

This great work was entered upon some years ago by one of our most eminent members. He began with the "History of Reynard the Fox," but neither lived to publish his essay nor to proceed farther in so useful an attempt, which is very much to be lamented, because the discovery he made and communicated to his friends is now universally received; nor do I think any of the learned will dispute that famous treatise to be a complete body of civil knowledge, and the revelation, or rather the apocalypse, of all state arcana. But the progress I have made is much greater, having already finished my annotations upon several dozens from some of which I shall impart a few hints to the candid reader, as far as will be necessary to the conclusion at which I aim.

The first piece I have handled is that of "Tom Thumb," whose author was a Pythagorean philosopher. This dark treatise contains the whole scheme of the metempsychosis, deducing the progress of the soul through all her stages.

The next is "Dr. Faustus," penned by Artephius, an author *bonæ notæ* and an adeptus; he published it in the nine hundred and eighty-fourth year[17] of his age; this writer proceeds wholly by reincrudation, or in the *via humida*; and the marriage between Faustus and Helen does most conspicuously dilucidate the fermenting of the male and female dragon.

"Whittington and his Cat" is the work of that mysterious Rabbi, Jehuda

Hannasi, containing a defence of the Gemara of the Jerusalem Misna, and its just preference to that of Babylon, contrary to the vulgar opinion.

"The Hind and Panther." This is the masterpiece of a famous writer now living,[18] intended for a complete abstract of sixteen thousand schoolmen from Scotus to Bellarmine.

"Tommy Potts." Another piece, supposed by the same hand, by way of supplement to the former.

The "Wise Men of Gotham," *cum* Appendice. This is a treatise of immense erudition, being the great original and fountain of those arguments bandied about both in France and England, for a just defence of modern learning and wit, against the presumption, the pride, and the ignorance of the ancients. This unknown author hath so exhausted the subject, that a penetrating reader will easily discover whatever has been written since upon that dispute to be little more than repetition. An abstract of this treatise has been lately published by a worthy member of our society.

These notices may serve to give the learned reader an idea as well as a taste of what the whole work is likely to produce, wherein I have now altogether circumscribed my thoughts and my studies; and if I can bring it to a perfection before I die, shall reckon I have well employed the poor remains of an unfortunate life. This indeed is more than I can justly expect from a quill worn to the pith in the service of the State, in pros and cons upon Popish Plots, and Meal Tubs, and Exclusion Bills, and Passive Obedience, and Addresses of Lives and Fortunes; and Prerogative, and Property, and Liberty of Conscience, and Letters to a Friend: from an understanding and a conscience, threadbare and ragged with perpetual turning; from a head broken in a hundred places by the malignants of the opposite factions, and from a body spent with poxes ill cured, by trusting to bawds and surgeons, who (as it afterwards appeared) were professed enemies to me and the Government, and revenged their party's quarrel upon my nose and shins. Fourscore and eleven pamphlets have I written under three reigns, and for the service of six-and-thirty factions. But finding the State has no farther occasion for me and my ink, I retire willingly to draw it out into speculations more becoming a philosopher, having, to my unspeakable comfort, passed a long life with a conscience void of offence towards God and towards men.

But to return. I am assured from the reader's candour that the brief specimen I have given will easily clear all the rest of our society's productions from an aspersion grown, as it is manifest, out of envy and ignorance, that they are of little farther use or value to mankind beyond the common entertainments of their wit and their style; for these I am sure have never yet been disputed by our keenest adversaries; in both which, as well as the more profound and most mystical part, I have throughout this treatise closely followed the most applauded originals. And to render all complete I have with much thought and application of mind so ordered that the chief title prefixed to it (I mean that under which I design it shall pass in the common conversation of court and town) is modelled exactly after the manner peculiar to our society.

I confess to have been somewhat liberal in the business of titles,[19] having observed the humour of multiplying them, to bear great vogue among certain writers, whom I exceedingly reverence. And indeed it seems not unreasonable that books, the children of the brain, should have the honour to be christened with variety of names, as well as other infants of quality. Our famous Dryden has ventured to proceed a point farther, endeavouring to introduce also a multiplicity of godfathers,[20] which is an improvement of much more advantage, upon a very obvious account. It is a pity this admirable invention has not been better cultivated, so as to grow by this time into general imitation, when such an authority serves it for a precedent. Nor have my endeavours been wanting to second so useful an example, but it seems there is an unhappy expense usually annexed to the calling of a godfather, which was clearly out of my head, as it is very reasonable to believe. Where the pinch lay, I cannot certainly affirm; but having employed a world of thoughts and pains to split my treatise into forty sections, and having entreated forty Lords of my acquaintance that they would do me the honour to stand, they all made it matter of conscience, and sent me their excuses.

SECTION II

Once upon a time there was a man who had three sons by one wife[21] and all at a birth, neither could the midwife tell certainly which was the eldest. Their father died while they were young, and upon his death-bed, calling the lads to him, spoke thus:—

"Sons, because I have purchased no estate, nor was born to any, I have long considered of some good legacies to bequeath you, and at last, with much care as well as expense, have provided each of you (here they are) a new coat. Now, you are to understand that these coats have two virtues contained in them; one is, that with good wearing they will last you fresh and sound as long as you live; the other is, that they will grow in the same proportion with your bodies, lengthening and widening of themselves, so as to be always fit. Here, let me see them on you before I die. So, very well! Pray, children, wear them clean and brush them often. You will find in my will (here it is) full instructions in every particular concerning the wearing and management of your coats, wherein you must be very exact to avoid the penalties I have appointed for every transgression or neglect, upon which your future fortunes will entirely depend. I have also commanded in my will that you should live together in one house like brethren and friends, for then you will be sure to thrive and not otherwise."

Here the story says this good father died, and the three sons went all together to seek their fortunes.

I shall not trouble you with recounting what adventures they met for the first seven years, any farther than by taking notice that they carefully observed their father's will and kept their coats in very good order; that they travelled through several countries, encountered a reasonable quantity of giants, and slew certain dragons.

Being now arrived at the proper age for producing themselves, they came up to town and fell in love with the ladies, but especially three, who about that time were in chief reputation, the Duchess d'Argent, Madame de Grands-Titres, and the Countess d'Orgueil.[22] On their first appearance, our three adventurers met with a very bad reception, and soon with great sagacity guessing out the reason, they quickly began to improve in the good qualities of the town. They wrote, and rallied, and rhymed, and sung, and said, and said nothing; they drank, and fought, and slept, and swore, and took snuff; they went to new plays on the first night, haunted the chocolate-houses, beat the watch; they bilked hackney-coachmen, ran in debt with shopkeepers, and lay with their wives; they killed bailiffs, kicked fiddlers down-stairs, ate at Locket's, loitered at Will's; they talked of the drawing-room and never came there; dined with lords they never saw; whispered a duchess and spoke never a word; exposed the scrawls of their laundress for billet-doux of quality; came ever just from court and were never seen in it; attended the levee *sub dio*; got a list of peers by heart in one company, and with great familiarity retailed them in another. Above all, they constantly attended those committees of Senators who are silent in the House and loud in the coffee-house, where they nightly adjourn to chew the cud of politics, and are encompassed with a ring of disciples who lie in wait to catch up their droppings. The three brothers had acquired forty other qualifications of the like stamp too tedious to recount, and by consequence were justly reckoned the most accomplished persons in town. But all would not suffice, and the ladies aforesaid continued still inflexible. To clear up which difficulty, I must, with the reader's good leave and patience, have recourse to some points of weight which the authors of that age have not sufficiently illustrated.

For about this time it happened a sect arose whose tenets obtained and spread very far, especially in the *grand monde*, and among everybody of good fashion. They worshipped a sort of idol,[23] who, as their doctrine delivered, did daily create men by a kind of manufactory operation. This idol they placed in the highest parts of the house on an altar erected about three feet. He was shown in the posture of a Persian emperor sitting on a superficies with his legs interwoven under him. This god had a goose for his ensign, whence it is that some learned men pretend to deduce his original from Jupiter Capitolinus. At his left hand, beneath the altar, Hell seemed to open and catch at the animals the idol was creating, to prevent which, certain of his priests hourly flung in pieces of the uninformed mass or substance, and sometimes whole limbs already enlivened, which that horrid gulph insatiably swallowed, terrible to behold. The goose was also held a subaltern divinity or *Deus minorum gentium*, before whose shrine was sacrificed that creature whose hourly food is human gore, and who is in so great renown abroad for being the delight and favourite of the Egyptian Cercopithecus.[24] Millions of these animals were cruelly slaughtered every day to appease the hunger of that consuming deity. The chief idol was also worshipped as the inventor of the yard and the needle, whether as the god of seamen, or on account of certain other mystical attributes, hath not been sufficiently cleared.

The worshippers of this deity had also a system of their belief which seemed to turn upon the following fundamental. They held the universe to be a large suit of clothes which invests everything; that the earth is invested by the air; the air is invested by the stars; and the stars are invested by the *Primum Mobile*. Look on this globe of earth, you will find it to be a very complete and fashionable dress. What is that which some call land but a fine coat faced with green, or the sea but a waistcoat of water-tabby? Proceed to the particular works of the creation, you will find how curious journeyman Nature hath been to trim up the vegetable beaux; observe how sparkish a periwig adorns the head of a beech, and what a fine doublet of white satin is worn by the birch. To conclude from all, what is man himself but a microcoat, or rather a complete suit of clothes with all its trimmings? As to his body there can be no dispute, but examine even the acquirements of his mind, you will find them all contribute in their order towards furnishing out an exact dress. To instance no more, is not religion a cloak, honesty a pair of shoes worn out in the dirt, self-love a surtout, vanity a shirt, and conscience a pair of breeches, which, though a cover for lewdness as well as nastiness, is easily slipped down for the service of both.

These *postulata* being admitted, it will follow in due course of reasoning that those beings which the world calls improperly suits of clothes are in reality the most refined species of animals, or to proceed higher, that they are rational creatures or men. For is it not manifest that they live, and move, and talk, and perform all other offices of human life? Are not beauty, and wit, and mien, and breeding their inseparable proprieties? In short, we see nothing but them, hear nothing but them. Is it not they who walk the streets, fill up Parliament-, coffee-, play-, bawdy-houses. It is true, indeed, that these animals, which are vulgarly called suits of clothes or dresses, do according to certain compositions receive different appellations. If one of them be trimmed up with a gold chain, and a red gown, and a white rod, and a great horse, it is called a Lord Mayor; if certain ermines and furs be placed in a certain position, we style them a judge, and so an apt conjunction of lawn and black satin we entitle a Bishop.

Others of these professors, though agreeing in the main system, were yet more refined upon certain branches of it; and held that man was an animal compounded of two dresses, the natural and the celestial suit, which were the body and the soul; that the soul was the outward, and the body the inward clothing; that the latter was *ex traduce*, but the former of daily creation and circumfusion. This last they proved by Scripture, because in them we live, and move, and have our being: as likewise by philosophy, because they are all in all, and all in every part. Besides, said they, separate these two, and you will find the body to be only a senseless unsavoury carcass. By all which it is manifest that the outward dress must needs be the soul.

To this system of religion were tagged several subaltern doctrines, which were entertained with great vogue; as particularly the faculties of the mind were deduced by the learned among them in this manner: embroidery was sheer wit, gold fringe was agreeable conversation, gold lace was repartee, a huge long periwig was humour, and a coat full of powder was very good raillery. All which required abundance of finesse and delicatesse to manage with advantage, as well as a strict observance after times and fashions.

I have with much pains and reading collected out of ancient authors this short summary of a body of philosophy and divinity which seems to have been composed by a vein and race of thinking very different from any other systems, either ancient or modern. And it was not merely to entertain or satisfy the reader's curiosity, but rather to give him light into several circumstances of the following story, that, knowing the state of dispositions and opinions in an age so remote, he may better comprehend those great events which were the issue of them. I advise, therefore, the courteous reader to peruse with a world of application, again and again, whatever I have written upon this matter. And so leaving these broken ends, I carefully gather up the chief thread of my story, and proceed.

These opinions, therefore, were so universal, as well as the practices of them, among the refined part of court and town, that our three brother adventurers, as their circumstances then stood, were strangely at a loss. For, on the one side, the three ladies they addressed themselves to (whom we have named already) were ever at the very top of the fashion, and abhorred all that were below it but the breadth of a hair. On the other side, their father's will was very precise, and it was the main precept in it, with the greatest penalties annexed, not to add to or diminish from their coats one thread without a positive command in the will. Now the coats their father had left them were, it is true, of very good cloth, and besides, so neatly sewn you would swear they were all of a piece, but, at the same time, very plain, with little or no ornament; and it happened that before they were a month in town great shoulder-knots came up. Straight all the world was shoulder-knots; no approaching the ladies' *ruelles* without the quota of shoulder-knots. "That fellow," cries one, "has no soul: where is his shoulder-knot?"[25] Our three brethren soon discovered their want by sad experience, meeting in their walks with forty mortifications and indignities. If they went to the playhouse, the doorkeeper showed them into the twelve-penny gallery. If they called a boat, says a waterman, "I am first sculler." If they stepped into the "Rose" to take a bottle, the drawer would cry, "Friend, we sell no ale." If they went to visit a lady, a footman met them at the door with "Pray, send up your message." In this unhappy case they went immediately to consult their father's will, read it over and over, but not a word of the shoulder-knot. What should they do? What temper should they find? Obedience was absolutely necessary, and yet shoulder-knots appeared extremely requisite. After much thought, one of the brothers, who happened to be more book-learned than the other two, said he had found an expedient. "It is true," said he, "there is nothing here in this will, *totidem verbis*, making mention of shoulder-knots, but I dare conjecture we may find them inclusive, or *totidem syllabis*." This distinction was immediately approved by all; and so they fell again to examine the will. But their evil star had so directed the matter that the first syllable was not to be found in the whole writing; upon which disappointment, he who found the former evasion took heart, and said, "Brothers, there is yet hopes; for though we cannot find them *totidem verbis* nor *totidem syllabis*, I dare engage we shall make them out *tertio modo* or *totidem literis*." This discovery was also highly commended, upon which they fell once more to the scrutiny, and soon picked out S, H, O, U, L, D, E, R, when the same planet, enemy to their repose, had wonderfully contrived that a K was not to be found. Here was a weighty difficulty! But the distinguishing brother (for whom we shall hereafter find a name), now his hand was in, proved by a very good argument that K was a modern illegitimate letter, unknown to the learned ages, nor anywhere to be found in ancient manuscripts. "It is true," said he, "the word *Calendæ*, had in Q. V. C.[26] been sometimes writ with a K, but erroneously, for in the best copies it is ever spelt with a C; and by consequence it was a gross mistake in our language to spell 'knot' with a K," but that from henceforward he would take care it should be writ with a C. Upon this all further difficulty vanished; shoulder-knots were made clearly out to be *jure paterno*, and our three gentlemen swaggered with as large and as flaunting ones as the best.

But as human happiness is of a very short duration, so in those days were human fashions, upon which it entirely depends. Shoulder-knots had their time, and we must now imagine them in their decline, for a certain lord came just from

Paris with ~~fifty yards of gold lace~~ upon his coat, exactly trimmed after the court fashion of that month. In two days all mankind appeared closed up in bars of gold lace. Whoever durst peep abroad without his complement of gold lace was as scandalous as a —, and as ill received among the women. What should our three knights do in this momentous affair? They had sufficiently strained a point already in the affair of shoulder-knots. Upon recourse to the will, nothing appeared there but *altum silentium*. That of the shoulder-knots was a loose, flying, circumstantial point, but this of gold lace seemed too considerable an alteration without better warrant. It did *aliquo modo essentiæ adhærere*, and therefore required a positive precept. But about this time it fell out that the learned brother aforesaid had read "Aristotelis Dialectica," and especially that wonderful piece *de Interpretatione*, which has the faculty of teaching its readers to find out a meaning in everything but itself, like commentators on the Revelations, who proceed prophets without understanding a syllable of the text. "Brothers," said he, "you are to be informed that of wills, *duo sunt genera*, nuncupatory and scriptory,[27] that in the scriptory will here before us there is no precept or mention about gold lace, *conceditur*, but *si idem affirmetur de nuncupatorio negatur*. For, brothers, if you remember, we heard a fellow say when we were boys that he heard my father's man say that he heard my father say that he would advise his sons to get gold lace on their coats as soon as ever they could procure money to buy it." "That is very true," cries the other. "I remember it perfectly well," said the third. And so, without more ado, they got the largest gold lace in the parish, and walked about as fine as lords.

A while after, there came up all in fashion a pretty sort of flame-coloured satin[28] for linings, and the mercer brought a pattern of it immediately to our three gentlemen. "An please your worships," said he, "my Lord C— and Sir J. W. had linings out of this very piece last night; it takes wonderfully, and I shall not have a remnant left enough to make my wife a pin-cushion by to-morrow morning at ten o'clock." Upon this they fell again to rummage the will, because the present case also required a positive precept, the lining being held by orthodox writers to be of the essence of the coat. After long search they could fix upon nothing to the matter in hand, except a short advice in their father's will to take care of fire and put out their candles before they went to sleep.[29] This, though a good deal for the purpose, and helping very far towards self-conviction, yet not seeming wholly of force to establish a command, and being resolved to avoid farther scruple, as well as future occasion for scandal, says he that was the scholar, "I remember to have read in wills of a codicil annexed, which is indeed a part of the will, and what it contains hath equal authority with the rest. Now I have been considering of this same will here before us, and I cannot reckon it to be complete for want of such a codicil. I will therefore fasten one in its proper place very dexterously. I have had it by me some time; it was written by a dog-keeper of my grandfather's, and talks a great deal, as good luck would have it, of this very flame-coloured satin." The project was immediately approved by the other two; an old parchment scroll was tagged on according to art, in the form of a codicil annexed, and the satin bought and worn.

Next winter a player, hired for the purpose by the Corporation of Fringemakers, acted his part in a new comedy, all covered with silver fringe,[30] and according to the laudable custom gave rise to that fashion. Upon which the brothers, consulting their father's will, to their great astonishment found these words: "Item, I charge and command my said three sons to wear no sort of silver fringe upon or about their said coats," &c., with a penalty in case of disobedience too long here to insert. However, after some pause, the brother so often mentioned for his erudition, who was well skilled in criticisms, had found in a certain author, which he said should be nameless, that the same word which in the will is called fringe does also signify a broom-stick, and doubtless ought to have the same interpretation in this paragraph. This another of the brothers disliked, because of that epithet silver, which could not, he humbly conceived, in propriety of speech be reasonably applied to a broom-stick; but it was replied upon him that this epithet was understood in a mythological and allegorical sense. However, he objected again why their father should forbid them to wear a broom-stick on their coats, a caution that seemed unnatural and impertinent; upon which he was taken up short, as one that spoke irreverently of a mystery which doubtless was very useful and significant, but ought not to be over-curiously pried into or nicely reasoned upon. And in short, their father's authority being now considerably sunk, this expedient was allowed to serve as a lawful dispensation for wearing their full proportion of silver fringe.

A while after was revived an old fashion, long antiquated, of embroidery with Indian figures of men, women, and children.[31] Here they had no occasion to examine the will. They remembered but too well how their father had always abhorred this fashion; that he made several paragraphs on purpose, importing his utter detestation of it, and bestowing his everlasting curse to his sons whenever they should wear it. For all this, in a few days they appeared higher in the fashion than anybody else in the town. But they solved the matter by saying that these figures were not at all the same with those that were formerly worn and were meant in the will; besides, they did not wear them in that sense, as forbidden by their father, but as they were a commendable custom, and of great use to the public. That these rigorous clauses in the will did therefore require some allowance and a favourable interpretation, and ought to be understood *cum grano salis*.

But fashions perpetually altering in that age, the scholastic brother grew weary of searching further evasions and solving everlasting contradictions. Resolved, therefore, at all hazards to comply with the modes of the world, they concerted matters together, and agreed unanimously to lock up their father's will in a strong-box, brought out of Greece or Italy[32] (I have forgot which), and trouble themselves no farther to examine it, but only refer to its authority whenever they thought fit. In consequence whereof, a while after it grew a general mode to wear an infinite number of points, most of them tagged with silver; upon which the scholar pronounced *ex cathedrâ*[33] that points were absolutely *jure paterno* as they might very well remember. It is true, indeed, the fashion prescribed somewhat more than were directly named in the will; however, that they, as heirs-general of their father, had power to make and add certain clauses for public emolument, though not deducible *todidem verbis* from the letter of the will, or else *multa absurda sequerentur*. This was understood for canonical, and therefore on the following Sunday they came to church all covered with points.

The learned brother so often mentioned was reckoned the best scholar in all that or the next street to it; insomuch, as having run something behindhand with the world, he obtained the favour from a certain lord[34] to receive him into his house and to teach his children. A while after the lord died, and he, by long practice upon his father's will, found the way of contriving a deed of conveyance of that house to himself and his heirs; upon which he took possession, turned the young squires out, and received his brothers in their stead.

SECTION III: A DIGRESSION CONCERNING CRITICS

Though I have been hitherto as cautious as I could, upon all occasions, most nicely to follow the rules and methods of writing laid down by the example of our illustrious moderns, yet has the unhappy shortness of my memory led me into an error, from which I must immediately extricate myself, before I can decently pursue my principal subject. I confess with shame it was an unpardonable omission to proceed so far as I have already done before I had performed the due discourses, expostulatory, supplicatory, or deprecatory, with my good lords the critics. Towards some atonement for this grievous neglect, I do here make humbly bold to present them with a short account of themselves and their art, by looking into the original and pedigree of the word, as it is generally understood among us, and very briefly considering the ancient and present state thereof.

By the word critic, at this day so frequent in all conversations, there have sometimes been distinguished three very different species of mortal men, according as I have read in ancient books and pamphlets. For first, by this term were understood such persons as invented or drew up rules for themselves and the world, by observing which a careful reader might be able to pronounce upon the productions of the learned, form his taste to a true relish of the sublime and the admirable, and divide every beauty of matter or of style from the corruption that apes it. In their common perusal of books, singling out the errors and defects, the nauseous, the fulsome, the dull, and the impertinent, with the caution of a man that walks through Edinburgh streets in a morning, who is indeed as careful as he can to watch diligently and spy out the filth in his way; not that he is curious to observe the colour and complexion of the ordure or take its dimensions, much less to be paddling in or tasting it, but only with a design to come out as cleanly as he may. These men seem, though very erroneously, to have understood the appellation of critic in a literal sense; that one principal part of his office was to praise and acquit, and that a critic who sets up to read only for an occasion of censure and reproof is a creature as barbarous as a judge who should take up a resolution to hang all men that came before him upon a trial.

Again, by the word critic have been meant the restorers of ancient learning from the worms, and graves, and dust of manuscripts.

Now the races of these two have been for some ages utterly extinct, and besides to discourse any further of them would not be at all to my purpose.

The third and noblest sort is that of the true critic, whose original is the most ancient of all. Every true critic is a hero born, descending in a direct line from a celestial stem, by Momus and Hybris, who begat Zoilus, who begat Tigellius, who begat Etcætera the elder, who begat Bentley, and Rymer, and Wotton, and Perrault, and Dennis, who begat Etcætera the younger.

And these are the critics from whom the commonwealth of learning has in all ages received such immense benefits, that the gratitude of their admirers placed their origin in heaven, among those of Hercules, Theseus, Perseus, and other great deservers of mankind. But heroic virtue itself hath not been exempt from the obloquy of evil tongues. For it hath been objected that those ancient heroes, famous for their combating so many giants, and dragons, and robbers, were in their own persons a greater nuisance to mankind than any of those monsters they subdued; and therefore, to render their obligations more complete, when all other vermin were destroyed, should in conscience have concluded with the same justice upon themselves, as Hercules most generously did, and hath upon that score procured for himself more temples and votaries than the best of his fellows. For these reasons I suppose it is why some have conceived it would be very expedient for the public good of learning that every true critic, as soon as he had finished his task assigned, should immediately deliver himself up to ratsbane or hemp, or from some convenient altitude, and that no man's pretensions to so illustrious a character should by any means be received before that operation was performed.

Now, from this heavenly descent of criticism, and the close analogy it bears to heroic virtue, it is easy to assign the proper employment of a true, ancient, genuine critic: which is, to travel through this vast world of writings; to peruse and hunt those monstrous faults bred within them; to drag out the lurking errors, like Cacus from his den; to multiply them like Hydra's heads; and rake them together like Augeas's dung; or else to drive away a sort of dangerous fowl who have a perverse inclination to plunder the best branches of the tree of knowledge, like those Stymphalian birds that ate up the fruit.

These reasonings will furnish us with an adequate definition of a true critic: that he is a discoverer and collector of writers' faults; which may be further put beyond dispute by the following demonstration:—That whoever will examine the writings in all kinds wherewith this ancient sect hath honoured the world, shall immediately find from the whole thread and tenor of them that the ideas of the authors have been altogether conversant and taken up with the faults, and blemishes, and oversights, and mistakes of other writers, and let the subject treated on be whatever it will, their imaginations are so entirely possessed and replete with the defects of other pens, that the very quintessence of what is bad does of necessity distil into their own, by which means the whole appears to be nothing else but an abstract of the criticisms themselves have made.

Having thus briefly considered the original and office of a critic, as the word is understood in its most noble and universal acceptation, I proceed to refute the objections of those who argue from the silence and pretermission of authors, by which they pretend to prove that the very art of criticism, as now exercised, and by me explained, is wholly modern, and consequently that the critics of Great Britain and France have no title to an original so ancient and illustrious as I have deduced. Now, if I can clearly make out, on the contrary, that the most ancient writers have particularly described both the person and the office of a true critic agreeable to the definition laid down by me, their grand objection—from the silence of authors—will fall to the ground.

I confess to have for a long time borne a part in this general error, from which I should never have acquitted myself but through the assistance of our noble moderns, whose most edifying volumes I turn indefatigably over night and day, for the improvement of my mind and the good of my country. These have with unwearied pains made many useful searches into the weak sides of the ancients, and given us a comprehensive list of them.[35] Besides, they have proved beyond contradiction that the very finest things delivered of old have been long since invented and brought to light by much later pens, and that the noblest discoveries those ancients ever made in art or nature have all been produced by the transcending genius of the present age, which clearly shows how little merit those ancients can justly pretend to, and takes off that blind admiration paid them by men in a corner, who have the unhappiness of conversing too little with present things. Reflecting maturely upon all this, and taking in the whole compass of human nature, I easily concluded that these ancients, highly sensible of their many imperfections, must needs have endeavoured, from some passages in their works, to obviate, soften, or divert the censorious reader, by satire or panegyric upon the true critics, in imitation of their masters, the moderns. Now, in the commonplaces[36] of both these I was plentifully instructed by a long course of useful study in prefaces and prologues, and therefore immediately resolved to try what I could discover of either, by a diligent perusal of the most ancient writers, and especially those who treated of the earliest times.

Here I found, to my great surprise, that although they all entered upon occasion into particular descriptions of the true critic, according as they were governed by their fears or their hopes, yet whatever they touched of that kind was with abundance of caution, adventuring no further than mythology and hieroglyphic. This, I suppose, gave ground to superficial readers for urging the silence of authors against the antiquity of the true critic, though the types are so apposite, and the applications so necessary and natural, that it is not easy to conceive how any reader of modern eye and taste could overlook them. I shall venture from a great number to produce a few which I am very confident will put this question beyond doubt.

It well deserves considering that these ancient writers, in treating enigmatically upon this subject, have generally fixed upon the very same hieroglyph, varying only the story according to their affections or their wit. For first, Pausanias is of opinion that the perfection of writing correct was entirely owing to the institution of critics, and that he can possibly mean no other than the true critic is, I think, manifest enough from the following description. He says they were a race of men who delighted to nibble at the superfluities and excrescences of books, which the learned at length observing, took warning of their own accord to lop the luxuriant, the rotten, the dead, the sapless, and the overgrown branches from their works. But now all this he cunningly shades under the following allegory: That the Nauplians in Argia learned the art of pruning their vines by observing that when an ass had browsed upon one of them, it thrived the better and bore fairer fruit. But Herodotus holding the very same hieroglyph, speaks much plainer and almost *in terminis*. He hath been so bold as to tax the true critics of ignorance and malice, telling us openly, for I think nothing can be plainer, that in the western part of Libya there were asses with horns, upon which relation Ctesias[37] yet refines, mentioning the very same animal about India; adding, that whereas all other asses wanted a gall, these horned ones were so redundant in that part that their flesh was not to be eaten because of its extreme bitterness.

Now, the reason why those ancient writers treated this subject only by types and figures was because they durst not make open attacks against a party so potent and so terrible as the critics of those ages were, whose very voice was so dreadful that a legion of authors would tremble and drop their pens at the sound. For so Herodotus tells us expressly in another place how a vast army of Scythians was put to flight in a panic terror by the braying of an ass. From hence it is conjectured by certain profound philologers, that the great awe and reverence paid to a true critic by the writers of Britain have been derived to us from those our Scythian ancestors. In short, this dread was so universal, that in process of time those authors who had a mind to publish their sentiments more freely in describing the true critics of their several ages, were forced to leave off the use of the former hieroglyph as too nearly approaching the prototype, and invented other terms instead thereof that were more cautious and mystical. So Diodorus, speaking to the same purpose, ventures no farther than to say that in the mountains of Helicon there grows a certain weed which bears a flower of so damned a scent as to poison those who offer to smell it. Lucretius gives exactly the same relation.

"Est etiam in magnis Heliconis montibus arbos,
Floris odore hominem retro consueta necare."—*Lib.* 6.[38]

But Ctesias, whom we lately quoted, has been a great deal bolder; he had been used with much severity by the true critics of his own age, and therefore could not forbear to leave behind him at least one deep mark of his vengeance against the whole tribe. His meaning is so near the surface that I wonder how it possibly came to be overlooked by those who deny the antiquity of the true critics. For pretending to make a description of many strange animals about India, he has set down these remarkable words. "Among the rest," says he, "there is a serpent that wants teeth, and consequently cannot bite, but if its vomit (to which it is much addicted) happens to fall upon anything, a certain rottenness or corruption ensues. These serpents are generally found among the mountains where jewels grow, and they frequently emit a poisonous juice, whereof whoever drinks, that person's brain flies out of his nostrils."

There was also among the ancients a sort of critic, not distinguished in specie from the former but in growth or degree, who seem to have been only the tyros or junior scholars, yet because of their differing employments they are frequently mentioned as a sect by themselves. The usual exercise of these young students was to attend constantly at theatres, and learn to spy out the worst parts of the play, whereof they were obliged carefully to take note, and render a rational account to their tutors. Fleshed at these smaller sports, like young wolves, they grew up in time to be nimble and strong enough for hunting down large game. For it has been observed, both among ancients and moderns, that a true critic has one quality in common with a whore and an alderman, never to change his title or his nature; that a grey critic has been certainly a green one, the perfections and acquirements of his age being only the improved talents of his youth, like hemp, which some naturalists inform us is bad for suffocations, though taken but in the seed. I esteem the invention, or at least the refinement of prologues, to have been owing to these younger proficients, of whom Terence makes frequent and honourable mention, under the name of Malevoli.

Now it is certain the institution of the true critics was of absolute necessity to the commonwealth of learning. For all human actions seem to be divided like Themistocles and his company. One man can fiddle, and another can make a small town a great city; and he that cannot do either one or the other deserves to be kicked out of the creation. The avoiding of which penalty has doubtless given the first birth to the nation of critics, and withal an occasion for their secret detractors to report that a true critic is a sort of mechanic set up with a stock and tools for his trade, at as little expense as a tailor; and that there is much analogy between the utensils and abilities of both. That the "Tailor's Hell" is the type of a critic's commonplace-book, and his wit and learning held forth by the goose. That it requires at least as many of these to the making up of one scholar as of the others to the composition of a man. That the valour of both is equal, and their weapons near of a size. Much may be said in answer to these invidious reflections; and I can positively affirm the first to be a falsehood: for, on the contrary, nothing is more certain than that it requires greater layings out to be free of the critic's company than of any other you can name. For as to be a true beggar, it will cost the richest candidate every groat he is worth, so before one can commence a true critic, it will cost a man all the good qualities of his mind, which perhaps for a less purchase would be thought but an indifferent bargain.

Having thus amply proved the antiquity of criticism and described the primitive state of it, I shall now examine the present condition of this Empire, and show how well it agrees with its ancient self.[39] A certain author, whose works have many ages since been entirely lost, does in his fifth book and eighth chapter say of critics that "their writings are the mirrors of learning." This I understand in a literal sense, and suppose our author must mean that whoever designs to be a perfect writer must inspect into the books of critics, and correct his inventions there as in a mirror. Now, whoever considers that the mirrors of the ancients were made of brass and fine mercurio, may presently apply the two principal qualifications of a true modern critic, and consequently must needs conclude that these have always been and must be for ever the same. For brass is an emblem of duration, and when it is skilfully burnished will cast reflections from its own superficies without any assistance of mercury from behind. All the other talents of a critic will not require a particular mention, being included or easily deducible to these. However, I shall conclude with three maxims, which may serve both as characteristics to distinguish a true modern critic from a pretender, and will be also of admirable use to those worthy spirits who engage in so useful and honourable an art.

The first is, that criticism, contrary to all other faculties of the intellect, is ever held the truest and best when it is the very first result of the critic's mind; as fowlers reckon the first aim for the surest, and seldom fail of missing the mark if they stay not for a second.

Secondly, the true critics are known by their talent of swarming about the noblest writers, to which they are carried merely by instinct, as a rat to the best cheese, or a wasp to the fairest fruit. So when the king is a horseback he is sure to be the dirtiest person of the company, and they that make their court best are such as bespatter him most.

Lastly, a true critic in the perusal of a book is like a dog at a feast, whose thoughts and stomach are wholly set upon what the guests fling away, and consequently is apt to snarl most when there are the fewest bones.[40]

Thus much I think is sufficient to serve by way of address to my patrons, the true modern critics, and may very well atone for my past silence, as well as that which I am like to observe for the future. I hope I have deserved so well of their whole body as to meet with generous and tender usage at their hands. Supported by which expectation I go on boldly to pursue those adventures already so happily begun.

SECTION IV: A TALE OF A TUB

I have now with much pains and study conducted the reader to a period where he must expect to hear of great revolutions. For no sooner had our learned brother, so often mentioned, got a warm house of his own over his head, than he began to look big and to take mightily upon him, insomuch that unless the gentle reader out of his great candour will please a little to exalt his idea, I am afraid he will henceforth hardly know the hero of the play when he happens to meet him, his part, his dress, and his mien being so much altered.

He told his brothers he would have them to know that he was their elder, and consequently his father's sole heir; nay, a while after, he would not allow them to call him brother, but Mr. Peter; and then he must be styled Father Peter, and sometimes My Lord Peter. To support this grandeur, which he soon began to consider could not be maintained without a better *fonde* than what he was born to, after much thought he cast about at last to turn projector and virtuoso, wherein he so well succeeded, that many famous discoveries, projects, and machines which bear great vogue and practice at present in the world, are owing entirely to Lord Peter's invention. I will deduce the best account I have been able to collect of the chief amongst them, without considering much the order they came out in, because I think authors are not well agreed as to that point.

I hope when this treatise of mine shall be translated into foreign languages (as I may without vanity affirm that the labour of collecting, the faithfulness in recounting, and the great usefulness of the matter to the public, will amply deserve that justice), that of the several Academies abroad, especially those of France and Italy, will favourably accept these humble offers for the advancement of universal knowledge. I do also advertise the most reverend fathers the Eastern missionaries that I have purely for their sakes made use of such words and phrases as will best admit an easy turn into any of the Oriental languages, especially the Chinese. And so I proceed with great content of mind upon reflecting how much emolument this whole globe of earth is like to reap by my labours.

The first undertaking of Lord Peter was to purchase a large continent, lately said to have been discovered in *Terra Australis incognita*. This tract of land he bought at a very great pennyworth from the discoverers themselves (though some pretended to doubt whether they had ever been there), and then retailed it into several cantons to certain dealers, who carried over colonies, but were all shipwrecked in the voyage; upon which Lord Peter sold the said continent to other customers again and again, and again and again, with the same success.

The second project I shall mention was his sovereign remedy for the worms, especially those in the spleen. The patient was to eat nothing after supper for three nights; as soon as he went to bed, he was carefully to lie on one side, and when he grew weary, to turn upon the other. He must also duly confine his two eyes to the same object, and by no means break wind at both ends together without manifest occasion. These prescriptions diligently observed, the worms would void insensibly by perspiration ascending through the brain.

A third invention was the erecting of a whispering-office for the public good and ease of all such as are hypochondriacal or troubled with the cholic, as likewise of all eavesdroppers, physicians, midwives, small politicians, friends fallen out, repeating poets, lovers happy or in despair, bawds, privy-counsellors, pages, parasites and buffoons, in short, of all such as are in danger of bursting with too much wind. An ass's head was placed so conveniently, that the party affected might easily with his mouth accost either of the animal's ears, which he was to apply close for a certain space, and by a fugitive faculty peculiar to the ears of that animal, receive immediate benefit, either by eructation, or expiration, or evomition.

Another very beneficial project of Lord Peter's was an office of insurance for tobacco-pipes, martyrs of the modern zeal, volumes of poetry, shadows . . . and rivers, that these, nor any of these, shall receive damage by fire. From whence our friendly societies may plainly find themselves to be only transcribers from this original, though the one and the other have been of great benefit to the undertakers as well as of equal to the public.

Lord Peter was also held the original author of puppets and raree-shows, the great usefulness whereof being so generally known, I shall not enlarge farther upon this particular.

But another discovery for which he was much renowned was his famous universal pickle. For having remarked how your common pickle in use among housewives was of no farther benefit than to preserve dead flesh and certain kinds of vegetables, Peter with great cost as well as art had contrived a pickle proper for houses, gardens, towns, men, women, children, and cattle, wherein he could preserve them as sound as insects in amber. Now this pickle to the taste, the smell, and the sight, appeared exactly the same with what is in common service for beef, and butter, and herrings (and has been often that way applied with great success), but for its many sovereign virtues was quite a different thing. For Peter would put in a certain quantity of his powder pimperlim-pimp, after which it never failed of success. The operation was performed by spargefaction in a proper time of the moon. The patient who was to be pickled, if it were a house, would infallibly be preserved from all spiders, rats, and weasels; if the party affected were a dog, he should be exempt from mange, and madness, and hunger. It also infallibly took away all scabs and lice, and scalled heads from children, never hindering the patient from any duty, either at bed or board.

But of all Peter's rarities, he most valued a certain set of bulls, whose race was by great fortune preserved in a lineal descent from those that guarded the golden-fleece. Though some who pretended to observe them curiously doubted the breed had not been kept entirely chaste, because they had degenerated from their ancestors in some qualities, and had acquired others very extraordinary, but a foreign mixture. The bulls of Colchis are recorded to have brazen feet; but whether it happened by ill pasture and running, by an alloy from intervention of other parents from stolen intrigues; whether a weakness in their progenitors had impaired the seminal virtue, or by a decline necessary through a long course of time, the originals of nature being depraved in these latter sinful ages of the world —whatever was the cause, it is certain that Lord Peter's bulls were extremely vitiated by the rust of time in the metal of their feet, which was now sunk into common lead. However, the terrible roaring peculiar to their lineage was preserved, as likewise that faculty of breathing out fire from their nostrils; which notwithstanding many of their detractors took to be a feat of art, and to be nothing so terrible as it appeared, proceeding only from their usual course of diet, which was of squibs and crackers. However, they had two peculiar marks which extremely distinguished them from the bulls of Jason, and which I have not met together in the description of any other monster beside that in Horace, "Varias inducere plumas," and "Atrum definit in piscem." For these had fishes tails, yet upon occasion could outfly any bird in the air. Peter put these bulls upon several employs. Sometimes he would set them a roaring to fright naughty boys and make them quiet. Sometimes he would send them out upon errands of great importance, where it is wonderful to recount, and perhaps the cautious reader may think much to believe it; an *appetitus sensibilis* deriving itself through the whole family from their noble ancestors, guardians of the Golden Fleece, they continued so extremely fond of gold, that if Peter sent them abroad, though it were only upon a compliment, they would roar, and spit, and belch, and snivel out fire, and keep a perpetual coil till you flung them a bit of gold; but then *pulveris exigui jactu*, they would grow calm and quiet as lambs. In short, whether by secret connivance or encouragement from their master, or out of their own liquorish affection to gold, or both, it is certain they were no better than a sort of sturdy, swaggering beggars; and where they could not prevail to get an alms, would make women miscarry and children fall into fits; who to this very day usually call sprites and hobgoblins by the name of bull-beggars. They grew at last so very troublesome to the neighbourhood, that some gentlemen of the North-West got a parcel of right English bull-dogs, and baited them so terribly, that they felt it ever after.

I must needs mention one more of Lord Peter's projects, which was very extraordinary, and discovered him to be master of a high reach and profound invention. Whenever it happened that any rogue of Newgate was condemned to be hanged, Peter would offer him a pardon for a certain sum of money, which when the poor caitiff had made all shifts to scrape up and send, his lordship would return a piece of paper in this form:—

"To all mayors, sheriffs, jailors, constables, bailiffs, hangmen, &c. Whereas we are informed that A. B. remains in the hands of you, or any of you, under the sentence of death. We will and command you, upon sight hereof, to let the said prisoner depart to his own habitation, whether he stands condemned for murder, sodomy, rape, sacrilege, incest, treason, blasphemy, &c., for which this shall be your sufficient warrant. And it you fail hereof, G— d—mn you and yours to all eternity. And so we bid you heartily farewell. Your most humble man's man,
"EMPEROR PETER."

The wretches trusting to this lost their lives and money too.

I desire of those whom the learned among posterity will appoint for commentators upon this elaborate treatise, that they will proceed with great caution upon certain dark points, wherein all who are not *verè adepti* may be in danger to form rash and hasty conclusions, especially in some mysterious paragraphs, where certain arcana are joined for brevity sake, which in the operation must be divided. And I am certain that future sons of art will return large thanks to my memory for so grateful, so useful an inmuendo.

It will be no difficult part to persuade the reader that so many worthy discoveries met with great success in the world; though I may justly assure him that I have related much the smallest number; my design having been only to single out such as will be of most benefit for public imitation, or which best served to give some idea of the reach and wit of the inventor. And therefore it need not be wondered if by this time Lord Peter was become exceeding rich. But alas! he had kept his brain so long and so violently upon the rack, that at last it shook itself, and began to turn round for a little ease. In short, what with pride, projects, and knavery, poor Peter was grown distracted, and conceived the strangest imaginations in the world. In the height of his fits (as it is usual with those who run mad out of pride) he would call himself God Almighty, and sometimes monarch of the universe. I have seen him (says my author) take three old high-crowned hats, and clap them all on his head, three storey high, with a huge bunch of keys at his girdle, and an angling rod in his hand. In which guise, whoever went to take him by the hand in the way of salutation, Peter with much grace, like a well-educated spaniel, would present them with his foot, and if they refused his civility, then he would raise it as high as their chops, and give them a damned kick on the mouth, which hath ever since been called a salute. Whoever walked by without paying him their compliments, having a wonderful strong breath, he would blow their hats off into the dirt. Meantime his affairs at home went upside down, and his two brothers had a wretched time, where his first *boutade* was to kick both their wives one morning out of doors, and his own too, and in their stead gave orders to pick up the first three strollers could be met with in the streets. A while after he nailed up the cellar door, and would not allow his brothers a drop of drink to their victuals.[41] Dining one day at an alderman's in the city, Peter observed him expatiating, after the manner of his brethren in the praises of his sirloin of beef. "Beef," said the sage magistrate, "is the king of meat; beef comprehends in it the quintessence of partridge, and quail, and venison, and pheasant, and plum-pudding, and custard." When Peter came home, he would needs take the fancy of cooking up this doctrine into use, and apply the precept in default of a sirloin to his brown loaf. "Bread," says he, "dear brothers, is the staff of life, in which bread is contained inclusive the quintessence of beef, mutton, veal, venison, partridge, plum-pudding, and custard, and to render all complete, there is intermingled a due quantity of water, whose crudities are also corrected by yeast or barm, through which means it becomes a wholesome fermented liquor, diffused through the mass of the bread." Upon the strength of these conclusions, next day at dinner was the brown loaf served up in all the formality of a City feast.

"Come, brothers," said Peter, "fall to, and spare not; here is excellent good mutton;[42] or hold, now my hand is in, I'll help you." At which word, in much ceremony, with fork and knife, he carves out two good slices of a loaf, and presents each on a plate to his brothers. The elder of the two, not suddenly entering into Lord Peter's conceit, began with very civil language to examine the mystery. "My lord," said he, "I doubt, with great submission, there may be some mistake." "What!" says Peter, "you are pleasant; come then, let us hear this jest your head is so big with." "None in the world, my Lord; but unless I am very much deceived, your Lordship was pleased a while ago to let fall a word about mutton, and I would be glad to see it with all my heart." "How," said Peter, appearing in great surprise, "I do not comprehend this at all;" upon which the younger, interposing to set the business right, "My Lord," said he, "my brother, I suppose, is hungry, and longs for the mutton your Lordship hath promised us to dinner." "Pray," said Peter, "take me along with you, either you are both mad, or disposed to be merrier than I approve of; if you there do not like your piece, I will carve you another, though I should take that to be the choice bit of the whole shoulder." "What then, my Lord?" replied the first; "it seems this is a shoulder of mutton all this while." "Pray, sir," says Peter, "eat your victuals and leave off your impertinence, if you please, for I am not disposed to relish it at present;" but the other could not forbear, being over-provoked at the affected seriousness of Peter's countenance. "My Lord," said he, "I can only say, that to my eyes and fingers, and teeth and nose, it seems to be nothing but a crust of bread." Upon which the second put in his word. "I never saw a piece of mutton in my life so nearly resembling a slice from a twelve-penny loaf." "Look ye, gentlemen," cries Peter in a rage, "to convince you what a couple of blind, positive, ignorant, wilful puppies you are, I will use but this plain argument; by G—, it is true, good, natural mutton as any in Leadenhall Market; and G— confound you both eternally if you offer to believe otherwise." Such a thundering proof as this left no further room for objection; the two unbelievers began to gather and pocket up their mistake as hastily as they could. "Why, truly," said the first, "upon more mature consideration"—"Ay," says the other, interrupting him, "now I have thought better on the thing, your Lordship seems to have a great deal of reason." "Very well," said Peter. "Here, boy, fill me a beer-glass of claret. Here's to you both with all my heart." The two brethren, much delighted to see him so readily appeased, returned their most humble thanks, and said they would be glad to pledge his Lordship. "That you shall," said Peter, "I am not a person to refuse you anything that is reasonable; wine moderately taken is a cordial. Here is a glass apiece for you; it is true natural juice from the grape; none of your damned vintner's brewings." Having spoke thus, he presented to each of them another large dry crust, bidding them drink it off, and not be bashful, for it would do them no hurt. The two brothers, after having performed the usual office in such delicate conjunctures, of staring a sufficient period at Lord Peter and each other, and finding how matters were like to go, resolved not to enter on a new dispute, but let him carry the point as he pleased; for he was now got into one of his mad fits, and to argue or expostulate further would only serve to render him a hundred times more untractable.

I have chosen to relate this worthy matter in all its circumstances, because it gave a principal occasion to that great and famous rupture[43] which happened about the same time among these brethren, and was never afterwards made up. But of that I shall treat at large in another section.

However, it is certain that Lord Peter, even in his lucid intervals, was very lewdly given in his common conversation, extreme wilful and positive, and would at any time rather argue to the death than allow himself to be once in an error. Besides, he had an abominable faculty of telling huge palpable lies upon all occasions, and swearing not only to the truth, but cursing the whole company to hell if they pretended to make the least scruple of believing him. One time he swore he had a cow at home which gave as much milk at a meal as would fill three thousand churches, and what was yet more extraordinary, would never turn sour. Another time he was telling of an old sign-post[44] that belonged to his father, with nails and timber enough on it to build sixteen large men-of-war. Talking one day of Chinese waggons, which were made so light as to sail over mountains, "Z—nds," said Peter, "where's the wonder of that? By G—, I saw a large house of lime and stone travel over sea and land (granting that it stopped sometimes to bait) above two thousand German leagues."[45] And that which was the good of it, he would swear desperately all the while that he never told a lie in his life, and at every word: "By G— gentlemen, I tell you nothing but the truth, and the d—l broil them eternally that will not believe me."

In short, Peter grew so scandalous that all the neighbourhood began in plain words to say he was no better than a knave; and his two brothers, long weary of his ill-usage, resolved at last to leave him; but first they humbly desired a copy of their father's will, which had now lain by neglected time out of mind. Instead of granting this request, he called them rogues, traitors, and the rest of the vile names he could muster up. However, while he was abroad one day upon his projects, the two youngsters watched their opportunity, made a shift to come at the will, and took a *copia vera*,[46] by which they presently saw how grossly they had been abused, their father having left them equal heirs, and strictly commanded that whatever they got should lie in common among them all. Pursuant to which, their next enterprise was to break open the cellar-door and get a little good drink to spirit and comfort their hearts.[47] In copying the will, they had met another precept against whoring, divorce, and separate maintenance; upon which, their next work was to discard their concubines and send for their wives.[48] Whilst all this was in agitation, there enters a solicitor from Newgate, desiring Lord Peter would please to procure a pardon for a thief that was to be hanged to-morrow. But the two brothers told him he was a coxcomb to seek pardons from a fellow who deserved to be hanged much better than his client, and discovered all the method of that imposture in the same form I delivered it a while ago, advising the solicitor to put his friend upon obtaining a pardon from the king. In the midst of all this platter and revolution in comes Peter with a file of dragoons at his heels, and gathering from all hands what was in the wind, he and his gang, after several millions of scurrilities and curses not very important here to repeat, by main force very fairly kicks them both out of doors, and would never let them come under his roof from that day to this.

SECTION V: A DIGRESSION IN THE MODERN KIND

We whom the world is pleased to honour with the title of modern authors, should never have been able to compass our great design of an everlasting remembrance and never-dying fame if our endeavours had not been so highly serviceable to the general good of mankind. This, O universe! is the adventurous attempt of me, thy secretary—

> "Quemvis perferre laborem
> Suadet, et inducit noctes vigilare serenas."

To this end I have some time since, with a world of pains and art, dissected the carcass of human nature, and read many useful lectures upon the several parts, both containing and contained, till at last it smelt so strong I could preserve it no longer. Upon which I have been at a great expense to fit up all the bones with exact contexture and in due symmetry, so that I am ready to show a very complete anatomy thereof to all curious gentlemen and others. But not to digress further in the midst of a digression, as I have known some authors enclose digressions in one another like a nest of boxes, I do affirm that, having carefully cut up human nature, I have found a very strange, new, and important discovery: that the public good of mankind is performed by two ways—instruction and diversion. And I have further proved my said several readings (which, perhaps, the world may one day see, if I can prevail on any friend to steal a copy, or on certain gentlemen of my admirers to be very importunate) that, as mankind is now disposed, he receives much greater advantage by being diverted than instructed, his epidemical diseases being fastidiosity, amorphy, and oscitation; whereas, in the present universal empire of wit and learning, there seems but little matter left for instruction.

However, in compliance with a lesson of great age and authority, I have attempted carrying the point in all its heights, and accordingly throughout this divine treatise have skilfully kneaded up both together with a layer of *utile* and a layer of *dulce*.

When I consider how exceedingly our illustrious moderns have eclipsed the weak glimmering lights of the ancients, and turned them out of the road of all fashionable commerce to a degree that our choice town wits of most refined accomplishments are in grave dispute whether there have been ever any ancients or no; in which point we are like to receive wonderful satisfaction from the most useful labours and lucubrations of that worthy modern, Dr. Bentley. I say, when I consider all this, I cannot but bewail that no famous modern hath ever yet attempted an universal system in a small portable volume of all things that are to be known, or believed, or imagined, or practised in life. I am, however, forced to acknowledge that such an enterprise was thought on some time ago by a great philosopher of O-Brazile. The method he proposed was by a certain curious receipt, a nostrum, which after his untimely death I found among his papers, and do here, out of my great affection to the modern learned, present them with it, not doubting it may one day encourage some worthy undertaker.

You take fair correct copies, well bound in calf's skin and lettered at the back, of all modern bodies of arts and sciences whatsoever, and in what language you please. These you distil in *balneo Mariæ*, infusing quintessence of poppy Q.S., together with three pints of lethe, to be had from the apothecaries. You cleanse away carefully the *sordes* and *caput mortuum*, letting all that is volatile evaporate. You preserve only the first running, which is again to be distilled seventeen times, till what remains will amount to about two drams. This you keep in a glass vial hermetically sealed for one-and-twenty days. Then you begin your catholic treatise, taking every morning fasting (first shaking the vial) three drops of this elixir, snuffing it strongly up your nose. It will dilate itself about the brain (where there is any) in fourteen minutes, and you immediately perceive in your head an infinite number of abstracts, summaries, compendiums, extracts, collections, medullas, excerpta quædams, florilegias and the like, all disposed into great order and reducible upon paper.

I must needs own it was by the assistance of this arcanum that I, though otherwise *impar*, have adventured upon so daring an attempt, never achieved or undertaken before but by a certain author called Homer, in whom, though otherwise a person not without some abilities, and for an ancient of a tolerable genius; I have discovered many gross errors which are not to be forgiven his very ashes, if by chance any of them are left. For whereas we are assured he designed his work for a complete body of all knowledge, human, divine, political, and mechanic,[49] it is manifest he hath wholly neglected some, and been very imperfect perfect in the rest. For, first of all, as eminent a cabalist as his disciples would represent him, his account of the *opus magnum* is extremely poor and deficient; he seems to have read but very superficially either Sendivogus, Behmen, or Anthroposophia Theomagica.[50] He is also quite mistaken about the *sphæra pyroplastica*, a neglect not to be atoned for, and (if the reader will admit so severe a censure) *vix crederem autorem hunc unquam audivisse ignis vocem*. His failings are not less prominent in several parts of the mechanics. For having read his writings with the utmost application usual among modern wits, I could never yet discover the least direction about the structure of that useful instrument a save-all; for want of which, if the moderns had not lent their assistance, we might yet have wandered in the dark. But I have still behind a fault far more notorious to tax this author with; I mean his gross ignorance in the common laws of this realm, and in the doctrine as well as discipline of the Church of England. A defect, indeed, for which both he and all the ancients stand most justly censured by my worthy and ingenious friend Mr. Wotton, Bachelor of Divinity, in his incomparable treatise of ancient and modern learning; a book never to be sufficiently valued, whether we consider the happy turns and flowings of the author's wit, the great usefulness of his sublime discoveries upon the subject of flies and spittle, or the laborious eloquence of his style. And I cannot forbear doing that author the justice of my public acknowledgments for the great helps and liftings I had out of his incomparable piece while I was penning this treatise.

But besides these omissions in Homer already mentioned, the curious reader will also observe several defects in that author's writings for which he is not altogether so accountable. For whereas every branch of knowledge has received such wonderful acquirements since his age, especially within these last three years or thereabouts, it is almost impossible he could be so very perfect in modern discoveries as his advocates pretend. We freely acknowledge him to be the inventor of the compass, of gunpowder, and the circulation of the blood; but I challenge any of his admirers to show me in all his writings a complete account of the spleen. Does he not also leave us wholly to seek in the art of political wagering? What can be more defective and unsatisfactory than his long dissertation upon tea? and as to his method of salivation without mercury, so much celebrated of late, it is to my own knowledge and experience a thing very little to be relied on.

It was to supply such momentous defects that I have been prevailed on, after long solicitation, to take pen in hand, and I dare venture to promise the judicious reader shall find nothing neglected here that can be of use upon any emergency of life. I am confident to have included and exhausted all that human imagination can rise or fall to. Particularly I recommend to the perusal of the learned certain discoveries that are wholly untouched by others, whereof I shall only mention, among a great many more, my "New Help of Smatterers, or the Art of being Deep

Learned and Shallow Read," "A Curious Invention about Mouse-traps," "A Universal Rule of Reason, or Every Man his own Carver," together with a most useful engine for catching of owls. All which the judicious reader will find largely treated on in the several parts of this discourse.

I hold myself obliged to give as much light as possible into the beauties and excellences of what I am writing, because it is become the fashion and humour most applauded among the first authors of this polite and learned age, when they would correct the ill nature of critical or inform the ignorance of courteous readers. Besides, there have been several famous pieces lately published, both in verse and prose, wherein if the writers had not been pleased, out of their great humanity and affection to the public, to give us a nice detail of the sublime and the admirable they contain, it is a thousand to one whether we should ever have discovered one grain of either. For my own particular, I cannot deny that whatever I have said upon this occasion had been more proper in a preface, and more agreeable to the mode which usually directs it there. But I here think fit to lay hold on that great and honourable privilege of being the last writer. I claim an absolute authority in right as the freshest modern, which gives me a despotic power over all authors before me. In the strength of which title I do utterly disapprove and declare against that pernicious custom of making the preface a bill of fare to the book. For I have always looked upon it as a high point of indiscretion in monstermongers and other retailers of strange sights to hang out a fair large picture over the door, drawn after the life, with a most eloquent description underneath. This has saved me many a threepence, for my curiosity was fully satisfied, and I never offered to go in, though often invited by the urging and attending orator with his last moving and standing piece of rhetoric, "Sir, upon my word, we are just going to begin." Such is exactly the fate at this time of Prefaces, Epistles, Advertisements, Introductions, Prolegomenas, Apparatuses, To the Readers's. This expedient was admirable at first; our great Dryden has long carried it as far as it would go, and with incredible success. He has often said to me in confidence that the world would never have suspected him to be so great a poet if he had not assured them so frequently in his prefaces, that it was impossible they could either doubt or forget it. Perhaps it may be so. However, I much fear his instructions have edified out of their place, and taught men to grow wiser in certain points where he never intended they should; for it is lamentable to behold with what a lazy scorn many of the yawning readers in our age do now-a-days twirl over forty or fifty pages of preface and dedication (which is the usual modern stint), as if it were so much Latin. Though it must be also allowed, on the other hand, that a very considerable number is known to proceed critics and wits by reading nothing else. Into which two factions I think all present readers may justly be divided. Now, for myself, I profess to be of the former sort, and therefore having the modern inclination to expatiate upon the beauty of my own productions, and display the bright parts of my discourse, I thought best to do it in the body of the work, where as it now lies it makes a very considerable addition to the bulk of the volume, a circumstance by no means to be neglected by a skilful writer.

Having thus paid my due deference and acknowledgment to an established custom of our newest authors, by a long digression unsought for and a universal censure unprovoked, by forcing into the light, with much pains and dexterity, my own excellences and other men's defaults, with great justice to myself and candour to them, I now happily resume my subject, to the infinite satisfaction both of the reader and the author.

SECTION VI: A TALE OF A TUB

We left Lord Peter in open rupture with his two brethren, both for ever discarded from his house, and resigned to the wide world with little or nothing to trust to. Which are circumstances that render them proper subjects for the charity of a writer's pen to work on, scenes of misery ever affording the fairest harvest for great adventures. And in this the world may perceive the difference between the integrity of a generous Author and that of a common friend. The latter is observed to adhere close in prosperity, but on the decline of fortune to drop suddenly off; whereas the generous author, just on the contrary, finds his hero on the dunghill, from thence, by gradual steps, raises him to a throne, and then immediately withdraws, expecting not so much as thanks for his pains; in imitation of which example I have placed Lord Peter in a noble house, given him a title to wear and money to spend. There I shall leave him for some time, returning, where common charity directs me, to the assistance of his two brothers at their lowest ebb. However, I shall by no means forget my character of a historian, to follow the truth step by step whatever happens, or wherever it may lead me.

The two exiles so nearly united in fortune and interest took a lodging together, where at their first leisure they began to reflect on the numberless misfortunes and vexations of their life past, and could not tell of the sudden to what failure in their conduct they ought to impute them, when, after some recollection, they called to mind the copy of their father's will which they had so happily recovered. This was immediately produced, and a firm resolution taken between them to alter whatever was already amiss, and reduce all their future measures to the strictest obedience prescribed therein. The main body of the will (as the reader cannot easily have forgot) consisted in certain admirable rules, about the wearing of their coats, in the perusal whereof the two brothers at every period duly comparing the doctrine with the practice, there was never seen a wider difference between two things, horrible downright transgressions of every point. Upon which they both resolved without further delay to fall immediately upon reducing the whole exactly after their father's model.

But here it is good to stop the hasty reader, ever impatient to see the end of an adventure before we writers can duly prepare him for it. I am to record that these two brothers began to be distinguished at this time by certain names. One of them desired to be called Martin, and the other took the appellation of Jack. These two had lived in much friendship and agreement under the tyranny of their brother Peter, as it is the talent of fellow-sufferers to do, men in misfortune being like men in the dark, to whom all colours are the same. But when they came forward into the world, and began to display themselves to each other and to the light, their complexions appeared extremely different, which the present posture of their affairs gave them sudden opportunity to discover.

But here the severe reader may justly tax me as a writer of short memory, a deficiency to which a true modern cannot but of necessity be a little subject. Because, memory being an employment of the mind upon things past, is a faculty for which the learned in our illustrious age have no manner of occasion, who deal entirely with invention and strike all things out of themselves, or at least by collision from each other; upon which account, we think it highly reasonable to produce our great forgetfulness as an argument unanswerable for our great wit. I ought in method to have informed the reader about fifty pages ago of a fancy Lord Peter took, and infused into his brothers, to wear on their coats whatever trimmings came up in fashion, never pulling off any as they went out of the mode, but keeping on all together, which amounted in time to a medley the most antic you can possibly conceive, and this to a degree that, upon the time of their falling out, there was hardly a thread of the original coat to be seen, but an infinite quantity of lace, and ribbands, and fringe, and embroidery, and points (I mean only those tagged with silver, for the rest fell off). Now this material circumstance having been forgot in due place, as good fortune hath ordered, comes in very properly here, when the two brothers are just going to reform their vestures into the primitive state prescribed by their father's will.

They both unanimously entered upon this great work, looking sometimes on their coats and sometimes on the will. Martin laid the first hand; at one twitch brought off a large handful of points, and with a second pull stripped away ten dozen yards of fringe. But when he had gone thus far he demurred a while. He knew very well there yet remained a great deal more to be done; however, the first heat being over, his violence began to cool, and he resolved to proceed more moderately in the rest of the work, having already very narrowly escaped a swinging rent in pulling off the points, which being tagged with silver (as we have observed before), the judicious workman had with much sagacity double sewn to preserve them from falling. Resolving therefore to rid his coat of a huge quantity of gold lace, he picked up the stitches with much caution and diligently gleaned out all the loose threads as he went, which proved to be a work of time. Then he fell about the embroidered Indian figures of men, women, and children, against which, as you have heard in its due place, their father's testament was extremely exact and severe. These, with much dexterity and application, were after a while quite eradicated or utterly defaced. For the rest, where he observed the embroidery to be worked so close as not to be got away without damaging the cloth, or where it served to hide or strengthened any flaw in the body of the coat, contracted by the perpetual tampering of workmen upon it, he concluded the wisest course was to let it remain, resolving in no case whatsoever that the substance of the stuff should suffer injury, which he thought the best method for serving the true intent and meaning of his father's will. And this is the nearest account I have been able to collect of Martin's proceedings upon this great revolution.

But his brother Jack, whose adventures will be so extraordinary as to furnish a great part in the remainder of this discourse, entered upon the matter with other thoughts and a quite different spirit. For the memory of Lord Peter's injuries produced a degree of hatred and spite which had a much greater share of inciting him than any regards after his father's commands, since these appeared at best only secondary and subservient to the other. However, for this medley of humour he made a shift to find a very plausible name, honouring it with the title of zeal, which is, perhaps, the most significant word that has been ever yet produced in any language, as, I think, I have fully proved in my excellent analytical discourse upon that subject, wherein I have deduced a histori-theo-physiological account of zeal, showing how it first proceeded from a notion into a word, and from thence in a hot summer ripened into a tangible substance. This work, containing three large volumes in folio, I design very shortly to publish by the modern way of subscription, not doubting but the nobility and gentry of the land will give me all possible encouragement, having already had such a taste of what I am able to perform.

I record, therefore, that brother Jack, brimful of this miraculous compound, reflecting with indignation upon Peter's tyranny, and further provoked by the despondency of Martin, prefaced his resolutions to this purpose. "What!" said he, "a rogue that locked up his drink, turned away our wives, cheated us of our fortunes, palmed his crusts upon us for mutton, and at last kicked us out of doors; must we be in his fashions? A rascal, besides, that all the street cries out against." Having thus kindled and inflamed himself as high as possible, and by consequence in a delicate temper for beginning a reformation, he set about the work immediately, and in three minutes made more dispatch than Martin had done in as many hours. For, courteous reader, you are given to understand that zeal is never so highly obliged as when you set it a-tearing; and Jack, who doted on that quality in himself, allowed it at this time its full swing. Thus it happened that, stripping down a parcel of gold lace a little too hastily, he rent the main body of his coat from top to bottom;[51] and whereas his talent was not of the happiest in taking up a stitch, he knew no better way than to darn it again with packthread thread and a skewer. But the matter was yet infinitely worse (I record it with tears) when he proceeded to the embroidery; for being clumsy of nature, and of temper impatient withal, beholding millions of stitches that required the nicest hand and sedatest constitution to extricate, in a great rage he tore off the whole piece, cloth and all, and flung it into the kennel, and furiously thus continuing his career, "Ah! good brother Martin," said he, "do as I do, for the love of God; strip, tear, pull, rend, flay off all that we may appear as unlike that rogue Peter as it is possible. I would not for a hundred pounds carry the least mark about me that might give occasion to the neighbours of suspecting I was related to such a rascal." But Martin, who at this time happened to be extremely phlegmatic and sedate, begged his brother, of all love, not to damage his coat by any means, for he never would get such another; desired him to consider that it was not their business to form their actions by any reflection upon Peter's, but by observing the rules prescribed in their father's will. That he should remember Peter was still their brother, whatever faults or injuries he had committed, and therefore they should by all means avoid such a thought as that of taking measures for good and evil from no other rule than of opposition to him. That it was true the testament of their good father was very exact in what related to the wearing of their coats; yet was it no less penal and strict in prescribing agreement, and friendship, and affection between them. And therefore, if straining a point were at all defensible, it would certainly be so rather to the advance of unity than increase of contradiction.

Martin had still proceeded as gravely as he began, and doubtless would have delivered an admirable lecture of morality, which might have exceedingly contributed to my reader's repose both of body and mind (the true ultimate end of ethics), but Jack was already gone a flight-shot beyond his patience. And as in scholastic disputes nothing serves to rouse the spleen of him that opposes so much as a kind of pedantic affected calmness in the respondent, disputants being for the most part like unequal scales, where the gravity of one side advances the lightness of the other, and causes it to fly up and kick the beam; so it happened here that the weight of Martin's arguments exalted Jack's levity, and made him fly out and spurn against his brother's moderation. In short, Martin's patience put Jack in a rage; but that which most afflicted him was to observe his brother's coat so well reduced into the state of innocence, while his own was either wholly rent to his shirt, or those places which had escaped his cruel clutches were still in Peter's livery. So that he looked like a drunken beau half rifled by bullies, or like a fresh tenant of Newgate when he has refused the payment of garnish, or like a discovered shoplifter left to the mercy of Exchange-women,[52] or like a bawd in her old velvet petticoat resigned into the secular hands of the mobile.[53] Like any or like all of these, a medley of rags, and lace, and fringes, unfortunate Jack did now appear; he would have been extremely glad to see his coat in the condition of Martin's, but infinitely gladder to find that of Martin in the same predicament with his. However, since neither of these was likely to come to pass, he thought fit to lend the whole business another turn, and to dress up necessity into a virtue. Therefore, after as many of the fox's arguments as he could muster up for bringing Martin to reason, as he called it, or as he meant it, into his own ragged, bobtailed condition, and observing he said all to little purpose, what alas! was left for the forlorn Jack to do, but, after a million of scurrilities against his brother, to run mad with spleen, and spite, and contradiction. To be short, here began a mortal breach between these two. Jack went immediately to new lodgings, and in a few days it was for certain reported that he had run out of his wits. In a short time after he appeared abroad, and confirmed the report by falling into the oddest whimsies that ever a sick brain conceived.

And now the little boys in the streets began to salute him with several names. Sometimes they would call him Jack the Bald, sometimes Jack with a Lanthorn, sometimes Dutch Jack, sometimes French Hugh, sometimes Tom the Beggar, and sometimes Knocking Jack of the North.[54] And it was under one or some or all of these appellations (which I leave the learned reader to determine) that he hath given rise to the most illustrious and epidemic sect of Æolists, who, with honourable commemoration, do still acknowledge the renowned Jack for their author and founder. Of whose originals as well as principles I am now advancing to gratify the world with a very particular account.

"Mellæo contingens cuncta lepore."

SECTION VII: A DIGRESSION IN PRAISE OF DIGRESSIONS

I HAVE sometimes heard of an Iliad in a nut-shell, but it has been my fortune to have much oftener seen a nut-shell in an Iliad. There is no doubt that human life has received most wonderful advantages from both; but to which of the two the world is chiefly indebted, I shall leave among the curious as a problem worthy of their utmost inquiry. For the invention of the latter, I think the commonwealth of learning is chiefly obliged to the great modern improvement of digressions. The late refinements in knowledge, running parallel to those of diet in our nation, which among men of a judicious taste are dressed up in various compounds, consisting in soups and olios, fricassees and ragouts.

It is true there is a sort of morose, detracting, ill-bred people who pretend utterly to disrelish these polite innovations. And as to the similitude from diet, they allow the parallel, but are so bold as to pronounce the example itself a corruption and degeneracy of taste. They tell us that the fashion of jumbling fifty things together in a dish was at first introduced in compliance to a depraved and debauched appetite, as well as to a crazy constitution, and to see a man hunting through an olio after the head and brains of a goose, a widgeon, or a woodcock, is a sign he wants a stomach and digestion for more substantial victuals. Further, they affirm that digressions in a book are like foreign troops in a state, which argue the nation to want a heart and hands of its own, and often either subdue the natives, or drive them into the most unfruitful corners.

But after all that can be objected by these supercilious censors, it is manifest the society of writers would quickly be reduced to a very inconsiderable number if men were put upon making books with the fatal confinement of delivering nothing beyond what is to the purpose. It is acknowledged that were the case the same among us as with the Greeks and Romans, when learning was in its cradle, to be reared and fed and clothed by invention, it would be an easy task to fill up volumes upon particular occasions without further expatiating from the subject than by moderate excursions, helping to advance or clear the main design. But with knowledge it has fared as with a numerous army encamped in a fruitful country, which for a few days maintains itself by the product of the soil it is on, till provisions being spent, they send to forage many a mile among friends or enemies, it matters not. Meanwhile the neighbouring fields, trampled and beaten down, become barren and dry, affording no sustenance but clouds of dust.

The whole course of things being thus entirely changed between us and the ancients, and the moderns wisely sensible of it, we of this age have discovered a shorter and more prudent method to become scholars and wits, without the fatigue of reading or of thinking. The most accomplished way of using books at present is twofold: either first to serve them as some men do lords, learn their titles exactly, and then brag of their acquaintance; or, secondly, which is indeed the choicer, the profounder, and politer method, to get a thorough insight into the index by which the whole book is governed and turned, like fishes by the tail. For to enter the palace of learning at the great gate requires an expense of time and forms, therefore men of much haste and little ceremony are content to get in by the back-door. For the arts are all in a flying march, and therefore more easily subdued by attacking them in the rear. Thus physicians discover the state of the whole body by consulting only what comes from behind. Thus men catch knowledge by throwing their wit on the posteriors of a book, as boys do sparrows with flinging salt upon their tails. Thus human life is best understood by the wise man's rule of regarding the end. Thus are the sciences found, like Hercules' oxen, by tracing them backwards. Thus are old sciences unravelled like old stockings, by beginning at the foot.

Besides all this, the army of the sciences hath been of late with a world of martial discipline drawn into its close order, so that a view or a muster may be taken of it with abundance of expedition. For this great blessing we are wholly indebted to systems and abstracts, in which the modern fathers of learning, like prudent usurers, spent their sweat for the ease of us their children. For labour is the seed of idleness, and it is the peculiar happiness of our noble age to gather the fruit.

Now the method of growing wise, learned, and sublime having become so regular an affair, and so established in all its forms, the number of writers must needs have increased accordingly, and to a pitch that has made it of absolute necessity for them to interfere continually with each other. Besides, it is reckoned that there is not at this present a sufficient quantity of new matter left in Nature to furnish and adorn any one particular subject to the extent of a volume. This I am told by a very skilful computer, who hath given a full demonstration of it from rules of arithmetic.

This perhaps may be objected against by those who maintain the infinity of matter, and therefore will not allow that any species of it can be exhausted. For answer to which, let us examine the noblest branch of modern wit or invention planted and cultivated by the present age, and which of all others hath borne the most and the fairest fruit. For though some remains of it were left us by the ancients, yet have not any of those, as I remember, been translated or compiled into systems for modern use. Therefore we may affirm, to our own honour, that it has in some sort been both invented and brought to a perfection by the same hands. What I mean is, that highly celebrated talent among the modern wits of deducing similitudes, allusions, and applications, very surprising, agreeable, and apposite, from the signs of either sex, together with their proper uses. And truly, having observed how little invention bears any vogue besides what is derived into these channels, I have sometimes had a thought that the happy genius of our age and country was prophetically held forth by that ancient typical description of the Indian pigmies whose stature did not exceed above two feet, *sed quorum pudenda crassa, et ad talos usque pertingentia.* Now I have been very curious to inspect the late productions, wherein the beauties of this kind have most prominently appeared. And although this vein hath bled so freely, and all endeavours have been used in the power of human breath to dilate, extend, and keep it open, like the Scythians,[55] who had a custom and an instrument to blow up those parts of their mares, that they might yield the more milk; yet I am under an apprehension it is near growing dry and past all recovery, and that either some new *fonde* of wit should, if possible, be provided, or else that we must e'en be content with repetition here as well as upon all other occasions.

This will stand as an uncontestable argument that our modern wits are not to reckon upon the infinity of matter for a constant supply. What remains, therefore, but that our last recourse must be had to large indexes and little compendiums? Quotations must be plentifully gathered and booked in alphabet. To this end, though authors need be little consulted, yet critics, and commentators, and lexicons carefully must. But above all, those judicious collectors of bright parts, and flowers, and observandas are to be nicely dwelt on by some called the sieves and boulters of learning, though it is left undetermined whether they dealt in pearls or meal, and consequently whether we are more to value that which passed through or what stayed behind.

By these methods, in a few weeks there starts up many a writer capable of managing the profoundest and most universal subjects. For what though his head be empty, provided his commonplace book be full? And if you will bate him but the circumstances of method, and style, and grammar, and invention; allow him but the common privileges of transcribing from others, and digressing from himself as often as he shall see occasion, he will desire no more ingredients towards fitting up a treatise that shall make a very comely figure on a bookseller's shelf, there to be preserved neat and clean for a long eternity, adorned with the heraldry of its title fairly inscribed on a label, never to be thumbed or greased by students, nor bound to everlasting chains of darkness in a library, but when the fulness of time is come shall happily undergo the trial of purgatory in order to ascend the sky.

Without these allowances how is it possible we modern wits should ever have an opportunity to introduce our collections listed under so many thousand heads of a different nature, for want of which the learned world would be deprived of infinite delight as well as instruction, and we ourselves buried beyond redress in an inglorious and undistinguished oblivion?

From such elements as these I am alive to behold the day wherein the corporation of authors can outvie all its brethren in the field—a happiness derived to us, with a great many others, from our Scythian ancestors, among whom the number of pens was so infinite that the Grecian eloquence had no other way of expressing it than by saying that in the regions far to the north it was hardly possible for a man to travel, the very air was so replete with feathers.

The necessity of this digression will easily excuse the length, and I have chosen for it as proper a place as I could readily find. If the judicious reader can assign a fitter, I do here empower him to remove it into any other corner he please. And so I return with great alacrity to pursue a more important concern.

SECTION VIII: A TALE OF A TUB

THE learned Æolists maintain the original cause of all things to be wind, from which principle this whole universe was at first produced, and into which it must at last be resolved, that the same breath which had kindled and blew up the flame of Nature should one day blow it out.

"Quod procul à nobis flectat Fortuna gubernans."

This is what the Adepti understand by their *anima mundi*, that is to say, the spirit, or breath, or wind of the world; or examine the whole system by the particulars of Nature, and you will find it not to be disputed. For whether you please to call the *forma informans* of man by the name of *spiritus*, *animus*, *afflatus*, or *anima*, what are all these but several appellations for wind, which is the ruling element in every compound, and into which they all resolve upon their corruption. Further, what is life itself but, as it is commonly called, the breath of our nostrils, whence it is very justly observed by naturalists that wind still continues of great emolument in certain mysteries not to be named, giving occasion for those happy epithets of *turgidus* and *inflatus*, applied either to the emittent or recipient organs.

By what I have gathered out of ancient records, I find the compass of their doctrine took in two-and-thirty points, wherein it would be tedious to be very particular. However, a few of their most important precepts deducible from it are by no means to be omitted; among which, the following maxim was of much weight: That since wind had the master share as well as operation in every compound, by consequence those beings must be of chief excellence wherein that primordium appears most prominently to abound, and therefore man is in highest perfection of all created things, as having, by the great bounty of philosophers, been endued with three distinct *animas* or winds, to which the sage Æolists, with much liberality, have added a fourth, of equal necessity as well as ornament with the other three, by this *quartum principium* taking in the four corners of the world. Which gave occasion to that renowned cabalist Bombastus[56] of placing the body of man in due position to the four cardinal points.

In consequence of this, their next principle was that man brings with him into the world a peculiar portion or grain of wind, which may be called a *quinta essentia* extracted from the other four. This quintessence is of catholic use upon all emergencies of life, is improveable into all arts and sciences, and may be wonderfully refined as well as enlarged by certain methods in education. This, when blown up to its perfection, ought not to be covetously boarded up, stifled, or hid under a bushel, but freely communicated to mankind. Upon these reasons, and others of equal weight, the wise Æolists affirm the gift of belching to be the noblest act of a rational creature. To cultivate which art, and render it more serviceable to mankind, they made use of several methods. At certain seasons of the year you might behold the priests amongst them in vast numbers with their mouths gaping wide against a storm. At other times were to be seen several hundreds linked together in a circular chain, with every man a pair of bellows applied to his neighbour, by which they blew up each other to the shape and size of a tun; and for that reason with great propriety of speech did usually call their bodies their vessels.[57] When, by these and the like performances, they were grown sufficiently replete, they would immediately depart, and disembogue for the public good a plentiful share of their acquirements into their disciples' chaps. For we must here observe that all learning was esteemed among them to be compounded from the same principle. Because, first, it is generally affirmed or confessed that learning puffeth men up; and, secondly, they proved it by the following syllogism: "Words are but wind, and learning is nothing but words; ergo, learning is nothing but wind." For this reason the philosophers among them did in their schools deliver to their pupils all their doctrines and opinions by eructation, wherein they had acquired a wonderful eloquence, and of incredible variety. But the great characteristic by which their chief sages were best distinguished was a certain position of countenance, which gave undoubted intelligence to what degree or proportion the spirit agitated the inward mass. For after certain gripings, the wind and vapours issuing forth, having first by their turbulence and convulsions within caused an earthquake in man's little world, distorted the mouth, bloated the cheeks, and gave the eyes a terrible kind of relievo. At which junctures all their belches were received for sacred, the sourer the better, and swallowed with infinite consolation by their meagre devotees. And to render these yet more complete, because the breath of man's life is in his nostrils, therefore the choicest, most edifying, and most enlivening belches were very wisely conveyed through that vehicle to give them a tincture as they passed.

Their gods were the four winds, whom they worshipped as the spirits that pervade and enliven the universe, and as those from whom alone all inspiration can properly be said to proceed. However, the chief of these, to whom they performed the adoration of Latria, was the Almighty North, an ancient deity, whom the inhabitants of Megalopolis in Greece had likewise in highest reverence. "Omnium deorum Boream maxime celebrant."[58] This god, though endued with ubiquity, was yet supposed by the profounder Æolists to possess one peculiar habitation, or (to speak in form) a *cælum empyræum*, wherein he was more intimately present. This was situated in a certain region well known to the ancient Greeks, by them called Σχοτία, the Land of Darkness. And although many controversies have arisen upon that matter, yet so much is undisputed, that from a region of the like denomination the most refined Æolists have borrowed their original, from whence in every age the zealous among their priesthood have brought over their choicest inspiration, fetching it with their own hands from the fountain-head in certain bladders, and disploding it among the sectaries in all nations, who did, and do, and ever will, daily gasp and pant after it.

Now their mysteries and rites were performed in this manner. It is well known among the learned that the virtuosos of former ages had a contrivance for carrying and preserving winds in casks or barrels, which was of great assistance upon long sea-voyages, and the loss of so useful an art at present is very much to be lamented, though, I know not how, with great negligence omitted by Pancirollus. It was an invention ascribed to Æolus himself, from whom this sect is denominated, and who, in honour of their founder's memory, have to this day preserved great numbers of those barrels, whereof they fix one in each of their temples, first beating out the top. Into this barrel upon solemn days the priest enters, where, having before duly prepared himself by the methods already described, a secret funnel is also conveyed to the bottom of the barrel, which admits new supplies of inspiration from a northern chink or cranny. Whereupon you behold him swell immediately to the shape and size of his vessel. In this posture he disembogues whole tempests upon his auditory, as the spirit from beneath gives him utterance, which issuing *ex adytis* and *penetralibus*, is not performed without much pain and griping. And the wind in breaking forth deals with his face as it does with that of the sea, first blackening, then wrinkling, and at last bursting it into a foam. It is in this guise the sacred Æolist delivers his oracular belches to his panting disciples, of whom some are greedily gaping after the sanctified breath, others are all the while hymning out the praises of the winds, and gently wafted to and fro by their own humming, do thus represent the soft breezes of their deities appeased.

It is from this custom of the priests that some authors maintain these Æolists to have been very ancient in the world, because the delivery of their mysteries, which I have just now mentioned, appears exactly the same with that of other ancient oracles, whose inspirations were owing to certain subterraneous effluviums of wind delivered with the same pain to the priest, and much about the same influence on the people. It is true indeed that these were frequently managed and directed by female officers, whose organs were understood to be better disposed for the admission of those oracular gusts, as entering and passing up through a receptacle of greater capacity, and causing also a pruriency by the way, such as with due management has been refined from carnal into a spiritual ecstasy. And to strengthen this profound conjecture, it is further insisted that this custom of female priests is kept up still in certain refined colleges of our modern

Æolists,[59] who are agreed to receive their inspiration, derived through the receptacle aforesaid, like their ancestors the Sybils.

And whereas the mind of man, when he gives the spur and bridle to his thoughts, does never stop, but naturally sallies out into both extremes of high and low, of good and evil, his first flight of fancy commonly transports him to ideas of what is most perfect, finished, and exalted, till, having soared out of his own reach and sight, not well perceiving how near the frontiers of height and depth border upon each other, with the same course and wing he falls down plump into the lowest bottom of things, like one who travels the east into the west, or like a straight line drawn by its own length into a circle. Whether a tincture of malice in our natures makes us fond of furnishing every bright idea with its reverse, or whether reason, reflecting upon the sum of things, can, like the sun, serve only to enlighten one half of the globe, leaving the other half by necessity under shade and darkness, or whether fancy, flying up to the imagination of what is highest and best, becomes over-short, and spent, and weary, and suddenly falls, like a dead bird of paradise, to the ground; or whether, after all these metaphysical conjectures, I have not entirely missed the true reason; the proposition, however, which has stood me in so much circumstance is altogether true, that as the most uncivilised parts of mankind have some way or other climbed up into the conception of a God or Supreme Power, so they have seldom forgot to provide their fears with certain ghastly notions, which, instead of better, have served them pretty tolerably for a devil. And this proceeding seems to be natural enough, for it is with men whose imaginations are lifted up very high after the same rate as with those whose bodies are so, that as they are delighted with the advantage of a nearer contemplation upwards, so they are equally terrified with the dismal prospect of the precipice below. Thus in the choice of a devil it has been the usual method of mankind to single out some being, either in act or in vision, which was in most antipathy to the god they had framed. Thus also the sect of the Æolists possessed themselves with a dread and horror and hatred of two malignant natures, betwixt whom and the deities they adored perpetual enmity was established. The first of these was the chameleon, sworn foe to inspiration, who in scorn devoured large influences of their god, without refunding the smallest blast by eructation. The other was a huge terrible monster called Moulinavent, who with four strong arms waged eternal battle with all their divinities, dexterously turning to avoid their blows and repay them with interest.[60]

Thus furnished, and set out with gods as well as devils, was the renowned sect of Æolists, which makes at this day so illustrious a figure in the world, and whereof that polite nation of Laplanders are beyond all doubt a most authentic branch, of whom I therefore cannot without injustice here omit to make honourable mention, since they appear to be so closely allied in point of interest as well as inclinations with their brother Æolists among us, as not only to buy their winds by wholesale from the same merchants, but also to retail them after the same rate and method, and to customers much alike.

Now whether the system here delivered was wholly compiled by Jack, or, as some writers believe, rather copied from the original at Delphos, with certain additions and emendations suited to times and circumstances, I shall not absolutely determine. This I may affirm, that Jack gave it at least a new turn, and formed it into the same dress and model as it lies deduced by me.

I have long sought after this opportunity of doing justice to a society of men for whom I have a peculiar honour, and whose opinions as well as practices have been extremely misrepresented and traduced by the malice or ignorance of their adversaries. For I think it one of the greatest and best of human actions to remove prejudices and place things in their truest and fairest light, which I therefore boldly undertake, without any regards of my own beside the conscience, the honour, and the thanks.

SECTION IX: A DIGRESSION CONCERNING THE ORIGINAL, THE USE, AND IMPROVEMENT OF MADNESS IN A COMMONWEALTH.

Nor shall it any ways detract from the just reputation of this famous sect that its rise and institution are owing to such an author as I have described Jack to be, a person whose intellectuals were overturned and his brain shaken out of its natural position, which we commonly suppose to be a distemper, and call by the name of madness or frenzy. For if we take a survey of the greatest actions that have been performed in the world under the influence of single men, which are the establishment of new empires by conquest, the advance and progress of new schemes in philosophy, and the contriving as well as the propagating of new religions, we shall find the authors of them all to have been persons whose natural reason hath admitted great revolutions from their diet, their education, the prevalency of some certain temper, together with the particular influence of air and climate. Besides, there is something individual in human minds that easily kindles at the accidental approach and collision of certain circumstances, which, though of paltry and mean appearance, do often flame out into the greatest emergencies of life. For great turns are not always given by strong hands, but by lucky adaptation and at proper seasons, and it is of no import where the fire was kindled if the vapour has once got up into the brain. For the upper region of man is furnished like the middle region of the air, the materials are formed from causes of the widest difference, yet produce at last the same substance and effect. Mists arise from the earth, steams from dunghills, exhalations from the sea, and smoke from fire; yet all clouds are the same in composition as well as consequences, and the fumes issuing from a jakes will furnish as comely and useful a vapour as incense from an altar. Thus far, I suppose, will easily be granted me; and then it will follow that as the face of Nature never produces rain but when it is overcast and disturbed, so human understanding seated in the brain must be troubled and overspread by vapours ascending from the lower faculties to water the invention and render it fruitful. Now although these vapours (as it hath been already said) are of as various original as those of the skies, yet the crop they produce differs both in kind and degree, merely according to the soil. I will produce two instances to prove and explain what I am now advancing.

A certain great prince[61] raised a mighty army, filled his coffers with infinite treasures, provided an invincible fleet, and all this without giving the least part of his design to his greatest ministers or his nearest favourites. Immediately the whole world was alarmed, the neighbouring crowns in trembling expectation towards what point the storm would burst, the small politicians everywhere forming profound conjectures. Some believed he had laid a scheme for universal monarchy; others, after much insight, determined the matter to be a project for pulling down the Pope and setting up the Reformed religion, which had once been his own. Some again, of a deeper sagacity, sent him into Asia to subdue the Turk and recover Palestine. In the midst of all these projects and preparations, a certain state-surgeon,[62] gathering the nature of the disease by these symptoms, attempted the cure, at one blow performed the operation, broke the bag and out flew the vapour; nor did anything want to render it a complete remedy, only that the prince unfortunately happened to die in the performance. Now is the reader exceeding curious to learn from whence this vapour took its rise, which had so long set the nations at a gaze? What secret wheel, what hidden spring, could put into motion so wonderful an engine? It was afterwards discovered that the movement of this whole machine had been directed by an absent female, who was removed into an enemy's country. What should an unhappy prince do in such ticklish circumstances as these? He tried in vain the poet's never-failing receipt of *corpora quæque*, for

> "Idque petit corpus mens unde est saucia amore;
> Unde feritur, eo tendit, gestitque coire."—*Lucr.*

Having to no purpose used all peaceable endeavours, the collected part of the semen, raised and inflamed, became adust, converted to choler, turned head upon the spinal duct, and ascended to the brain. The very same principle that influences a bully to break the windows of a woman who has jilted him naturally stirs up a great prince to raise mighty armies and dream of nothing but sieges, battles, and victories.

The other instance is what I have read somewhere in a very ancient author of a mighty king,[63] who, for the space of above thirty years, amused himself to take and lose towns, beat armies and be beaten, drive princes out of their dominions, fright children from their bread and butter, burn, lay waste, plunder, dragoon, massacre subject and stranger, friend and foe, male and female. It is recorded that the philosophers of each country were in grave dispute upon causes natural, moral, and political, to find out where they should assign an original solution of this phenomenon. At last the vapour or spirit which animated the hero's brain, being in perpetual circulation, seized upon that region of the human body so renowned for furnishing the *zibeta occidentalis*,[64] and gathering there into a tumour, left the rest of the world for that time in peace. Of such mighty consequence is it where those exhalations fix, and of so little from whence they proceed. The same spirits which in their superior progress would conquer a kingdom descending upon the anus, conclude in a fistula.

Let us next examine the great introducers of new schemes in philosophy, and search till we can find from what faculty of the soul the disposition arises in mortal man of taking it into his head to advance new systems with such an eager zeal in things agreed on all hands impossible to be known; from what seeds this disposition springs, and to what quality of human nature these grand innovators have been indebted for their number of disciples, because it is plain that several of the chief among them, both ancient and modern, were usually mistaken by their adversaries, and, indeed, by all, except their own followers, to have been persons crazed or out of their wits, having generally proceeded in the common course of their words and actions by a method very different from the vulgar dictates of unrefined reason, agreeing for the most part in their several models with their present undoubted successors in the academy of modern Bedlam, whose merits and principles I shall further examine in due place. Of this kind were Epicurus, Diogenes, Apollonius, Lucretius, Paracelsus, Des Cartes, and others, who, if they were now in the world, tied fast and separate from their followers, would in this our undistinguishing age incur manifest danger of phlebotomy, and whips, and chains, and dark chambers, and straw. For what man in the natural state or course of thinking did ever conceive it in his power to reduce the notions of all mankind exactly to the same length, and breadth, and height of his own? Yet this is the first humble and civil design of all innovators in the empire of reason. Epicurus modestly hoped that one time or other a certain fortuitous concourse of all men's opinions, after perpetual jostlings, the sharp with the smooth, the light and the heavy, the round and the square, would, by certain clinamina, unite in the notions of atoms and void, as these did in the originals of all things. Cartesius reckoned to see before he died the sentiments of all philosophers, like so many lesser stars in his romantic system, rapt and drawn within his own vortex. Now I would gladly be informed how it is possible to account for such imaginations as these in particular men, without recourse to my phenomenon of vapours ascending from the lower faculties to overshadow the brain, and there distilling into conceptions, for which the narrowness of our mother-tongue has not yet assigned any other name beside that of madness or frenzy. Let us therefore now conjecture how it comes to pass that none of these great prescribers do ever fail providing themselves and their notions with a number of implicit disciples, and I think the reason is easy to be assigned, for there is a peculiar string in the harmony of human understanding, which in several individuals is exactly of the same tuning. This, if you can dexterously screw up to its right key, and then strike gently upon it whenever you have the good fortune to light among those of the same pitch, they will by a secret necessary sympathy strike exactly at the same time. And in this one circumstance lies all the skill or luck of the matter; for, if you chance to jar the string among those who are either above or below your own height, instead of subscribing to your doctrine, they will tie you fast, call you mad, and feed you with bread and water. It is therefore a point of the nicest conduct to distinguish and adapt this noble talent with respect to the differences of persons and of times. Cicero understood this very well, when, writing to a friend in England, with a caution, among other matters, to beware of being cheated by our hackney-coachmen (who, it seems, in those days were as arrant rascals as they are now), has these remarkable words, *Est quod gaudeas te in ista loca venisse, ubi aliquid sapere viderere.*[65] For to speak a bold truth, it is a fatal miscarriage so ill to order affairs as to pass for a fool in one company, when in another you might be treated as a philosopher; which I desire some certain gentlemen of my acquaintance to lay up in their hearts as a very seasonable innuendo.

This, indeed, was the fatal mistake of that worthy gentleman, my most ingenious friend Mr. Wotton, a person in appearance ordained for great designs as well as performances, whether you will consider his notions or his looks. Surely no man ever advanced into the public with fitter qualifications of body and mind for the propagation of a new religion. Oh, had those happy talents, misapplied to vain philosophy, been turned into their proper channels of dreams and visions, where distortion of mind and countenance are of such sovereign use, the base, detracting world would not then have dared to report that something is amiss, that his brain hath undergone an unlucky shake, which even his brother modernists themselves, like ungrates, do whisper so loud that it reaches up to the very garret I am now writing in.

Lastly, whoever pleases to look into the fountains of enthusiasm, from whence in all ages have eternally proceeded such fattening streams, will find the springhead to have been as troubled and muddy as the current. Of such great emolument is a tincture of this vapour, which the world calls madness, that without its help the world would not only be deprived of those two great blessings, conquests and systems, but even all mankind would unhappily be reduced to the same belief in things invisible. Now the former postulatum being held, that it is of no import from what originals this vapour proceeds, but either in what angles it strikes and spreads over the understanding, or upon what species of brain it ascends, it will be a very delicate point to cut the feather and divide the several reasons to a nice and curious reader, how this numerical difference in the brain can produce effects of so vast a difference from the same vapour as to be the sole point of individuation between Alexander the Great, Jack of Leyden, and Monsieur Des Cartes. The present argument is the most abstracted that ever I engaged in; it strains my faculties to their highest stretch, and I desire the reader to attend with utmost perpensity, for I now proceed to unravel this knotty point.

There is in mankind a certain . . . *Hic multa . . . desiderantur.* . . and this I take to be a clear solution of the matter.

Having, therefore, so narrowly passed through this intricate difficulty, the reader will, I am sure, agree with me in the conclusion that, if the moderns mean by madness only a disturbance or transposition of the brain, by force of certain vapours issuing up from the lower faculties, then has this madness been the parent of all those mighty revolutions that have happened in empire, in philosophy, and in religion. For the brain in its natural position and state of serenity disposeth its owner to pass his life in the common forms, without any thought of subduing multitudes to his own power, his reasons, or his visions, and the more he shapes his understanding by the pattern of human learning, the less he is inclined to form parties after his particular notions, because that instructs him in his private infirmities, as well as in the stubborn ignorance of the people. But when a man's fancy gets astride on his reason, when imagination is at cuffs with the senses, and common understanding as well as common sense is kicked out of doors, the first proselyte he makes is himself; and when that is once compassed, the difficulty is not so great in bringing over others, a strong delusion always operating from without as vigorously as from within. For cant and vision are to the ear and the eye the same that tickling is to the touch. Those entertainments and pleasures we most value in life are such as dupe and play the wag with the senses. For if we take an examination of what is generally understood by happiness, as it has respect either to the understanding or the senses we shall find all its properties and adjuncts will herd under this short definition, that it is a perpetual possession of being well deceived. And first, with relation to the mind or understanding, it is manifest what mighty advantages fiction has over truth, and the reason is just at our elbow: because imagination can build nobler scenes and produce more wonderful revolutions than fortune or Nature will be at the expense to furnish. Nor is mankind so much to blame in his choice thus determining him, if we consider that the debate merely lies between things past and things conceived, and so the question is only this: whether things that have place in the imagination may not as properly be said to exist as those that are seated in the memory? which may be justly held in the affirmative, and very much to the advantage of the former, since this is acknowledged to be the womb of things, and the other allowed to be no more than the grave. Again, if we take this definition of happiness and examine it with reference to the senses, it will be acknowledged wonderfully adapt. How sad and insipid do all objects accost us that are not conveyed in the vehicle of delusion! How shrunk is everything as it appears in the glass of Nature, so that if it were not for the assistance of artificial mediums, false lights, refracted angles, varnish, and tinsel, there would be a mighty level in the felicity and enjoyments of mortal men. If this were seriously considered by the world, as I have a certain reason to suspect it hardly will, men would no longer reckon among their high points of wisdom the art of exposing weak sides and publishing infirmities—an employment, in my opinion, neither better nor worse than that of unmasking, which, I think, has never been allowed fair usage, either in the world or the playhouse.

In the proportion that credulity is a more peaceful possession of the mind than curiosity, so far preferable is that wisdom which converses about the surface to that pretended philosophy which enters into the depths of things and then comes gravely back with informations and discoveries, that in the inside they are good for nothing. The two senses to which all objects first address themselves are the sight and the touch; these never examine farther than the colour, the shape, the size, and whatever other qualities dwell or are drawn by art upon the outward of bodies; and then comes reason officiously, with tools for cutting, and opening, and mangling, and piercing, offering to demonstrate that they are not of the same consistence quite through. Now I take all this to be the last degree of perverting Nature, one of whose eternal laws it is to put her best furniture forward. And therefore, in order to save the charges of all such expensive anatomy for the time to come, I do here think fit to inform the reader that in such conclusions as these reason is certainly in the right; and that in most corporeal beings which have fallen under my cognisance, the outside hath been infinitely preferable to the in, whereof I have been further convinced from some late experiments. Last week I saw a woman flayed, and you will hardly believe how much it altered her person for the worse. Yesterday I ordered the carcass of a beau to be stripped in my presence, when we were all amazed to find so many unsuspected faults under one suit of clothes. Then I laid open his brain, his heart, and his spleen, but I plainly perceived at every operation that the farther we proceeded, we found the defects increase upon us, in number and bulk; from all which I justly formed this conclusion to myself, that whatever philosopher or projector can find out an art to sodder and patch up the flaws and imperfections of Nature, will deserve much better of mankind and teach us a more useful science than that so much in present esteem, of widening and exposing them (like him who held anatomy to be the ultimate end of physic). And he whose fortunes and dispositions have placed him in a convenient station to enjoy the fruits of this noble art, he that can with Epicurus content his ideas with the films and images that fly off upon his senses from the superfices of things, such a man, truly wise, creams off Nature, leaving the sour and the dregs for philosophy and reason to lap up. This is the sublime and refined point of felicity called the possession of being well-deceived, the serene peaceful state of being a fool among knaves.

But to return to madness. It is certain that, according to the system I have above deduced, every species thereof proceeds from a redundancy of vapour; therefore, as some kinds of frenzy give double strength to the sinews, so there are of other species which add vigour, and life, and spirit to the brain. Now it usually happens that these active spirits, getting possession of the brain, resemble those that haunt other waste and empty dwellings, which for want of business either vanish and carry away a piece of the house, or else stay at home and fling it all out of the windows. By which are mystically displayed the two principal branches of madness, and which some philosophers, not considering so well as I, have mistook to be different in their causes, over-hastily assigning the first to deficiency and the other to redundance.

I think it therefore manifest, from what I have here advanced, that the main point of skill and address is to furnish employment for this redundancy of vapour, and prudently to adjust the seasons of it, by which means it may certainly become of cardinal and catholic emolument in a commonwealth. Thus one man, choosing a proper juncture, leaps into a gulf, from thence proceeds a hero, and is called the saviour of his country. Another achieves the same enterprise, but unluckily timing it, has left the brand of madness fixed as a reproach upon his memory. Upon so nice a distinction are we taught to repeat the name of Curtius with reverence and love, that of Empedocles with hatred and contempt. Thus also it is usually conceived that the elder Brutus only personated the fool and madman for the good of the public; but this was nothing else than a redundancy of the same vapour long misapplied, called by the Latins *ingenium par negotiis*, or (to translate it as nearly as I can), a sort of frenzy never in its right element till you take it up in business of the state.

Upon all which, and many other reasons of equal weight, though not equally curious, I do here gladly embrace an opportunity I have long sought for, of recommending it as a very noble undertaking to Sir Edward Seymour, Sir

Christopher Musgrave, Sir John Bowles, John Howe, Esq., and other patriots concerned, that they would move for leave to bring in a Bill for appointing commissioners to inspect into Bedlam and the parts adjacent, who shall be empowered to send for persons, papers, and records, to examine into the merits and qualifications of every student and professor, to observe with utmost exactness their several dispositions and behaviour, by which means, duly distinguishing and adapting their talents, they might produce admirable instruments for the several offices in a state, . . . civil and military, proceeding in such methods as I shall here humbly propose. And I hope the gentle reader will give some allowance to my great solicitudes in this important affair, upon account of that high esteem I have ever borne that honourable society, whereof I had some time the happiness to be an unworthy member.

Is any student tearing his straw in piecemeal, swearing and blaspheming, biting his grate, foaming at the mouth, and emptying his vessel in the spectators' faces? Let the right worshipful the Commissioners of Inspection give him a regiment of dragoons, and send him into Flanders among the rest. Is another eternally talking, sputtering, gaping, bawling, in a sound without period or article? What wonderful talents are here mislaid! Let him be furnished immediately with a green bag and papers, and threepence in his pocket,[66] and away with him to Westminster Hall. You will find a third gravely taking the dimensions of his kennel, a person of foresight and insight, though kept quite in the dark; for why, like Moses, *Ecce cornuta erat ejus facies.* He walks duly in one pace, entreats your penny with due gravity and ceremony, talks much of hard times, and taxes, and the whore of Babylon, bars up the wooden of his cell constantly at eight o'clock, dreams of fire, and shoplifters, and court-customers, and privileged places. Now what a figure would all these acquirements amount to if the owner were sent into the City among his brethren! Behold a fourth in much and deep conversation with himself, biting his thumbs at proper junctures, his countenance chequered with business and design; sometimes walking very fast, with his eyes nailed to a paper that he holds in his hands; a great saver of time, somewhat thick of hearing, very short of sight, but more of memory; a man ever in haste, a great hatcher and breeder of business, and excellent at the famous art of whispering nothing; a huge idolator of monosyllables and procrastination, so ready to give his word to everybody that he never keeps it; one that has forgot the common meaning of words, but an admirable retainer of the sound; extremely subject to the looseness, for his occasions are perpetually calling him away. If you approach his grate in his familiar intervals, "Sir," says he, "give me a penny and I'll sing you a song; but give me the penny first" (hence comes the common saying and commoner practice of parting with money for a song). What a complete system of court-skill is here described in every branch of it, and all utterly lost with wrong application! Accost the hole of another kennel, first stopping your nose, you will behold a surly, gloomy, nasty, slovenly mortal, raking in his own dung and dabbling in his urine. The best part of his diet is the reversion of his own ordure, which expiring into steams, whirls perpetually about, and at last reinfunds. His complexion is of a dirty yellow, with a thin scattered beard, exactly agreeable to that of his diet upon its first declination, like other insects, who, having their birth and education in an excrement, from thence borrow their colour and their smell. The student of this apartment is very sparing of his words, but somewhat over-liberal of his breath. He holds his hand out ready to receive your penny, and immediately upon receipt withdraws to his former occupations. Now is it not amazing to think the society of Warwick Lane[67] should have no more concern for the recovery of so useful a member, who, if one may judge from these appearances, would become the greatest ornament to that illustrious body? Another student struts up fiercely to your teeth, puffing with his lips, half squeezing out his eyes, and very graciously holds out his hand to kiss. The keeper desires you not to be afraid of this professor, for he will do you no hurt; to him alone is allowed the liberty of the ante-chamber, and the orator of the place gives you to understand that this solemn person is a tailor run mad with pride. This considerable student is adorned with many other qualities, upon which at present I shall not further enlarge. . . . Hark in your ear. . . . I am strangely mistaken if all his address, his motions, and his airs would not then be very natural and in their proper element.

I shall not descend so minutely as to insist upon the vast number of beaux, fiddlers, poets, and politicians that the world might recover by such a reformation, but what is more material, beside the clear gain redounding to the commonwealth by so large an acquisition of persons to employ, whose talents and acquirements, if I may be so bold to affirm it, are now buried or at least misapplied. It would be a mighty advantage accruing to the public from this inquiry that all these would very much excel and arrive at great perfection in their several kinds, which I think is manifest from what I have already shown, and shall enforce by this one plain instance, that even I myself, the author of these momentous truths, am a person whose imaginations are hard-mouthed and exceedingly disposed to run away with his reason, which I have observed from long experience to be a very light rider, and easily shook off; upon which account my friends will never trust me alone without a solemn promise to vent my speculations in this or the like manner, for the universal benefit of human kind, which perhaps the gentle, courteous, and candid reader, brimful of that modern charity and tenderness usually annexed to his office, will be very hardly persuaded to believe.

SECTION X: A FARTHER DIGRESSION

It is an unanswerable argument of a very refined age the wonderful civilities that have passed of late years between the nation of authors and that of readers. There can hardly pop out a play, a pamphlet, or a poem without a preface full of acknowledgments to the world for the general reception and applause they have given it, which the Lord knows where, or when, or how, or from whom it received. In due deference to so laudable a custom, I do here return my humble thanks to His Majesty and both Houses of Parliament, to the Lords of the King's most honourable Privy Council, to the reverend the Judges, to the Clergy, and Gentry, and Yeomanry of this land; but in a more especial manner to my worthy brethren and friends at Will's Coffee-house, and Gresham College, and Warwick Lane, and Moorfields, and Scotland Yard, and Westminster Hall, and Guildhall; in short, to all inhabitants and retainers whatsoever, either in court, or church, or camp, or city, or country, for their generosity and universal acceptance of this divine treatise. I accept their approbation and good opinion with extreme gratitude, and to the utmost of my poor capacity shall take hold of all opportunities to return the obligation.

I am also happy that fate has flung me into so blessed an age for the mutual felicity of booksellers and authors, whom I may safely affirm to be at this day the two only satisfied parties in England. Ask an author how his last piece has succeeded, "Why, truly he thanks his stars the world has been very favourable, and he has not the least reason to complain." And yet he wrote it in a week at bits and starts, when he could steal an hour from his urgent affairs, as it is a hundred to one you may see further in the preface, to which he refers you, and for the rest to the bookseller. There you go as a customer, and make the same question, "He blesses his God the thing takes wonderful; he is just printing a second edition, and has but three left in his shop." "You beat down the price; sir, we shall not differ," and in hopes of your custom another time, lets you have it as reasonable as you please; "And pray send as many of your acquaintance as you will; I shall upon your account furnish them all at the same rate."

Now it is not well enough considered to what accidents and occasions the world is indebted for the greatest part of those noble writings which hourly start up to entertain it. If it were not for a rainy day, a drunken vigil, a fit of the spleen, a course of physic, a sleepy Sunday, an ill run at dice, a long tailor's bill, a beggar's purse, a factious head, a hot sun, costive diet, want of books, and a just contempt of learning,—but for these events, I say, and some others too long to recite (especially a prudent neglect of taking brimstone inwardly), I doubt the number of authors and of writings would dwindle away to a degree most woeful to behold. To confirm this opinion, hear the words of the famous troglodyte philosopher. "It is certain," said he, "some grains of folly are of course annexed as part in the composition of human nature; only the choice is left us whether we please to wear them inlaid or embossed, and we need not go very far to seek how that is usually determined, when we remember it is with human faculties as with liquors, the lightest will be ever at the top."

There is in this famous island of Britain a certain paltry scribbler, very voluminous, whose character the reader cannot wholly be a stranger to. He deals in a pernicious kind of writings called "Second Parts," and usually passes under the name of "The Author of the First." I easily foresee that as soon as I lay down my pen this nimble operator will have stole it, and treat me as inhumanly as he has already done Dr. Blackmore, Lestrange, and many others who shall here be nameless. I therefore fly for justice and relief into the hands of that great rectifier of saddles and lover of mankind, Dr. Bentley, begging he will take this enormous grievance into his most modern consideration; and if it should so happen that the furniture of an ass in the shape of a second part must for my sins be clapped, by mistake, upon my back, that he will immediately please, in the presence of the world, to lighten me of the burthen, and take it home to his own house till the true beast thinks fit to call for it.

In the meantime, I do here give this public notice that my resolutions are to circumscribe within this discourse the whole stock of matter I have been so many years providing. Since my vein is once opened, I am content to exhaust it all at a running, for the peculiar advantage of my dear country, and for the universal benefit of mankind. Therefore, hospitably considering the number of my guests, they shall have my whole entertainment at a meal, and I scorn to set up the leavings in the cupboard. What the guests cannot eat may be given to the poor, and the dogs under the table may gnaw the bones.[68] This I understand for a more generous proceeding than to turn the company's stomachs by inviting them again to-morrow to a scurvy meal of scraps.

If the reader fairly considers the strength of what I have advanced in the foregoing section, I am convinced it will produce a wonderful revolution in his notions and opinions, and he will be abundantly better prepared to receive and to relish the concluding part of this miraculous treatise. Readers may be divided into three classes—the superficial, the ignorant, and the learned, and I have with much felicity fitted my pen to the genius and advantage of each. The superficial reader will be strangely provoked to laughter, which clears the breast and the lungs, is sovereign against the spleen, and the most innocent of all diuretics. The ignorant reader (between whom and the former the distinction is extremely nice) will find himself disposed to stare, which is an admirable remedy for ill eyes, serves to raise and enliven the spirits, and wonderfully helps perspiration. But the reader truly learned, chiefly for whose benefit I wake when others sleep, and sleep when others wake, will here find sufficient matter to employ his speculations for the rest of his life. It were much to be wished, and I do here humbly propose for an experiment, that every prince in Christendom will take seven of the deepest scholars in his dominions and shut them up close for seven years in seven chambers, with a command to write seven ample commentaries on this comprehensive discourse. I shall venture to affirm that, whatever difference may be found in their several conjectures, they will be all, without the least distortion, manifestly deducible from the text. Meantime it is my earnest request that so useful an undertaking may be entered upon (if their Majesties please) with all convenient speed, because I have a strong inclination before I leave the world to taste a blessing which we mysterious writers can seldom reach till we have got into our graves, whether it is that fame being a fruit grafted on the body, can hardly grow and much less ripen till the stock is in the earth, or whether she be a bird of prey, and is lured among the rest to pursue after the scent of a carcass, or whether she conceives her trumpet sounds best and farthest when she stands on a tomb, by the advantage of a rising ground and the echo of a hollow vault.

It is true, indeed, the republic of dark authors, after they once found out this excellent expedient of dying, have been peculiarly happy in the variety as well as extent of their reputation. For night being the universal mother of things, wise philosophers hold all writings to be fruitful in the proportion they are dark, and therefore the true illuminated (that is to say, the darkest of all) have met with such numberless commentators, whose scholiastic midwifery hath delivered them of meanings that the authors themselves perhaps never conceived, and yet may very justly be allowed the lawful parents of them, the words of such writers being like seed, which, however scattered at random, when they light upon a fruitful ground, will multiply far beyond either the hopes or imagination of the sower.

And therefore, in order to promote so useful a work, I will here take leave to glance a few innuendos that may be of great assistance to those sublime spirits who shall be appointed to labour in a universal comment upon this wonderful discourse. And first, I have couched a very profound mystery in the number of 0's multiplied by seven and divided by nine. Also, if a devout brother of the Rosy Cross will pray fervently for sixty-three mornings with a lively faith, and then transpose certain letters and syllables according to prescription, in the second and fifth section they will certainly reveal into a full receipt of the *opus magnum*. Lastly, whoever will be at the pains to calculate the whole number of each letter in this treatise, and sum up the difference exactly between the several numbers, assigning the true natural cause for every such difference, the discoveries in the product will plentifully reward his labour. But then he must beware of Bythus and Sigè, and be sure not to forget the qualities of Acamoth; *a cujus lacrymis humecta prodit substantia, à risu lucida, à tristitiâ solida, et à timore mobilis,* wherein Eugenius Philalethes[69] hath committed an unpardonable mistake.

SECTION XI: A TALE OF A TUB

After so wide a compass as I have wandered, I do now gladly overtake and close in with my subject, and shall henceforth hold on with it an even pace to the end of my journey, except some beautiful prospect appears within sight of my way, whereof, though at present I have neither warning nor expectation, yet upon such an accident, come when it will, I shall beg my reader's favour and company, allowing me to conduct him through it along with myself. For in writing it is as in travelling. If a man is in haste to be at home (which I acknowledge to be none of my case, having never so little business as when I am there), if his horse be tired with long riding and ill ways, or be naturally a jade, I advise him clearly to make the straightest and the commonest road, be it ever so dirty; but then surely we must own such a man to be a scurvy companion at best. He spatters himself and his fellow-travellers at every step. All their thoughts, and wishes, and conversation turn entirely upon the subject of their journey's end, and at every splash, and plunge, and stumble they heartily wish one another at the devil.

On the other side, when a traveller and his horse are in heart and plight, when his purse is full and the day before him, he takes the road only where it is clean or convenient, entertains his company there as agreeably as he can, but upon the first occasion carries them along with him to every delightful scene in view, whether of art, of Nature, or of both; and if they chance to refuse out of stupidity or weariness, let them jog on by themselves, and be d—n'd. He'll overtake them at the next town, at which arriving, he rides furiously through, the men, women, and children run out to gaze, a hundred noisy curs run barking after him, of which, if he honours the boldest with a lash of his whip, it is rather out of sport than revenge. But should some sourer mongrel dare too near an approach, he receives a salute on the chaps by an accidental stroke from the courser's heels, nor is any ground lost by the blow, which sends him yelping and limping home.

I now proceed to sum up the singular adventures of my renowned Jack, the state of whose dispositions and fortunes the careful reader does, no doubt, most exactly remember, as I last parted with them in the conclusion of a former section. Therefore, his next care must be from two of the foregoing to extract a scheme of notions that may best fit his understanding for a true relish of what is to ensue.

Jack had not only calculated the first revolution of his brain so prudently as to give rise to that epidemic sect of Æolists, but succeeding also into a new and strange variety of conceptions, the fruitfulness of his imagination led him into certain notions which, although in appearance very unaccountable, were not without their mysteries and their meanings, nor wanted followers to countenance and improve them. I shall therefore be extremely careful and exact in recounting such material passages of this nature as I have been able to collect either from undoubted tradition or indefatigable reading, and shall describe them as graphically as it is possible, and as far as notions of that height and latitude can be brought within the compass of a pen. Nor do I at all question but they will furnish plenty of noble matter for such whose converting imaginations dispose them to reduce all things into types, who can make shadows—no thanks to the sun—and then mould them into substances—no thanks to philosophy—whose peculiar talent lies in fixing tropes and allegories to the letter, and refining what is literal into figure and mystery.

Jack had provided a fair copy of his father's will, engrossed in form upon a large skin of parchment, and resolving to act the part of a most dutiful son, he became the fondest creature of it imaginable. For although, as I have often told the reader, it consisted wholly in certain plain, easy directions about the management and wearing of their coats, with legacies and penalties in case of obedience or neglect, yet he began to entertain a fancy that the matter was deeper and darker, and therefore must needs have a great deal more of mystery at the bottom. "Gentlemen," said he, "I will prove this very skin of parchment to be meat, drink, and cloth, to be the philosopher's stone and the universal medicine." In consequence of which raptures he resolved to make use of it in the most necessary as well as the most paltry occasions of life. He had a way of working it into any shape he pleased, so that it served him for a nightcap when he went to bed, and for an umbrella in rainy weather. He would lap a piece of it about a sore toe; or, when he had fits, burn two inches under his nose; or, if anything lay heavy on his stomach, scrape off and swallow as much of the powder as would lie on a silver penny—they were all infallible remedies. With analogy to these refinements, his common talk and conversation ran wholly in the praise of his Will, and he circumscribed the utmost of his eloquence within that compass, not daring to let slip a syllable without authority from thence. Once at a strange house he was suddenly taken short upon an urgent juncture, whereon it may not be allowed too particularly to dilate, and being not able to call to mind, with that suddenness the occasion required, an authentic phrase for demanding the way to the back, he chose rather, as the more prudent course, to incur the penalty in such cases usually annexed; neither was it possible for the united rhetoric of mankind to prevail with him to make himself clean again, because, having consulted the will upon this emergency, he met with a passage near the bottom (whether foisted in by the transcriber is not known) which seemed to forbid it.[70]

He made it a part of his religion never to say grace to his meat, nor could all the world persuade him, as the common phrase is, to eat his victuals like a Christian.[71]

He bore a strange kind of appetite to snap-dragon and to the livid snuffs of a burning candle,[72] which he would catch and swallow with an agility wonderful to conceive; and by this procedure maintained a perpetual flame in his belly, which issuing in a glowing steam from both his eyes, as well as his nostrils and his mouth, made his head appear in a dark night like the skull of an ass wherein a roguish boy hath conveyed a farthing-candle, to the terror of his Majesty's liege subjects. Therefore he made use of no other expedient to light himself home, but was wont to say that a wise man was his own lanthorn.

He would shut his eyes as he walked along the streets, and if he happened to bounce his head against a post or fall into the kennel (as he seldom missed either to do one or both), he would tell the gibing apprentices who looked on that he submitted with entire resignation, as to a trip or a blow of fate, with whom he found by long experience how vain it was either to wrestle or to cuff, and whoever durst undertake to do either would be sure to come off with a swingeing fall or a bloody nose. "It was ordained," said he,[73] "some few days before the creation, that my nose and this very post should have a rencounter, and therefore Providence thought fit to send us both into the world in the same age, and to make us countrymen and fellow-citizens. Now, had my eyes been open, it is very likely the business might have been a great deal worse, for how many a confounded slip is daily got by man with all his foresight about him. Besides, the eyes of the understanding see best when those of the senses are out of the way, and therefore blind men are observed to tread their steps with much more caution, and conduct, and judgment than those who rely with too much confidence upon the virtue of the visual nerve, which every little accident shakes out of order, and a drop or a film can wholly disconcert; like a lanthorn among a pack of roaring bullies when they scour the streets, exposing its owner and itself to outward kicks and buffets, which both might have escaped if the vanity of appearing would have suffered them to walk in the dark. But further, if we examine the conduct of these boasted lights, it will prove yet a great deal worse than their fortune. It is true I have broke my nose against this post, because Providence either forgot, or did not think it convenient, to twitch me by the elbow and give me notice to avoid it. But let not this encourage either the present age of posterity to trust their noses unto the keeping of their eyes, which may prove the fairest way of losing them for good and all. For, O ye eyes, ye blind guides, miserable guardians are ye of our frail noses; ye, I say, who fasten upon the first precipice in view, and then tow our wretched willing bodies after you to the very brink of destruction. But alas! that brink is rotten, our feet slip, and we tumble down prone into a gulf, without one hospitable shrub in the way to break the fall—a fall to which not any nose of mortal make is equal, except that of the giant Laurcalco,[74] who was Lord of the Silver Bridge. Most properly, therefore, O eyes, and with great justice, may you be compared to those foolish lights which conduct men through dirt and darkness till they fall into a deep pit or a noisome bog."

This I have produced as a scantling of Jack's great eloquence and the force of his reasoning upon such abstruse matters.

He was, besides, a person of great design and improvement in affairs of devotion, having introduced a new deity, who has since met with a vast number of worshippers, by some called Babel, by others Chaos, who had an ancient temple of Gothic structure upon Salisbury plain, famous for its shrine and celebration by pilgrims.

When he had some roguish trick to play, he would down with his knees, up with his eyes, and fall to prayers though in the midst of the kennel. Then it was that those who understood his pranks would be sure to get far enough out of his way; and whenever curiosity attracted strangers to laugh or to listen, he would of a sudden bespatter them with mud.

In winter he went always loose and unbuttoned, and clad as thin as possible to let in the ambient heat, and in summer lapped himself close and thick to keep it out.[75]

In all revolutions of government, he would make his court for the office of hangman-general, and in the exercise of that dignity, wherein he was very dexterous, would make use of no other vizard than a long prayer.

He had a tongue so musculous and subtile, that he could twist it up into his nose and deliver a strange kind of speech from thence. He was also the first in these kingdoms who began to improve the Spanish accomplishment of braying; and having large ears perpetually exposed and erected, he carried his art to such a perfection, that it was a point of great difficulty to distinguish either by the view or the sound between the original and the copy.

He was troubled with a disease the reverse to that called the stinging of the tarantula, and would run dog-mad at the noise of music, especially a pair of bagpipes.[76] But he would cure himself again by taking two or three turns in Westminster Hall, or Billingsgate, or in a boarding-school, or the Royal Exchange, or a state coffee-house.

He was a person that feared no colours, but mortally hated all, and upon that account bore a cruel aversion to painters, insomuch that in his paroxysms as he walked the streets, he would have his pockets loaded with stones to pelt at the signs.[77]

Having from his manner of living frequent occasions to wash himself, he would often leap over head and ears into the water, though it were in the midst of the winter, but was always observed to come out again much dirtier, if possible, than he went in.[78]

He was the first that ever found out the secret of contriving a soporiferous medicine to be conveyed in at the ears.[79] It was a compound of sulphur and balm of Gilead, with a little pilgrim's salve.

He wore a large plaister of artificial caustics on his stomach, with the fervour of which he could set himself a groaning like the famous board upon application of a red-hot iron.

He would stand in the turning of a street, and calling to those who passed by, would cry to one, "Worthy sir, do me the honour of a good slap in the chaps;" to another, "Honest friend, pray favour me with a handsome kick in the rear;" "Madam, shall I entreat a small box in the ear from your ladyship's fair hands?" "Noble captain, lend a reasonable thwack, for the love of God, with that cane of yours over these poor shoulders." And when he had by such earnest solicitations made a shift to procure a basting sufficient to swell up his fancy and his sides, he would return home extremely comforted, and full of terrible accounts of what he had undergone for the public good. "Observe this stroke," said he, showing his bare shoulders; "a plaguy janissary gave it me this very morning at seven o'clock, as, with much ado, I was driving off the Great Turk. Neighbours mine, this broken head deserves a plaister; had poor Jack been tender of his noddle, you would have seen the Pope and the French King long before this time of day among your wives and your warehouses. Dear Christians, the Great Moghul was come as far as Whitechapel, and you may thank these poor sides that he hath not—God bless us —already swallowed up man, woman, and child."

It was highly worth observing the singular effects of that aversion or antipathy which Jack and his brother Peter seemed, even to affectation, to bear towards each other. Peter had lately done some rogueries that forced him to abscond, and he seldom ventured to stir out before night for fear of bailiffs. Their lodgings were at the two most distant parts of the town from each other, and whenever their occasions or humours called them abroad, they would make choice of the oddest, unlikely times, and most uncouth rounds that they could invent, that they might be sure to avoid one another. Yet, after all this, it was their perpetual fortune to meet, the reason of which is easy enough to apprehend, for the frenzy and the spleen of both having the same foundation, we may look upon them as two pair of compasses equally extended, and the fixed foot of each remaining in the same centre, which, though moving contrary ways at first, will be sure to encounter somewhere or other in the circumference. Besides, it was among the great misfortunes of Jack to bear a huge personal resemblance with his brother Peter. Their humour and dispositions were not only the same, but there was a close analogy in their shape, their size, and their mien; insomuch as nothing was more frequent than for a bailiff to seize Jack by the shoulders and cry, "Mr. Peter, you are the king's prisoner;" or, at other times, for one of Peter's nearest friends to accost Jack with open arms: "Dear Peter, I am glad to see thee; pray send me one of your best medicines for the worms." This, we may suppose, was a mortifying return of those pains and proceedings Jack had laboured in so long, and finding how directly opposite all his endeavours had answered to the sole end and intention which he had proposed to himself, how could it avoid having terrible effects upon a head and heart so furnished as his? However, the poor remainders of his coat bore all the punishment. The orient sun never entered upon his diurnal progress without missing a piece of it. He hired a tailor to stitch up the collar so close that it was ready to choke him, and squeezed out his eyes at such a rate as one could see nothing but the white. What little was left of the main substance of the coat he rubbed every day for two hours against a rough-cast wall, in order to grind away the remnants of lace and embroidery, but at the same time went on with so much violence that he proceeded a heathen philosopher. Yet after all he could do of this kind, the success continued still to disappoint his expectation, for as it is the nature of rags to bear a kind of mock resemblance to finery, there being a sort of fluttering appearance in both, which is not to be distinguished at a distance in the dark or by short-sighted eyes, so in those junctures it fared with Jack and his tatters, that they offered to the first view a ridiculous flaunting, which, assisting the resemblance in person and air, thwarted all his projects of separation, and left so near a similitude between them as frequently deceived the very disciples and followers of both . . . *Desunt nonnulla*, . . .

The old Sclavonian proverb said well that it is with men as with asses; whoever would keep them fast must find a very good hold at their ears. Yet I think we may affirm, and it hath been verified by repeated experience, that—

"Effugiet tamen hæc sceleratus vincula Proteus."[80]

It is good, therefore, to read the maxims of our ancestors with great allowances to times and persons; for if we look into primitive records we shall find that no revolutions have been so great or so frequent as those of human ears. In former days there was a curious invention to catch and keep them, which I think we may justly reckon among the *artes perditæ*; and how can it be otherwise, when in these latter centuries the very species is not only diminished to a very lamentable degree, but the poor remainder is also degenerated so far as to mock our skilfullest tenure? For if only the slitting of one ear in a stag hath been found sufficient to propagate the defect through a whole forest, why should we wonder at the greatest consequences, from so many loppings and mutilations to which the ears of our fathers and our own have been of late so much exposed? It is true, indeed, that while this island of ours was under the dominion of grace, many endeavours were made to improve the growth of ears once more among us. The proportion of largeness was not only looked upon as an ornament of the outward man, but as a type of grace in the inward. Besides, it is held by naturalists that if there be a protuberancy of parts in the superior region of the body, as in the ears and nose, there must be a parity also in the inferior; and therefore in that truly pious age the males in every assembly, according as they were gifted, appeared very forward in exposing their ears to view, and the regions about them; because Hippocrates[81] tells us that when the vein behind the ear happens to be cut, a man becomes a eunuch, and the females were nothing backwarder in beholding and edifying by them; whereof those who had already used the means looked about them with great concern, in hopes of conceiving a suitable offspring by such a prospect; others, who stood candidates for benevolence, found there a plentiful choice, and were sure to fix upon such as discovered the largest ears, that the breed might not dwindle between them. Lastly, the devouter sisters, who looked upon all extraordinary dilatations of that member as protrusions of zeal, or spiritual excrescences, were sure to honour every head they sat upon as if they had been cloven tongues, but especially that of the preacher, whose ears were usually of the prime magnitude, which upon that account he was very frequent and exact in exposing with all advantages to the people in his rhetorical paroxysms, turning sometimes to hold forth the one, and sometimes to hold forth the other; from which custom the whole operation of preaching is to this very day among their professors styled by the phrase of holding forth.

Such was the progress of the saints for advancing the size of that member, and it is thought the success would have been every way answerable, if in process of time a cruel king had not arose, who raised a bloody persecution against all ears above a certain standard;[82] upon which some were glad to hide their flourishing sprouts in a black border, others crept wholly under a periwig; some were slit, others cropped, and a great number sliced off to the stumps. But of this more hereafter in my general "History of Ears," which I design very speedily to bestow upon the public.

From this brief survey of the falling state of ears in the last age, and the small care had to advance their ancient growth in the present, it is manifest how little reason we can have to rely upon a hold so short, so weak, and so slippery; and that whoever desires to catch mankind fast must have recourse to some other methods. Now he that will examine human nature with circumspection enough may discover several handles, whereof the six[83] senses afford one apiece, beside a great number that are screwed to the passions, and some few riveted to the intellect. Among these last, curiosity is one, and of all others affords the firmest grasp;

curiosity, that spur in the side, that bridle in the mouth, that ring in the nose of a lazy, an impatient, and a grunting reader. By this handle it is that an author should seize upon his readers; which as soon as he hath once compassed, all resistance and struggling are in vain, and they become his prisoners as close as he pleases, till weariness or dulness force him to let go his grip.

And therefore I, the author of this miraculous treatise, having hitherto, beyond expectation, maintained by the aforesaid handle a firm hold upon my gentle readers, it is with great reluctance that I am at length compelled to remit my grasp, leaving them in the perusal of what remains to that natural oscitancy inherent in the tribe. I can only assure thee, courteous reader, for both our comforts, that my concern is altogether equal to thine, for my unhappiness in losing or mislaying among my papers the remaining part of these memoirs, which consisted of accidents, turns, and adventures, both new, agreeable, and surprising, and therefore calculated in all due points to the delicate taste of this our noble age. But alas! with my utmost endeavours I have been able only to retain a few of the heads. Under which there was a full account how Peter got a protection out of the King's Bench, and of a reconcilement between Jack and him, upon a design they had in a certain rainy night to trepan brother Martin into a spunging-house, and there strip him to the skin. How Martin, with much ado, showed them both a fair pair of heels. How a new warrant came out against Peter, upon which Jack left him in the lurch, stole his protection, and made use of it himself. How Jack's tatters came into fashion in court and city; how he got upon a great horse and ate custard.[84] But the particulars of all these, with several others which have now slid out of my memory, are lost beyond all hopes of recovery. For which misfortune, leaving my readers to condole with each other as far as they shall find it to agree with their several constitutions, but conjuring them by all the friendship that has passed between us, from the title-page to this, not to proceed so far as to injure their healths for an accident past remedy, I now go on to the ceremonial part of an accomplished writer, and therefore by a courtly modern least of all others to be omitted.

THE CONCLUSION

Going too long is a cause of abortion as effectual, though not so frequent, as going too short, and holds true especially in the labours of the brain. Well fare the heart of that noble Jesuit[85] who first adventured to confess in print that books must be suited to their several seasons, like dress, and diet, and diversions; and better fare our noble notion for refining upon this among other French modes. I am living fast to see the time when a book that misses its tide shall be neglected as the moon by day, or like mackerel a week after the season. No man has more nicely observed our climate than the bookseller who bought the copy of this work. He knows to a tittle what subjects will best go off in a dry year, and which it is proper to expose foremost when the weather-glass is fallen to much rain. When he had seen this treatise and consulted his almanac upon it, he gave me to understand that he had manifestly considered the two principal things, which were the bulk and the subject, and found it would never take but after a long vacation, and then only in case it should happen to be a hard year for turnips. Upon which I desired to know, considering my urgent necessities, what he thought might be acceptable this month. He looked westward and said, "I doubt we shall have a bit of bad weather. However, if you could prepare some pretty little banter (but not in verse), or a small treatise upon the it would run like wildfire. But if it hold up, I have already hired an author to write something against Dr. Bentley, which I am sure will turn to account."

At length we agreed upon this expedient, that when a customer comes for one of these, and desires in confidence to know the author, he will tell him very privately as a friend, naming whichever of the wits shall happen to be that week in the vogue, and if Durfey's last play should be in course, I had as lieve he may be the person as Congreve. This I mention, because I am wonderfully well acquainted with the present relish of courteous readers, and have often observed, with singular pleasure, that a fly driven from a honey-pot will immediately, with very good appetite, alight and finish his meal on an excrement.

I have one word to say upon the subject of profound writers, who are grown very numerous of late, and I know very well the judicious world is resolved to list me in that number. I conceive, therefore, as to the business of being profound, that it is with writers as with wells. A person with good eyes can see to the bottom of the deepest, provided any water be there; and that often when there is nothing in the world at the bottom besides dryness and dirt, though it be but a yard and half under ground, it shall pass, however, for wondrous deep, upon no wiser a reason than because it is wondrous dark.

I am now trying an experiment very frequent among modern authors, which is to write upon nothing, when the subject is utterly exhausted to let the pen still move on; by some called the ghost of wit, delighting to walk after the death of its body. And to say the truth, there seems to be no part of knowledge in fewer hands than that of discerning when to have done. By the time that an author has written out a book, he and his readers are become old acquaintance, and grow very loathe to part; so that I have sometimes known it to be in writing as in visiting, where the ceremony of taking leave has employed more time than the whole conversation before. The conclusion of a treatise resembles the conclusion of human life, which has sometimes been compared to the end of a feast, where few are satisfied to depart *ut plenus vitæ conviva*. For men will sit down after the fullest meal, though it be only to dose or to sleep out the rest of the day. But in this latter I differ extremely from other writers, and shall be too proud if, by all my labours, I can have any ways contributed to the repose of mankind in times so turbulent and unquiet as these. Neither do I think such an employment so very alien from the office of a wit as some would suppose; for among a very polite nation in Greece[86] there were the same temples built and consecrated to Sleep and the Muses, between which two deities they believed the strictest friendship was established.

I have one concluding favour to request of my reader, that he will not expect to be equally diverted and informed by every line or every page of this discourse, but give some allowance to the author's spleen and short fits or intervals of dulness, as well as his own, and lay it seriously to his conscience whether, if he were walking the streets in dirty weather or a rainy day, he would allow it fair dealing in folks at their ease from a window, to criticise his gate and ridicule his dress at such a juncture.

In my disposure of employments of the brain, I have thought fit to make invention the master, and to give method and reason the office of its lackeys. The cause of this distribution was from observing it my peculiar case to be often under a temptation of being witty upon occasion where I could be neither wise nor sound, nor anything to the matter in hand. And I am too much a servant of the modern way to neglect any such opportunities, whatever pains or improprieties I may be at to introduce them. For I have observed that from a laborious collection of seven hundred and thirty-eight flowers and shining hints of the best modern authors, digested with great reading into my book of common places, I have not been able after five years to draw, hook, or force into common conversation any more than a dozen. Of which dozen the one moiety failed of success by being dropped among unsuitable company, and the other cost me so many strains, and traps, and ambages to introduce, that I at length resolved to give it over. Now this disappointment (to discover a secret), I must own, gave me the first hint of setting up for an author, and I have since found among some particular friends that it is become a very general complaint, and has produced the same effects upon many others. For I have remarked many a towardly word to be wholly neglected or despised in discourse, which hath passed very smoothly with some consideration and esteem after its preferment and sanction in print. But now, since, by the liberty and encouragement of the press, I am grown absolute master of the occasions and opportunities to expose the talents I have acquired, I already discover that the issues of my observanda begin to grow too large for the receipts. Therefore I shall here pause awhile, till I find, by feeling the world's pulse and my own, that it will be of absolute necessity for us both to resume my pen.

1. The number of livings in England.—*Pate.*
2. "Distinguished, new, told by no other tongue."—*Horace.*
3. "Reading prefaces, &c."—*Swift's note in the margin.*
4. Plutarch.—*Swift's note in the margin.*
5. Xenophon.—*Swift's note in the margin, marked, in future, S.*
6. Spleen.—*Horace.*
7. "But to return, and view the cheerful skies,
      In this the task and mighty labour lies." — Dryden's *"Virgil"*
8. "That the old may withdraw into safe ease."
9. In his subsequent apology for "The Tale of a Tub," Swift wrote of these machines that, "In the original manuscript there was a description of a fourth, which those who had the papers in their power blotted out, as having something in it of satire that I suppose they thought was too particular; and therefore they were forced to change it to the number three, whence some have endeavoured to squeeze out a dangerous meaning that was never thought on. And indeed the conceit was half spoiled by changing the numbers; that of four being much more cabalistic, and therefore better exposing the pretended virtue of numbers, a superstition then intended to be ridiculed."
10. "Under the rainy sky, in the meetings of three and of four ways."
11. Lucretius, lib. 2.—S.
12. "'Tis certain, then, the voice that thus can wound;
      Is all material body, every sound."
13. To be burnt or worm-eaten.
14. The Royal Society first met at Gresham College, the resort of men of science. Will's Coffee-House was the resort of wits and men of letters.
15. Viz., about moving the earth.—S.
16. "Virtuoso experiments and modern comedies."—S.
17. He lived a thousand.—S.
18. Viz., in the year 1697.—S. Dryden died in 1700, and the publication of the "Tale of a Tub," written in 1697, was not until 1704.
19. The title-page in the original was so torn that it was not possible to recover several titles which the author here speaks of.—S.
20. See Virgil translated, &c.—S.
21. Peter, the Church of Rome; Martin, the Reformed Church as established by authority in England; Jack, the dissenters from the English Church Establishment. Martin, named probably from Martin Luther; Jack, from John Calvin. The coats are the coats of righteousness, in which all servants of God should be clothed; alike in love and duty, however they may differ in opinion.
22. Covetousness, ambition, and pride, which were the three great vices that the ancient fathers inveighed against as the first corruptions of Christianity.— *W. Wotton.*
23. The tailor.
24. A sacred monkey.
25. The Roman Catholics were considered by the Reformers to have added to the simple doctrines of Christianity inventions of their own, and to have laid especial stress on the adoption of them. Upon Swift's saying of the three brothers, "Now the coats their father had left them were, it is true, of very good cloth, and besides so neatly sewn that you would swear they were all of a piece, but, at the same time, very plain, with little or no ornament," W. Wotton observes: "This is the distinguishing character of the Christian religion. *Christiana religio absoluta et simplex*, was Ammianus Marcellinus's description of it, who was himself a heathen." But the learned Peter argues that if a doctrine cannot be found, *totidem verbis*, in so many words, it may be found in so many syllables, or, if that way fail, we shall make them out in a third way, of so many letters.
26. *Quibusdam veteribus codicibus* [some ancient MSS.].—S.
27. There are two kinds—oral tradition and the written record,—reference to the value attached to tradition in the Roman Church.
28. The flame-coloured lining figures the doctrine of Purgatory; and the codicil annexed, the Apocryphal books annexed to the Bible. The dog-keeper is said to be an allusion to the Apocryphal book of Tobit.
29. Dread hell and subdue their lusts.
30. Strained glosses and interpretations of the simple text.
31. Images in churches.

32. The locking up of the Gospel in the original Greek or in the Latin of the Vulgate, and forbidding its diffusion in the language of the people.
33. The Pope's bulls and decretals, issued by his paternal authority, that must determine questions of interpretation and tradition, or else many absurd things would follow.
34. Constantine the Great, from whom the Church of Rome was said to have received the donation of St. Peter's patrimony, and first derived the wealth described by our old Reformers as "the fatal gift of Constantine."
35. See Wotton "Of Ancient and Modern Learning."—S.
36. Satire and panegyric upon critics.—S.
37. *Vide* excerpta ex eo apud Photium—S.
38. "Near Helicon and round the learned hill
    Grow trees whose blossoms with their odour kill."—*Hawkesworth*.
39. A quotation after the manner of a great author. *Vide* Bentley's "Dissertation," &c.—S.
40. "And how they're disappointed when they're pleased."—*Congreve, quoted by Pate*.
41. Refusing the cup of sacrament to the laity. Thomas Warton observes on the following passage its close resemblance to the speech of Panurge in Rabelais, and says that Swift formed himself upon Rabelais.
42. Transubstantiation.
43. The Reformation.
44. The cross (*in hoc signo vinces*). Pieces of the wood said to be part of it were many in the churches.
45. One miracle to be believed was that the Chapel of Loretto travelled from the Holy Land to Italy.
46. Made a true copy of the Bible in the language of the people.
47. Gave the cup to the laity.
48. Allowed marriages of priests.
49. Homerus omnes res humanas poematis complexus est.—*Xenophon in Conviv.*—S.
50. A treatise written about fifty years ago by a Welsh gentleman of Cambridge. His name, as I remember, Vaughan, as appears by the answer to it by the learned Dr. Henry More. It is a piece of the most unintelligible fustian that perhaps was ever published in any language.—S. This piece was by the brother of Henry Vaughan, the poet.
51. After the changes made by Martin that transformed the Church of Rome into the Church of England, Jack's proceedings made a rent from top to bottom by the separation of the Presbyterians from the Church Establishment.
52. The galleries over the piazzas in the old Royal Exchange were formerly filled with shops, kept chiefly by women. Illustrations of this feature in London life are to be found in Dekker's "Shoemaker's Holiday," and other plays.
53. The contraction of the word mobile to mob first appeared in the time of Charles the Second.
54. Jack the Bald, Calvin, from calvus, bald; Jack with a Lanthorn, professing inward lights, Quakers; Dutch Jack, Jack of Leyden, Anabaptists; French Hugh, the Huguenots; Tom the Beggar, the Gueuses of Flanders; Knocking Jack of the North, John Knox of Scotland. Æolists pretenders to inspiration.
55. Herodotus, l. 4.—S.
56. Bombast von Hohenheim—Paracelsus.
57. Fanatical preachers of rebellion.
58. Pausanias, l. 8.—S.
59. The Quakers allowed women to preach.
60. The worshippers of wind or air found their evil spirits in the chameleon, by which it was eaten, and the windmill, Moulin-à-vent, by whose four hands it was beaten.
61. Henry IV. of France.
62. Ravaillac, who stabbed Henry IV.
63. Swift's contemporary, Louis XIV. of France.
64. Western civet. Paracelsus was said to have endeavoured to extract a perfume from human excrement that might become as fashionable as civet from the cat. It was called *zibeta occidentalis*, the back being, according to Paracelsus, the western part of the body.
65. Ep. Fam. vii. 10, to Trebatius, who, as the next sentence in the letter shows, had not gone into England.
66. A lawyer's coach-hire.—S.
67. The College of Physicians.
68. The bad critics.

69. A name under which Thomas Vaughan wrote.
70. Revelations xxii. 11: "He which is filthy, let him be filthy still;" "phrase of the will," being Scripture phrase, of either Testament, applied to every occasion, and often in the most unbecoming manner.
71. He did not kneel when he received the Sacrament.
72. His inward lights.
73. Predestination.
74. *Vide* Don Quixote.—S.
75. Swift borrowed this from the customs of Moronia—Fool's Land—in Joseph Hall's *Mundus Alter et Idem*.
76. The Presbyterians objected to church-music, and had no organs in their meeting-houses.
77. Opposed to the decoration of church walls.
78. Baptism by immersion.
79. Preaching.
80. "This wicked Proteus shall escape the chain."—*Francis's Horace.*
81. Lib. de Aëre, Locis, et Aquis.—S.
82. Charles II., by the Act of Uniformity, which drove two thousand ministers of religion, including some of the most devout, in one day out of the Church of England.
83. "Including Scaliger's," is Swift's note in the margin. The sixth sense was the "common sense" which united and conveyed to the mind as one whole the information brought in by the other five. Common sense did not originally mean the kind of sense common among the people generally. A person wanting in common sense was one whose brain did not properly combine impressions brought into it by the eye, the ear, &c.
84. Reference here is to the exercise by James II. of a dispensing power which illegally protected Roman Catholics, and incidentally Dissenters also; to the consequent growth of feeling against the Roman Catholics. "Jack on a great horse and eating custard" represents what was termed the occasional conformity of men who "blasphemed custard through the nose," but complied with the law that required them to take Sacrament in the Church of England as qualification for becoming a Lord Mayor or holding any office of public authority.
85. Père d'Orleans.—S.
86. Trazenii, Pausan. L. 2.—S.

THE HISTORY OF MARTIN

THE HISTORY OF MARTIN

GIVING AN ACCOUNT OF HIS DEPARTURE
FROM JACK, AND THEIR SETTING UP FOR
THEMSELVES, ON WHICH ACCOUNT THEY
WERE OBLIGED TO TRAVEL, AND MEET MANY
DISASTERS; FINDING NO SHELTER NEAR
PETER'S HABITATION, MARTIN SUCCEEDS IN
THE NORTH; PETER THUNDERS AGAINST
MARTIN FOR THE LOSS OF THE LARGE
REVENUE HE USED TO RECEIVE FROM
THENCE; HARRY HUFF SENT MARLIN A
CHALLENGE IN FIGHT, WHICH HE RECEIVED;
PETER REWARDS HARRY FOR THE
PRETENDED VICTORY, WHICH ENCOURAGED
HARRY TO HUFF PETER ALSO; WITH MANY
OTHER EXTRAORDINARY ADVENTURES OF
THE SAID MARTIN IN SEVERAL PLACES WITH
MANY CONSIDERABLE PERSONS.

How Jack and Martin, being parted, set up each for himself. How they travelled over hills and dales, met many disasters, suffered much from the good cause, and struggled with difficulties and wants, not having where to lay their head; by all which they afterwards proved themselves to be right father's sons, and Peter to be spurious. Finding no shelter near Peter's habitation, Martin travelled northwards, and finding the Thuringians, a neighbouring people, disposed to change, he set up his stage first among them, where, making it his business to cry down Peter's powders, plasters, salves, and drugs, which he had sold a long time at a dear rate, allowing Martin none of the profit, though he had been often employed in recommending and putting them off, the good people, willing to save their pence, began to hearken to Martin's speeches. How several great lords took the hint, and on the same account declared for Martin; particularly one who, not having had enough of one wife, wanted to marry a second, and knowing Peter used not to grant such licenses but at a swingeing price, he struck up a bargain with Martin, whom he found more tractable, and who assured him he had the same power to allow such things. How most of the other Northern lords, for their own private ends, withdrew themselves and their dependants from Peter's authority, and closed in with Martin. How Peter, enraged at the loss of such large territories, and consequently of so much revenue, thundered against Martin, and sent out the strongest and most terrible of his bulls to devour him; but this having no effect, and Martin defending himself boldly and dexterously, Peter at last put forth proclamations declaring Martin and all his adherents rebels and traitors, ordaining and requiring all his loving subjects to take up arms, and to kill, burn, and destroy all and every one of them, promising large rewards, &c., upon which ensued bloody wars and desolation.

How Harry Huff,[1] lord of Albion, one of the greatest bullies of those days, sent a cartel to Martin to fight him on a stage at Cudgels, quarter-staff, backsword, &c. Hence the origin of that genteel custom of prize-fighting so well known and practised to this day among those polite islanders, though unknown everywhere else. How Martin, being a bold, blustering fellow, accepted the challenge; how they met and fought, to the great diversion of the spectators; and, after giving one another broken heads and many bloody wounds and bruises, how they both drew off victorious, in which their example has been frequently imitated by great clerks and others since that time. How Martin's friends applauded his victory, and how Lord Harry's friends complimented him on the same score, and particularly Lord Peter, who sent him a fine feather for his cap,[2] to be worn by him and his successors as a perpetual mark for his bold defence of Lord Peter's cause. How Harry, flushed with his pretended victory over Martin, began to huff Peter also, and at last downright quarrelled with him about a wench. How some of Lord Harry's tenants, ever fond of changes, began to talk kindly of Martin, for which he mauled them soundly, as he did also those that adhered to Peter. How he turned some out of house and hold, others he hanged or burnt, &c.

How Harry Huff, after a deal of blustering, wenching, and bullying, died, and was succeeded by a good-natured boy,[3] who, giving way to the general bent of his tenants, allowed Martin's notions to spread everywhere, and take deep root in Ambition. How, after his death, the farm fell into the hands of a lady,[4] who was violently in love with Lord Peter. How she purged the whole country with fire and sword, resolved not to leave the name or remembrance of Martin. How Peter triumphed, and set up shops again for selling his own powders, plasters, and salves, which were now declared the only true ones, Martin's being all declared counterfeit. How great numbers of Martin's friends left the country, and, travelling up and down in foreign parts, grew acquainted with many of Jack's followers, and took a liking to many of their notions and ways, which they afterwards brought back into ambition, now under another landlady,[5] more moderate and more cunning than the former. How she endeavoured to keep friendship both with Peter and Martin, and trimmed for some time between the two, not without countenancing and assisting at the same time many of Jack's followers; but finding, no possibility of reconciling all the three brothers, because each would be master, and allow no other salves, powders, or plasters to be used but his own, she discarded all three, and set up a shop for those of her own farm, well furnished with powders, plasters, salves, and all other drugs necessary, all right and true, composed according to receipts made by physicians and apothecaries of her own creating, which they extracted out of Peter's, and Martin's, and Jack's receipt-books, and of this medley or hodge-podge made up a dispensatory of their own, strictly forbidding any other to be used, and particularly Peter's, from which the greatest part of this new dispensatory was stolen. How the lady, farther to confirm this change, wisely imitating her father, degraded Peter from the rank he pretended as eldest brother, and set up herself in his place as head of the family, and ever after wore her father's old cap with the fine feather he had got from Peter for standing his friend, which has likewise been worn with no small ostentation to this day by all her successors, though declared enemies to Peter. How Lady Bess and her physicians, being told of many defects and imperfections in their new medley dispensatory, resolve on a further alteration, to purge it from a great deal of Peter's trash that still remained in it, but were prevented by her death. How she was succeeded by a North-Country farmer,[6] who pretended great skill in the managing of farms, though he could never govern his own poor little farm, nor yet this large new one after he got it. How this new landlord, to show his valour and dexterity, fought against enchanters, weeds, giants, and windmills, and claimed great honour for his victories. How his successor, no wiser than he, occasioned great disorders by the new methods he took to manage his farms. How he attempted to establish in his Northern farm the same dispensatory[7] used in the Southern, but miscarried, because Jack's powders, pills, salves, and plasters were there in great vogue.

How the author finds himself embarrassed for having introduced into his history a new sect different from the three he had undertaken to treat of; and how his inviolable respect to the sacred number three obliges him to reduce these four, as he intends to do all other things, to that number; and for that end to drop the former Martin and to substitute in his place Lady Bess's institution, which is to pass under the name of Martin in the sequel of this true history. This weighty point being cleared, the author goes on and describes mighty quarrels and squabbles between Jack and Martin; how sometimes the one had the better and sometimes the other, to the great desolation of both farms, till at last both sides concur to hang up the landlord,[8] who pretended to die a martyr for Martin, though he had been true to neither side, and was suspected by many to have a great affection for Peter.

A DIGRESSION ON THE NATURE, USEFULNESS, AND NECESSITY OF WARS AND QUARRELS

This being a matter of great consequence, the author intends to treat it methodically and at large in a treatise apart, and here to give only some hints of what his large treatise contains. The state of war, natural to all creatures. War is an attempt to take by violence from others a part of what they have and we want. Every man, fully sensible of his own merit, and finding it not duly regarded by others, has a natural right to take from them all that he thinks due to himself; and every creature, finding its own wants more than those of others, has the same right to take everything its nature requires. Brutes, much more modest in their pretensions this way than men, and mean men more than great ones. The higher one raises his pretensions this way, the more bustle he makes about them, and the more success he has, the greater hero. Thus greater souls, in proportion to their superior merit, claim a greater right to take everything from meaner folks. This the true foundation of grandeur and heroism, and of the distinction of degrees among men. War, therefore, necessary to establish subordination, and to found cities, kingdoms, &c., as also to purge bodies politic of gross humours. Wise princes find it necessary to have wars abroad to keep peace at home. War, famine, and pestilence, the usual cures for corruption in bodies politic. A comparison of these three—the author is to write a panegyric on each of them. The greatest part of mankind loves war more than peace. They are but few and mean-spirited that live in peace with all men. The modest and meek of all kinds always a prey to those of more noble or stronger appetites. The inclination to war universal; those that cannot or dare not make war in person employ others to do it for them. This maintains bullies, bravoes, cut-throats, lawyers, soldiers, &c. Most professions would be useless if all were peaceable. Hence brutes want neither smiths nor lawyers, magistrates nor joiners, soldiers or surgeons. Brutes having but narrow appetites, are incapable of carrying on or perpetuating war against their own species, or of being led out in troops and multitudes to destroy one another. These prerogatives proper to man alone. The excellency of human nature demonstrated by the vast train of appetites, passions, wants, &c., that attend it. This matter to be more fully treated in the author's panegyric on mankind.

THE HISTORY OF MARTIN—CONTINUED

How Jack, having got rid of the old landlord, set up another to his mind, quarrelled with Martin, and turned him out of doors. How he pillaged all his shops, and abolished his whole dispensatory. How the new landlord[9] laid about him, mauled Peter, worried Martin, and made the whole neighbourhood tremble.

How Jack's friends fell out among themselves, split into a thousand parties, turned all things topsy-turvy, till everybody grew weary of them; and at last, the blustering landlord dying, Jack was kicked out of doors, a new landlord[10] brought in, and Martin re-established. How this new landlord let Martin do what he pleased, and Martin agreed to everything his pious landlord desired, provided Jack might be kept low. Of several efforts Jack made to raise up his head, but all in vain; till at last the landlord died, and was succeeded by one[11] who was a great friend to Peter, who, to humble Martin, gave Jack some liberty. How Martin grew enraged at this, called in a foreigner[12] and turned out the landlord; in which Jack concurred with Martin, because this landlord was entirely devoted to Peter, into whose arms he threw himself, and left his country. How the new landlord secured Martin in the full possession of his former rights, but would not allow him to destroy Jack, who had always been his friend. How Jack got up his head in the North, and put himself in possession of a whole canton, to the great discontent of Martin, who finding also that some of Jack's friends were allowed to live and get their bread in the south parts of the country, grew highly discontented with the new landlord he had called in to his assistance. How this landlord kept Martin in order, upon which he fell into a raging fever, and swore he would hang himself or join in with Peter, unless Jack's children were all turned out to starve. Of several attempts to cure Martin, and make peace between him and Jack, that they might unite against Peter; but all made ineffectual by the great address of a number of Peter's friends, that herded among Martin's, and appeared the most zealous for his interest. How Martin, getting abroad in this mad fit, looked so like Peter in his air and dress, and talked so like him, that many of the neighbours could not distinguish the one from the other; especially when Martin went up and down strutting in Peter's armour, which he had borrowed to fight Jack.[13] What remedies were used to cure Martin's distemper . . .

Here the author being seized with a fit of dulness, to which he is very subject, after having read a poetical epistle addressed to . . . it entirely composed his senses, so that he has not writ a line since.

N.B.—Some things that follow after this are not in the MS., but seem to have been written since, to fill up the place of what was not thought convenient then to print.

A PROJECT FOR THE UNIVERSAL BENEFIT OF MANKIND

The author, having laboured so long and done so much to serve and instruct the public, without any advantage to himself, has at last thought of a project which will tend to the great benefit of all mankind, and produce a handsome revenue to the author. He intends to print by subscription, in ninety-six large volumes in folio, an exact description of *Terra Australis incognita*, collected with great care, and prints from 999 learned and pious authors of undoubted veracity. The whole work, illustrated with maps and cuts agreeable to the subject, and done by the best masters, will cost but one guinea each volume to subscribers, one guinea to be paid in advance, and afterwards a guinea on receiving each volume, except the last. This work will be of great use for all men, and necessary for all families, because it contains exact accounts of all the provinces, colonies, and mansions of that spacious country, where, by a general doom, all transgressors of the law are to be transported; and every one having this work may choose out the fittest and best place for himself, there being enough for all, so as every one shall be fully satisfied.

The author supposes that one copy of this work will be bought at the public charge, or out of the parish rates, for every parish church in the three kingdoms, and in all the dominions thereunto belonging. And that every family that can command £10 per annum, even though retrenched from less necessary expenses, will subscribe for one. He does not think of giving out above nine volumes nearly; and considering the number requisite, he intends to print at least 100,000 for the first edition. He is to print proposals against next term, with a specimen, and a curious map of the capital city with its twelve gates, from a known author, who took an exact survey of it in a dream. Considering the great care and pains of the author, and the usefulness of the work, he hopes every one will be ready, for their own good as well as his, to contribute cheerfully to it, and not grudge him the profit he may have by it, especially if he comes to a third or fourth edition, as he expects it will very soon.

He doubts not but it will be translated into foreign languages by most nations of Europe, as well as Asia and Africa, being of as great use to all those nations as to his own; for this reason he designs to procure patents and privileges for securing the whole benefit to himself from all those different princes and states, and hopes to see many millions of this great work printed in those different countries and languages before his death.

After this business is pretty well established, he has promised to put a friend on another project almost as good as this, by establishing insurance offices everywhere for securing people from shipwreck and several other accidents in their voyage to this country; and these officers shall furnish, at a certain rate, pilots well versed in the route, and that know all the rocks, shelves, quicksands, &c., that such pilgrims and travellers may be exposed to. Of these he knows a great number ready instructed in most countries; but the whole scheme of this matter he is to draw up at large and communicate to his friend.

---

1. Henry VIII.
2. "Fidei Defensor."

3. Edward VI.
4. Queen Mary.
5. Queen Elizabeth.
6. James I.
7. Episcopacy.
8. Charles I.
9. Cromwell.
10. Charles II.
11. James II.
12. William III.
13. High Church against Dissent.

Made in the USA
Las Vegas, NV
29 December 2024

15540438R10215